The Transmutation of Noah

BY

C. S. ROYCE

the Peppertree Press
Sarasota, Florida

No part of this book may be used or reproduced by any means, graphic, electronic, or mechanical, including photocopying, recording, taping or by an information storage retrieval system without written permission of the author, except in the case of brief quotations embodied in articles and reviews.

The historical and statistical facts in this book are as accurate as possible. The characters are fictitious. Any similarity to real persons, living or dead, is coincidental and not intended by the author.

Copyright © C. S. Royce, 2014

All rights reserved. Published by the Peppertree Press, LLC. the Peppertree Press and associated logos are trademarks of the Peppertree Press, LLC.

No part of this publication may be reproduced, stored in a retrieval system, transmitted in any form or by any means, electronic, mechanical, photocopying, recording, or otherwise, without prior written permission of the publisher and author/illustrator. Graphic design by Rebecca Barbier.

For information regarding permission,
call 941-922-2662 or contact us at our website:
www.peppertreepublishing.com or write to:
the Peppertree Press, LLC.
Attention: Publisher
1269 First Street, Suite 7
Sarasota, Florida 34236

ISBN: 978-1-61493-205-5

Library of Congress Number: 2014900147

Printed in the U.S.A.

Printed July 2014

To Ray, with much love always.

Chapter 1

THE FLORIDA EVERGLADES AT NIGHT IS A PLACE SO dark a person can't see anything, not an outstretched hand or a foot on the ground. It is a place where Seminole Indians once hid, where alligators submerge in black swampy waters, and panthers search for prey, where the light from tiny stars and the half halo of a new moon does not reach. It is a place so dark at night that a vehicle from space could land without detection, which has happened, although not often.

On January 11, 2000, a black metallic ship extinguished its cabin lights and decelerated. The craft made a slight humming noise, not as loud as the buzzing, croaking, chirping cadences of the night sounds of the Everglades. It touched a rock road in silence to deliver two passengers beneath the unfamiliar stars.

"I cannot fathom why you would elect to visit Earth, but you are here," the pilot said in brief, deliberate tones using Universal language. She was short in stature, wearing a gray jumpsuit and a small gray cap with a pilot's insignia, a black craft superimposed on a white world. She depressed a smooth button on the control panel with her left thumb, and the door of the ship slid silently open.

William Blake took his first step onto a new and dangerous world with a feeling of intense curiosity. The pull of gravity against his body was similar to his home planet of Abidan, but the smell of delicious cool moisture was vastly different. He had read everything about Earth that was available on his home planet. Although it was not a great amount and it was cleansed, it was enough information to intrigue him with the creativity, athletic power and natural beauty that flourished there. He offered his hand to his companion, Irina Vega, as she stepped from the craft. The ground was almost completely black.

Blake felt a sensation he had not known in his 25 years of life, a sensation he had never needed to know. It was fear. No one he knew had ever known fear, but it was fear that rattled deep inside and shook him to the edge of his being. It was fear that grew larger, like the world had appeared outside the huge display windows of his craft.

As they had approached Earth, he had watched the beautiful planet change like a painting-in-progress as detail is added. Reddish brown colors appeared on the blue and white tableau; then recognizable continents, the outline of North America, the East Coast of the United States, and finally, the distinctive coastline of Florida, looking like the head of a giant sea turtle, with the big southern lake as its eye, or the head of a serpent.

From his view, Earth had not looked like a dangerous place for a research mission. It was a sparkling blue world swirled in white clouds, a distant jewel suspended in velvety blackness, a soliloquy in the emptiness of space.

Would he survive this mission? Would Irina Vega, his mission companion, survive?

"I believe the lights appearing on the road are those of your agent's vehicle," the pilot continued, "I signaled from the ship two hours ago to advise him of our estimated time of arrival and location. If it is he, I will be gone. I seek no experience with violent planets or with detection."

The headlights split the dark night like vectors of light as they approached the craft and extinguished. A man in sandaled feet stepped from the door of a silvery vehicle, casting a triangle of light on the dark ground. In the shadows, Blake got the impression of a man of medium height, wearing a short sleeved shirt covering his broad chest, and shorts reaching to the knees of his muscular legs.

The agent and pilot exchanged formal greetings using a Universal code. "This is Agent Eugene Barios," the pilot said. "You are delivered to Earth."

The agent acknowledged their greeting with a silent nod.

Blake turned to the pilot. "Thank you. It was a beautiful flight and we appreciate your work. Maybe you will be our pilot on our return flight?"

The pilot did not acknowledge the question and summarily returned to the spacecraft. The black door closed and the ship vanished as smoothly and quietly as it had arrived.

Chapter 2

The vehicle's headlights provided their only light as they bounced along a rough road in the black night.

"Where are we, Mr. Barios?" Blake could barely distinguish the outline of the agent's face as he half-turned toward them.

"Call me Eugene. We're in the Big Cypress Swamp. This rock road we're on connects with the Tamiami Trail in the Everglades. It's a National Park, some think it's interesting, I don't, just one more place I don't want to be on this cursed planet."

"How long have you been here, Eugene?"

"Five years too long." The agent cleared his throat. "I don't know why they maintain outposts on evil planets, anyway, I'm just waitin' for my transfer."

"Do you have many visitors?" Blake felt relieved that Barios had survived on Earth five years.

"Not since I've been here, a few map makers, curiosity seekers, never had any researchers like you, don't know why anyone'd want to research this Godforsaken place. It's a doomed planet, that's for sure, and it won't take much research to find that out."

Blake took a deep breath, "have you been in personal danger?"

"Not so much but I'm careful, you should be too," Eugene said.

"Have you seen any deaths?"

"People die here everyday, a few even die from natural causes. I stay away from it and I don't talk about it." Eugene's tone sounded like a warning.

Blake rubbed his moist palms against the nanotech material of the jumpsuit he wore. Its tiny silicon filaments repelled the moisture on his hands; the feel of his strong thighs beneath his clothing soothed his fear. He recalled the warnings of Professor Shem. His major professor on their home planet of Abidan, a planet of peace, had stringently opposed Blake's chosen thesis topic. Dr. Shem had warned him that Earth was a treacherous place to conduct research. Blake tried to develop interest in another topic, but his theory that Earth was worth preserving held him like a strong and powerful magnet. Dr. Shem approved his thesis only because the Great Creator of Life had granted permission.

Planets served as God's experiments in the Universe. Some experiments were successful and some were not. They were generally classified with the nomenclature Planet of Peace or Planet of Evil. Those in the latter category faced extinction. Generally this was accomplished by allowing the failed experiment to annihilate itself. God had judged Earth as a failure, scheduled to be annihilated in the year 2070, by nuclear holocaust in World War III.

It had been four months since Blake had faced God. He could almost conjure the blessing of that warm white cloud upon his frigid meeting spot, as he sat in a folding chair among patches of snow and tufts of brown grass on the cold ground of Abidan.

He had been right. Earth was unique. Something extraordinarily good existed among the evils, although it was a strange paradox that the violent planet was the one that had generated the greatest creative energy. He believed that it was not a coincidence that Earth was the last planet of evil remaining in this galaxy group. New experimental worlds were continuously developing, but it was less likely that another violent planet would evolve. God's Universal Law had obliterated most evil. Original Sin was practically extinct.

Blake turned to Vega, "Does the verbal communication in English feel awkward to you?"

"Yes, it does feel awkward," she concurred. "Thoughtcom is easier."

"I agree," he said, "but it is good for us to practice."

Blake studied her quiet profile, her plain brown hair and hazel eyes. He scanned her thought patterns and knew that she was experiencing similar doubts about her choice of Earth. She was questioning the value of her thesis on genetic variations and the causes of human violence.

Professor Shem had arranged for her to accompany him when his girlfriend Bekah had refused to come. He did not know Vega well. He knew she was 28, and considered an excellent geneticist by her colleagues. She lived at home with her parents and one brother.

Eugene's voice interrupted his thoughts. "Those polymedia computer cards on your car seat have all the orientation info you need. You can connect 'em to your main computers at home. They're good, yobibytes of storage, superfast transfer speeds, you know how to activate 'em, just fold out the touch screen holograms. I've also got drivers' licenses, social securities, bank cards, hard copies of maps and stuff. It'll be daylight soon, I was gonna give you yer paperwork then."

"That sounds good," Blake said, "do you mind if I open the window?"

The agent shrugged. "Be my guest. There's a button on your armrest."

Blake absorbed the cool, crisp air of the Everglades through his open window, the choir of night sounds, the faint pinkish light from the east filtering through the lacy bare branches of cypress trees, and the wispy beard-like strands of Spanish moss. There was a foggy mist on the ground and the air had the fresh smell of soil, grass, trees and sweet wildflowers. The ambience was heavenly after weeks of confinement in two different crafts of reformulated air.

Blake thought of his petition meeting with God about his proposed research. It was his first time to meet the Great Creator, Who appeared in Plasma form. The Plasma cloud had been a warm comfort on the chilly plain of Abidan, but making his presentation was strenuous. Blake felt no fear then, only anxiety over advancing his theories, and the conviction that he was right.

Blake was intrigued by the biblical stories, the story of Noah, and the concept of purging the world of evil. He argued that Earth's unique creative power should be preserved by eliminating its culture of violence through the combined methodology of genetic engineering of the human species and environmental remediation.

In every conceivable way, Blake was at a disadvantage in presenting his thesis to God. His greatest impediment was that he did not understand violence because he was from a planet of peace, where all knowledge of evil was blocked. He vividly remembered God's strong voice and even stronger translated words:

> ...For over 50,000 years, the people of Earth have committed heinous atrocities in a vast, cruel history of terror and tragedy. Their tribes have waged wars where tens of millions of human beings have savagely murdered each other. Every nation has been involved. In the 20th century, over 200 million people died in wars and genocides. Dictators named Hitler, Stalin and Mao have caused the murders of millions of innocent people and caused their followers to murder. Whole populations have enslaved others.
>
> The people of Earth have committed hideous individual crimes: crimes of sex, crimes against children, crimes of hate, crimes against humanity, crimes against the Prophets, crimes against God.
>
> In your chosen country of the United States, there were 21 million violent crimes in the past two decades: serial murders, mass shootings, stabbings, crimes of passion, tortures, rapes, pornography, child molestations, murders of children, murders by children.
>
> The attempts to purge and cure the tribes of Earth have failed. Earth is a deeply flawed experiment and must be allowed to annihilate itself. I will not intervene.

They drove east into the glowing sunrise through miles of green-gold saw grass swaying in a gentle breeze. Small green hammocks of hardwood trees and cabbage palms dotted the expanse, like little islands among waves of grass. For miles and miles it looked that way, golden grass and tufts of green islands, empty and open and beautiful.

The ground beneath the grass was dry in some areas and shallow water stood in others. The sky was dark blue with streaks of pink, gold, and orange. Puffs of white clouds rising from the horizon reflected the rosy colors of dawn. The ground dripped with early morning dew. A large flock of pink birds seemed to erupt into the sky from a small tree island where they had been roosting.

Blake used his polymedia card to identify the birds as Roseate Spoonbills. "There's some fantastic plant and animal life here," he said.

"Yeah, if you like alligators and mosquitoes," Eugene grumbled, "guess they're not so bad, a lot better'n what you'll find in Miami."

Vega clenched her lips together.

"We don't have large animals at home," Blake said.

"You two are from a planet of peace. You'll see a lot of things here you don't expect." Eugene's stark warning seemed out of place in the peaceful Everglades.

Blake wiped his face again. He felt hot although the temperature in the car was cool. He had been awestruck by God's message and the unbelievable litany of Earth's violence, yet strangely, he had not abandoned his iconoclastic thesis idea. He did not know why. It made him feel singular and different.

He did not know why he was different, why he possessed a thing called curiosity that no one else he knew had. He did not know why he was driven to understand the answers to questions no one else asked. In Abidan, no one seemed curious about ideas. Even his mission companion, Irina Vega, who was certainly more inquisitive than most people of Abidan, did not possess the same curiosity. He thought of his girlfriend whom he had left behind. Bekah had insisted that he should not have curiosity, as though it were something he could select like a grocery item. He did not feel he had a choice.

Blake had been given permission for his research mission when he had reminded God of the promise of the Second Coming of a Prophet Messiah to save the just people of Earth. Blake knew then that God still loved Earth. The Creator's rejection of the planet was not total. There was a scintilla of a chance to save it.

Blake recalled the commandments God had given him for his mission to Earth. He was required to return within six months. He was required to take a woman with him. Social contact was permitted. Procreation was not permitted. He was forbidden to touch any instrument of violence or become involved in the commission of any violent act. Before returning to Abidan, he must have his brain dusted at the transport station to obliterate the memory of the evil he saw. No one except his travel companion was allowed to return with him. He knew he would be careful. If he transgressed any commandment, he could never return to Abidan or any other planet of peace.

Blake returned his thoughts to the mission. "Is this our rental car?" he asked.

"Yep, I brought it so you can learn to drive on an empty road. It's not hard. Thought we'd wait for more light."

"I didn't expect to see vehicles riding on roads."

Eugene grunted.

"What kind of vehicle is it?" Blake asked.

"Lexus SUV, sport utility vehicle, good safety record, handy to carry stuff."

"I like this quaint car. Do you have a car, Eugene?"

"Yep, left it at your rental house."

They passed a group of buildings next to a large parking area and a big yellow sign topped with small flags of white, black, red and yellow. The sign read "Welcome to Miccosukee Indian Village."

"What's Miccosukee?" Blake asked.

"Indians, descended from Creek Indians, also called Native Americans, 'cause they came here before this was the United States. Miccosukee are part of the Seminole Tribe. They hid in the Everglades when the rest of 'em were being conquered and forced to move out west in the 1800's. When this road was built, they got themselves recognized as a separate tribe, started this village so they could support themselves. They also have a big gaming hall closer to town. There're about 500 of 'em, nice people, I feel sorry for 'em for the way they were treated, but they've done violence too. That yellow building's a restaurant, sorry they're not open this early, their fry bread's real good. If you want to eat, we can stop in Miami."

Blake looked at Vega. "We're fine."

"They eat three times a day here, more'n we do, but their food's real good, lot of variety, meat's not engineered, but it's good too. I'm sure the food's not as healthy as what you're used to, but it's sure tasty. I stocked your kitchen with some local stuff."

"Thanks. I'd like to try the food," Blake said. "I'd also like to meet the Miccosukee."

"You can if you want. It's only about an hour from Miami, once you get outta traffic," Barios sounded ambivalent. "They sleep more here too. I recommend you get at least six hours. It'll help with the stress of living here."

They passed a small brown sign that read "Shark Valley," and Blake asked Eugene if there were sharks there.

"Supposedly there're some at Shark River Slough, a real shallow river nearby, never seen 'em here, just in the ocean."

"Is there a river here?"

"There was an interesting journalist named Marjorie Stoneman Douglas," Eugene said, "wrote a book about the Everglades called *River of Grass*. Her point was this part of the park is a 50 mile wide very shallow river critical to the ecology of the whole state. She died two years ago at 108, which is old for here."

"What's the life expectancy here?"

"In the U.S. it's 77, that is if you're lucky. People look old here too, it's a little shocking at first, but you get used to it."

"I see," Blake thought about how it would feel to be old on Earth. People aged on Abidan, but it was gradual and not apparent until they neared 130. "Have you read Douglas's book?"

"Yeah, I read it back when I was interested in things here. It's a good book."

They passed a dark man, wearing a tan shirt and green trousers and holding a pole in his hands. He tossed the line from his pole into a wide canal cut through limestone banks next to the road.

"What's that man doing?" Blake asked.

"Catching fish to eat," Barios said.

Blake was mesmerized by his first glimpse of a person from Earth.

"Okay, it's light enough, here're your papers I was telling you about, contracts, keys and such." Blake got a quick look at Eugene's tan skin and sad hazel eyes as he handed them their paperwork. "I rented a four bedroom, four and a half bath house in Coral Gables, bigger than you need, but near the university like you wanted, good neighborhood, and it's furnished. You specified one car, you can rent another if you want. It's not hard driving on roads, you just gotta know the rules and watch out for other drivers. They have somethin' here they call 'road rage' where someone will come after you for a small thing like cutting them off in another lane. You gotta be careful."

A man in a red truck with oversized tires drove toward them in the other lane. Blake observed him curiously as he passed. From what he knew, the man did not appear to have road rage.

"Did you have any problem transferring your money from the station to the Foundation?" Eugene asked.

"No, there didn't seem to be any problem."

"No problem on my end either. I set up accounts for both of you at the Foundation in Switzerland, and here at a local bank. You'll have to sign for everything since I don't have access to your money. I set up an appointment for both of you at the private banking section of your Miami bank. Shouldn't be a problem, the Foundation's solid, and private banks are used to handling all kinds of transactions. You're from a wealthy planet, so you'll have a lot of American money here."

"They don't take advantage of their wealth," Blake said, "at least not by traveling."

"Haven't been there," Eugene said, "but from what I've heard your planet's got a stable government, pretty good standard of living, plenty of natural resources, and it's safe."

"It's a good place," Blake agreed, "but don't you think they're some good things on Earth by comparison?"

"Not that I've seen, but your money'll go a long way here, guess that's the one good thing you can say about Earth, and the women, I've never seen such beautiful women as there are in Miami." He looked at Blake, "I don't mean to interfere or get too personal, but just a word of advice, a good looking guy like you's gonna to get a lot of attention, which can get complicated."

"How do you mean?" Blake asked.

"Hard to say exactly, just be careful." Eugene cleared his throat and glanced in the rear view mirror at Irina. "Anyway, you also need to be careful with your money. I gottcha several hundred dollars each. I wouldn't go around with more cash than that, they'll likely steal your money or think you're a drug dealer."

"Drug dealer?" Blake looked at Vega who shook her head.

"All part of the violence here," Eugene grumbled, "a really sad thing, you'll learn about it soon enough, just be careful you don't get hurt."

"We've never learned about violence," Blake said.

"You oughta keep it that way is my advice," Eugene snarled.

"But wouldn't you agree that the creative power and natural beauty of Earth is unique and worth preserving?" Blake persisted.

"Nope." Eugene cleared his throat. "There's all kinds of visitor information, tips on safety, where to shop, stuff like wear sunscreen so you don't get a sunburn. That's another thing you're not used to," the agent said, "yer rent includes yard service, garbage pickup and utilities. If you want someone to clean the house, that's extra."

"If the homes aren't self-cleaning, is there much to do?" William asked.

Eugene shrugged. "It's more than where you came from, you can see for yourself."

"What about our clothing?" William looked at their jumpsuits, "are we okay until we have a chance to buy some local clothes?"

"You should be okay, jumpsuits may be kinda' odd, but you can't really tell they're advanced fabric by looking at 'em," Eugene adjusted his grip on the steering wheel. "People might stare some, but they'll probably think you're military or a mechanic or something like that. People here wear almost anything, and it's no indication you're from elsewhere."

"Okay for now then." Blake looked at his fold-out screen, "I see there's plenty of clothing stores here, I've never paid any attention to clothes, but it should be interesting to try some different things."

"Their clothes are okay, I guess," Eugene shrugged, "as far as my services, I've got an itemized bill at the house, I wrote down my phone number in case you need to get a hold of me."

"Thanks for doing a great job." Blake tried to sound friendly. He felt sorry for his agent who sounded so sad.

"Before we get in traffic, you need to learn to drive, who wants to go first?" Eugene asked.

Blake turned to Vega.

"I'll drive," she said.

She placed her smooth strong hands on the steering wheel, and Eugene gave her instructions from the passenger side of the front seat. Vega suddenly swerved and stopped, distracted by the sight of a huge alligator lying on the canal bank across the road. The enormous reptile was dark gray, like charcoal, with scaly skin and spiked ridges on its back. Its four legs and feet were tipped with huge claws at the end of each sprawling toe, and its huge open jaw was full of massive teeth.

"Alligator," Eugene said, "they look slow and lazy most of the time, but they can run faster'n any man. Its jaws are so strong when they're shut, if it grabs you, it's almost impossible to get away."

Blake estimated that the ancient-looking beast was four meters in length. "What do they eat?"

"Flesh."

Blake traded places with Irina for his turn to drive. He fastened his seatbelt and asked Irina, "Was it hard to be confined to roads?"

"It wasn't bad," she said.

A few people in Abidan owned individual antigravity vehicles, but most used AGV Public Transportation. The vehicles did not require roads, and there was little traffic among the domed neighborhoods.

"The main thing here is the traffic, like I said," Eugene added.

"You're right, it's not hard," Blake relaxed his hands on the wheel. "What do you do with your time, Eugene?"

"Not much. I fish, watch basketball, go to concerts, do some odd jobs. I didn't come with much money and I don't make much, there's not much outpost work here. Hope I get a busier post next time."

"I hope you do too," Blake said.

Chapter 3

"I'll drive now," Eugene motioned Blake to stop in the Miccosukee Tobacco Shop parking lot. Eugene turned the car onto Tamiami Trail, and Blake noticed the Miccosukee Resort and Gaming Hall, a cream colored building trimmed in terracotta, blue and aqua.

As they neared town, Blake unfolded his paper map so they could make an eyepik of it. He observed that the Tamiami Trail was also called 41, SW 8th Street and Calle Ocho.

Miami was more different from their native planet than any place he could imagine. Abidan was a land of cloud cover, frozen lakes and rivers, and a chilly ocean, where most of life was lived in huge grey buildings and under massive domes. Although there were trees and small gardens and blue skies under the domes, compared to Miami, Abidan was cold and dull and much the same. Even the people were the same, with brown hair and hazel eyes and fixed patterns of thought.

Miami sparkled with color – lovely pastels and dazzling bright colors. The sky was a brilliant blue, and the flowers were many shades of red, yellow, orange, pink and purple. The grass and tropical trees were spring green, and the buildings blossomed in unimaginable colors, sizes and shapes. The people and cars on the streets were as varied as the buildings. The traffic was another curious thing: people driving in cars, looking at the road ahead, some talking on phones or playing loud music, stopping and going and turning and changing lanes and sometimes shouting at other drivers. It was all vastly different from anything he had ever seen, and loud compared to Abidan, or even with the quiet dawn of the Everglades.

"What's that noise?" Blake asked.

Eugene explained what sirens were, and Blake noticed them roaring and whining almost constantly, an unsettling sound signifying troubling things.

They passed under a large highway. On their right they got a quick look at the stone archway entrance to Florida International University, contemporary gray buildings, trimmed in pink and yellow, in a garden of palms and green grass. Further on, random names and signs advertised: Burgers, Tacos, Pizza, La Bomba Check Cashing, Motel Presidente, Guns.Armas, Banzai Judo Self-Defense, Botanica, Bahamas Fish Restaurant, Librerias Impactos, Small Daddy's Liquor, Paintball, Catholic Bookstore, Miami Police Supply. The people along the sidewalks and road were as varied as the signs.

"Are you surprised by all this variety in Miami?" he asked Vega.

"I am," she nodded.

"There's so much I want to know about," Blake said, "what's a botanica?"

Eugene changed lanes. "Botanicas sell all kinds of strange stuff like bones, crosses, black candles, Voodoo dolls, stuffed monkey heads, salves, herbs, Christian stuff."

"What's it for?" asked Blake.

"I don't know much about it," the agent said, "supposedly some of the stuff is for religions like Voodoo, where they chant and curse their enemies and Santeria, where they sacrifice goats and chickens."

"It's all so different," Blake shook his head, "even the weather doesn't seem like winter."

"No it doesn't." Vega looked through her car window.

"Like I said, you're in for a lot of surprises," Barios repeated. "You gotta watch for crime all the time. Roads marked with a bright orange sun are supposed to be safe, I wouldn't count on it, but it's a help. It's a good idea to plan where you're gonna' go first so you don't get lost, be sure ya' park in well-lit areas where there's people around. If anybody bumps your car, don't get out; drive to a gas station, if you can. There's been a lot of robberies when people get bumped. They stop and get outta their cars to see what happened and get robbed, or worse."

"Have you had any problems?" Blake asked.

"Not much. Had my house broken into a few times. Fortunately, I wasn't there. They didn't take much 'cause I don't have much, but be careful, and college campuses may look nice, but there's crime there too."

"Have you seen instruments of violence?"

"Oh, yeah," sadness returned to the agent's voice.

"How do you learn about violence? How do you understand it?" Blake felt questions rising in him like steam in a geyser, but Eugene did not respond.

Vega was also silent.

Barios turned onto Columbus Drive, a road covered by a lovely canopy of green leafed ficus trees. Their trunks were huge tan clusters of roots.

"What's that building?" Blake pointed to a spectacular peach and white colored structure and tower that suddenly appeared in front of them. It had creamy white columns, rows of windows, arches and cupolas.

"Biltmore Hotel and golf course," Eugene said, "built in the 1920's, to look like buildings in Spain. It's got a swimming pool covering one side of the hotel, supposed to be the largest hotel swimming pool in the U.S. Your rental includes a pool and spa membership there."

"Is that information in our orientation?"

"Yep." Eugene turned south on Granada past the beautiful hotel, "another thing, we do the best we can on your documents, but they're not perfect. They call people from other planets 'aliens,' but there's no widespread belief we exist." Eugene gave a gruff laugh, "their idea of aliens are little blue or green guys with big heads, big eyes, no ears, hardly any mouth, but I think it's mostly a joke," Eugene shifted in his seat, "like I said, there's no real belief we exist, and since most people look similar enough, they won't suspect your papers are fake by looking at you, but be careful. You don't want anyone to find out you're from another planet, that'd be real bad."

Eugene turned into the driveway of an attractive two story painted brick house. It was yellow with white trim and a white wrought iron balcony on the second floor. The light at the front door was turned on. Shady oak trees lined a circular drive and the front yard was landscaped with flowering bushes of red, purple and blue. Eugene opened the garage door with a clicker and parked next to his white Ford Taurus.

They set their suitcases and computer screen rolls on the floor of the large kitchen, and Eugene showed them around. The house had a pleasant interior with high ceilings, off-white carpet, and light-colored furniture. The walls were of pickled cypress, wood rubbed with light paint to show its grain. Easy chairs and a loveseat stood in the living room next to a fireplace, with a carved wooden mantle painted in white. A mahogany grand piano stood in another corner of the room. The family room centered around a large television housed in an oak wall unit, which also displayed blue glass vases and picture books. On the second floor, at the top of the stairs was a spacious loft area with couches and a big screen TV. Two bedrooms connected to the loft and a third and larger bedroom was located down a hallway.

Blake felt out of place in his long-sleeved jumpsuit when they stepped through the open French doors in the family room onto a stone patio. Tall bronze birds spouted water from their long beaks into a round pool in the center of the patio. The fountain made a pleasant sound of continuous splashing water. Several lounge chairs and a table with chairs were arranged on the patio that faced a lush green golf course. Tropical flower bushes on each side of the patio gave it both beauty and privacy.

"The technology should be pretty easy," Eugene said as they went back into the kitchen. "There're manuals on everything in this drawer, there's basic electric outlets in each room, I'm assuming you got adaptor capability at the transport station for your computers and stuff."

Blake and Vega nodded.

Eugene opened the refrigerator door. "I got orange juice, cream cheese, pastrami, corned beef, Yellowtail Snapper, I caught that, it needs to be cooked soon - or you can freeze it." He pointed to a basket on the counter. "Got some local fruits, guavas, mangos, avocados, papayas, limes, bananas, tomatoes, strawberries."

He opened the pantry. "Cuban bread, bagels, guava shells, tacos, refried beans, like I said, food's pretty good. There's a market on U.S. 1, plenty of other grocery stores, and more restaurants than you'll have time to eat at, Jewish, Cuban, Nuevo Latino, Nicaraguan, Chinese, Vietnamese, just about anything."

"What's your favorite?" Blake asked.

"I think Haitian, but it's all pretty good. Well, that about covers what I've got to say. I'm sure I forgot somethin' but you can always call me, I don't mind if you call anytime."

They paid Eugene and thanked him.

"Thanks, also for the gratuity." Eugene folded the check, put it in the front pocket of his flowered shirt and walked toward the garage, "be real careful, and good luck to you both."

"Thanks again, and good luck to you too," Blake shook his hand. "I hope you find the job you want."

Eugene grunted and drove away.

Vega asked, "What do we do now?"

"We have a full day ahead of us. Why don't you pick the rooms you want? Then I'd like to unpack and go swimming. You're welcome to join me. After that, I'd like to explore Miami. Is that okay with you?"

"Fine, although I won't swim now." She selected a bedroom and office at the end of the hall on the first floor, and he chose the upstairs for his bedroom and office.

Chapter 4

THE WALK THROUGH THEIR GOLF COURSE NEIGHBORhood to the Biltmore Hotel was approximately one mile. For Blake, it was an enchanting scene of trees, flowers, soft green grass and bright blue sky. The elegant façade of the old hotel and tower spread before him like a huge tropical flower in a garden of palms. To one side of the hotel was a spectacular L-shaped swimming pool, a gorgeous expanse of turquoise water surrounded by a tropical garden patio.

As he approached the pool, Blake noticed many people staring at him. The attention from the beautiful women in bikinis felt good, but he also felt self-conscious. The swim trunks he purchased at the hotel gift shop felt bare compared to swimwear on Abidan, which covered most of the body, even though it was light weight material. He was glad he hadn't taken the saleslady's advice to buy a brief. She was adamant that he had the physique to wear a man's bikini, unlike most people she had seen buy them.

People continued to stare at him as he stretched his chest, shoulders and arms into a diving position near the deep end of the pool. He flexed his knees and sprung into a high swan dive that left the suggestion of a splash. When he surfaced at the opposite end of the pool, everyone nearby was clapping their hands.

The cool, luxurious water was as wonderful as the environment of bright blue sky, swaying palms, tropical plants, inviting lounge chairs, cozy cabanas, beautiful people and a loggia decorated with graceful statutes of nude women. He swam for a long time, pondering the meaning of all he saw, what the attention meant, why Earth was so beautiful, why there was violence here, what it was and when he would learn about it.

When he returned to their house, Vega appeared content to be settled into her downstairs bedroom and office. The roll-up flexible screen of her computer had filled the four walls of her office.

"I hope I didn't keep you waiting," he said, "swimming outdoors is amazing."

"I might try it sometime," she looked unsure, "but what are you wearing?"

"This is an Earth swim suit," he explained, "surprising isn't it?"

Vega agreed.

He moved toward the stairs. "I'll get changed now."

"No hurry," she responded, "I'll activate the travel information when you're ready."

"Thanks."

He bounded to his upstairs bedroom, and pulled off his swim trunks. He thought about how much he would like to share his experiences with his family and girlfriend. He remembered the day he left his worried family, his quiet, kind father, his dear mother who was crying, his sisters, Ruth and Margaret, and brother, Isaac. They were all afraid of his mission, although Isaac had been especially impressed that he had met the Great Creator of Life to obtain permission for the voyage.

Thinking of his little sister Ruth touched him the most. She was 13. He had nicknamed her the "family philosopher," because she was often reflective. He would always remember her small worried face. He would be glad when his dissertation was finished and he could return to his family. Maybe then, his demon curiosity would be satisfied.

He did not miss Bekah as much as he would have thought. He missed their physical contact, but when he tried to picture her, it was her scowling face and frequent lectures that he saw.

Chapter 5

"Are you ready to see Miami?" Blake asked as they studied the multidimensional map on the walls of Vega's computer room.

"Yes, but I'm worried about what Eugene said to us."

"Me too," he rotated his chair, "that's why it's important to plan. What would you like to see first?"

"I'm okay with anything safe. Would you choose?"

"I'd like to see everything today, but we can't," he turned. "I suggest Brickell Avenue, downtown Miami and South Beach. They're safe areas. Is that okay?"

"Yes." She was worried.

"I'm worried too," he said as he started the car, "but we'll be careful."

Shady trees lined the pretty streets of Coral Gables by a small green waterway, churches and attractive homes. They noticed some homes had decorative metal bars on their windows and doors.

"What do you think the bars are for?" Irina asked.

"Must be for security." He turned onto U.S. Highway 1, and pointed to a sign that said, "Move Accident Vehicles From Travel Lanes." "How would someone in an accident be able to do that?" he asked.

"I was wondering the same thing," Vega said.

The skyline of tall buildings grew larger as they approached, like Earth had appeared from their craft, only that morning.

Brickell Avenue was a striking scene of diverse architecture, blue glass, tropical flowers, stately Royal Palms, white concrete, colors, balconies and construction cranes. Glimpses of the bright blue bay sparkled between the high buildings. The sky was as blue as the water.

"How far have we come from Abidan to see such wonders?" He slowed their car.

"It is amazing," Vega agreed.

They crossed the Miami River into downtown. Horns honked and big buses thumped and squeaked, stopping or shifting gears. Palm trees swayed in the gentle breeze among wonderful smells of food, and the little people-mover bus danced around on rails on a concrete track above the street. Stores bombarded them with offerings. Loud music blared with energy. Sirens whined in the distance.

A black man wearing a white hard hat, sun glasses, yellow tee shirt, jeans and a black shoulder bag walked past an olive skinned middle-aged lady wearing a red blouse, a flowered skirt and black stiletto heels.

"They don't have one blended race like in Abidan," Vega noted, "I wonder what that will do to my genetic models."

He was about to respond when he saw two tall boys in front of the Dade County Courthouse hit an old woman so hard she fell on the steps. Red blood spurted from the back of her head, soaking her white hair. They grabbed her straw purse and ran away as she yelled "mi bolsa, mi bolsa!"

He said to Vega, "Please drive around the block and pick me up in a little while."

He rushed toward the white-haired woman and helped her sit on the steps. She looked very wrinkled and old, but she seemed tough. He thought of what Eugene said about having to get used to aging on Earth, and realized that this woman may have been only in her 60's or 70's, even though she looked very old. He pressed his gray handkerchief against the cut on her head. Two boys hurried away in a flash of dark baggy clothes. One carried the woman's bolsa and they laughed as they ran. Blake felt his face flush with an unfamiliar sensation. He made sure the woman was all right, and chased after the boys, finding them three blocks away. They were both about six feet tall, almost as tall as he was. Blake caught them from behind, gripping them each by the shoulder, one in each hand.

"Let go o' me you mutha," one boy said, "that hurt like hell."

The second boy sounded the same as the first, "turn me loose you son of a bitch. Yo hurtin me bad."

Blake forced the youths to walk back as they kept yelling angrily at him. When he reached the old woman, he turned the boys around and faced them.

He addressed the boy holding the handbag, "Return this lady's bolsa and tell her you're sorry."

A middle-aged man approached them. He had light skin and was wearing a white shirt with a silver badge, black pants, and a black hat with an emblem.

"Sorry," the boy mumbled as he returned the purse to the old woman.

"Yeah, sorry," the other boy added.

Blake felt good to make the youths return the elderly woman's purse to her. She scolded the boys, speaking loudly and rapidly in her own language. They listened and did not speak.

The man in the uniform looked at Blake, "these the perpetrators?"

"Yes."

The man clamped handcuffs around the boys' wrists. "Thanks for your help, don't know how you managed to hold one in each hand like that. You must have some pretty strong hands."

"I'm glad to help, it made me very angry to see this," Blake said, "may I please ask who you are?"

"Casen, Officer Frank Casen."

"I'm pleased to meet you," Blake shook his hand. "What do you do?"

The man was puzzled. "I'm a cop. I'm supposed to try to stop this stuff but it's usually not this easy, pretty bad when an old lady gets mugged in broad daylight right in front of the courthouse."

"It's very bad," Blake had never heard of a "cop."

"By the way, you need to throw that bloody handkerchief away," the cop said, "wash yourself real good, with all the AIDS around here you can't be too careful around blood."

"I'm not familiar with AIDS or cops, but I'll do as you suggest. What language is this woman speaking?"

"Spanish," the cop was scrutinizing him. "I need to get your contact information since you're a witness."

"Here's my phone number."
"You new in town?" the cop asked.
Blake felt the cop measuring him with puzzlement, "yes."
"Where're ya' from?" the cop asked.
"Far away," he ventured.
"I see," the cop said.
"I guess I should get my ride." Blake began walking.
"Sure, have a nice day." The cop was looking at a man driving a black and white vehicle slowly toward them. He had dark skin and was dressed the same.
"Got a witness?" The man helped Officer Casen shove the boys into the back seat of his police car.
"Not sure," Officer Casen said, "got his cell phone number. Strangest thing I've seen in a long time. He apprehended both these criminals with one hand each, grip like a vise, then forced them to walk several blocks to get back here, still holding each one only by the shoulder, made 'em apologize and give the purse back too. Then he says he doesn't know what a cop is, never heard of AIDS, and didn't know people in Miami speak Spanish. I don't know whether to encourage him to join the force or go to the funny farm."
"Hasta la vista," the other cop said and they both laughed.
Blake stopped at a garbage receptacle attached to a pole on the sidewalk. He started to throw his bloody handkerchief away when he noticed a man with wild black hair grasping a piece of bread from the other side of the can. The man was poorly dressed and smelled badly.
"Giv' me some money man, I'm homeless an' hungry."
"Why are you homeless?" Blake handed him a $100 bill.
The homeless man looked so shocked Blake thought he must have done something wrong, but the man was gone before he could ask him. Blake wiped his hands with the clean side of his bloody handkerchief and tossed it in the can. He was happy to see Vega on the street ahead.
As he resumed driving, Vega told him about the difficulty she had finding her way back.

She described how a woman in another car ran into her bumper, and how she remembered Eugene's warning to stay in her car. The woman did not get out, instead she yelled "asshole" and drove away.

He told her about the very old looking Spanish woman whose purse was stolen, the cops, AIDS and blood. "I learned another new emotion," he said. "It's anger."

"What does anger feel like?" she asked.

"You feel hot and completely focused on the thing that's wrong, like a very exaggerated reaction. Does that explain it?"

"I don't know."

"I made them apologize to the woman and return her purse," he added, "that was very satisfying."

"It's hard to comprehend these emotions," Vega said.

"I guess I'm not explaining them well."

"It's all right," she said.

"There's a cop." He pointed as he drove toward the beach. "There sure are a lot of cops, must be a big need for them."

"I guess so," she said. "I like their uniforms. They remind me of uniforms in Abidan."

On the next corner they were shocked to see a man sitting in a wheelchair. There were bare stumps where the man's legs should have been, and he held a cup in his hand.

"That's really hard to see that isn't it?" Blake looked toward the man in the wheelchair, "certainly nothing like that could ever happen where we come from, but if it did, it would be healed."

Irina nodded

A siren whined in the distance.

Chapter 6

The waters of Biscayne Bay shimmered in aqua and turquoise as they drove across the MacArthur Causeway between cruise ships on one side and small white bridges to Palm, Hibiscus and Star Islands on the other. Turquoise waters sloshed against sailboats anchored in the shallow bay, and waves lapped the private docks and seawalls of the islands where glamorous yachts and pastel-colored mansions stood in opulent luxury. The sky was a brilliant blue.

At the end of the causeway was South Beach, a place where small, decorative buildings with pastel colors and artistic designs seemed to exist at least partly for fun. Blake turned onto Ocean Drive, a scene of outdoor revelry among rows of palm trees, rhythmic music, bronze bodies, and gorgeous girls skating and flying colorful kites in the sea breeze. The Atlantic Ocean was a tantalizing glimpse of blue beyond the grassy park and white sand.

"Shall we find a place to eat?" he asked.

Irina nodded. "It smells so good here."

They searched for a parking place along Ocean Drive and its side streets, without success, until a valet with shiny black hair waved them down and parked their car for $25.

On the sidewalk, a statuesque dark-haired girl in a tiny brown and black print bathing suit posed for photographers with large cameras. The tall girl had black eyes, smooth bronze skin, beautiful curves and full coral-colored lips. Blake thought about the contrast between this glamorous model and the little old woman who had been robbed and injured not far away.

"This looks like a good place to eat. Is this okay?" he approached an outdoor restaurant adjacent to a three-story building in pale green, aqua and lavender colors.

"Fine," she answered.

A young girl with long blond hair and blue eyes, like the sky, asked if they would like a table inside or outside. She wore black shorts, a small white top and white sandals.

"I think we should be outside, is that okay?" he asked.

When Vega nodded yes, the pretty hostess showed them to a round table under a sea grape, a small graceful tree with big heart-shaped leaves. As the girl handed them menus, she touched Blake's arm and smiled. Her smile and touch felt good, like the gentle ocean breeze that caressed his face.

The indoor restaurant featured a bar and newsstand. Outside, green and white striped awnings were attached to the building near the patio tables. Three large girls with olive skin and long, dark hair sitting at a table next to them stared and pointed at Blake as though they recognized him. Their table was loaded with platters of fried food and tall drink glasses full of green limes and leaves.

"Hi guys." A dark haired young man approached their table. "I'm Ben, your waiter. Welcome to The Café. Can I start you off with something to drink?" Ben wore a white shirt, white apron, black trousers, and white sneakers.

"A waiter is someone who brings you food and drink?" Blake asked.

"Good one, man," Ben laughed. "So what drinks can I bring you?"

"Water, please," said Vega.

"Pellegrino, Fiji, or tap water?"

"Tap water," she responded.

"Would you like lemon in that water?" Ben asked.

"No thank you."

Blake considered, "What drink do you suggest, Ben?"

"Alcohol or no alcohol?" Ben asked.

"Is alcohol good or bad?"

"That's a good question, man. If this was a serious discussion, I'd have to say it's both, but this is South Beach, so it's good, it's all good," Ben said.

"But it's bad to drive after drinking alcohol, isn't it?"

"Well, yeah, if you drink too much, but your friend here's drinking water, so you got yourself a designated driver."

Vega nodded.

"Then I'll have an alcohol in South Beach."

The waiter grinned, "what kind of an alcohol?"

One of the three dark-haired girls at the next table motioned to Ben.

"Problem solved, man," Ben said, "these girls want to buy you a Mojito, which is my personal favorite, and they want to know if you're an actor, model or athlete."

"Please thank them for me." Blake acknowledged the girls. "I'll be glad to have a Mojito, but I'm not sure how to answer them."

"Even in that jumpsuit, a ripped, good looking guy like you could be all of the above, not that it does anything for me," Ben laughed, "but if you'd rather not say, I can handle it." Ben stopped at the girls' table, as they kept staring and pointing at Blake.

Blake felt amused and slightly perplexed, but he enjoyed the girls' attention.

"Now this, my friend, is a Mojito," Ben said as he set the drinks on the table.

Blake tasted the refreshing mint, lime and sugary rum drink. "This is delicious," he said, as he waved to the girls who waved back as they laughed.

"Would you like to order an appetizer to go with that?"

"Yes," Blake looked at Vega who nodded, "we'll try mango salsa, soft shell crab, and conch fritters, will that be too much if we have an entrée and dessert?"

"Probably not. One of the great things about this place is we're open 24 hours a day and we don't rush you. This your first trip to South Beach?"

"We just arrived here."

"How did I know?" Ben chuckled.

They stayed for several hours enjoying the tasty and unusual food and fascinating parade of people. The girls sent him a second Mojito, and after that they blew kisses and left. He didn't know if it was the day, the nice girls, or the rum that made him feel happy.

He asked Ben about things to see in South Beach, curious about the Holocaust Memorial listed in his orientation.

Ben winced, "I wouldn't see that today, man. I'm Jewish and it's very important no one ever forgets about it, I guess that's why I'm studying history in college, but you're having a good day, and haven't even seen the beach yet, save it for another time."

"Why's that?"

"It's just so sad, so brutal." Ben set the bill on the table, "I don't know, man, you seem like you don't know much about this area. You just learned about alcohol and had your first taste of Cuban coffee and Key lime pie, I think you should wait."

"Then we'll see the beach first."

"Good choice, man."

Blake paid the bill by credit card and added a generous tip.

"Thanks very much, man." Ben picked up the bill, "I hope you'll come back soon. We have lots more alcohol." They both laughed.

Lummus Park on the beach was vibrant with activity. Bright neon jewelry was for sale under colorful, rippling umbrellas next to a stand of motorcycles for rent. Young girls in tiny bright colored bathing suits were bouncing a ball over a net, their tan, bare feet half-concealed in the white sand. The shore was dotted with people who were bathing or walking along. Irina and Blake dabbed sunscreen on their faces and hands.

The ocean was a spectacular light and dark blue color and the salty breeze felt wonderful, even in their jumpsuits. They watched the beautiful ocean and eternal waves scatter the small pink and brown shells along the shoreline. Busy little sandpipers constantly darted back and forth, probing for food between the breaking waves.

Blake watched a bubbly wave come toward them and spread out like lace on the wet sand. He touched the clear water and it felt pleasantly cool, but not cold. The water near the beach was a gorgeous aqua color topped with frothy white waves that pressed continuously toward the shore in a soft roaring motion. Further out in the ocean, dark blue water delineated where the deeper water began and continued to the horizon.

After a pleasant hour had passed, Blake turned to Vega, "I'd like to visit the Art Deco Welcome Center, and also buy some clothes, would you like to join me?"

"You are a fine and inquisitive person," she answered, "but I don't have your energy or your curiosity, I'll be happy to sit in the park and wait."

"Many people tell me I make them feel tired because I have too much energy. I'm sorry."

"It's not a bad thing," she said, "but nevertheless I'm content to sit."

"Here's a good bench with shade, is this okay?" he asked

"It'll be fine." She sat down.

"Then I'll return in three hours, but call me if you need me."

"Okay."

Chapter 7

THE ART DECO WELCOME CENTER WAS A GIFT SHOP selling posters, blue glass vases, flamingos, books and scarves. In one corner, a man in a red shirt and tan shorts with ear phones danced by himself.

"Welcome, my name is Charles," a friendly man spoke from behind a counter scattered with picture books and brochures. "May I have the pleasure of assisting you?" Charles had red curly hair, pink skin, bright blue eyes and gold stud earrings in his ears.

"Thanks," said Blake, "I assume you're here to welcome people to the art district."

"Of course, you silly boy," Charles said. "May I tell you about Art Deco?"

"Yes, please, I'm new in town and curious about it."

"How interesting," Charles said. "Well, in a nutshell, you are in Sobe's Art Deco District, which comprises about 800 buildings preserved through the efforts of one amazing woman named Barbara Capitman. The Art Deco style captivated the world at the 1925 Exposition in Paris. Miami adopted its own version, we call Tropical Deco, which became popular during the Great Depression, as a wonderful way to lift people's spirits. It features ice-cream colors, fantasy towers, curves, lines, chrome, neon, glass blocks and tropical motifs. There are variations, like Deco Dazzle, popularized by Leonard Horowitz in the 1980's. May I book you for a tour?"

"I'd like that, but first I need to know my schedule at the University of Miami," Blake said. An older man and woman approached the counter with a brightly colored scarf and a credit card.

When Charles completed the transaction he asked Blake, "Will you be visiting one of our clubs later this evening?"

"I'm not familiar with the clubs. Do you have a recommendation?"

"I find Fantasy very creative, although it's rather straight," Charles said.

"What's straight?"

Charles laughed. "Oh you're too cute."

"Thank you," Blake said, "where is Fantasy?"

"It's on the 14th block of Washington Street, several blocks north of here," Charles said, "it's open quite late. I may go there myself."

"Then I'll go there too."

"Good," said Charles. "I'm sure they'll admit you. Your clothes are, well, if you don't mind my saying so, a little dated, but original anyway. I think jumpsuits with wide collars went out in the seventies, of the last century, and your shoes, are they made of flubber?" Charles laughed, "but you are a beautiful man."

"Thank you."

"If you have any trouble getting in just tell the doorman you're meeting Charles."

"Thanks again," said Blake. "Do you know where I can purchase some clothes nearby?"

"Yes," Charles looked at his body. "There is so much here, you might try DecoDeco, it's close by on Eighth Street. You could stop by Wet Willie's on the way and have 'Sex on the Beach,'" Charles giggled.

"What's that?"

"Wet Willie's is a place where they have frozen drinks with funny names."

"Oh," Blake said, "well, thank you."

"I hope to see you again quite soon," Charles waved.

The white walls of DecoDeco glistened in the sunshine. The afternoon light added to the charm of its black and white awnings and low front wall trimmed with silver rails and purple bougainvillea flowers. Blake checked his watch and opened the front door onto shiny white marble floors, a rotunda with white columns, dark lounge chairs and a staircase accented by a bright red and purple mural along its back wall. Spotlights from the ceiling illuminated clothing displays on body forms with no heads and arms.

He looked around. These were the casual clothes that would make him look American. The labels read China, Turkey, Dominican Republic, India.

A girl with dark hair, dark eyes and red lips appeared. She wore a tight black dress and tall black shoes. Her body had a beautiful shape and her bare legs were tan.

"May I help you?" she asked.

"Yes, I want to look American, but I can't find any clothes made in America."

She shrugged her shoulders and picked up a belt made of Italian leather and manufactured in the U.S. "This is it," she tossed the belt back on the table. "It's not important. You don't have to have clothes made in America to look American. I'm Cuban. What's important is that you get something to wear besides that jumpsuit you have on."

"Do you speak Spanish?"

"Si."

"But you speak English too. I saw a woman earlier today who didn't speak English."

"Was she older?" she asked.

"Yes, she looked very old," he said.

"A lot of older people don't speak English because they came from Cuba, my generation speaks Spanish at home, but we were born here, we're third generation so we all speak English. You won't get the good jobs if you don't, and we Cuban Americans pretty much run things in Miami. We're hard workers, and you can get ahead in this country if you work hard."

"I'd like to learn about Cuba and your life here, but I don't have much time now," he apologized. "I need to meet my friend in two hours and twenty minutes; she's waiting for me at the beach. Can you help me pick some shirts, shorts, slacks and shoes?"

"Sure," she appraised his body. "You must be a slim fit, extra large. Is that your girlfriend at the beach?"

"No. She's my friend and college roommate."

"I'm in college too," she held up some shirts against his chest, "Madre de Dios, you're good looking! You want to try these on?" She pointed to the dressing room.

He walked out of the dressing room wearing a fitted silky blue shirt, jeans, a brown leather belt, and brown Italian leather shoes.

"You look so hot. I wish I didn't have a jealous boyfriend," the Cuban girl said. "Do you dance?"

"I'm not sure."

She squinted, "my boyfriend's my dance partner, that's not always a good thing. We dance for the Latin Dance Show. The money's good. We compete once a year in Puerto Rico."

"How do you compete in dance?"

"A panel of judges gives you scores based on how good they think you did, the couple with the highest score wins. It's fun, but hard work, for competitions, we dance Salsa."

"Like the food?" He asked.

"Yeah, they call it Salsa cuz it's danced to Salsa music."

"You must be a beautiful dancer," he said.

"Tell my boyfriend that. He's always making me work harder. I complain cuz I'm a full-time student at FIU and that takes a lot of time."

"I saw the FIU campus on Tamiami Trail this morning."

"Yeah, it's a pretty good university. Anyway, my boyfriend says I'm not the only one busy, he says he's busy too cuz he works two jobs, and we have won several times. So, do you like the clothes?"

"Yes, I'll buy all of them. May I wear what I have on?"

"Sure, how do you want to pay, credit card, debit card?"

"I haven't used my debit card yet."

"It's not stolen, is it?"

"Definitely not."

"Sorry, but you have to be careful, there's so much crime around, you need to know your pin number to use your debit card, you know that?"

"Yeah," he answered

She smiled, "okay, just swipe the card like this and enter your pin number on the keypad. You know, you need to be careful when you enter your pin number, if someone gets your number, they can get your money."

"I read a warning about that, but I trust you."

She handed him his receipt and used scissors to cut the tags off the new clothes he was wearing. When she moved closer to him he could hear her breathing and smell her perfume. "The cleaning instructions are in your garments," she said, "but I guess you know that."

"The clothes need to be cleaned?"

"Yeah," she laughed, "you know, laundry."

"Oh, yeah," he smiled.

"You're really different, but I like you." She looked thoughtful as she wrapped his new clothes in tissue paper and placed them in two large shopping bags. She put the jumpsuit in a separate bag. As she handed it to him she was surprised at how lightweight it was, "I hope you ditch this in the first garbage can you see," she laughed.

"I'm not sure if I'll do that, but thanks for your help. What's your name?"

"Marielena, Marielena Gonzalez, and yours?"

"William Blake, pleased to meet you Marielena Gonzalez."

"Thanks, William Blake, a pleasure to meet you too," she said as she flashed him a smile that made him feel wistful. She glanced at her watch, took a deep breath and looked at him "so where do you go next?"

"I'm not sure, I think I'll walk around until it's time to meet my friend."

"I have a better idea," she pulled a key from a drawer near the cash register. "I can get off work soon, I'd like you to meet me." She whispered, "I'd like to be with you, but only once," she breathed, "no matter what."

"I have to meet my friend," he said.

"I know."

She gave him directions to a nearby apartment belonging to a friend of hers. She said she would meet him there in several minutes, which she did.

When Blake returned to the sidewalk, he felt lost in a dreamy haze of Marielena's perfume and pleasure, as he relived the memory of every steamy moment with her. He wondered if all sex on Earth was that exciting, and why she treated it in such a casual way. She did not want to change anything or tell her boyfriend, but she'd obviously wanted to have sex with him, once, and then she was so ecstatic about it, she told him to leave immediately before she changed her mind. As he walked along in a daze, feeling the breeze on his skin, he remembered every detail of her shapely naked body, and every exciting motion she made. He wanted to see Marielena again and have more sex with her, but she did not want to change her relationship with her boyfriend and he had to respect that. He thought of the difference between the steamy, instantaneous and casual sex with Marielena, and the relationship he had with his girlfriend on Abidan. Being with Bekah was very pleasant, but it had none of the wild excitement he had just experienced. Relationships on Abidan were tame in comparison, at least in comparison with Marielena. Casual sex on Abidan was rare and always discouraged. As he walked, he felt a heightened sensitivity toward each woman he passed and wondered if there would be more sexual invitations.

To protect his thoughts, Blake enabled a privacy shield before he returned to Loomis Park. Vega was still sitting on the shaded bench.

She regarded him in his new clothes. "I prefer our jumpsuits, but I'm happy for you that you like your new clothes."

He grinned, "I might change my mind after I do my laundry."

"Laundry?"

He told her what he had learned about the need to wash clothes, which surprised them, since nanotech clothing from Abidan was self-cleaning.

They wandered the streets and saw many new things they had never seen before, tattoos, Erotic Art Museum, surf rentals, body piercing, and a condom store. At dusk, the vibrant city glowed with bold neon colors shining brightly on the exciting world of South Beach. Blake continued to reflect on his dreamy sexual encounter, but he did not disclose it.

When they retrieved their car from the valet, Vega drove. They traveled south on Washington Street where it was less crowded, and there was more renovation and construction of old and new buildings in the Art Deco style.

"This has been the most amazing day of my life," he breathed the salty air from his window.

Vega followed the curve of the road near the water. "There's an amazing variety of individuals here, I'll likely need several genetic maps. I would not have thought that the structure of the genome would vary greatly, since evolution is similar on earthlike planets throughout the Universe, but I'm not sure. What should we do now?"

Blake utilized his eyepik, "Let's drive toward North Miami Beach and see some more of this fabulous place."

"Good idea." She turned the car toward the wonderful hotels, striking buildings, bright lights, lush tropical landscaping and endless parade of fascinating humanity and beautiful women.

Chapter 8

"Do you want to see Fantasy?" Blake pointed to a white Art Deco building. A crowd of mostly young people waited next to a velvet rope. A big man stood near the door with his arms folded across his chest, not looking at anyone's eyes.

"I'd like to see it briefly," Vega answered, "it may be helpful in our research."

The girls waiting in line at the club made Blake think of Marielena. They had pretty faces, perfect white teeth, silky hair, curving breasts and tiny waists. They wore tall shoes that showed off beautiful tan legs and feet. The men were also young, with eager faces and easy clothes, silky shirts and dark slacks or jeans. One dark woman was very tall with large shoulders and stiff black hair. She wore a huge, billowing, red ruffled dress that parted the crowd as she walked about. Blake continued to be amazed at the variety of people on Earth.

Slowly, the man with the crossed arms permitted small groups to enter. Blake watched many of the lovely girls gracefully disappear behind the club doors and wondered what it would be like inside. He steered himself and Vega close to the man at the door and mentioned Charles. The man motioned them in.

The first room was dark, humid, crowded and smoky. Soft music played in the background, and attractive young people lounged on large comfortable chairs and sofas. Blake and Vega had not seen many people smoking cigarettes, and the smell of their smoke was acrid and unpleasant. Several men served drinks at a square bar in the center of the room. Many girls stared at him, and a few brushed against him as he passed by. One very pretty brunette said hi and flashed him a dazzling white smile. He wondered what she would be like.

They climbed a staircase at the back of the room that opened into another large room emanating a blast of loud music. Bright white lights flashed through the darkness and a misty fog filled the room. Young people were dancing in an almost frantic way. No one looked at anyone; they stared ahead as if they were in a dream state of continuous motion. Many of them had necklaces or short sticks that glowed in green neon colors in the dark. Several of them opened their mouths to show the glowing sticks inside their mouths. It was excessively humid. He turned to ask Vega her opinion of the dancing and saw that she was ahead of him in the crowd. He tried to push toward her direction.

"Nice buns," a woman said to him as she grabbed his backside. She made her voice loud to be heard over the music. She was not one of the pretty young girls. Her face looked painted and there were deep lines around her purple mouth. Her body was hard and freckled.

She held tightly to the right cheek of his buttocks through his jeans.

"Thanks," he was not sure what to say. "I must go find my friend now."

"That figures," the girl let go of him and stumbled off through the crowd bumping into people as she went.

He spotted Vega entering a doorway to another room. When he attempted to push through the crowd to catch up with her, he felt someone touch his crotch, but he could not tell who it was in the throng of people.

The room where he found Vega was not as loud and bright as the room where the people danced. The music, played by a young boy from a booth, had a rhythmic, talking sound and there were more large chairs and couches in the room. Lovely young girls with long blond hair and tight black clothes were serving drinks at the bar. Blake ordered a Bacardi Pina Colada. He liked it and offered Vega a taste, but she was content with water. He liked the beat of the music even though he could not distinguish many of the words. He had never heard music like that before. Music on Abidan was more structured, although it was also pleasing.

Vega sighed, "I'm ready to go when you are."

"Me too." He signaled their waitress for the check. "I think it would be difficult to find Charles anyway, there's such a crowd."

"Maybe you can help me," he paid for the drink, "I'm looking for a sweet man named Charles. He was supposed to meet me here."

"Haven't seen him," the waitress abruptly walked away to join the other waitress behind the bar.

"What a waste of manhood," he heard her say as they were leaving, "and look how gorgeous he is."

"What did you think of Fantasy?" Blake looked at the glittering lights of Miami as Vega drove them across the Causeway.

"It seemed decadent," she said. "I'm even confused about the genetic makeup of some of the people in the crowd."

"A very physical crowd," he said. "It did seem decadent, especially compared with recreation on Abidan, but I'm not certain what to take from it. It wasn't violent, the music was good, I found it interesting to see them socialize, it makes me wonder what they do when they're not at Fantasy."

"That's a good observation," she said, "the diversity was surprising too."

"Yeah, lots of variety, not just the faces, but the clothes."

"I even got a few compliments on my jumpsuit," she said.

He smiled, "Tomorrow, we register at the University of Miami. That should improve our understanding of all the strange things we've experienced. I look forward to it."

"I do too."

Chapter 9

THE UNIVERSITY OF MIAMI CAMPUS SPARKLED IN sunshine, like a tropical Garden of Eden, among beautiful fountains, colorful flowers, abundant shade and palm trees, and college students talking and laughing. Girls lay on towels on the green grass, reading books and sunning the backs of their slim legs. Mockingbirds sang beautiful trills from the treetops.

"May I help you?" asked a middle-aged woman from behind a counter at the Registrar's Office. She had a wide face, pink cheeks, short black hair held in place by a pink headband, and a precise way of speaking through her broad mouth and the gap between her front teeth.

"Yes, thank you," William Blake said, "my friend and I want to register for some courses."

"Well, you're too late," the woman rested her stout arms on the counter. "Classes start next week. You should have registered by telephone anyway."

"How do you register by telephone?" he asked.

"Well, you need your pin number and your spring schedule," she announced. "We mailed those out to all of our students in November."

"When do spring classes start?" he asked.

"January 19," she stated.

"Isn't that winter?" he asked. "Students seem to be going to class now."

"That's the inter-session," she sounded impatient, "and we don't have winter here sir.

Now what degree are you seeking?"

"I don't want a degree. I'm here only for six months," he said.

"Why would you come if you are only going to be here six months?" she asked.

"That's all the time I was allowed," he started to explain.

"Where did you come from?" she asked nervously.

"I'd rather not say," he knew he should have a better answer. She was frightened.

"Are you armed?" she almost whispered.

He was unsure what to say, but he knew he had to respond. "Yes, I have arms."

"Oh my God. Someone call security," she raised her voice.

"There's no need to be afraid," he said, "I just want to sign up for some courses."

"Are you threatening me?" the woman asked.

An older man with white hair and a big stomach appeared. He was dressed like the cops downtown.

"What seems to be the problem, Miss Parsons?" he asked.

"Officer, this man is threatening me. He wants me to register him without proper paperwork and he's armed!"

The man turned to Blake, "Is that true, sir?"

"Yes sir, I was trying to find out information about attending classes here at the University, and I do have arms, a right one and a left one."

The man chuckled as Miss Parsons tightened her jaw.

Blake realized that arms must mean weapons and his answer had been foolish. He had not anticipated that a question about weapons would arise so spontaneously.

The officer continued, "What do you want to study here?"

"I'm writing a graduate dissertation for my doctorate in Sociology on the need to preserve creativity on Earth, while eliminating its culture of violence through genetic and environmental engineering," Blake said.

The man whistled. "Well, I sure wish you luck, and what is it you want here?"

"I want to audit some classes and use the library and laboratories for research," Blake responded, "and my friend here is focusing on genetic variations and causes of violence, and she wants to do the same."

The officer looked at Miss Parsons, "I don't think there's any need to be alarmed about these two, ma'am, but I'm sure you can't be too careful these days. There're a lot of strange things in this world, that's for sure."

"Well, he's not even in the right building," Miss Parsons said pointedly, "and he'll never audit anything without permission from the individual professors, and then that's only lecture courses…"

"Well, Miss Parsons, if you'll just tell me where they need to go, I'll be glad to take them there," the man said gently.

"I'm William Blake and this is my friend, Irina Vega." Blake shook hands with the officer as they walked toward the bus stop.

"Good to meet you, I'm Stubbs, Officer Lou Stubbs. Miss Parsons is a nice woman, just has a little overactive imagination sometimes, but it's good to be careful. It can be a dangerous place all right. Well, here's your bus. It'll take you to the graduate school at Pick Hall, good luck to both of you."

"Thanks for your help." Blake followed Vega onto the bus.

When they met later that afternoon, Vega was pleased with the contacts she made in the Department of Biomedical Engineering. Blake was also pleased. He had met a Biochemistry Professor named Dr. James Harmon, who was very interested in his theories. Dr. Harmon arranged for Blake to audit classes in Molecular Biology, Genetics, World History and Advanced Criminology.

They went to the campus bookstore, where Blake purchased Miami Hurricanes tee shirts for his family and Vega browsed the merchandise. The Otto G. Richter Library was nearby. There was a large banner across the front of the building announcing a rape crisis seminar. Vega chose to stay on the first floor of the library in a large reading room lined with computer terminals, while Blake explored upstairs.

Blake took the elevator to the third floor. The door opened onto a sign posted on a pastel colored column, "Prevent crime, protect your valuables." He looked around. The stacks of books were dark, musty smelling and empty. He felt excited. Inside this building was access to all of Earth's recorded knowledge.

He walked toward the first row of books and a long tube light hanging from the ceiling illuminated. When he left the first row of books, the tube light extinguished. He reached the next stack, and another light shined. The fourth, fifth and sixth floors had the same warning sign and dark rows of musty books. Beyond the stacks on each floor were desks against windows overlooking the palm trees outside. The floors were mostly empty; only an occasional row was lit in the dark rooms.

He wanted to read everything, but he did not want to leave Vega for long. He spent a few minutes looking through an atlas and decided the next time someone asked where he was from, he'd say Belgium. It was a small country and different enough from Miami to help account for his lack of knowledge of local customs.

He used his new student ID to check out books: *River of Grass, A Guide to Belgium, The Holy Bible, American History, Florida History, En Espanol, World Atlas, David Copperfield, Letters from the Earth, Anna Karenina, Salsa Dancing Made Easy,* and *The Miccosukee Tribe.* He would get more books soon.

Vega was working at the computer station on the first floor. She showed Blake the digital patterns of DNA on her monitor, and they studied them together until it was almost dark. When they left the library, spotlights on the walkway shined brightly.

Chapter 10

On the way home from campus, they stopped at Milam's grocery. In front of the store a small group of men paced back and forth carrying signs that read, "Boycott sugar. Aliens are taking our jobs." Vega looked around nervously.

"Who you bumpin'?" one of the men with the signs said.

"I beg your pardon," Blake said, "I guess I wasn't looking where I was going."

"You don't be bumpin' me no mo', ya' heah? Or I be thinkin' you dissin' me."

"Sure," Blake said, feeling not quite sure. "Can I ask you what your sign means?"

"It means what it say. Don't buy no shuga'," the man answered.

"But what about the aliens?"

"What you think I'm talkin' 'bout, man?"

"I don't know."

"I'm talkin' about J'makins. They takin' our jobs," the man said.

"What are Jamaicans?"

"They come here from the islands."

"Oh," Blake nodded. "I guess that's a problem, but aren't there enough jobs for everyone?"

"Where you come from, man? You don't know much."

"Belgium."

"That's a long way off ain't it? Well at least you ain't no damn J'makin be takin' our jobs, huh?" The man laughed and held up his light palm toward him.

Blake smiled at the man.

"You suppose' to giv' me five, like this." The man showed him. Blake liked slapping hands with the man.

"Good luck to you," Blake said. "I hope you get a job."

"Shor' man, you have a nice evenin' too."

Blake pushed their grocery cart into a store that appeared as different from their home planet as everything else they'd experienced.

"We need only a few things to make dinner," Blake looked at Vega, "and I think we shouldn't buy any sugar for now. I know there are at least two sides to each conflict, but I liked the people with the signs."

"At first I was worried about the word aliens on their signs," she said.

"Yeah, me too, but they meant people from other places on Earth."

"Once I realized that, I also liked them." Vega put a box of black beans and rice in the grocery cart.

At home, Blake sautéed the fresh Yellowtail Snapper in olive oil and lemon and sliced a mango, while Vega fixed black beans and rice according to the package directions. He suggested they watch television while they ate dinner.

> *A man was put to death in Texas for strangling a woman and child who had lived next door to him. A Canadian woman was arrested on the Vermont border with suspected links to an Algerian terrorist organization planning a possible bombing in the Seattle area. An airport baggage handler accused of trying to smuggle three hand grenades and one pistol on an American Airlines flight was acquitted. Police used tear gas on demonstrators arguing about a little Cuban boy who was found floating on a tire in the ocean. His mother had drowned trying to get them to the United States. UNICEF reported that, in the last decade, two million children had been killed and six million disabled in armed conflicts, including injuries from land mines.*
>
> *And a baby rhinoceros was born at the Metro Zoo.*

On Abidan, they were familiar with the word "violence," but no one understood what it meant. What a strange, sick, horrible thing that people would hurt each other and cause death on each other, especially on children. He did not understand how that could happen, but he knew that is why Earth was classified as a failed experiment. Very, very failed. That was why God had refused them intervention and why Eugene hated the planet. It was what Professor Shem had warned him against. Was Earth worth saving? Maybe it should destroy itself and the horrible, horrible violence with it.

He thought of the people he'd met. They were kind and good and helpful and some of them were very creative. They did not appear to be violent, but the people in the news were immersed in a terrible culture of hate and violence. There must be something very wrong with their genetics and their environments.

How much better would this strange world be if there was no violence? To what beautiful heights could it ascend? What wonderful things could be achieved? What beauty that had never before existed in the Universe could be created? That was his thesis, but was it valid?

He turned off the television. "I could not have imagined anything like this. I see why we were warned so stringently about the dangers of Earth."

She nodded. They sat in silence for a long time.

"I think we have no choice but to complete our research here," he finally said. "I'll try to complete my work more quickly than six months so that we can leave here as soon as feasible."

"I agree, and I'll make the same effort," she said quietly.

Chapter 11

Several days following the newscast, Blake was able to gain some insight from Dr. Harmon, the professor who had helped him secure courses to audit.

"This is a world of extremes," the professor said over a cup of coffee at the student union, "being from Belgium, you may not have seen as much trouble as we have in this country. My dad was a policeman, killed in the line of duty when I was 14," Dr. Harmon rested his cup on the table, "after that, we had to work hard to hold it together. I had to work after school to help Mama raise my little brother. When he got older, he worked too. I became a professor because my dad always wanted me to go to college."

Blake listened as Dr. Harmon continued.

"Life can be so cruel it makes you cry. It can also be so beautiful, it makes you cry, like the day I married my wife, the day my daughter was born, or the day my little brother graduated from college… and all the times as a kid, holidays with my dad, the day I hit my first home run in Little League, my father was at the game. He was always there for me until he died. He retrieved the baseball where it landed when I hit it over the fence. I still have it."

Blake set his coffee down. "Did you play a lot of baseball?"

The professor smiled. "Every year of my life from the time I was five until I graduated from college. Actually, I still play on a team, for recreation now. I also coach some kids in Little League. I don't have a son, maybe I will someday, but I love my baseball kids like they're my own. They don't have much, they're poor kids, baseball means a lot to them, it even motivates them to learn to read."

"You must be a fine coach."

Harmon smiled again.

"I've never played baseball, but I'd like to try it," Blake said.

"I admire your curiosity," the professor said, "it's essential in academic research, of course, but you're curious about everything. We've got baseball practice tomorrow night, as a matter of fact, tryouts for the adult recreational league are in a few weeks, so our season's just getting started. It might not be possible to do much if you've never played before, but you're welcome to come see what it's all about. It's a great game."

"I'd like to do that, thank you."

The next evening, Blake followed the professor's directions to a park where clusters of silver lights on tall poles shined brightly. There were four baseball fields enclosed in tall fences, connected by a concrete area with walkways and silver bleachers. At the center was a small round building, a closed concession stand, and a storage area with an open door.

Blake found Field 3, where the professor and 20 or more men were paired up throwing baseballs into each other's gloves. Blake recognized the "diamond" with its orange lanes and white equidistant bases, having read numerous books about baseball the previous night. As he took a seat on the bleachers, the professor nodded and waved.

Blake watched the men rhythmically throwing to each other, and listened to the pop of baseballs as they hit their large black or brown gloves. They sometimes missed and had to run back for the ball, but mostly they caught it. The men wore a variety of old uniforms, colorful numbered jerseys, long pants, dark socks, large black shoes with cleats and different colored caps sporting team symbols. The air was pleasant and cool, and the short green grass in the outfield smelled fresh.

Blake was intrigued by baseball and the idea of competition. Competition was not permitted in Abidan, but baseball seemed to be centered around that idea. Baseball was about winning and losing, mostly about winning.

Blake found the game's history to be surprising. It had excluded "black" players until a man named Jackie Robinson, who was black, joined the Brooklyn Dodgers in 1947. Before that, there were separate black and white leagues of teams. Robinson was a great baseball player and the first black man to be voted into the Baseball Hall of Fame. He had changed things by opening the way for blacks and whites to play together.

To Blake, everyone and everything on Earth was so different from what he knew that he would not have thought of skin color as something that made them appear different to each other.

Their skin colors were all a shade of tan or brown. He could not see that "black" was actually black, the same with "white."

It did not seem to be a problem now. There were black, white and Hispanic players on the field, making friendly jokes and getting along fine. The problem seemed to be in the past, but Blake realized that if Dr. Harmon had wanted to play baseball in Robinson's day, he would not have been allowed on a white team. What did skin color have to do with baseball, or anything, for that matter?

It related to freedom, a fragile and beautiful concept. Blake had studied the Civil War, civil rights and the ongoing struggle for freedom. He did not know if he would ever understand it. In present times, the concept of freedom seemed overindulged with excesses like pornography and the right to own all manner of dangerous weapons. These were overblown freedoms that fed the beast of evil and caused it to grow into a terrible culture of hate and violence on Earth, like what he witnessed on the evening news. Yet to the slaves of history, freedom was everything. To the little Cuban boy's mother, freedom was worth dying for.

A pitcher approached the mound and began throwing to a catcher squatting behind home plate. The catcher wore protective gear covering his face, neck, chest and legs. When the pitcher threw the baseball, it made a thunking sound as it hit the catcher's big, tan glove.

Blake was curious as to why Dr. Harmon, whom his teammates called Jim, loved the game so well. They were clearly having a good time, and that must be part of it, but it was also the competition.

Half the men lined up along the baseline where Blake was sitting, each holding a metallic bat. The other half took the field. The first batter strode to home plate, planted his feet apart, cocked his bat, and faced the white square that was dusty with orange dirt. The pitcher zinged the ball across the plate, and the man tried to hit it and missed. The catcher caught the ball. The men in line chattered and teased the batter. They were quiet for the next pitch.

The players took turns trying to bat the balls the pitcher threw toward home plate. He observed many styles of throws, sliders, sinkers, changeups, fast balls, curve balls. It looked difficult to hit the baseball, but the players were able to do it, at least some of the time.

When the players took a water break, Jim Harmon strode over to the bleachers to talk to him. Blake asked if he could try hitting.

"Okay, if you're sure, but first you need to go in that storage room and see if you can find some clothes." Jim pointed to the door of the round building. "I'm sure the guys can probably find you some. There's lots of old stuff in there. Tell them you're my friend."

Blake returned wearing gray clay-stained pants and a navy jersey with a number ten and the name "Homer" on the back. He wore one long black and one shorter navy sock under his baseball pants, and black shoes with cleats that clinked when he walked across the concrete. He liked the sound of the cleats; it made him feel like one of the players.

He overheard a player say to Jim, "This's a bad idea, the guy doesn't even know how to put on baseball pants, doesn't have a cup, not that you could find one to fit him."

"What's the harm in letting the guy try?" Jim asked.

"Better get him a helmet, and a supersized cup."

Jim found Blake a black batter's helmet and let him use his own dark green and black metal bat. He showed him how to stand at home plate and how to hold the bat.

"Which side should I hold it on?" Blake asked.

"Are you right or left handed?" Jim asked.

"I'm not sure."

"Well, which hand do you write with?"

"Either," Blake felt confused.

"Oh," Jim said. "Well, try both then, start with the right, most people are right-handed, bat that way for a while, and then switch. See which one feels better to you. If you can do both, that's a good thing."

"Okay," Blake liked his encouraging tone.

Jim took his bat to demonstrate, "Now, when you swing, rotate your hips and transfer your weight from the back foot to the front foot, like this. Take your hands to the ball, like this, with your chin down, and follow through with the bat. Don't try to smash the ball, just try to make contact. The power comes from the rotation of your hips." Jim got out of the way and the pitcher threw the ball.

Blake felt excited as he watched the pitch come toward him. He swung the bat and missed. The players laughed and made good natured chatter about the rookie at bat. They called him "Homer," the name on his borrowed shirt. He swung and missed the next pitch and there was more chatter and laughter. Blake reviewed what Jim told him and realized he was swinging early. On the third pitch, he connected. He watched the ball sail over the fence. Everyone did. He understood what to do. The guys were quiet.

On the next pitch and the next, he hit the ball over the fence. On the sixth throw, he hit the fence. He assumed a rhythm of hitting the pitches hard and most of them flew over the fence.

Jim stepped toward him. "You sure you've never played before?"

Blake nodded, glad Jim was pleased.

Jim shook his head and stepped back, "try it left handed."

It was the same. Blake hit the ball as well left handed as right handed. When the pitcher stopped, Blake noticed everyone staring at him and talking about something called steroids.

"Man, Homer's too good for us," one of the players said.

"That's what I was thinking," said Jim.

Chapter 12

ONE OF THE STRANGEST PARADOXES ON EARTH WAS that people were surrounded by terrible acts of violence every day, yet they found happiness and contentment in their lives. After seeing horrible things during one newscast on one ordinary night, Blake would not have believed that he and Vega would find a measure of peace in their daily routines, but they did.

They shared the household chores of cooking, shopping and cleaning, and ate evening meals together, which gave them a chance to discuss their research and to become friends. Sometimes they ate at home. At other times, they enjoyed the tantalizing variety of Miami's restaurants. It was good to have a friend in this strange and perplexing world, especially a friend from Abidan.

Vega developed a schedule of studying and spending time at the lab or library in her research into the intricacies of human genomics. She did not watch television or read the newspaper.

Blake spent his days attending classes, studying, reading, swimming and playing baseball. Although he also avoided television and newspapers, he could not avoid learning about violence in his research. From the discovery of the knowledge of good and evil in the Garden of Eden, violence was embedded in the story of Earth. He was continually shocked by what he learned about violence, even as he was constantly reminded of the stunning dichotomy between good and evil.

Even the idea of capitalism had different facets. The idea that a person like Bill Gates could use brain power and talent to achieve wonderful innovations was a great concept, further enhanced by Bill and Melinda Gates' charity work to help people all over the world. But capitalism had also been twisted to oppress the weak and cause great suffering and poverty, even slavery, in the historical struggle between the "haves" and "have-nots." The struggle existed even in the animal world with the predatory survival of the fittest. There was much for his mind to process.

He studied Earth's vast history of war and tried to understand it. Being from a planet of peace, he had never known war. What he learned about the true nature of war blasted his mind with its horror. Not only did these humans kill each other, but throughout their history they organized killing to an incredible level of sophistication, wasting their technology and resources and the lives of their young men, and women, in horrible attempts to resolve issues. Sometimes the issues were a struggle of good versus evil, but more often the reasons were purely economic and political. It was the leaders who caused the wars. The unfortunate soldiers had to fight and die in them. In World War I, an estimated 20 million people died. In World War II, 50 million or more people died.

And World War III was coming.

Genocide by individuals was closely related to war. It was hard to imagine anyone worse than Hitler, who was responsible for the deaths of 12 million people, but Joseph Stalin was responsible for the deaths of 23 million, due to purges and Ukraine's famine. Mao Ze Dong, considered the worst genocider in the 20th century, was responsible for the deaths of between 49 to 78 million in China and Tibet.

The list of genociders did not stop with Hitler, Stalin and Mao. Ismail Enver in Turkey was responsible for the deaths of 2.5 million Armenians, Greeks and Assyrians; Pol Pot in Cambodia, 1.7 million of his people; Yakubu Gowon, 1 million Biafrans. The list surpassed meaning. It continued in the Western Hemisphere, Fidel Castro killed 30,000 Cubans; Papa Doc Duvalier killed 60,000 Haitians; Rafael Videla killed 20,000 Argentinians; Augusto Pinochet killed 3,000 Chileans.

Except for the American Revolution and Civil War in the United States, most wars were not fought on their soil, but it was a warlike country. During Richard Nixon's presidency, 70,000 Vietnamese civilians were killed, and 30,000 died in Viet Nam during Lyndon

Johnson's tenure. It was staggering. That was in the 20th century. In primitive wars, an estimated 400 million died. The history of human warfare had recorded 1,763 wars.

Blake learned how people sometimes used religion to justify whatever terrible atrocities they wanted to commit. He found many examples: the Crusades, the French Wars of Religion, the Muslim conquests, the Taiping Rebellion and the Reconquista of the Iberian Peninsula.

A more recent example was Jim Jones, who founded a religion because he saw it as the best way to promote his political views. In 1978, at his People's Temple in Guyana, when things started to go wrong for him, he coerced over 900 followers, including 276 children, to commit "revolutionary suicide." He made them drink a grape flavored drink containing a poisonous combination of sedatives and cyanide. It was unbelievable that such things could happen.

And there was horrid individual crime - serial murderers like Ted Bundy, John Wayne Gacy and Jeffrey Dahlmer. He learned what happened to the tourists in Miami whose car had been bumped. Mrs. Jensen was a German tourist with a rental car license plate who took a wrong turn into a bad neighborhood. Her attackers bumped her car from behind and when she got out of the car to see about it, they ran over her and killed her, while her mother and children, aged 2 and 6, watched. She was the third German tourist to be murdered in Miami. There were five other tourists killed, including two Canadians and one Venezuelan. He understood why Eugene had not given them those details.

He did not think his mind could ever process how and why these terrible things could happen. The people of Earth had formulated laws against these horrors, and punishments for those who committed them. God's commandments forbade these terrible actions. Yet they continued to take place. He understood why God had turned away.

And yet, in the midst of all this horror, he was amazed that people were able to put the atrocities aside and live as though these terrible things did not happen. He reasoned that a protective mechanism in the brain enabled this phenomenon. Otherwise, no one would want to live. Instead, he saw people live with hope and optimism and kindness and laughter and even joy. It was astounding.

Not only did they live happily, there were so many giving, loving and kind people. He learned that in 1998 alone, 70.1% of American households made charitable contributions averaging $1,075, and 55.5% of Americans volunteered their time to help others for a total of 19.9 billion hours. That too, was staggering. He had seen it in his friend, Jim, who volunteered many hours to help poor children in the inner city learn to read and to play baseball.

Blake also found a measure of happiness on Earth. His friendship with Jim, his participation in sports, and the novelty of being outdoors gave him great pleasure.

He swam several times a week at the Biltmore Hotel pool, and played baseball six days each week. When he passed a drug test and a physical exam, Jim arranged for him to work out with the University of Miami baseball team. The drug test had been no problem, but the physical had made him nervous.

The young doctor performing his physical exam became keenly interested in the rate and size of his heart. Because Blake had no history of participation in sports, the doctor was intrigued by his resting rate of 34 beats per minute and maximal oxygen uptake of 70. The doctor wanted to do further testing on him to check things like his maximal heart rate, muscle myosin and lactic acid. He was also perplexed that he was unable to palpate the regular pattern of internal organs. Blake was worried about arousing the young doctor's suspicions, and he used his busy schedule as an excuse to avoid further contact.

Blake loved everything about playing baseball with the Miami Hurricanes, how hard the players worked, what good friends they were to each other, and how friendly they were to him. They practiced at Mark Light Field on the edge of campus adjacent to the football practice field, track and Hecht Athletic Center. The baseball team shared the weight room with the football players, and other athletes, and he found those athletes to be as friendly and dedicated as the baseball players. The idea of competition continued to intrigue him as well as the concept of a contact sport like football. If only all of this intense competition could somehow substitute for the contest of war.

He grew accustomed to the dank smell of the baseball locker room and he loved the friendliness of the athletes in the weight room. They also called him "Homer," somehow the name had followed him from the rec league. His teammates taught him to field the ball, and his strong hands were exceptional. One of the ways he helped the team was to pitch to players in the batting cages. The players preferred his pitching to the machines, and unlike most pitchers, he never had to ice or rest his arm.

He was surprised to learn that baseball, like all sports, required a tremendous amount of practice. That seemed unusual, especially because the game had come so easily for him. During his physical, Blake learned that he had superior strength, vision and reflexes, which explained why he was able to hit and field the baseball so well, without practice. He admired the young athletes who had to work so hard at their sports, at the same time laboring to be good students.

He loved everything about the field: the clay pitcher's mound and batter's box, the green mesh fence, the two billowing leafy ficus trees shading the bleachers, and the little commuter trains across the street that passed every few minutes along elevated tracks, as if they traveled in the treetops.

He was not eligible to join the team since he was not enrolled as a student. The players often teased that they needed "his bat." He enjoyed teasing them back that they really did not need him because they were last year's national champions.

During practice, he would often hear the whine of sirens in the distance signaling the ever present troubles on Earth. The noise made him think of his research, but each day when the late afternoon breeze rose from the nearby ocean he felt a balm to his soul. He was happy within the perimeter of that special field. He was grateful to Jim, the wonderful professor who had made his life on Earth better.

Blake's daily routine also included time at the library. He loved the stories he found there. One that seemed so unusual to him was

Romeo and Juliet. The language of love was beautiful, but he did not understand suicide or why Romeo killed others, another manifestation of the paradox of good and evil.

He sometimes drove to South Beach to walk the beach at Lummus Park. He loved the warmth, the gentle breeze, the salty smell, the little shore birds scurrying for food, the eternal pressing of the frothy waves, the attention from the beautiful bronze and gold girls.

He had not seen Marielena again, but there were propositions from other women. When he accepted, he could not deny that he enjoyed the encounters, but casual sex often felt like something was missing. He did not go out in the evenings, because he knew Vega did not have other friends on Earth.

He and Vega often ran in their neighborhood in Coral Gables. He would caution her about safety and she would do the same to him, but their neighborhood seemed like a peaceful place. In spite of all the horrors, their time on Earth passed more pleasantly and quickly than they would have ever thought was possible.

Chapter 13

"I'm doubtful about completing my research before our six months' deadline," Vega said one night at home when they were having Sushi take-out. They had been on Earth for two months. "The working draft sequence of the Human Genome Project will likely be completed soon, but the bulk of scientific work in deciphering how the approximately three billion base pairs of the human haploid gene will take years to complete, which complicates my efforts to identify and map aggressor genes and gene variants."

"Yes, the completed human sequence identifying the gene locations is probably three years away." Blake passed a serving plate to her, "but research is beginning to show a genetic propensity for human violence. For example, dysfunctional MAO-A genes been have been correlated with heightened levels of violent aggression and antisocial behavior."

She nodded, "That was the study of the large Dutch family where the 14 male members were mildly retarded, extremely violent and lacked the MAO-A gene."

"Yes," he said, "the Brunner study in 1993. Since then, they've found that the correlation is stronger if the carrier had experienced some sort of childhood trauma."

Vega took a bite of Sushi. "Aggression, like most behaviors, is plastic, attributable to multiple segregating genes sensitive to the environment."

"The cause of human violence is complex," Blake agreed, "it must be both environmental and genetic."

"That's what my research is pointing toward," she said.

"Should we reverse our decision to leave before our six months is up?" he asked.

"I think so."

"So far, the culture of violence has not touched us."

"Thank God," Vega said.

"Then it's decided," he said, "I'm okay with the decision as long as you are. I've been enjoying a lot of things here."

"I've enjoyed some things too," she said, "and my studies of human genetics have been very interesting."

"I wanted to ask you what you think about the biblical stories," he put some Sushi on his plate. "I've been examining them and it seems like they would likely be based on actual historical events. What do you think?"

"I've read some of them, but I haven't formulated a definitive opinion," she took a bite of food.

"If the stories do derive from historical events, I'm trying to reconcile them with hereditary and environmental influences, specifically, which begat the other. If the first murderer was Cain," Blake continued, "and he was described as the second generation of man on Earth, even if there were others on Earth at the time, was he the first to possess aggressor genes, as mutations, and what was the extent of his environmental influence? If the first murder transpired because of mutant genes, did that subsequently create the environmental stimulus for aggressive behavior?"

"I see your point," she answered.

"Or do you think Adam and/or Eve first possessed the mutant gene and that was what lead to their discovery of evil?"

"The cause certainly originates from environment and heredity," she said, "although I'm not sure if they spawned separately or simultaneously, but I don't believe it's possible to reconcile these two factors with biblical stories."

"If you pursue the thesis that there is an historical basis for the Bible, wouldn't aggressor genes have to be a part of Cain's genome, and wouldn't that propensity have been passed on, even through Noah's family?"

"If you give a literal interpretation to those stories," Vega countered.

"It's difficult to decipher what actually occurred, but I think there may be some basis to believe Adam and Eve were the first to obtain the knowledge of evil," he said.

"That might be," she said.

"Yes, and Noah was a real character," he smiled, "or else my theories about the need for a second Noah experiment will be harder to prove."

"Or he was a real symbol," she said.

"One thing seems fairly certain to me, some of my research and experience at the University, in class, the library, the baseball team proves that there are many good and caring people on Earth. They vastly outnumber the criminals. It's something like .5% of Americans commit violent crimes, and 18% of homicides are committed by people with serious psychiatric disorders. It seems like a small number of the population to cure in order to make things right. Genetic and environmental engineering appear to be a worthy goal after all." He looked up, "where're you going?"

"Campus lab, I have a sequence theory I want to explore."

"It'll be dark soon, can't it wait until morning?" he picked up their plates from the table.

"I really want to go now to verify an idea I have. It may be a breakthrough. I'll tell you about it later," she stood up.

"You want me to go with you?"

"No, that's all right. I won't be long." She slung her bag over her shoulder. "Do you mind cleaning the dishes by yourself?"

"Not at all," he said. "Why don't you take the car?"

She shook her head, "it's so close."

"You sure? I'm not going to use it."

She shook her head again.

"I'll be glad to go with you."

"Thanks, but you don't need to, I won't be long." She waved and was off.

He picked up the rest of the dishes, activated his computer and sat down to the piano. He played Beethoven's Eighth Symphony.

At dark, he turned the front porch light on for Irina.

Chapter 14

Irina Vega took a deep breath, as if inhaling the quiet satisfaction she felt about her remarkable discovery. The smell of chemicals in the biolab was like a familiar constant in a place that thrived on change. Seated at her work station, Vega scrutinized the digital DNA sequence on her screen, the images from the transmission electron microscope, and the black and white bars of chromosomes on the human gene map. She pushed her brown hair back from her face. The ceiling lights shined brightly against the darkness outside. She smiled. Alone, in this small lab at the University of Miami, she had discovered the genetic causes of human violence.

Vega recorded her groundbreaking research in her blue notebook, describing the 19 genes and gene variants that elevated the risk of violent human behavior. She affirmed their connection with adverse environmental factors, and wrote of the impact of childhood trauma on gene function. Vega predicted how her discovery might produce a cure for human aggression through a combination of mutagenesis, synthetic genomics and gene therapy. She dated the entry March 11, 2000.

Vega checked her watch. She had been at the lab for several hours. She didn't want Blake to worry, and she was anxious to tell him the news of her discovery. Her research affirmed his theory that the cause of human violence was both genetic and environmental. She stowed her blue spiral notebook in her shoulder bag, shut down the equipment and lights, placed her hand against the door handle and locked the lab door.

When she left the campus, the neighborhood was dark. Although she could see well, she did not see the three men who jumped at her from the bushes. She soon felt the frightening terror of their attack, and the awful pain, as they dragged her into the tall vegetation and slammed her on the hard ground. A rough hand covered her mouth. She was horrified that they ripped away her shirt and slacks and even her underwear. They stuffed her underwear in her mouth and covered her with their stinking bodies. She fought back with all of her strength, but her strong hands had little power against their savage attack. She twisted, turned, pushed, kicked and struggled to free herself, but there were three of them and she could not fight them off.

Irina felt pain, terrible pain, terror and humiliation, more intense than she could have ever imagined. Her throat was searing; her body was assaulted with a frightening pain. She felt hands around her throat, and she screamed without the ability to make any noise. She struggled to breathe, and felt the dig of fingernails against her throat. She choked. Everything hurt with a frightening intensity as they continued to brutalize her.

She could no longer breathe. She felt herself drifting away, drifting into darkness, deeper, trying to escape in any way that she could.

Vega thought of her home planet of Abidan as she floated away from the pain. She thought of her family and her friends at home as she drifted closer and closer to the darkness.

She thought of her research on Earth, her roommate and what would happen to her discovery.

As she drifted away from life, through the sounds of exquisite music, she reached a place where there was no anxiety or pain, only a peaceful, spiritual sensation of transmuting through darkness, toward a strong and powerful blessing of Light.

Chapter 15

Even though Vega had said she would not be long, Blake didn't worry at first when she had not returned. He knew that research often takes longer than anticipated. When she didn't answer her phone around midnight, he decided to run to campus to check on her.

As he was about to leave the house, a squad of investigators from the Miami-Dade County Homicide Bureau appeared at his front door. What Sergeant John O'Neal told him exploded whatever tranquility Blake had ever felt on Earth.

"Are you sure?" Blake asked repeatedly as the horrible news penetrated first one level and then the next of his consciousness, until it sank deeper and deeper into his mind and he began to understand the full horror of what the sergeant told him. Irina Vega had been murdered, probably raped.

"Unfortunately, I'm very sure it happened," the sergeant responded. When Blake didn't speak, O'Neal cleared his throat. "Got some business to do here, need your cooperation, some routine questions, need to search your place for clues." O'Neal was a stocky man with a friendly square face, thinning red blonde hair and ruddy skin. He sat at the kitchen table across from Blake and began asking questions.

To Blake, each question felt like it pounded him further into the grizzly night. The kitchen lights seemed unusually bright, glaring at him through the dark of the evil night. Where was she from, how long have you known her, where was she going that night, what was your relationship with the deceased, did you know she had a false social security number, who did she socialize with on campus, was there anyone who appeared to dislike her, had she had any fights with anyone he knew of, did she have any enemies, did she go to the laboratory often, where else did she go besides the campus? On and on, the questions pounded upon his shattered soul into the night. He answered the sergeant's questions carefully, trying to be helpful but noncommittal. He knew he should not say they were from another planet.

One of the women with the team asked him to sign a consent to search. When he cooperated, they rifled through everything in his house, through his closet, his drawers, his bedroom, his office. It made him feel violated, especially when the investigators handled their Universal passports. Since the documents were not activated, they did not reveal anything unusual.

After what felt like hours of questions, Blake said to the sergeant, "Sir, I've never been close to murder before, how do I cope with it?"

O'Neal paused for a moment before he spoke, "you just do." Blake saw competence and kindness in the slightly opaque blue eyes, and experience. This was a man who had seen things, who had buried loved ones.

"You just do," the sergeant repeated kindly, "time will pass and you'll heal, some."

"But I could have saved her." Tears filled Blake's eyes.

"Maybe, maybe not," the sergeant said. "Time will heal that too. God has a plan, you can't take too much responsibility on yourself. That's just the way it is, you're 25, you're lucky not to have been close to something like this before. You have anyone you can call, family, friends?"

Blake shook his head.

"You said earlier you weren't having a romantic relationship with Ms. Vega, that'll make it easier in the long run." O'Neal studied his face, "you a movie star, play sports or something?"

"No, I'm a scholar," Blake said, "but I get that question a lot."

"Where'd you say you're from?" O'Neal paced toward the next room which had been Vega's office.

"Belgium." Blake followed, feeling the need to be careful.

"That's right, same place as Ms. Vega. I would have thought maybe Mediterranean, except for your blue-green eyes, can't quite place your accent."

O'Neal peered into the next room and whistled. "That's some fancy equipment she had there. How's it work?"

"It's activated by thought, voice, or touch, mostly by thought."

"That's a new one, never seen anything covering the walls like that, that come from Belgium?" O'Neal crossed his arms in front of him.

"I believe so."

"You know, we think we're such a great country here, but look what they're doing in Europe, Asia too, with high speed trains and all. We don't even notice they're ahead of us," O'Neal cleared his throat, "What kind of work was Ms. Vega doing?"

"Research in genetics. She was studying genetic variations and causes of human aggression and violence."

The sergeant shook his head, "Now there's some sad irony for you, poor woman."

Tears clouded Blake's eyes. He blinked.

O'Neal took a breath, "There're some more details we need to take care of, the body's at the medical examiner's now. That takes about 24 hours. We can get a lab technician at UM to confirm our identification of the body, save you that. From you, we need help identifying next of kin, and we'll need a funeral home, lawyer to handle her estate. If she doesn't have anyone, you can make the arrangements, otherwise the county'll take care of it."

"She has no next of kin that I know of, so I'll make the arrangements for her, but I'm not familiar with a funeral home," Blake began.

"We can give you some names."

"I'd appreciate that," Blake said.

"They can assist you with the arrangements," O'Neal added.

"That would help, I guess, I really don't know what to do."

The sergeant followed his squad toward the front door. "Since you're taking care of things, we'll give you her personal effects that we're through with." He handed Blake a white plastic bag. "And don't leave town, you'll be wanted for further questioning… again, my condolences on your loss."

"Thanks." Blake recognized Irina's shoulder bag inside the plastic bag.

O'Neal turned to Blake, the others were ahead of him, "I know this just happened and it'll take time, but you need to remember that life goes on. Give yourself time to heal, but there comes a time when you have to let go, you gotta' move on." He offered his hand. "Good luck to you."

Blake shook O'Neal's hand, "Thank you, I'll try to remember what you said."

When they left, Blake felt as empty as the house. He had nothing inside himself but pain, and guilt and regret. He turned off the front porch light, and carried the plastic bag to Irina's bedroom where he quickly set it inside the door, as if to get away from it.

He wandered into Vega's office. The wall screens were covered with rows of letters in different combinations of A, C, T, G, nucleotide base pairs of DNA. He sat at her revolving work station at the center of the room, and touched the penciled notes on the small desk. He held her pencil and stroked the papers where she had written. He touched the words "genetic causes" inscribed in her neat handwriting.

He recalled Shakespeare's line from *Othello*, "It is the cause. It is the cause, my soul. Let me not name it to you, you chaste stars." He thought of the contrast between violence on Earth and the chaste stars of the innocent Universe. He wished he had never come to Earth, and above all, that Irina had never come to Earth. He wished they had never chosen to study the causes of human violence here. His theory that the creativity and goodness on Earth should be preserved was a tragic mistake. The world that killed Irina did not deserve redemption. The cause no longer mattered. Their research no longer mattered.

Although Sergeant O'Neal had told him not to leave town, he didn't think he could stay. He wanted to go home. What could he accomplish by staying? Could he apprehend the murderers and bring them to justice? The homicide bureau would likely do that.

He called his agent. Eugene was not there, so Blake left a message about what happened to Irina and his desire to depart as soon as he had taken care of the necessary details for her. Once he had left Earth to return to Abidan, the bureau would never know what happened to him. There was no point in staying. He could not change what had happened.

He would have to pack Irina's things. He would also have to notify her family, but he couldn't do that until he traveled to the transport station. Those tasks were going to be very hard. He was not ready to do either.

Blake sought a way to say goodbye to Irina. At daylight, he walked to the nearby church, but the door was locked, so he wandered the neighborhood where they used to run together. Nothing he did mattered. He did not want to say goodbye to his friend. He wanted to change what had happened to her.

He wondered if Irina's soul would be transmuted from Earth, or recycled, as it would have been if she had died on Abidan. All he knew was that everything was silent, and he was more alone than he had ever been, and her soul was somewhere else where he could not communicate with it, and that she had likely suffered in a gruesome way. The suffering she must have felt and the regret that he was not there to save her hurt him the most. He never knew what the idea was that sent her to the lab that terrible night. Whatever it was, it no longer mattered.

Eugene telephoned while Blake was out and left a message. "I'm real sorry about what happened," his recorded voice said, "but since it has happened, looking back and second guessing yourself won't do a bit of good now, it'll only drive you nuts. You're smart to want to leave, but I can't get a goddamned flight for you yet, I'll keep trying. It'd be best if you could arrange for Vega's burial here. It's temporary, we'll send her back with her things as soon as we can. I'll be gone for a week and I'll give you a call soon as I get back. Meanwhile, be careful, real careful, and try not to let this destroy you. I know it's hard, but we'll get you home soon. Take care, and don't forget to erase this message. Talk to you soon."

Blake erased the message, went to Irina's room and lay down on her bed. He had not been in her room before. The closeness made the pain of her loss even more intense, if that was possible. He lay there sobbing. Of all the things he experienced since coming to Earth two months ago, this eclipsed everything.

Chapter 16

STATE ATTORNEY'S OFFICE, MIAMI

Janna Anderson felt slightly annoyed and slightly amused.

"Ah, my loveliest lady, how are you this morning?"

"Busy, K. J., I've got a caseload of 35 active homicides, the customary truckload of administrative paperwork, and I just opened a new homicide."

"The UM grad student?"

"Yes, apparently she had left a campus lab and was walking home by herself in a nice neighborhood in Coral Gables when she was attacked, raped and strangled. The police got a tip, and they've got three suspects," Janna said. "I'm going to see that they pay for what they did."

"If anyone can do it, you can," he handed her a cup of black coffee, "but let's forget about that for a moment and talk about us. You know we can't ever really win as long as most of the laws protect the criminals. Sure there're some minor changes, a little show from the politicians now and then. But let's face it, they passed the three strikes rule, the crime stats are down this month, so the pressure's off, and the laws won't really change in my lifetime, or in yours, my truly lovely girl. Did anyone ever tell you that you look like a young Jackie Kennedy? You're wasting yourself, Jan-An, on a system that doesn't work and we can't fix," he drank his coffee, "and if you're not going to marry a billionaire, which you should, you can at least go out with me." He leaned across her desk. His breath smelled like fresh coffee and there was mischief in his dark eyes. "I could take you to new heights."

"Is your proposition du jour finished? I have work to do."

"You shouldn't talk to your boss that way. Think of all the

unprecedented amount of responsibility I give you for someone fresh out of law school."

"Someone's got to do some real work around this office," she grinned.

"Well, what can I say? When you're old and your boobies are sagging and you lose all your fabulous looks, you'll wish you'd gone out with good ole' K.J. when you had the chance."

"K.J., why do you bother? You know I'm just going to say no?"

"Strange, isn't it?" He shrugged. "I don't know, you're just so beautiful and intelligent, and so good at what you do, I guess I'd rather be turned down by you than accepted by most women, and you're always so serious, it must be the challenge."

"Well, why don't you get a new challenge?" she suggested.

"You know I could fire you." His dark eyes sparkled.

"You wouldn't dare," she smiled. For all his antics, he was a fine State Attorney. "There is something odd about this woman," she picked up another page from the report, "no relatives, no college transcript, no friends except a roommate in this fancy home they were renting in Coral Gables where they'd lived for two months. Her social security number was fake, so was the roommate's."

"You know I'll review the case with you, but you're circumventing my 'prop du jour,' which was enjoyable, at least for me, and we have to take our enjoyment where we can on this job, since it frequently comes up short in the job satisfaction category. Case in point, you'll bust your extremely attractive little butt prosecuting these murderers, and they'll likely slip through some loophole and be back on the streets before you can turn me down again. Or one juror just won't be able to get beyond the old reasonable doubt, or the district court will reverse us." He shook his head.

"And you campaigned for this job?"

"Yeah, I used to believe," he looked sad, "and I have to be somewhere."

"How about out of my office?"

"Okay, but you don't know what you're missing."

"You know, I've got a darned good sexual harassment case against you," she said. "I might just prosecute the pants off you if I thought you could really do any of the things you talk about."

"I love it when you talk dirty," he smiled.

She opened the door and gently pushed him out of her office.

"Told ya' she was busy," Moira said from a nearby desk. Moira was Ms. Anderson's legal assistant.

K.J. checked his watch. "Eight o'clock, time to play State Attorney."

Janna Anderson spent most of the morning building a paper file for the new homicide. There was something especially compelling about this case. She had asked the head of major crimes to assign her to it. It was a travesty for anyone to be murdered, but this woman was a university student walking home from a bioscience lab.

Janna had been on beeper for the South County last night when the police called about the need for a homicide investigation. She was there when the squad examined, photographed and bagged the body. The victim had her own underwear stuffed in her mouth and she had been stripped. The cause of death appeared to be strangulation. The Miami-Dade Homicide Bureau was one of the most sophisticated crime units in the country. She hoped they would help her be successful in bringing the murderers to justice.

She had been with the squad when they went to the roommate's home to inform him. There was something unusual and different about him. He did not even seem to understand much about murder and rape. She felt she should have been more professional than to notice how handsome he was, especially under the circumstances, but she had to admit that he was the best looking man she'd ever seen. There was an intriguing quality about him, an intense awareness and innocence combined, like eloquent grief.

She wondered if she were to see him again if she would like him. He was cooperative and did not object to signing the consent to search, but he was obviously in shock about what had happened. She silently chided herself for spending so much time thinking about this stranger.

Moira interrupted her thoughts. Sergeant John O'Neal, from the homicide bureau, was there. Janna stood up at her desk and shook hands. She liked the ruddy-faced man. He had been a dedicated law man for a long time. They exchanged greetings and he sat down. Moira got him a cup of black coffee.

"Any witnesses?" Janna asked as they sat down.

"No one's come forward."

"Was the rape of the victim confirmed?" she asked.

"Appears that way, at least by one of them. The DNA's should be ready in a few weeks."

She looked in the file the sergeant handed her and scrutinized the student I.D. photo, "she had a kind face."

"Yep, it's too bad, there's too damn much of this stuff happening and that's a fact."

Janna turned to the next page, "no doubt intelligent, too, she was studying biochemistry, cell biology, molecular biology, genetics and microbiology."

"They weren't regular students, just auditing courses, still and all, a pretty impressive list of courses," O'Neal added.

"Yes, wonder what her career goals were."

"She did a lot of genetics research in the labs, but no one seems to know exactly what she was working on."

Janna looked through more pages, "did they find any family?"

"Nope." He sipped his hot coffee. "You saw the roommate last night, didn't seem to know much about her, wasn't sure where in Belgium she was from. Says he only knew her a couple of months, says he's from Belgium too. I checked immigration but they don't seem to have any records on either of them."

"Was he having sexual relations with her?"

"Says they just roomed together. Nice guy, just kinda' different."

"Yes, he was," Janna said.

"Well, I guess that's about it for now. Thanks for the coffee." He stood up.

"Thanks, John, please let me know when the DNA's are available, and if you find anything else," she said.

"Sure, Ms. Anderson. If you don't mind my saying so, ma'am, you get prettier every time I see you."

"Thank you again, John, please let me hear what you find out."

Anderson ate a tuna wrap at her desk, and continued working on the file until she reached a stopping place by mid-afternoon. She kept thinking about the foreign roommate. Although she usually relied on the police reports, she suddenly decided to visit the man whose roommate was raped and murdered.

Chapter 17

Anderson parked her black BMW in the circular driveway in Coral Gables, and rang the front door bell. No response. She rang it again. Still no response. She was about to leave, when William Blake half opened the door. He looked as if he had just gotten out of bed, thick brown hair swirled around his head, several days' growth of whiskers, white bathrobe held to his body. She saw the suffering in his eyes, but the quality she had noticed before was there, something kind, intelligent, understanding, and deeply appealing. His scruffy appearance added to his charm. She felt an amazing attraction.

"Hi, I'm Janna Anderson, the prosecutor for Ms. Vega's case. I'd like to talk to you for a few minutes, if it's convenient."

"Yes, of course, I apologize for my appearance, I haven't been out of the house for some time, what day it is?"

"March 15, Wednesday," Janna responded.

"It's been four days then. If you don't mind waiting, I'll dress."

"If it's not convenient, I could come back another time," she felt bad for disturbing him.

"No, it's okay, if you don't mind waiting."

"Okay."

He showed her into the living room, and excused himself.

There were no personal items in the neatly decorated room she had seen the night of the murder, the end tables were still heaped with a variety of library books. She wanted to wander around, but hesitated. He wasn't a suspect, and his house had already been searched. She recalled from the night of the search that Vega's room and office had been in the master suite on the first floor, at the end of the hall. That door was closed. Blake's room and office was upstairs.

When he returned, clean-shaven and dressed in a black shirt and khaki shorts, she knew she had been right about him. He was handsome. Really handsome. She chided herself for noticing, the man was clearly grieving, but how could she not notice? He was drop-dead gorgeous, with smooth tan skin, a perfectly proportioned body, breathtaking blue-green hazel eyes and phenomenal lashes. Even his hands and legs were beautiful.

"May I get you something to drink? Iced tea?"

"Please." She felt comfortable around him.

"I don't have any sugar, can I get you some lemon?"

"Lemon's good, thanks."

They sat across from each other at a rattan table with a glass top.

"Since Ms. Vega had no family that we know of, I just wanted to come by, ask a few questions. I was here the night the police told you about the murder, I don't know if you remember."

He sat looking at her intently. She felt breathless. He shook his head, "no."

"Of course."

"You said you're a prosecutor. Do you know who murdered my friend?"

"We have three suspects," she answered, "that's the other reason I came by, to let you know we're going to do all we can to see that these three pay for this horrible crime."

"Irina may not have died if I'd been there. I'm a strong man, I could have stopped them," he said.

"Or they could have killed you too, at least one of them had a gun, which is always a more dangerous situation."

He paused in thought before he spoke. "Why would they do it? Why would they murder such a nice, kind person like Irina?" He blinked back tears.

She sighed, "that's such a good question, I work every day to try to answer it, and especially to keep it from ever happening again."

"Do you see a lot of crime?"

"Oh yes. There were 27,281 violent crimes in Miami-Dade last year, our office probably sees at least a third of them in one way or another, maybe more, unfortunately, Ms. Vega's murder was only one of about 200 murders last year. The people I see, they're always guilty of something. I've never seen an innocent man or woman in my job yet."

"It's more terrible than I thought."

"If you don't mind my asking, how are you coping? I know you asked Sergeant O'Neal for advice the other night. I do a lot of volunteer work with crime victims and their families, and I know that healing is a terribly long and difficult process."

He started to cry, "I doubt that healing is possible. Have you ever seen anyone really heal?"

"It's very hard, but people eventually do find the strength to go on."

"That's what Sergeant O'Neal said. He was very kind."

"He is kind, and he's right."

The mention of Sergeant O'Neal made him feel nervous about more questions he could not answer, but this time it was not under the glaring kitchen light in the middle of the night. This was a lovely young woman with wide dark eyes and an exquisite figure carefully dressed in a smart gray suit, with pearls around her elegant throat, sipping iced tea in the golden sunlit afternoon. "You said you came here to ask some questions?"

"I mainly came by to see if you had the help you needed to cope with your grief."

Large tear drops ran down his face. "Thank you, that's very kind."

Janna did not think she had ever seen any man so attractive, even when he was crying, "I also felt concerned about your lack of family, finding support after a loss is critical." She handed him her card, "if you need help let me know, I can refer you to support groups, therapists, grief counselors. There are a lot of good, dedicated people out there who can help."

"I think that is what perplexes me the most. How this world can be so evil as to murder my friend, and how it can be so kind."

"I wish I could explain it, but there are no easy answers. Criminals make up only a small percentage of who we are, but the impact of their crimes, not only on the victims, but their friends and families, is permanent and life-changing."

"Have you ever experienced death of a friend or loved one?"

She looked thoughtful, "My grandfather died a year ago. His was the first death of anyone close in our family. I tell myself how lucky I am to have had all four grandparents until I was 23, but it hit me very hard, and he was old and in poor health, but he'd always been there. I guess intellectually I knew he would die, but emotionally I guess I thought he would always be there. I had such an idyllic childhood I didn't really understand death until I had to experience it. You think you do, but you really don't, at least I didn't." She liked the way he listened, but she didn't want to monopolize the conversation. "Death is very hard even when you lose someone gradually from old age, like my grandfather. Murder is so much worse. Murder is such a shock, it brings a whole set of grief concerns, including anger at those who did it, and regret that the circumstances of the event can never change."

"That's all true."

"I brought some reading material and lists of resources that may help." She retrieved a folder from her large Gucci tote, and passed it across the table to him.

"Thank you."

"People who're religious usually cope the best. Faith can be a great comfort, praying, meditation, going to a church or synagogue, belief in the afterlife."

"I'm certain there's an afterlife," he said.

"That can definitely help. Do you have a minister or rabbi you could talk to?"

"I tried to go to a church a few days ago, but it was locked. Can you recommend one?"

"There's a list here," she opened the folder.

"Thank you, I'll be sure to look at it. Do you go to a church or synagogue?" he asked.

"I was raised Catholic, but I can't say I go much. I've gone to St. Hugh's in Coconut Grove a few times."

"I'd like to go to church. I don't wish to intrude, but if you have the time, I'd be grateful if you'd go with me."

He looked so sweet that she said yes, not quite sure why she said yes, but it had been so long since she had taken any time from her work, and so long since she had been invited out by a gentleman, especially to church. She didn't think that had ever happened.

They agreed to meet for 5:30 Mass at St. Hugh's on Saturday.

Chapter 18

"Happy St. Patty's Day," K.J. pushed the door to Janna's office with his foot, so he could hand a cup of coffee to her and to Moira. He glanced at their dark professional looking suits. "No wearin' of the green?"

"I may have an Irish sounding first name, but I'm pure Italian," Moira said, "what are you Janna, French, English?"

"But you don't have to be Irish, to be doing a wee bit of celebratin'" K.J.'s black eyes sparkled, "you're coming to the party tonight, aren't ya?"

"I am," Moira said. Janna shook her head.

K.J. scowled at Janna, "What you're working tonight? It's Friday! Talk to her, Moira, talk to her. Going to be a fine party, lots of drinking and dancing."

"But you are Irish, Mr. Carey," Moira pointed out.

"Like I was saying, you don't have to be Irish…oh well, I'll save my arguments for court," he grimaced, "big day today. Wish me luck."

Janna winced, "good luck."

"Yeah, good luck," Moira added.

He shook his head, "child murderer, poor little girl, he molested her, killed her, dumped her body in a canal. Can you imagine what that poor little girl's last hours must have been like? Let's hope we can get some real justice."

"Amen," Janna said.

"For sure," Moira added.

After he left, they each paused in silent thought about K.J.'s murder trial.

Moira took a sip of coffee, "so, you're not going tonight?"

"You know I'm not much of a partier."

"You could say that. Other than a few happy hours, you hardly ever go out."

"I know, I guess I'm not much fun, but I am going out tomorrow night," Janna sipped her coffee, "well, it's not a date or anything, I'm meeting someone at church."

"Really? Who?"

"Well, it's more like grief counseling."

"Huh? Who're you going to church with?"

"William Blake."

"The guy who's roommate was murdered? How'd that happen?" Moira asked.

"You know I was on beeper the night of Vega's murder, I was at his house with the squad, he was really overcome with grief, so I just dropped by with some grief literature for him on the way home from work the other night."

Moira started to say something and stopped. She finished her coffee.

She doesn't fully believe me, Janna thought. I wonder if I believe myself. Janna looked at the clock, "Eight o'clock," she announced, "as K.J. would say, time to play State Attorney."

"Okay, but be careful."

"I'm just meeting a guy at church."

"Like I said, be careful."

Saint Hugh Catholic Church had a distinctive sloping roof outside which made for a dramatic sloping ceiling inside and a beautiful triangle of blue stained glass behind the altar.

Janna could not remember the last time she'd been to Mass, but she was glad to be there. Church reminded her of her childhood and gave her a feeling of tranquility. She hoped it would help William Blake, although she could not tell what he was thinking and feeling. She knew almost nothing about him, but she discovered he could read music well and sang in a beautiful voice. She found herself thinking more about him than the Mass.

When the congregation recited the Our Father, she looked into his eyes and shook his hand with the ritual greeting, "peace be with you." It was only a few seconds before they turned to wish peace to others in the congregation, but the touch of his hand in hers felt like a warm electric current, not shocking, but wonderful. She thought he might have felt a connection too, but she could not tell.

After Mass, he asked her if she would like to get something to eat and she suggested TuTu Tango. It was close by in CocoWalk, a Mediterranean style open mall with three levels. TuTu Tango was a Spanish café on the second level of CoCoWalk, decorated like an artist's studio with original paintings on the walls and unfinished canvases suspended from the high ceiling. They ordered white wine sangria and tapas.

"I want to thank you for the information you gave me about grieving," he said, "it was very kind of you to bring it to me."

"I hope it helped."

He shrugged slightly, "it's the fact that it happened at all, the fact that something so horrible could happen at all."

"I know. I fight against violence every day, and it just keeps happening. How are you coping?"

"I really don't think about anything but Irina's murder," he said.

"It's only been a week. It takes time. Unfortunately you may never completely get over your loss, but counselors advise that you shouldn't keep from enjoying life, even while you continue to have periods of deep sadness. When you reach a point when you aren't constantly dwelling on sadness, it's a sign you're starting to heal, but there's no set timeline, you have to go at your own pace."

He blinked away tears, "that's what the grief literature advises. It's just very hard."

"I'm sorry," she said. "Your strong belief in the afterlife will ultimately help you come to terms with it."

"I don't think I'll ever come to terms with it," he drank some sangria, "thanks for going to Mass with me. I was glad to be there."

"Me too, I enjoy the peaceful feeling of church, even though

I'm a skeptic."

He felt many emotions converging in his wounded mind. He wished, he wished so much that nothing bad had ever happened, that he would not have to continue to face this awful death of Irina, but suddenly he was aware of the beautiful dusky night and the lovely face of the woman sitting across from him, and it seemed to him that something like the sign of peace had come to his troubled soul. "Do you like your job?" he asked.

"Yes and no. I always made A's in school and my professors told me I could do most anything, but I feel that fighting crime and my volunteer work with victims and their families is the most important thing I can do right now. There're a lot of people in my profession who feel it's hopeless, that crime is totally out of control, but I try not to feel that way. I believe I can make a difference." She sipped her sangria, feeling excited as she always did when she talked about her work. She felt another thing, a subtle pulsing that seemed mindless of her small efforts to right the world, even as she continued to ask questions. "Tell me about your research at the University of Miami, weren't you and Ms. Vega studying behavioral genetics?"

He shook his head. "I've decided not to finish my dissertation. I was studying how to eliminate violence on Earth through genetic engineering and environmental remediation. It was my thesis that if the genetic and environmental causes of criminal aggression could be eliminated in the people of Earth, then it would result in a new Renaissance across the Universe."

"How would that work, I mean, what would you do with all the criminals we have now? Would you modify their genetics and their environments or would you have to phase out violence and work on the next generation?"

"It would likely be generational, because the research is not currently in place to achieve such results, but it's not out of the question to treat violent criminals with gene therapy. The goal of my dissertation was to raise awareness and direct research toward those possibilities."

"Is it possible?" she asked.

"Yes it is. Progress in this area will necessitate an understanding of both gene-gene and gene-environment interactions. Scientists are currently mapping the human genome, which is several years off, and the genes that cause the predisposition for human violence will eventually be identified, although research on specific pathways from individual genes to aggressive behavior is still in its infancy."

"Isn't it tricky to study the genetics of human aggression due to ethical concerns?" she asked.

"Definitely. Current research is confined mostly to twin, family and adoption studies, but these studies do suggest that the biological characteristics that increase the risk for criminal convictions and aggression are transmitted from biological parents to their offspring. Animal studies point to the same conclusions."

"How do you study aggression?"

"Another good question. It's hard, because the term itself includes a huge range of behaviors. Aggression is generally defined as 'externalizing behavior that directs problematic energy outward,' such as defiance, bullying, vandalism, and theft, but it also includes war, genocides and other atrocities and neuropsychiatric disorders, like traumatic brain injury, neurogenerative diseases, alcohol and substance abuse."

She took a sip of wine. "What are the future implications of your thesis?"

"One is to create neuroprediction, which is testing individual genotypes and identifying those who are more at risk towards aggression," he explained. "That information could be applied to aggression prevention programs, which would include curing aggressive tendencies through strategies like gene therapy and mutagenesis."

"What's mutagenesis?" she asked, "I haven't studied biology in a while."

"Mutagenesis is using mutagens, like radiation and chemicals, to artificially increase the chance of mutations, in this case, mutations that would cure aggressive behavior."

She paused in thought. "Of course, any treatment would undoubtedly get into more ethical questions, like should unborn children be tested for aggression? If they test positive, should they be allowed to be born? Should parents with the aggressive gene be allowed to have children and so forth."

"Yes, lots of complications," he said, "further complicated by the fact that there isn't just one aggressor gene. The cause is likely from multiple genes and variants, called alleles."

"But so much potential for good. You're really not going to finish your dissertation?"

"I don't know if it matters. Irina's death has made me rethink a lot of things. It's made decide to leave here as soon as I can."

"You mean, return to Belgium?"

"Not exactly there, but far from here."

"I'd hate to see you go," she paused, "your thesis is such a profound idea. If it could actually rid the world of violence, its impact would be beyond belief."

He poured another glass of sangria for her, but not for himself. He looked thoughtful. Her mind was also full of thought.

She sipped her wine. "If you don't mind my asking, what was your relationship with Ms. Vega?"

"She was a wonderful companion and fine researcher, and I loved her as my friend and roommate, but we did not have a physical relationship. What about you, are you in a relationship?"

"No, everyone at work gives me a hard time because I don't go out much, but I'm always so busy with work. I was disappointed once or twice," she confided, "so I'm more careful now."

"I would think they'd be waiting in line for you."

She was surprised and pleased by his compliment, but she changed the subject, "William Blake, like the English poet."

"No relation," he smiled slightly, "although I appreciate the irony that the poet whose name I share wrote 'Songs of Innocence and Experience,' kind of like my story on Earth."

"The two states of the human condition, I studied that," she smiled thoughtfully, "I also memorized one of his poems in school, 'Tyger! Tyger! Burning bright, In the forests of the night, What immortal hand or eye, Could frame thy fearful symmetry?' Have you read his work?"

He nodded, "a very unique, creative mind, typical of what Earth can produce."

"You have a different sort of outlook, like you're judging Earth like you don't really belong here," she said.

He recited the next stanza, "'In what distant deeps or skies, Burnt the fire of thine eyes? On what wings dare he aspire? What the hand, dare seize the fire?'"

The waitress showed up with the check, and William paid the bill.

He offered to escort her home. Her condo-hotel was several blocks away. As they walked, they looked up at the stars. Janna listened to William's voice that sounded as far away as the stars he described. "There're more than 500 million galaxies that can be seen from Earth, 100 billion solar masses in our galaxy, 350 billion in the next galaxy and how quaint that people on Earth think theirs is the only inhabited planet in the Universe."

"You're right, there must be life on other planets, but why haven't we seen it?"

"I guess that's a subject for another time," he said.

"But if you're leaving, there may not be another time."

He looked pensive.

They said good night at the entrance of her building. He asked if she would go to church and dinner with him next Saturday. She said yes.

Chapter 19

On Saturday, William brought sunflowers when he met Janna in the lobby of her building. He waited while she took them upstairs to her condo. She thought the cheerful flowers might be a sign his grief was healing. He had gone back to his baseball team that week. She told him she had spent the week working. She did not tell him how much time she had spent thinking about seeing him again.

They went to the Church of the Little Flower, St. Therese of Lisieux, in Coral Gables. He had not been inside, but he had admired it often when he ran in his neighborhood. The church was 75 years old, with a magnificent marble sanctuary, the longest nave of any church in Miami, and a gold reredos behind the main altar. It was a popular place for formal weddings and Janna had attended several there.

Like the church, the music was more elaborate. Janna thought it was a good setting for William's beautiful voice. She tried to concentrate on the readings and homily, like William did, but she found herself thinking more about how handsome he looked in his black sport coat, and about touching his hand again.

After Mass, he took her to the elegant Palm D'Or Restaurant in the Biltmore Hotel. She was glad she had worn a pretty new dress. The stylish black and white dress made her feel very feminine, or was it William that made her feel that way? She told herself not to get interested, he'd be moving soon. When she spoke aloud, she said, "the Biltmore's such a classic, lovely place, isn't it? It's always a treat to be here."

"Do you come here often?" he asked.

"No, a few parties, bar association events, but I always love seeing it."

"I used to swim here almost every day. My rental house came with a pool and spa membership."

"Nice," she smiled.

He began to smile and stopped.

"So how are you coping?" she asked.

"About the same, maybe a little better, being back to the baseball team seems to have helped."

"Even a little better is good. Are you still planning to leave?"

He nodded, "I'm not sure exactly when. In the meantime, I'm trying to act on the grieving advice, and attempt to take some small joy from things again, even while I still cope with intense sadness."

She looked down at her menu.

He opened his menu and thought of what Eugene said about the food on Earth being almost like an art form: wild Alaskan sockeye salmon, halibut with wild morel mushrooms, asparagus and blood orange, so different from the plainer food on Abidan, and delicious, if he could let himself enjoy it. "What would you like to have?" he asked.

She ordered Florida lobster and he chose grilled swordfish. He suggested pairing their food with Chardonnay, and selected a 1997 Calcaire Vineyard, Clos du Bois. He asked her about herself.

"I'm from Tallahassee," she said, "my dad owns a European car dealership there."

"Is that why you drive a BMW?"

"Of course," she tasted her wine, "this is very good, are you interested in wine?"

"Some, I used to enjoy trying new things." He looked down, "Do you have brothers and sisters?"

"Yes, my parents and one brother live in Tallahassee. He's married to a really wonderful woman who does all kinds of volunteer work and they have two little boys. I also have a sister who lives in Maryland, outside of Washington D.C. She's a lawyer like me, but a corporate lawyer, and she's married to a U.S. Senator, which is pretty exciting. They don't have kids. Where's your family?"

"Some in Belgium, they're scattered about." He was thinking about what else he should say when their entrees arrived.

They made small talk during dinner, but she felt a distance between them. He was still grieving and preoccupied, but she felt there was something else going on, something that he did not want to talk about and he had his guard up against it. He did not want to get close, perhaps because he would be leaving, or he just didn't like her. They spoke about the baseball team, which seemed to be a comfortable topic, and travel, her travel, not his.

She thought she should skip dessert and not prolong the evening since he didn't seem interested in being with her, but he insisted. "In that case," she said, "I'll have 'retour en enfance.' "

"French for return to childhood."

"Yes, and look at what's in it, fresh strawberries, pistachio ice cream, soft pistachio financier cake, whatever that is, and warm chocolate sauce. Would you like to split it?"

"Who could resist?" He smiled politely. "Would you like some coffee to go with it? I think I'll have Ethiopian Moka." It still seemed like he was somewhere else.

"I'll try the Jamaican Blue Mountain."

When he took her to her front door, she was not surprised that he made no effort to touch her, not even a handshake or a friendly pat on the shoulder.

She was surprised that he invited her out again, this time not to church, but to play tennis at the Biltmore Hotel courts next Saturday. She considered his invitation only for a few seconds before she said yes. She thought later that she probably should have said no.

Chapter 20

Looking at him in tennis shorts and shirt, Janna was glad she had said yes to his invitation. She didn't know if it was a cheerful sign that he was not in black, or just the uniform for tennis, but he looked good, from every angle.

From his first volley, it was apparent that his tennis form was as perfect as his body, and she was more out of practice than she had thought. He was patient with her, and when they played a set, he seemed to be holding back in each game.

"You're good," he said, as they were putting their tennis rackets away.

She smiled, "maybe at one time, not lately. Why do I feel like you were holding back? I'm pretty sure the only games I won were because you let me win."

"I'm taking it slowly with you."

He suggested the 19th Hole Sports Bar and Grill at the Biltmore golf course for a light supper. She noticed that he held back in conversation, like in his tennis game. She had told him so much about herself, and had learned hardly anything about him. It made her feel uncomfortable. She made up her mind that no matter how attracted to him she was, if he asked her out again, she would say no.

She had been so lost in her own thoughts she had not noticed that he had placed a small box wrapped in turquoise tied with a white ribbon next to her plate.

"What's this?" She was truly shocked to see a Tiffany's package. "Is this an April Fool's Day joke?"

"What's that?" he asked.

"I guess not," she said, "but what's this for?"

He smiled, but he looked sad. "This is a gift from me to thank you for your friendship at the most difficult time of my life, and something to remember me by when I'm gone." His beautiful blue-green eyes glistened. "Please open it."

She started to unwrap the gift, not sure what to think, "oh my gosh, it's a tennis bracelet. This's way too expensive. I can't accept this."

"There were others that cost more, but I didn't want you to feel uncomfortable. You know I'll be leaving soon and I can't offer you much, but I can give you this gift. Please accept it." He looked so anxious that she smiled and said yes and thanked him as much as she could.

When he asked her to go out with him next Sunday, she said yes without even thinking.

"A tennis bracelet! Good God, what on earth?" Moira sat in the chair across from Janna's desk. K.J. had just brought them coffee and had gone to court with his assistant Frank Alvarez. Moira drank some coffee, "so tell me what happened."

"Well, he picked me up and took me to the Biltmore tennis courts."

"So he knows where you live," Moira frowned, "continue."

"And after we played tennis, I'm so rusty, we went for a light dinner at the 19th Hole at the Biltmore and he gave me this bracelet."

Moira leaned forward, "personal question, have you had sex with him?"

"No, he's never touched me at all, unless you count church where we shake everyone's hands and say peace be with you."

"Doesn't count. So he gives you a tennis bracelet and he's never touched you. He's a freak."

"I am very perplexed, something definitely doesn't add up, but he's not a freak," Janna paused.

"You think he stole it?"

Janna shook her head. "It was in the classic Tiffany's wrap, but it could be fake, or he may have stolen it. I don't know. I'm so confused."

"Well, he doesn't have a record, I Googled him. There's nothing on him. I mean no pictures, nothing."

"You Googled him?"

"Of course. What's he look like?"

Janna blushed crimson. No one ever got anything past Moira for very long.

"Wow, you must like him. So tell me, what's he look like?"

Janna took a deep breath, "He is without a doubt the most gorgeous, appealing, hottest guy I've ever seen." She leaned her forehead against her hand. "If the truth be known, I'm so hot for him I can hardly stand it."

"Really? What else?"

"I recognize something doesn't add up, he's hard to talk to, I mean he's not hard to talk to, he just never talks about himself, he's clearly holding back about something, which has me worried, but he's the best looking man I've ever met, and he's absolutely brilliant, he's read everything, he knows everything. There's no subject he can't discuss intelligently. The two times I've been to his place, the night of the murder and when I dropped the grief material by, his house was stacked with every kind of book, and he sounds like he's read all of them, I'm so confused, what should I do?"

"Are you going to see him again?"

"He invited me to Lowe's Art Museum next Sunday."

"You going?"

"I always say yes. I keep thinking I shouldn't because he's holding something back and he's hard to talk to, and he says he's moving away sometime soon, and I don't think he's interested in me, and then every time he asks, I say yes."

"He's definitely interested in you if he gave you the bracelet, but that may not be a good thing. He could be a weirdo, and he knows where you live."

"Yeah, but I have security."

"Yeah, and he's probably gotten to know them, gained their trust, you know."

"You're right."

"Janna, you don't have to go far from this office to know how many sick people there are out there. He could be a serial murderer for all you know."

Janna winced. "I don't see how that could be. There's nothing about him that would indicate anything like that. He's researching the genetic causes of violence, and it's his thesis that our culture of violence can be eliminated through genetic and environmental manipulation."

"He may have a dark side. He may be studying how to eliminate violence in himself. Didn't Ted Bundy study criminal law?"

"Don't say that!"

"Well, you gotta be careful. You just don't know about people. Ted Bundy was charming, and gained people's trust, and he allegedly murdered 36 women," Moira said.

"That scares me, but I still think it's something else, something peaceful. He's not a serial murderer."

"Why take a chance? Be careful, girlfriend."

"I will, thanks. I guess I'd better get to work. It's almost 8:00 o'clock."

"Think about cancelling."

"I will."

"And at least take the bracelet to Tiffany's, see if it's real."

Janna smiled, "okay."

Chapter 21

She wore the Tiffany's tennis bracelet that was 5.5 carats, worth $14,000. She had been apprehensive all week, but when she was with William, she felt comfortable and safe. She fervently hoped the things that he held back about were something she could accept.

"I haven't been to Lowe's Art Museum since I first moved here, thanks for bringing me," she said lightly.

"Thanks for joining me, I've never seen it, even though I've been by it often enough on campus, I understand it's a good collection. Look at the number 76 football player, oil on polyvinyl," he said. "He looks so real."

"He really does," she agreed, "the Miami Dolphins used to be a great team."

"The only NFL team to finish an entire season undefeated."

"Yes," she said as they walked into the Greco-Antiquities room. A nude slave girl carved in white marble stood under a spotlight in the center of the room. The girl clutched a cloth between her clenched legs to cover part of herself, and there were marble ropes around her wrists. The expression on her downcast face was compelling. Her beautifully carved wavy hair was tied back.

"Her face illustrates the anguish of slavery," he said. "That's something I've studied. It was very terrible, especially for the black people of history."

"It was, and so was segregation. Fortunately, that's improved," she said. "It may be hard to believe but a lot of the past is even worse than some things today."

"That's what I've learned."

"I want you to see the El Greco," she took his hand and led him in the direction of the painting entitled *Christ Carrying the Cross, 1590-95*. "What do you think?" she asked.

Still holding her hand, he studied the painting of Christ in a red garment. Christ was painted with a crown of thorns and a few drops of blood on his neck and forehead, with a graceful left hand curved across a wooden plank of the cross.

"It's fine art," he said, "a difficult subject, the brutalization of God's son."

"Yeah, but I like the painting, don't you?" She loved holding his hand.

"I do," he said. "The face is at an odd angle for a portrait, almost a side view, maybe it's turned that way to show great suffering, but it's spiritual too with the three triangles of light behind his head, and his eyes looking toward heaven. The story of Jesus, like your Mass, is intriguing."

"It's a hard thing to understand," she said, "but there's more than we can fathom in an afternoon. Let's go see the Native American Art before they close." He did not let go of her hand as they went to the adjoining room.

He liked the tall Raven Totem Pole of carved animalistic figures painted in bold red, yellow, green and black. A birdlike creature with large outstretched wings and wolf-like ears sat on top of another creature that was holding a fish. It was a modern carving from the Northwest Coast showing how raven brought salmon to the bear.

"This Native American art is also fascinating," he said. "They have such a keen sense of the afterlife and reverence for their ancestors."

An intercom voice announced that the museum would close in fifteen minutes.

"Thanks again for bringing me here," she said.

"Thanks for coming," he smiled and held her by the hand to the exit, as they walked along the sidewalk, and to his car.

She thought he looked worried or wistful or both.

"Do you like Spanish food?" he asked, "I've learned to cook garbanzo bean soup, arroz con pollo and flan."

"Impressive," she smiled.

"Would you like to come to dinner?"

She hesitated, "sure, but could you drop me by my place so I can get my car?"

"If that's what you want, of course, but I'm glad to drive you."

"No, that's okay, I prefer to drive my own car and all, being it's a work night." She thought Moira would approve, at least in part.

"Then I will take you to your condo and go start dinner." As he opened his car door for her, he seemed reluctant to let go of her hand.

William opened a bottle of 1999 Rioja from the Penedas region of Spain, and he played several Spanish songs on the piano for her. She was enchanted, even as she told herself to be careful. He seemed too good to be true, and he was leaving.

The house looked the same as it did on her two previous visits. The door at the end of the hall was still closed.

They sat at the patio table to taste their wine and talk. Janna loved the gentle breeze on her legs, the bright stars beginning to light the evening sky, the gentle noise of the bubbling fountain and nighttime crickets, and the lucious scent of night-blooming jasmine. He served their food outdoors.

"This is good," she said, "you're a very good cook."

"I'm glad you like it."

After dinner, they moved to the chaise lounge chairs and held hands across the chairs. "I've been to Brussels before," she said.

"Brussels?"

"Yeah, isn't that where you're from?"

He looked troubled. "No, Janna, I'm not from Belgium."

"Oh, you don't have that fair-skinned Northern European look, now that I think about it. Are you from the Mediterranean, maybe?" She smiled. "I guess I've told you about most of my travels, in Italy and all. What's the matter?"

"Just thinking." He looked at her lovely face in the glow of moonlight. "There's something I should tell you, but I don't know how you will take it. I'm not sure you'll understand."

Here it is, she thought, even before he spoke again. Here's a reality I don't want to hear. The thing he's been holding back. The reality that will spoil my perfect moment. But it was worse than she could have guessed. Worse, when he quietly, gently tried to explain to her that he was from another planet, and she felt the mirror of her illusion breaking all around her until the imagined sound of breaking glass that crashed in her ears seemed more real than anything else that was happening to her. She hastily arose from the table.

"I'm sorry, I'm very sorry, but I have to get to work early tomorrow. Thank you for everything. It was lovely. I must go. I really must go." She grabbed her purse and left through the front door as fast as she could. She did not look back and tried not to hear William's troubled voice.

"Janna, don't leave. I can explain more to you. I can help you understand."

She managed to start her car in spite of her shaking hands and then she no longer heard the pleading voice. "Oh my God," she said out loud, but as she drove, she heard his voice come back to her from that night after dinner in the Grove when they had looked at the stars. "…One hundred billion solar masses, three hundred fifty billion in the next galaxy. How quaint that people on Earth think theirs is the only inhabited planet in the Universe."

Chapter 22

It was early Monday morning when Janna got to her office. K.J. was not there, she was grateful that Moira was.

"What happened, are you okay? This is about William Blake, isn't it, is he psycho? He didn't hurt you, did he? Your eyes are so red, you've been crying a lot. What happened? Talk to me."

Just then K.J. showed up. He saw Janna's red eyes. "Are you okay?"

Janna nodded weakly.

"Can I help?" K.J. asked.

"Thanks, but I probably need to talk to Moira."

K.J. nodded, "girl talk, why don't you all go to the Pickle?"

"Thanks, we won't be too long."

"You sure you're okay, you're shaking?"

"Thanks K.J., I really appreciate your concern, I'll be okay," Janna wiped her eyes with a tissue.

"Well, if you two weren't so brilliant, I'd hire two men to replace you, then I wouldn't have to worry about girl talk," his black eyes twinkled, and he earned a weak smile from Janna, as he had intended.

"You forgot beautiful," Moira added, "and I think it would take three or four men to replace us, don't you Janna?"

K.J. rolled his eyes.

The Pickle Barrel in the criminal courthouse was not crowded. It smelled of good Cuban coffee and frying onions. They chose one of the black and white tables in the far corner of the room. Over café con leche, Janna told Moira what happened.

"You think you've heard every lie in the book, but this is a new one," Moira said, "gotta give him a little credit for originality."

Janna wiped her eyes.

Moira stirred her coffee, "I knew something was up, but I never would have guessed, he buys you a tennis bracelet and by the way, he's from another planet. I'm freaked out."

"I can't believe I fell for him, but I did," Janna felt tears in her eyes again, "he's probably got a wife and kids stashed away somewhere."

"Yeah, but he must be separated, he was rooming with Vega."

"I always thought I was a good judge of character, but I guess not, he seemed so thoughtful."

"Maybe he is from another planet."

Janna managed a weak laugh.

"What are you gonna do about him?" Moira asked.

"Stay away, I guess," Janna wiped more tears away. "It feels good to talk about it, makes me feel more normal."

"Where's he say he's from? How'd he get here?"

"I didn't stay for details. He told me last night after he cooked dinner at his place. I left as fast as I could. I had my own car, thanks to your warnings."

"Good! You feel like you were in any danger?"

"Not at all."

"And he doesn't look any different?"

"Only that he's drop-dead gorgeous, but he certainly looks human, just a really gorgeous con man, I guess."

"You think there's any chance it could be true? After all, there's gotta' be other life out there, the Universe being so huge and all," Moira considered.

"I always thought so, but I just can't accept that this gorgeous guy, who looks so completely human, is from another planet. I just don't see how it could be the case. Although, he doesn't have finger prints, he said it was an inherited skin condition, like Naegeli syndrome. That was kind of strange."

"Anything else?"

"I accidently locked us out last night on his patio, and he opened the locked door by just putting his hand over it. I asked him about it, he said it was simple magnetism. His computer screen covers four walls and it's this hologram thing that's activated by thought, which is kind of strange but that's no proof he's an alien, and he doesn't sneeze."

"That's strange."

"Yeah, I sneezed one time and he got all worried about me like something bad was happening, and when I tried to explain what a sneeze was, he gets this credit card looking thing out of his wallet, and unfolds this pretty big, hologram type computer screen and searches for a definition of sneezing. When I asked him about it, he said it was some kind of Euro technology, but he put it away pretty quickly. And he's never been sick."

"Never?"

Janna shook her head, "That's why he didn't know about sneezing, I guess." She looked thoughtful. "He's got great vision. I think he has night vision too."

"Anything else?"

He's amazingly athletic, no proof there either, and well, I shouldn't have noticed, but he had this enormous," she lowered her voice to a whisper, "you know, hard on, which seemed unusual."

"But then, you don't have much to compare him to," Moira pointed out.

"That could be, but it was huge. I'm embarrassed to have noticed."

"Sounds like you couldn't miss it."

They laughed.

"Of course none of that proves anything," Janna took a sip of coffee. "He's a perfect gentleman, he's brilliant, he can sing, he can cook, he knows every wine by year, he can play the piano, play tennis, play baseball, he's got great manners, very considerate, kind of old-fashioned."

"Definitely from another planet."

Janna smiled.

"Do you think he does drugs?" Moira asked.

Janna shook her head, "didn't see any evidence."

"You sure he doesn't have a brother, any friends just like him?"

They laughed again. "Please don't say anything to anyone. Not even a hint."

"Don't worry. I wouldn't wanta have to tell this story to anyone," Moira shook her head. "People we know would freak, especially if it did happen to be true."

"I think he's just a con man, and I was fooled, big time," Janna said.

"Don't cry, Jan-An, you've cried enough, at least you didn't go to bed with him," Moira said philosophically.

"In all honesty, I find myself feeling sorry that I didn't, unless of course it's too weird," Janna said, "and that makes me feel ashamed."

"It's okay, we all have things we're not proud of," Moira sipped her coffee, "it's called life."

Janna reached across the table and squeezed her hand, "thanks for being such a good friend."

"Glad to be there for you."

Janna said, "I guess I'd better get back to work. That was nice of K.J. to give us some time, but I don't want to take advantage, and work'll be a good distraction."

"Always plenty to do. You know Vega's murderers are still roaming free while the police have to get their files perfect so they can arrest them? Makes me angry."

Janna shook her head, "me too, and I need to get to work."

"Are you gonna see him again?"

"I don't see how I can."

"Probably a good idea," Moira said, "but that's sad, isn't it?"

"Why do you think I've been crying all night?" she sighed, "seriously, thanks girlfriend."

Chapter 23

Blake decided to stay on Earth long enough to complete his dissertation, having personalized it in a way he never could have predicted. Now, he was trying to save a world that contained Janna, her family and friends.

In the past month, he had experienced more revulsion and deep sadness than he had ever imagined possible when Irina was murdered, to a love greater than he could have imagined possible. He knew that nothing as terrible as Irina's murder could ever happen on Abidan, but he had never come close, or known anyone who had come close to the love he discovered that he felt for Janna. No experience in his life could have prepared him for her.

He knew she returned his love, because he could read the passion in her thoughts. Knowing her feelings tested all of his powers of control, but he had not felt he could act on his love until she knew he was an alien and that he was required to leave Earth in 13 weeks. He had felt strongly that Janna deserved the truth, even though the truth was proving to be very difficult for her to accept.

He desperately longed to see her again, even as he longed to find a way to help her understand his alien origin. He was surprised that her reaction was so strong against the idea of life from other planets, and tried to imagine why it was such a shock for her.

He telephoned her many times, sometimes he left a message, sometimes not, but if she was there, she never answered.

Moira stayed with her the first night. They listened to his messages. Janna felt as though she were frozen, unable to face the reality of what had happened and not knowing what to do.

"Why don't you call him?" Moira asked. "He sounds rational. I'm sure you could find a good drug rehab program for him."

Janna shook her head.

"Well, get him to a good shrink. A little medication might do wonders. He sounds like he's worth saving. Maybe he needs a divorce lawyer."

But she did not call.

He waited, knowing that his time on Earth was running out, yearning with all he had for the phone to ring from Janna.

The phone did ring. It was Eugene.

"Good news, my friend, I got you a flight. It's on my flight, as a matter of fact. I got my blessed transfer."

"That's wonderful, Eugene, I'm happy for you," he felt good to hear Eugene sound almost cheerful.

"Well, the timing's not perfect, like everything else on this perverse planet," his agent's voice turned sad, "I've met a woman, a good woman, not good enough, I guess, for me to stay. Wish I could take her with me, but, of course, I can't." He cleared his throat. "Anyway, my friend, come next Tuesday we're out of here, forever. I'm on permanent, no return transfer."

"Thanks so much, Eugene," Blake said, "and I'm sorry for all your trouble, but I've decided to wait until my original flight. I've also met a woman, and ... I can't go, just yet."

"Well, I guess you're free to make your own choices, but I think it's a big mistake."

"I appreciate your concern. I just can't go yet. I hope to see her again."

"I see, well, yer time's up July 11, will you be ready then?" Eugene asked.

"I don't know, but I guess I'll have to go then," Blake said.

"Yep, that you will, my friend, that you will. Strange place, this planet. I can't say I'll miss it. Spent most of my time hating it, but I'll never forget it, that's for sure."

"Yeah, I know what you mean. Where will you go, Eugene?"

"Not sure yet, I'll be reassigned at the station. Alls I know is it'll be a peaceful planet, and it won't be here."

"That's great, Eugene, I wish you very well and I thank you for all you did for me, and Irina."

"Well, if you change your mind about leaving next week, call me any time before Tuesday. They may not fill my position here for a while, or they may even close the post in Miami, I don't know, but I know a driver I can trust. Before I leave, I'll arrange for transportation so you can catch yer flight. That way you're covered if they don't get a new agent. Just lock the house from the inside, leave the rental car in the garage, take all your stuff with you."

"Thanks, you've been a great help. I must write a message to Irina's family. I would appreciate it if you will signal it for me from the transport station, and messages to my family."

"Sure. Just call when they're ready. I'll take all her stuff, that way you won't have to deal with it, when you leave here. I think we should send the body back, if that's okay with you. It's not likely to get much notice, but there're some physiological differences they may pick up on in the autopsy report. Pro'bly better to get the body out of here in case they decide to study it further, the family'll likely want it sent home anyway. Where's it now?"

"I had Irina's body interred in a mausoleum west of town," Blake answered.

"Okay, if you'll give me the address, I'll get some help and take care of it," Eugene said.

"Thanks, Eugene, thanks for everything. And best wishes to you always."

"Thanks, pal, I'd feel better if you were going with me, but I guess 13 more weeks isn't too long. Don't miss that flight, okay?"

"Okay."

Chapter 24

Janna did not try to contact William in the week after she left him, although he was never far from her conflicted thoughts. She longed to be with him, and felt the need to avoid him at the same time.

Her professional life was in order as much as possible in a career of prosecuting criminals. She won a tough case that week which made her feel good. She hated to lose and blamed herself when she did. She was also satisfied with their progress in the Vega case. The three suspects had been arrested and were in jail without bond. She thought the DNA results would give her an airtight case, and she intended to seek the death penalty. Things in the office were temporarily in order. It was her personal life that was not.

She knew the whole strange story had been hard for Moira too. They had both tried to resume their work, as usual, until Moira walked into her office one afternoon with papers in her hands and a serious expression on her face.

"What is it?" Janna asked.

"The Vega autopsy report, look at this," Moira pointed to some words on one of the pages.

Janna read, "unknown physical anomalies, exhibiting highly irregular internal features…Absence of vestigial organs without evidence of excision…Apparent hand-foot Naegeli syndrome…Heart 30% enlarged without evidence of heart disease…Irregular DNA, 52 chromosomes reported…Atypical brain, denser, more convoluted, heavier at 2.1 kg…Mutations suggestive of evolutionary characteristics…"

"You think the P.D. will make anything of this?" Moira asked nervously.

"No, I don't think so," she responded. "It's possible they could raise a legal issue by alleging that the victim was not a human being, but I don't think so. I think they'll be more interested in trying to cut a deal because they know their clients are guilty."

"But you know what this means," Moira said, "he could be for real."

"I know."

"How do you feel?"

"Afraid, and still very much in love with him."

"If he calls tonight will you talk to him?" Moira asked.

"I think so," Janna said.

"Do you think you'll make love to him?"

"I don't know," Janna shook her head, "I really haven't thought that far."

"And which organs would you say had those anomalies?"

"I can't say for sure."

Moira chuckled. "Unless you consider size an anomaly, just think, if the relationship doesn't work out, you can always sell your story to the tabloids."

Janna tried not to laugh.

"Of course, they may not be buying, they probably already have their quota of 'an alien gave me a tennis bracelet' stories."

Janna laughed in spite of herself, "enough! I need time to think."

"Sorry, Jan-An, you're right, you do need time to think. You should go home. It's 4:30 and it's Friday."

"Good idea. It's not like I'm getting any work done with my brain in total chaos. I think I'll go, please don't say anything, especially now that this whole thing has gotten more confusing than ever."

"Not a problem. I'm too freaked to talk about this anyway," Moira said. "Good luck."

"Thanks, I'll need it."

Janna walked out of her office, past the security guards, down the elevators and by the metal detectors with more confusion in her mind than she had ever experienced. Where did he come from? And what was he really doing here studying human genetics?

She drove her vehicle out of the parking lot. What was his mission?

She turned onto the road by the pink walls of the jail topped with rolls of barbed wire. She had to wait for one of the white buses moving prisoners. Where was he from? How did he get here?

She turned onto 12th Street past the Gerstein Justice Building, where the criminal court business was winding down that afternoon. People in different groups were still gathered around the building, in the yard, on the steps, on the benches under the shade of the palms and flowering trees. The ground was full of litter. A piece a newspaper blew in front of her car. The colorful umbrellas of the street vendors fluttered in the breeze. Was he performing some experiment here? Was that why touching his hand felt electric? Would he try to do more than hold her hand? Would he try to have sex with her or impregnate her? What was really going on? What were his plans? Did he have friends here? Would he stay here? Would he return to his planet, wherever that was?

A truck at the corner honked loudly and the driver yelled at her. Apparently she had turned into his path. She tried to pay better attention to her driving, but she felt terribly distracted. She had heard plenty of weird and amazing stories in her line of work. But this was very strange. And it wasn't happening to someone she was prosecuting or someone else she knew. It was her story. It was her chapter. And she did not have any idea what would happen next.

She did not drive home. She drove to his house.

Chapter 25

THEY DID NOT TOUCH. THEY RECLINED IN LOUNGE chairs on his patio as the twinkling stars began to appear in the sky above them. The splashing waters of the fountain provided a gentle background for their conversation. It felt natural to be talking together, but she wanted him to touch her.

"What went wrong here?" her mind was full of questions, "why do some planets work and some don't?"

"Planets are God's experiments," he gazed at her, "a kind of spiritual and cultural testing ground. Some experiments don't pass the test." He felt so happy she had come back.

"Who is God?" she asked.

"God is the Great Creator of Life who selects planets, makes them habitable, and then sets evolution in motion. God doesn't get involved in day to day life on the planets, but monitors their progress, and is present when humans evolve in order to infuse them with a spirit soul." He watched her serious and beautiful face, "at least that's what we believe."

"Hmm," she gazed at him, "and you don't use gender when you talk about God."

He shook his head, "no need to."

"So, getting back to the main point, God created life, and planets are experiments, but didn't God also make the Universe?"

"The Universe exists," he said thoughtfully, "it always is, always was, and always will be. Of course, individual stars, planets and galaxies are created and annihilated, but the Universe is constant. The Creator is the author of life."

"That's enough, I guess, but I was always taught God created the Universe and life in it."

"What do you believe?" he asked.

"I'm not sure, I believe in God, but you know I'm not much of a Catholic."

"You're pretty good with the sign of peace," he smiled.

She felt glad that he probably couldn't see her face flush, even with night vision. "I'd like to believe, but I kind of approach religion in a superstitious way, I'm afraid not to believe," she folded up her knees on the chaise lounge, "so God creates worlds like they're experiments, what happens to the planets that fail?"

"God allows them to annihilate themselves," he answered carefully, "I'm afraid that's the fate planned for Earth in 2070."

"Wow," she felt shocked, "although I might agree with God, Earth probably is a mistake, I see examples of our violent culture every day, but there're so many good people here, what about them?"

"According to our religion, the soul of every just person on Earth or any planet of evil is transmuted, which means their souls transform to inhabit another body on another planet of peace."

"Amazing," she said, "so that's why you're so certain about the afterlife?"

"Yes, there's definitely an afterlife, although we don't know exactly how transmutation of the soul works, like recycling of souls on planets of peace. We know it happens, just not exactly how."

"Is it like reincarnation?"

"It could be similar. On Abidan, we have ceremonies for the Recycling of the Soul when the body of a person reaches 130 years. The ceremonies are very beautiful and peaceful. In both processes, transmutation and recycling, the souls begin new corporal lives as babies. The soul transits from one body to another, and although memory goes away, the essential energy and personality remains intact. It's a comfort knowing that Irina's soul lives on."

"Definitely," she agreed, "so why 130?"

"Ages are capped at 130 on Abidan," he shifted in his lounge chair, "to allow for the continuum of life. Aging is very gradual there, but by the time people reach 130 years, they're considered old." He felt acutely aware of the confusion in her thoughts, and the passion.

"Have you been to other planets?"

He shook his head, "this is my first trip."

"I'm glad it was here, but you've learned so many bad things," she took a deep breath, "and Earth's gonna end in 70 years?"

"That's why I came here, when Earth is annihilated, its uniquely creative culture will be lost for all time. It's my thesis that it should be preserved."

"But you have superior technology, like space travel and supercomputers and other advances we don't have, why do you need us?"

"We have shared knowledge among certain planets of peace," he said, "but we really haven't invented or discovered anything significant ourselves."

"So you would save Earth in spite of what God thinks?" she asked.

He nodded, "admittedly, a bold and probably foolish idea, but I can't let go of the idea that Earth should be preserved."

She was thoughtful, "but if the souls of the just on Earth are transmuted, won't something of Earth be preserved in another place?"

"Yes, but the new lives will be scattered in many places in the Universe and no longer exist as a single culture."

"My mind feels like it's orbiting," she said, "and how come you don't look any different, except for being amazingly handsome?"

"Thanks," he smiled. "The pattern of evolution for planets with similar chemistry is much the same everywhere. There aren't any Star Wars creatures roaming the Universe as far as I know, although I love their characters. On any given planet, humanoids have the same genes as each other. They look similar but scientists can measure the differences in their genetic codes. It's the alleles, the variations of their genes, that change the way the genes work and account for the variety in people, which is especially evident on Earth."

"And that's how Genetic Code Scanners work to keep people from violent planets out?" she asked.

"Yes, they have a GCS at every transport station and every

checkpoint throughout the Universe."

"Are we in danger?"

"You're not in danger from any planet of peace," he gazed at her silhouette and thought how beautiful and desirable she was, "they don't even know what it is to harm someone, there aren't any other evil planets in this galaxy group, the only real danger is from Earth itself."

"I see, do you really think God will let Earth perish?"

"Yes, unfortunately, I think so," he shifted his legs, "unless, of course, my dissertation can persuade otherwise."

"Maybe it will, and fortunately it's a long way off. When you think about our nuclear arsenals, it may be good news we can last until 2070." She stretched out her legs on the lounge chair, "so are there other visitors here now?"

"There used to be travelers here, but not any that I know of now, there may be a few travel agents."

"Travel agents?"

He smiled as he tried to explain interplanetary travel agents. There was something wistful in his smile. He was patient with her questions. He knew she would need to ask many of them.

He dreaded the one about how long he could stay on Earth, but he knew it would come.

"It seems amazing that we've actually had aliens here and no one really knows it," she leaned back against her chair, "I guess there're books and programs about 'ancient aliens.' Those theories sound credible at first, but then the arguments usually break down. And what about the evolutionary mutations that Irina had? Do you have them too?"

"Yes," he shifted his position, "our genetic makeup is more evolved, larger hearts and brains, augmented vision and muscular coordination, advanced cognitive capabilities, enhanced immune systems, more chromosomes, no vestigial organs. Things like computational skills, learning a language, managing thought patterns, telepathic conversations, and information processing are much easier for us. We also have a genetic predisposition to athletics I was not aware of until I tried baseball, which seems kind of strange since we don't have competition."

"And no fingerprints," she touched his smooth hand, "and you have telepathic thought. How does that work?"

"I'm not sure how to explain it, it's so second nature to us. We just do it with others in our proximity," he held onto her hand, "but we use verbal communication for social gatherings, especially celebrations, which adds to their significance."

"So can you read thoughts?"

"Oh yes," he grinned. She had not seen a happier expression on his face since she had met him.

She felt the warmth of his hand and she felt self-conscious. "Can you read my thoughts?"

"I love your thoughts, especially the ones about me," he took a deep breath and held her hand firmly, "don't feel embarrassed, my sweet, your love is returned ten-fold."

"I thought you didn't like me."

"I know, I'm sorry, but I didn't feel free to act on my love until you knew about my origin."

She breathed deeply, "and do you feel free to act now?"

"One more question."

"I think I know what that one is," she took another breath, "how long are you here for?"

He squeezed her hand gently, "I have to leave here in 12 weeks and 4 days if I'm ever to return to Abidan or any planet of peace."

"It's worse than I thought."

"Don't cry, darling," he used his handkerchief to wipe her tears.

"Can you come back?" she asked.

"No. It's one of God's commandments to me. Please don't cry." He put his arms around her as they stood together, and blinked at the tears in his own eyes. She held him tightly.

"Something could happen," he said after a long while. "I could stay."

"And leave your home and your family for a violent world where your friend was murdered? A world God wants destroyed because it's a mistake? No, there must be a way I can go with you. I'm not a violent person. I'm a prosecutor. You're sure there isn't a way I can get through the scanner? What would they do to me if I got caught?"

"It could be very difficult. You would likely be detained permanently."

She looked up at his face in the darkness. His expression was so sad that she knew she had to give it a rest, even as everything inside her screamed for her to solve the problem right away.

"Now you know everything," he sighed.

She paused in thought while he waited. She loved the strong feel of his chest. "So, do you feel free to act now?"

"I do, but it's completely up to you."

Her mind was racing, "and if we were to have a relationship, is it possible for me to get pregnant?"

"No, I have a birth control implant that should be good for the duration of my visit here," he sighed again.

"Implant? That sounds a little creepy."

"It's really quite simple, a small chemical pellet under the skin on my thigh. It dissolves in time, but it's very effective in the meantime," he looked intently at her, "whether or not we have a physical relationship is your choice, I'll always love you no matter what."

"And you know I love you," she smiled, "I feel like Juliet in the balcony scene. It's kind of like you overheard me and you know how I feel about you," she tilted her head, "so if I follow Juliet's reasoning, I guess I don't need to be coy, you know I want you."

"And I, you, but I want you to think carefully about it, like *Romeo and Juliet*, it will not end well. It will have to end soon with my departure. Please be sure."

"I've been sure since I met you, and if you think about it, no love ends well, it's the journey that matters. 'Better to have loved and lost than never to have loved at all.'"

"You're so sweet. Please think about it overnight."

"And lose another night?"

He smiled, "but you're not just some casual encounter, you mean everything to me whether or not we have a physical relationship. Think it over tonight, my little love, and if you still want us to have a relationship, let's go to church first. I know that's kind of quaint, but I think it'd be nice for us."

She smiled. "You want me to lust after you in church again?"

He took a deep breath. She had the sweetest, most adorable grin, and she was so charmingly unaware of how sexy it was. He took another deep breath and said, "it worked for Romeo."

"Okay, Romeo, I'll meet you at St. Therese at 5:00. I've already thought about it."

"I'll be there."

Chapter 26

He wore white to church. So did she. Being there was like a declaration of love.

After Mass, they went to his house. He opened a bottle of 1996 Louis Roederer Cristal Champagne, "you're still sure?"

"Oh yes," she touched his glass with hers and smiled, "this is nice."

He also tasted his champagne, thinking how lovely and desirable she looked.

He carried her upstairs. She felt like a bride when he undressed her and looked at every part of her, without touching her. He smiled sweetly in the soft light from his bedroom window and as gently as an evening breeze he caressed her bare skin. It felt so good to be touched by such a strong and tender man. The touch of his hands was warm and incredible. She undressed him. He was as beautiful as she had imagined.

He was sensual and passionate, loving her with a beauty and grace she had never known. The physical experience was amazing, pulsating, electric, almost spiritual. She had never felt like this before, so completely taken with a deep, penetrating sensation of enduring love. The whole time she felt that he was only there to please her. After, as they lay together panting and catching their breath, she hoped that she had pleased him. To say that he had pleased her would be an abysmal understatement. He had changed her.

Later, he made love to her again, strong and powerful and sweet and gentle all at once, with a pulsing in their bodies that reverberated in their souls. She was exhausted. She fell asleep first, and after several hours of cradling her, he slept too. It was a natural, peaceful sleep in the warmth and comfort of two beings coming across all time and matter and distance to be together.

In the morning, she woke alone. She felt shock at all that had happened, and fear that he was not there, that it may have been a dream and he was gone. She heard noise in the kitchen and looked over the second floor railing. He waved from the kitchen entrance; he was cooking breakfast. She saw his face, tender and smiling and that was all she wanted, all she felt she ever wanted. She had never known the kind of desire she felt for him. She drifted toward the shower. The steamy, warm water was like the pleasant remembrance of the previous evening. Janna leaned back and savored the feeling that this was love, and it was beautiful and good and worth the wait. She wanted him with a passion she did not know was even possible. As she grabbed a towel, she noticed a paper taped to the mirror.

To Janna

You came to me like spring to winter,

To soothe the terrible sadness in my shattered soul,

You made me know, fully and completely, that I have always reached across the eons and light years with the particles of my soul

For you.

That the atoms of my being lay scattered across the Universe

only to be assembled for one reason.

To exist by your side.

To hold your warm hand

and rejoice in your bright beauty.

To fill the silent void of your aloneness as

you have filled mine, and I know too

That I have spent all my life waiting for one thing.

Waiting only for the chance to say

I love you.

She toweled off, and snuggled back into her beautiful daydream and enjoyed breakfast with the man she truly loved. Later, they made love again and it was a different and more powerful experience in the half daylight of the drawn blinds to see the beautiful face of this wonderful man who loved her. Afterwards, she rested into the afternoon. He made love to her again in the late afternoon. She was exhausted but she could not get enough of him.

He felt concern. "I can do as little or as much as you want, tell me if it's too much. I would never want to hurt you."

She smiled a contented smile as she stared at the ceiling fan above them. She pulled the covers around them and rested her head against his bare shoulder. She supposed she should go to work tomorrow morning. She buried her head in his shoulder.

"I'd love to go to Abidan," she said. "I'd love to see a place where there's no violence."

"I wish it were not against Universal Law," he said. "You can't know how much I wish I could take you."

The melancholy in his tone made her sad. She did not want to feel sad now. "Well, maybe it's just as well," she said.

"Why's that?"

"Because I'd be out of a job."

"Earth humor?" he laughed.

"Speaking of jobs, I guess I should go back to work tomorrow."

But she did not go to work on Monday. She called in sick, and gave Moira a rambling excuse. Moira knew. She wanted details, and Janna gave her some. At least Moira could not see her blushing face, this time. She was able to reassure Moira that she was okay, way more than okay, she was in heaven. Moira was happy for her and sorry that he would be leaving.

I need one more day, Janna thought, one more perfect day, before she could let reality shatter the beauty of the existence she had known since they first made love. She knew it was inevitable that she would have to return to work soon, rejoin her crude reality, and that he too would have to resume work on his dissertation. But a voice inside her said not now, not yet. Love was too new and must be nurtured and enjoyed. And imprinted, imprinted so well that it would become her total reality, that she could take it with her into the world and it would still be safe.

He cooked Red Snapper. Eugene had brought it to him on Friday, when he had come to pick up William's messages and all of Irina's things.

"We have 12 weeks. We need to make the most of it," Janna straightened her graceful shoulders and smiled at him across the dinner table.

He loved the sweet way she did that.

"We ought to take some time off and go somewhere," she said "New York, Paris, London, Grand Canyon, Florida Keys... Abidan."

He smiled, "I'd love to go on a trip with you."

"I'd be glad to pay for a trip," she said.

"No, I'll pay."

"I was thinking maybe you might be running out of money, not being from here and so forth."

"I have money. How do you think I bought the tennis bracelet?"

"Oh yeah, but that may have depleted your resources."

"My agent, Eugene, the one who brought the fresh fish, took care of finances for me. I've got credit cards, a checkbook, an ATM card, a Swiss bank account, and cash."

"Quite the man about town," she teased, "okay, how about New York next week?"

"That'd be wonderful, like you."

"Can we stop talking now?"

He took her upstairs and opened his bedroom window and the sweet perfume of night blooming jasmine filled their room. In the long, lovely tender evening they made exquisite love. A soothing breeze cooled them afterwards until he finally closed the window to shut out the night chill.

He snuggled beside his sleeping Janna to get some rest himself. Sadly, it was already time to return to work.

Before Janna left, they agreed that they would spend every

evening and night together. That week, they took long walks, they talked, they swam in the Biltmore pool, and he gave her wonderful massages when she was tired from work. They drank wine, they cooked dinner, they laughed together and they made love that was so thrilling and perfect that they hoped it would last forever, even though they knew it could not.

Chapter 27

"You want two days off?" K.J. sounded surprised. He studied her face. "Is there a problem, Jan-An?"

She shifted in her chair that was opposite his desk. "No, I just need some time off. This would be an okay week since I don't have any trials scheduled, and Moira and Frank can cover for me. I was on beeper last week, so that's done for a while, it just seems like a good time."

"Yeah, but you never take any leave time. You sure you're not having some problem?"

"Yes, I'm sure. But thanks for asking."

"It must be a man then."

She could feel her face flush.

"I see, is it serious?"

"I'd like it to be," she answered.

He shook his head. "You're going to take all the fun out of my propositions. How am I gonna start my day?"

"How about with work, same as everyone else?"

"I should have noticed, the tears, the girl talk, calling in sick last Monday, who is he?" K.J. asked.

"I'm pretty sure you've never met him, but he's nice, very nice."

"Well, it breaks my heart, but I can't stand in the way. Go ahead and have a great time. Hard as you work, you deserve it. Don't worry about anything here, it'll all be here when you get back. But do me one favor, okay?"

"What's that?" she asked.

"Make sure he's good enough for you. You're really a class act."

"Thanks, K.J." She felt touched.

He stood up. "Well, I guess you've got a lot to do. Where're you going?"

"New York, we'll try to get a flight Wednesday night, be home Sunday night."

She walked toward his office door.

"One more thing, if it doesn't work out, don't forget there's always good old K.J."

"Thanks again." She felt sad. She knew for certain that it would not work out, since William would be leaving.

Chapter 28

"Alone at last," she grinned, after the bellman left them in their suite at the Trump International Hotel in New York City, "so what did you think of your first airplane ride and your first New York cab ride?"

"Both a little quaint and bumpy," he smiled as he held her in his arms.

"Now that we're here, I'm torn between trying to show you everything in the City, and keeping you in this room all weekend."

"We could stay here, it's a beautiful hotel, isn't it?" He looked around at the tasteful gold and bronze décor and the beautiful view of Central Park.

"It is," she felt her heart beating rapidly as they moved toward the bedroom. "We have some time before dinner."

He undressed her gently and touched her with his strong hands and his smooth lips and gave her all the sweetness she could handle. When he made love to her he levitated her slightly and caressed every part of her, from every angle.

She lost track of time, she lost track of everything but the pleasure from every part of him. When he thought it was time for her to rest, he massaged her with great gentleness where she lay, until her breathing returned to normal. After they showered together, he asked if he could dress her for dinner.

"That'd be wonderful," she said, "I'm still a little tired from everything you did. Was that levitation?"

"Yes, I hope you enjoyed the energy fields as much as I did."

She smiled happily. "What's that?" She saw him bring a shopping bag from their closet.

"I bought you an outfit," he opened her robe and dressed her with elaborate care in deep red colored panties and bra. He turned her around, "you're so beautiful," he said.

"You seem pretty knowledgeable about underwear, seen a lot of it?"

"It's everywhere, and certainly one of my favorite examples of Earth's creativity." He smiled and kissed her beautiful lips softly, "is my Earth humor improving?"

She laughed, "maybe a little too much."

"I hope you know the only underwear I ever want to see is what is on or off of you."

"I don't worry about anything that happened before us, but I really wouldn't want you to see anyone else for now. How do you feel about that?" she asked.

"Being faithful to you is my greatest joy and my greatest desire. You were thinking about Bekah but you don't need to worry, that relationship's over."

"I guess it may not matter, our time together is so short." She looked down so he couldn't see her sadness, even though he would read her thoughts, "so, what else should I wear? Is this it?"

He held up a dress in the same deep red color with a ruffle from neck to hem, and almost reluctantly pulled it over her sexy curves and slim waist, "a Givenchy creation from a Jackie Kennedy style."

"You sound like K.J., comparing me to Jackie Kennedy."

"You do resemble her."

She looked thoughtful, "I guess you've studied American history and know what happened to John Kennedy?"

"The ever-recurring theme of evil and good. There seems to be no end to it."

She walked to a full-length mirror in her bare feet, trying not to be sad, and admired her couture. "Thanks, it fits perfectly."

"So how do you like Windows on the World?" she asked when they were seated for dinner.

"I love it. This whole World Trade Center is spectacular. Where I come from buildings are limited to five stories." He glanced at the striking view from the windows, "this restaurant is well named."

"When it first opened in 1976, *The New Yorker* called it the most spectacular restaurant in the world. Originally, this was one of five bars and restaurants covering an acre on two floors here."

"I've read about how the World Trade Center was constructed; it has redundant design, but the steel is very lightweight."

"Some critics don't think much of the architecture," she said, "they say the twin towers look like the boxes the Chrysler and Empire State Buildings came in, but I think this is one of the most stunning building complexes ever."

"The height to which humans can reach."

She smiled, "how do you like being on the 107th floor?"

"I love it, the 60 second elevator ride was worth the trip all by itself, and the view of New York harbor and the Statue of Liberty is inspiring. I've read there're 22 restaurants in this complex and over 190,000 people work or pass through here every day, like a small city. Earth is amazing, and you're the most amazing part of it."

"Thanks, my love." She looked around.

It was a relatively small restaurant, decorated in warm colors of orange, navy, green and brown. Tables and chairs stood precipitously close to the tall windows across from booths upholstered with striped cloth in the same colors.

"We're lucky not to be in the clouds this evening," she said as they watched a brightly glowing New York City at night through the floor to ceiling vertical windows.

"Gorgeous."

In the center of the room was a parquet dance floor, next to a round bar with different colored stools and a large, swirling wooden light fixture overhead. Near the dance floor was a distinctive carpet of black and white squares.

"Of course, on Earth there's always the bad with the good," she sipped water "in 1993, some terrorists drove a van with a 1,500 pound bomb into the basement here. They exploded the bomb and killed six people and wounded more than a thousand. It did millions of dollars worth of damage, mainly in the basement, but this restaurant was closed for structural repairs for three years. Terrorists who trained at Al Queda camps in Afghanistan were convicted for it.

They were trying to kill as many Americans as they could. That's pretty bad, but we have terrorists in this country too. In Oklahoma City a few years ago, a deranged person named Timothy McVeigh bombed a federal building and destroyed it. Another truck bomb. He killed 168 people, including children in a day care center in the building, and he injured over 800 people. They're going to get him, though. He's due to be executed next year."

"Executed?"

"Yeah, capital punishment, I know that sounds awful, but they execute some of the worst criminals to punish them for their crimes. They'll give McVeigh a lethal injection, which is what almost all states do now, it's a lot kinder than what his victims got, but I shouldn't be talking about all this with you," she sighed, "in 11 weeks, you'll never be a part of this ever again."

"I understand retribution, but capital punishment is very difficult."

"Like I say, you don't have to understand it," she said.

"I had hoped to understand Earth, I always felt so curious about things."

"And you've learned so many bad things here," she touched his hand.

"I've learned that innocent people can suffer terrible fates, and violence is horrible and must be eliminated if Earth is going to have any chance at all for a future. It should be possible because there's such a small percentage of violent criminals – my research shows it's only about .5% in the U.S." He paused. "I've also learned many beautiful things," he raised his glass of wine to toast her, "that it's possible to have one great love that can endure forever."

She raised her glass and smiled. They both sat thoughtfully and quietly, savoring their 1982 Mouton-Rothchild Bordeaux. "Do you know everything about wine too?"

"Mostly," he smiled, "but it's very individual, I know my palate, and I think I know yours."

She flushed, "and then some."

A small band in the corner began playing Latin music. She glanced at the musicians, "do you like to dance?"

"I've never danced, but I'd like to try." He held her hand as they walked to the dance floor.

"You're such a good dancer, I thought you said you'd never danced before?"

"I haven't, but I read a book on Salsa dancing."

"Most people can't just read a book and dance Salsa, but then, everything about you is amazing." When they returned to their table she asked him how he liked New York.

"Very interesting," he said. "I like the contrast with Miami, I thought buildings in Miami were big until I saw the ones here, like this World Trade Center. The ride from LaGuardia had some rough-looking places and people, like Miami, and some beautiful areas, also like Miami, but it's surprisingly different, northern, definitely not tropical, much faster, bigger, and much cooler. There's an incredible variety here. I'm fascinated by the skyscrapers."

"If you like buildings, we should see Trump Plaza on Fifth Avenue. It's really beautiful, lots of marble. I met Donald Trump once in South Beach. He's actually quite the gentleman, especially for a famous person."

"I've read about him, a very original and creative man, and a great builder. I'd definitely like to see Trump Plaza."

"I'm also looking forward to seeing *The Lion King* tomorrow night, it's such a good story, kind of like Macbeth," she said.

He nodded, "and the music's very good too, what else do you think we should see?"

"It's really up to you, since I've been here a few times. Hopefully, you'll want to spend some time in our hotel," she said playfully.

"Most definitely," he said, "it's so wonderful being with you. I truly wish it could last forever."

"Me too. With all my heart."

Chapter 29

After New York, they returned with an urgency to get their work done in order to have more time together in the ten weeks they had left.

Blake was determined to finish his dissertation before he was required to leave Earth, but it was a difficult task. The record of the atrocities in human history was overwhelming, disturbing and tragic. Irina's murder made it more personal and intense.

There were multitudes of inexplicable evils, staggering statistics of atrocities, genocides and war. He did not feel that he had the ability to understand and process all of the evils that he studied. He wondered if anyone really did. The story of abuses was without end.

The litany of wars he studied advanced like a charging army. He counted 115 separate wars in the 20th century. He learned about the concentration camps of World War II, and the unfathomable horrors that took place there. He read about how the Allies had fought to stop Hitler, who had been responsible for the deaths of 12 million Jews, Poles and other innocents.

He recalled the Holocaust Memorial in South Beach that Ben, the waiter, had told Irina and him not to see on their first day. He was not sure if he should go now, but Ben had said that it was important that no one ever forget what happened. He decided to go.

Blake drove to South Beach and parked near the convention center. He walked a short block to Meridian Road that lead to a walkway of white stones and small palms at the entrance of the memorial. A huge bronze hand and arm rose from a small island in the center of a pond. Life-sized bronze statues of humans in all frightening forms of agony clung to the massive arm. A large number tattooed on the wrist of the huge arm, beginning with

A-13, disappeared into the mass of human suffering.

A green patina on the bronze sculpture added to its somber effect, like the semicircular black granite wall behind it. The wall told the awful history of the Holocaust. The first panel began with a picture and explanation beneath it. "Gassed naked bodies are loaded by prisoners under the watchful eye of a German guard to be brought to the crematoria for burning." That must be a picture of hell.

He tried to focus on the tiny hopeful message of the good people who had built such a moving memorial, "In memory of the six million innocent Jewish men, women, and children who perished by the hands of the Nazis...Though their bodies have perished, their souls and their spirit will forever remain immortal."

At the center of the structure was a narrowing tunnel-like walkway that listed the names of the death camps on its walls. There were so many, so many. The walkway opened onto the sculpture on the island. The great hand and arm covered with statues of human agony was 42 feet tall. It reached from a plaza paved in pink blocks of Jerusalem stone, enclosed by a wall of the same blocks. There were other statues on the plaza, placed in family groups and surrounding the huge arm. The statues represented victims writhing in anguish and despair, reacting to the intense horror of human torture. The rest of the memorial continued with the black granite semicircle listing the names of victims submitted by survivors.

He felt almost as shocked as he had been by Irina's death. He silently addressed her, "Irina, we can never understand this, but I'm grateful that we did not go to this place that pretty day we spent together in South Beach. We can never comprehend this any more than we can understand the extremes of beauty and evil on this planet, but I must try to eliminate the evil and carry on the work you did, as well as my own."

And yet, the English, the Americans, and their allies fought to rid the world of Hitler and all of his atrocities. Hundreds of thousands of these noble people were killed or wounded in that great struggle of good versus evil.

He also knew that no matter how much he loved Janna, and how much he longed to be with her always, he must return to his home, to his Planet of Peace. That was his personal tragedy.

He began to cry. What about Janna? What could he do for his love?

Chapter 30

No matter how many wonderful memories they tried to create in the waning days and nights they had together, the inevitable day of parting on July 11 arrived.

In late May, they had taken a beautiful five day trip to Las Vegas and the Grand Canyon. William continued to be enchanted by the creativity and natural beauty of Earth. Most of all, he was enchanted to be anywhere with Janna. As the days grew shorter, they spent most of their time at home. Even playing tennis seemed too distant.

They made love like there was no tomorrow, because that's how it was for them. He was gentle with her when he needed to be and he always took good care of her. They loved and laughed together and tried to keep their spirits bright, but they laughed a little less with each passing day.

He completed his dissertation and was proud of his work. He did not know if it would save Earth, only the Great Creator of Life could do that, but he held a tiny hope that he might be an effective advocate for the planet.

He would have liked for Professor Harmon to read it, except that the extraterrestrial information would be too revealing. Instead, he paid Jim a farewell visit and brought him the new baseball bat he knew he wanted.

William had stopped practicing with the Miami baseball team in order to have more time with Janna. He explained to the team members that he was moving soon. He and Janna went to see the Hurricanes play in the Super Regionals in early June. The University of Miami lost to Florida State University by a score of 6-1. William learned about winning and losing on Earth, how good winning felt to the team and how bad it felt for them to lose.

He bought many gifts for his family members, books, jewelry, Waterford crystal, Lenox china, Gucci leather, American Impressionist paintings, and Buell Whitehead lithographs of Florida scenes. He looked forward to seeing his family, even though it would mean that he could no longer see his love.

Janna had read his dissertation. He wanted her to read his work, and be prepared for Earth's ending. Considering life spans on Earth and the dangers always present, she could be gone in the year 2,070. If she survived until then, she would be 94, but certainly her children and her grandchildren would be in grave danger. Would there be any? What would happen to her? What would happen to his love?

William arrived at her condo for their last dinner together.

He gave her a small wrapped package. "I hope you like it."

"I'm sure I will," she smiled, "looks like more Tiffany's." It was a lovely gold star pin covered with diamonds. "This is so beautiful!"

"I thought a star would have special meaning," he blinked away tears.

They embraced and kissed with great longing, and they made love the same way, overwhelmed by the knowledge they had only a few hours left.

Afterwards, Janna put on a tee shirt and shorts and went to the kitchen, deep in thought. What was there to say that could be important enough for such a little amount of time? The words I love you sounded so insignificant. What to say? What to say that would count enough, that would express the deep emotions of a lifetime? What was there to say in these last few hours that would really count, that would really matter, that would really be enough?

Maybe there were no words. If there were, she did not know them. But small talk seemed so inadequate, so trivial, so oblivious to the reality of the situation. And yet what else was there when all the words of love had been tenderly spoken?

William's decision to return home was the right one. Earth was wrong. God had judged it as a mistaken experiment. The fact that God had spoken to William made it slightly easier for her to accept, but it was still very hard, like the death of a loved one who was ill and suffering, and you knew it was for the best even though the loss was deeply painful. He had changed her life forever. She would never, never, never again experience the deep love they had.

"So what's for dinner?"

"You startled me!" she said.

"I'm sorry, truly a day to be deep in thought."

"Definitely." She checked the saucepan on the stove, "we're having a little menu I picked up in Rome."

"Smells delicious."

"Hope so, I don't take the time to cook much, but I enjoy it."

They sat on her balcony before dinner looking at the small, colorful sailboats on Biscayne Bay.

"The Grove has a lot of nice things about it," he said.

"I've loved sharing it with you," she sighed.

"We've had some good times here." He felt concern. "The neighborhood seems safe. Do you think it is?"

"For the most part."

"You'll be careful won't you, my love?"

"Oh yeah," she said.

"What will happen to you?"

"I'll keep working. Oh, I've had some good news. My brother and his family are moving here, so I'll get to enjoy being an aunt close by."

"That is good news." He gazed at her, she was so beautiful. "I'm glad you'll have family here. I look forward to being an uncle on Abidan, since I'll never marry."

She took an uneven breath, "I think we'll make a fine aunt and uncle."

"Where will they live in Miami?"

"They're looking in Aventura. I just found out." She took another breath, "shall we have dinner?"

As they stood to go inside, he took her in his arms. They hugged each other for a long time, trying to seal up all the empty places that their words did not seem to be able to fill.

"This's the hardest thing I've ever tried to do," she sighed, "but what choice do we have? Come, darling, I hope you don't mind dining in the living room."

"That's fine," he smiled, "your dinner's great."

"I'm glad."

"I wonder what Jesus ate at his Last Supper, besides bread and wine, of course."

"Whatever it was He couldn't have enjoyed it knowing what was going to happen. At least I can feel glad you're going to a safe place." She shook her head. "I've always wondered why God would let his son be killed for us."

"We don't know what really happened," he said, "it may have even been in another dimension. When I talked to God, I was very aware of the existence of a deep universe that we do not comprehend."

She nodded, "it's certainly beyond my understanding, like God letting us destroy ourselves, unless your dissertation can change His mind."

"Not likely, but I still have hope."

"Your dissertation's amazing," she said, "I like what you wrote about the dichotomy of good and evil, and how much good there is on Earth, even among all the wars and atrocities. Another thing I found really interesting is how we're able to turn our minds off to all the horrible things that surround us. Your dissertation's excellent. I'd vote to save Earth."

"Thanks, I truly hope it will, but it's not likely."

"So, assuming World War III happens, will our planet itself be destroyed, like a Star Wars movie, or will it be just the people, and will it be all the people?" she asked.

"I don't know. I believe it'll be all life forms on Earth, and what will be left will be a dark, cold, radioactive, extinct planet," he shook his head. "Promise me you'll be careful when the war comes. There'll likely be some extra-planetary options then."

"Like the International Space Station?"

"Maybe not that particular station, NASA plans to de-orbit it in early 2016," he said.

"Really? It seems like they've just started it."

"They'll likely extend that date or they might use parts from it to build another station, but there'll be some options when the time comes, possible colonies elsewhere, a giant space elevator to facilitate space travel." He helped her clear the dishes, "promise me, you'll take care."

"I'll try, but it's a long way off. So much could happen, and it's such a long time to live without you." She blinked.

"Yes." He put his arms around her and held her gently.

"Oh dear, it's nine o'clock already," she said, "we need to go to your house like we planned. I'll follow in my car."

He nodded because he was too full of tears to speak.

When they reached his house, he placed his luggage in the front hall except for his carry on bag. He had two bags, several large bundles of gifts and a number of long computer screen rolls.

They sat outside remembering the nights they had spent together on that same patio, when the crickets chirped, and the night air was sometimes full of the delicious scent of jasmine. That night, a stiff breeze kept the mosquitoes away, the jasmine was not in bloom and it was not cool. Summer had changed that. Everything else had changed too. They had three hours left. The driver was due at 1:00 a.m.

"How many stars are there?" she asked.

"That's hard even for astronomers. There are new stars forming and old ones dying all the time."

"Can you see Abidan from here?"

"No, but maybe some day with your orbiting telescopes. What will you do?"

"Work harder, keep trying to fight crime," she sighed, "I hope when you're back on Abidan, you'll look at Earth through one of your telescopes and think of me."

Tears filled his eyes again. "I'll always think of you and I'll always be in love with you, forever, but darling, if you find someone else..."

Tear also filled her eyes as she quietly reflected on the connection they had, what it meant to have her lover know her thoughts, how peaceful and loving they could be to each other without any reason for conflict or disagreement or discord, what it meant to be completely understood by another individual. How could she ever find that again? Why would she even want to? She shook her head. "There won't be anyone else. I'll love you, will all my soul, forever."

He looked at his love trying to remember everything about her.

"I should be happy you're returning to a place where crime doesn't even exist," she sighed, "and I guess if you have your brain dusted you won't even know about it anymore. How does that work? You won't have your memory of me wiped out, will you?"

He smiled, "no, it's very target-specific, utilizing advanced neuron technology. Don't worry, I'll never forget you, I'm sorry, I just don't know how I can leave my family forever…"

She touched his lips. "I know. There's no need to apologize. I know."

"You like your job, don't you?" he asked.

"I feel like I have to try. Like the old Chinese proverb, 'Better to light one candle than curse the darkness.' I just hope I can continue, after, do you think you could ever come back and visit?"

He shook his head sadly.

"If not in this life, at least there's an afterlife."

"Yes, and the souls of the just are transmuted."

"Then the souls of the just don't carry the seeds of violence?" she asked.

"Not once they've been transmuted."

"It comforts me just knowing about the afterlife."

He took her in his arms for one of the last times, holding her in an embrace whose memory he hoped would last a lifetime, an eon, an eternity. He glanced at his watch, and carried her to his room where they each tried to remember every touch of lips and hands and minds and bodies, every gentle moment of passion, every piece of heaven that the memory could hold.

Chapter 31

She sat quietly watching him dress in his jumpsuit, trying to memorize everything about him.

"I brought you something, well actually two things," she smiled shyly.

He looked into her perfect face, loving the way she tried to be cheerful.

The large package was a volume of empty pages bound in red leather. The front was imprinted in gold letters that read "The Journal of William Aaron Blake." She had enclosed two photographs, one of herself and the other of the two of them in New York. Another tourist had taken the picture of them standing in front of the fountain in the plaza of the World Trade Center. It was late afternoon and the sun glistened on their smiling faces and on the golden-colored bronze sculpture above the water in the center of the fountain. The water bubbled from the center of the pool and spilled over its smooth black edge.

"Thank you, sweetheart, these pictures are lovely," he said.

"The picture of me was from the Pro Bono Awards, I guess it's okay."

"It's beautiful," he looked sad.

"The other one's from our trip to New York."

"They're both great pictures. I'll put them in a special place when I get home. The bronze sculpture in the fountain's interesting isn't it?"

"Yeah, I haven't studied it," she said, "wonder what it's supposed to mean."

"It's called 'The Sphere' by a German sculptor named Fritz Koenig. It's supposed to symbolize world peace through world trade, but like a lot of art, it's subject to interpretation."

"It's neat. The base looks like a spindly Atlas, and the sphere has cracks in it. So, it's a weakened Atlas trying to support a broken world," she said. "How's that interpretation?"

"Very good," he said as he tucked the photos inside the front of the journal and flipped through its empty pages.

"You write so beautifully," she said. "I thought you might want to write about your visit to Earth, or whatever you like."

There was a solid gold St. Christopher's medal in the second box. "It's beautiful, but it looks expensive. I don't want you to have to go without food or something. You rarely have any food in your refrigerator now."

She shook her head. "I want you to have it. He's the patron saint in charge of keeping traveler's safe."

"Thank you, for everything." He slipped the medal in his pocket and folded her in his arms, overcome by the feel of her, the taste of her, the wonderful scent of her, her thoughts, her emotions, the deep connection he felt with her. Everything about this woman thrilled him. And the terrible choice he had faced over and over smothered him again. He could not leave and he could not stay. It was time for his personal tragedy.

An older man wearing a gray uniform arrived at 12:45 a.m. He parked his bronze Yukon in front of Janna's car. He had a military bearing and spoke little as he waited at the door, making a final farewell awkward. William thought it was just as well. There was no easy way to ever say goodbye to his darling. He put his luggage in the back of the Yukon and locked the house from the inside, as Eugene had said. He left the keys on the kitchen counter along with his car key, and stepped over the beam so the garage door could close.

Janna waited in her car in the driveway until the man she loved was gone. She cried as much as it was possible for a person to cry, until her eyes stung badly and she was tired and shook all over in gasping breaths, and she cried until she knew she could cry no more, because it didn't do any good.

She gripped the steering wheel she had been leaning on, and

knew that there was nothing at all to do but somehow go on with her life. And when she thought of that, she cried again.

Chapter 32

When the driver did not answer several easy questions, William opted for silence. He had wanted to know if this driver knew anything about Eugene, and if Eugene was happy. Blake had seen Eugene shortly before he left when had come by to get Irina's things and the messages he had written for Irina's family and his own family. Eugene had seemed content, but preoccupied. He wondered if Eugene had made the right decision, and how badly he missed the woman he had left behind.

They drove on the dark road illuminated only by car headlights, tiny bright stars, and a first quarter moon that would not be full for another six nights. He recalled the predawn darkness when he and Irina had arrived six months ago. He thought of Irina, and how she had left her life on Earth.

He had intended to return to the Everglades while he was on Earth, but he had never taken the time. So much left undone, small regrets when he thought of the whole lifetime with Janna he had left behind.

The metallic black spacecraft was waiting. He was the sole passenger. The pilot was a young man who did not appear to want conversation any more than the driver. It was just as well. Every minute, every mile away from Janna felt wrong, but he could not leave his family forever. He thought of his parents, sisters and brother. They would be living their lives. How could he not be there? And how could he transgress God's commandments?

But it felt wrong. The farther they traveled from Earth the more he felt it, the awful choice, the decision he had to make that could never make him happy. He thought again of ways to bring Janna to Abidan, but they would stop her, and detain her. She would never be permitted to leave an evil planet to go to a planet of peace. The laws of the Universe were inflexible, even though Janna would never spread violence anywhere. He had been warned against going to Earth, but he could never be sorry that he had known Janna, never sorry that he had had one great love.

His mind did not rest during his journey to the Milky Way Transport Station. He decided to try to gain another appointment with the Great Creator of Life to request permission to bring Janna to Abidan. He knew it was a bold move to ask the Great Creator to change the rules, no matter how unfair to the individual they seemed, but the intense mental exercise of preparing a petition helped his troubled mind.

There was space traffic congestion at the transport station when they arrived. They had to cruise for several hours before being cleared to dock. When they docked, he thanked the pilot who seemed pleased to be at the station. Blake also felt good to leave the cramped craft and walk about.

The first thing he did at the station, after clearing the Genetic Code Scanner, was to post the signal of his dissertation to the Great Creator, as he had been earlier instructed by Professor Shem. Even though he had no experience with such a transmission, it was a surprisingly simple process. He checked his messages. There were signals from his family responding to the ones Eugene had sent for him. His family was fine, they missed him and were concerned about his safety. He loved the connection with them. The signal from Irina's family was very sad. They were as devastated as they were confused by a young death on a violent planet that they had no way of understanding. They thanked him for arranging to have the body returned to Abidan.

Blake chose a mountain motif hotel, avoiding the tropical motif where he and Irina had stayed during their travels to Earth. He registered for seven days, the same amount of time he and Irina had spent on their earlier trip. This time, he carried a heavy burden of double grief.

He was not sure how to obtain a meeting with the Great Creator. Professor Shem had arranged his one and only meeting with God.

He went to the station chapel, a small building with two side walls of stained glass windows intersecting in a tall pointed ceiling at the front of the room. The windows were illuminated from behind with a yellow-gold light. He sat for a moment on one of the soft chairs, organizing his thoughts, when the double doors at the entrance opened.

A Prayer Guide walked toward him and asked him if he could be of help. The guide was of medium height, with a kindly face, brown hair and hazel eyes. Blake told him why he had come, and the guide offered to elevate the request for an appointment. William thanked him and gave him his contact information.

Blake returned by shuttle to his hotel room. He wrote in his journal, read books, watched television, listened to music, ordered room service and looked at Janna's picture and their photo together in New York, all the while, hoping for a message from the Creator.

He went by the chapel but the Prayer Guide could tell him nothing new. He extended his hotel stay for another seven days. He sent signals to his family assuring them he was all right. This time, he wrote them about Janna. When he began to describe her, the words came as easily as water rushing in the strong current of a beautiful mountain creek. He told them he was waiting to seek permission to bring her home to Abidan. He knew the message would worry them, but they would already be worried because he had not yet returned to Abidan.

He signaled another message to Irina's family, trying to be as comforting as possible, but there was no real solace for what had happened to Irina on Earth. He reviewed the procedure for brain dusting, but he did not schedule it.

As time passed without a message from the Creator, he began to feel listless. He made no plans. He quit writing, reading, eating and listening to music. He spent hours lying on the hotel bed. He felt that he was drifting away.

Chapter 33

THE PRAYER GUIDE'S MESSAGE BROUGHT HIM BACK. Blake had an appointment tomorrow at 11:00 Universal Time. He showered, dressed and went for something to eat. When he exercised at the winter sports arena, he felt stiff from his period of inactivity, but his mind was energized with arguments, that he sensed were inadequate.

The designated meeting place was a greenhouse restaurant under a domed ceiling of artificial light and blue sky. The seating was interspersed with colorful fruits and vegetables growing on leafy plants and vines. A young couple sat in one corner. In the opposite corner a man in a white suit sat by himself. He had alert brown eyes, neat shoulder-length brown hair and a kind expression. He directed Blake to sit down.

"I am a Messenger from the Great Creator." The gaze in the quiet brown eyes was steady. "The Creator has no reason to see you. The evidence of evil on Earth is incontrovertible. The Creator will not intervene."

Blake cleared his throat. "The good people of Earth are remarkably gifted, talented and generous. Only a minute percentage of them commit evil. It is possible to remediate their behavioral genetics and their culture of violence and enable them to produce a Universal Renaissance."

"You assume that a planet that gave birth to evildoers like Hitler deserves still another chance. Our Creator does not."

"But Hitler was beaten by people on Earth who knew how evil he was," Blake countered, "they gave their lives to defeat him."

"Yes, and your record of their sacrifice is quite beautiful," the Messenger said, "but consider the legacy of Hitler. Look at the genetic composition that created that man. Consider the environment. Review your record of the genocides and atrocities that have taken place since that time. There is no hope of peace. The culture of violence controls Earth."

"Is it written that Earth will end in nuclear annihilation?"

"Yes, just as it is written that people from evil planets may never go to planets of peace." The man regarded him carefully.

"What about a Messiah? Will God not save the Earth for even one just man?"

"Irrelevant to this discussion. You came for two things, Mr. Blake, to champion your dissertation, which you have done, and to decide what to do about the woman on Earth. You cannot take her to Abidan. The laws of the Universe are inflexible."

"Then I do not know what to do," Blake said sadly.

The voice was kind and soothing. "I know. You came to ask the Creator to change the laws of the Universe for this one woman. This will never happen. You are the one who must choose."

Yes, Blake thought, I must decide between the two irreconcilable choices in my mind.

The messenger touched his arm. "Do not be despondent, William Blake. The souls of the just are transmuted, and the spirit love you have experienced will never be truly obliterated. Perhaps your souls will join again, in another state, in another time."

"But I am not making a decision for the next life. I am making it for this one, now."

"Yes. But one choice will affect the next."

"What would you do?" Blake asked the kind eyes.

"Go to Abidan, of course."

Blake gave a long, troubled sigh. "Of course, but then you do not know Janna."

"Yes."

"If I choose Earth would I be permitted to visit my family in Abidan beforehand?"

The man in white shook his head. "The rules do not change. You have surpassed your timeline. If you choose Earth you cannot return to any planet of peace. You should consider this a permanent decision."

"If I select Earth, how does that occur?"

"If you select Earth, you must take one-way transportation there. You must take this time-sensitive code for permission to re-enter Earth." He handed him a piece of silvery metallic paper with three numbers and three letters on it. "If you go to Earth, I suggest you send your dissertation to Abidan. You should also send anything else you choose, as it would be your last chance for communication with Abidan."

Blake looked down, still paralyzed by indecision. The Messenger held his arm at the wrist. He glanced at it.

"The power of spirit love is remarkably strong. It is the only thing in the Universe that endures. I am sorry for you and wish you well."

He looked at the hand holding his wrist. He thought he saw a reddish scar in the center of that hand, but he was not sure. He looked again and the Messenger was gone.

He sat at the empty table thinking of the power of love. Love of his family, love of his woman, one balanced against the other on some kind of mystical scale that he did not think he could tip one way or the other. He looked at the code on the silver piece of paper. He had to depart for Earth by no later than August 1, Earth time. That was two 24-hour days from now. He had a deadline. He could not dwell in uncertainty forever. It would be resolved. But how?

He realized he had not thanked the Messenger for his kindness.

Chapter 34

JANNA OPENED HER EYES AND LOOKED AT THE CLOCK. IT was 7:30. She stared at the mahogany posts of her bed and decided not to go to work. She glanced at the Grand Canyon picture calendar on her wall, August 12, a Saturday. Maybe she'd go to work later. Maybe not.

She made coffee, heated a bagel and sat on the balcony in her sleep shirt. She stared absently at the water, hardly noticing the pretty view of boats in the bay and the graceful drive lined with palm trees. An hour or more passed.

She thought of William, like she always did. He would be sad that her life had so little meaning. She wondered how he was, if he missed her, if he had seen Rebekah.

She took a sip of coffee. Action is the way to overcome depression, but she'd lost her drive to do anything. Loss of love had changed everything. No, she would not go to work today.

She had told Moira that he left; it was a small comfort to be able to talk about him with a friend. Moira had kept her word and never told anyone where William was from or where he had returned.

K.J. knew only that her lover had left. He had proposed marriage to her with apologies for his tasteless timing. He told her that he had loved her from the first time he saw her, but he had not wanted to interfere with her career. He knew she might need someone now, and that he would never forgive himself if he had never asked. As much as she appreciated his friendship, it had felt good to be able to gently tell him that she would never marry.

She should probably go see her brother and his family today, but it was hard to see anyone when she felt so depleted, and so hard to fake not feeling that way. Maybe she would sit for a few hours and then sleep.

There was a tap at the door. That was odd because the front desk was good about keeping solicitors out. The only neighbor she knew was Miss Abbey Lou Hyer. She often helped the elderly lady walk to the library, but Janna knew she was busy with her visiting daughter.

The knock sounded again, a little louder. "Oh, go away," she thought, "I don't feel like talking to anyone."

It was louder the next time. She got up slowly, set her coffee mug down on the little round table on the balcony, and made her way to her door.

It was William. At least it looked like him through the peephole in her door. She unlatched the door as fast as her shaking hands could and flung it open to make sure. Dear God, it was! She threw her arms around him and allowed herself to feel every molecule of joy at seeing him again. They laughed and cried and kissed and hugged for a long time. There would be time for questions later. All that mattered now was that her love had come back to her. She felt overwhelmed at the touch of his arms, his lips, his skin, his beautiful hands. He smiled a wide, deep, happy smile with only a hint of sadness just around the edges and tiny corners.

"You've got your stuff!" She looked at the two large bags and long rolled containers extending off a brass luggage cart.

"Yes, I suppose I'm officially what you'd call homeless, although your front desk recognized me and let me in."

"So you're staying?" She felt giddy, deliriously happy, and tearful all at once as she hurried him inside and locked the door. He kissed her tears away and they made love as if they had been lost forever, as if trying to erase all of the sadness they had felt, the sadness she knew he must feel at leaving his family and his home, all placed on hold for now, as they thought only of their passion for each other. They spent the afternoon together in her four post bed, and it was more exciting than either of them had remembered.

"Welcome home, Superman," she kissed his lips.

The golden afternoon had faded into dinner time when they showered and dressed.

"I'm afraid the fridge is empty," she confessed.

He grinned. "Some things don't change, but you need to eat, you've lost weight. Where'd you like to go?"

"Is CocoWalk okay, it's close?"

Over dinner, he told her about his trip to the transport station, his unusual meeting with the Messenger, and how he made his decision.

"It was hard to write my family," he said, "but I knew this time it was the right decision. I don't want you to ever feel that it was your fault, or feel guilty. I made this decision of my own free will."

"How'd your family react?" she felt bad in spite of what he had said.

"They were as sad as you would expect, but I think they understood. My father transmitted a beautiful letter to me, full of words of kindness and wisdom. They were happy about you and said to send you all their love, and if they can ever signal us, they will. The hardest thing is that I can't see them and I have to live on a dangerous planet. I tried to reassure them that there are safe places even on Earth."

"Do you think they could visit Earth like you did?"

He shook his head, "Universal law prohibits family visits to expatriates, but I'd love it if they could send me a message."

Janna felt guilty, but all she could think to say was, "a message would be great."

"Yes, it would."

"I'm sorry," she reached across the table to touch his hand, "my dear expat."

"Thanks, but please don't be sorry," he held her hand.

"How did you get here?" She changed the subject because she could not change the facts.

"I took a flight to the Everglades with a no-return Earth code the Messenger gave me. The same driver met me and brought me here. Of course, I no longer have my house."

"But you have mine," she felt happier, "and, what did you do with your dissertation that you worked so hard on?"

"I sent it in a signal to the Great Creator, that was prearranged."

"You sent your dissertation to God? How does that work?" she asked.

"It's not as weird as it sounds, the transport station is pretty advanced."

"That's so amazing, I'd love to see the place, but that's where the scanners would catch me, and it would be kind of silly to go there, if you're here."

"I sent Professor Shem the original," he said, "it will be cleansed so there probably won't be much left."

"Is that like censoring all the bad stuff?" She took a bite of food.

"Yes, it gave me a feeling of closure to send it, like signaling Irina's family. They had signaled to thank me for arranging with Eugene to return her body and her things. They were devastated because Irina had a young, violent death, which they can't even understand."

"It was a terrible thing," she paused, "and how'd they get Irina's body back to Abidan?"

"Eugene arranged it before he left here. It traveled on the same vehicle with him."

"That's interesting, at least I won't have to worry about public defenders wanting to exhume her body and study it for anomalies, which I wasn't really worried about. I guess it was good to return the body."

"Yes, anything that could make the family feel better would be a help."

"It seems so strange to try to explain a violent death," she took a sip of water, "to someone on a planet of peace who doesn't even know what violence is."

He nodded, "I used some of the ideas in the grief material you gave me after Irina was murdered."

"Abidan sounds like a good place."

"It is," he said carefully, "but it's a much colder planet, no pretty green outdoors and warm ocean like here, and the people have so little imagination, but much more importantly, it was missing you and I've learned that I cannot live without you."

She looked down, "thanks, I'll try to deserve such an extraordinary love, and sacrifice."

"You do, without question."

She blinked away happy tears and changed the subject again, "what about all those nice gifts you bought your family?"

He smiled. "I sent them. That was a bright spot, knowing they'll have something from me and picturing them opening their gifts."

"I'm sure they'll love having something from you," she smiled, "so, did you have your brain dusted?"

"I never got that far."

"Then you haven't forgotten anything."

He shook his head. "No."

They talked for a long time and did not rush their meal.

"I hope you'll have dessert," he said, "how much weight have you lost?"

"Not much," she shrugged, "but dessert sounds good."

When they walked back to her condo in the warm August night, he looked up, "I always feel comfort when I look at the stars," he said. "The Universe is incredibly vast, but we all belong to one Universe."

She stepped along the sidewalk, feeling the comfort of the oneness of the Universe, along with a whirl of conflicting emotions about this wonderful man who had made an incredible sacrifice to be with her.

Chapter 35

IN THOSE SWEET DAYS OF HIS RETURN, THEY LIVED almost without worries as each day flowed in gentle succession, like the rippling currents of a beautiful river.

William successfully enrolled at the University of Miami, after several visits to the International Admissions Office. Since he had no school records, he had to take the GED, the General Educational Development exam, for high school equivalency, and the SAT, the Scholastic Aptitude Test, for college admission. He made perfect scores on both tests. Not long after that, he was admitted to undergraduate school.

He chose to double major in Biochemistry & Molecular Biology and in Criminology, and he planned to attend grad school, teach and conduct research in behavioral genetics. He did not mind starting as an undergraduate freshman. It was a useful transition from his former role as an observer, writing a dissertation about Earth. He was now a researcher collaborating with scientists in many parts of Earth, like Bulgaria, England, California, and China. He learned that current research in behavioral genetics varied from measuring aggression in people consuming different amounts of hot sauce to studying people's willingness to mete out punishment on others. He also learned that all research required funding.

He was sorry he had given Irina's notes and computer to Eugene to be sent to Abidan, as they would have been useful. Nevertheless, he had benefitted from their discussions and he felt good to continue her work. He hoped to make a contribution to science that would eliminate the genetic and environmental predisposition for human aggression.

He was happy to return to the Miami Hurricanes' baseball team. As a full-time student, he was eligible to try out for the team, and the players and coaches encouraged him to join. The 'Canes were very disappointed they had not advanced to the College World Series last summer. They had hoped to be the fifth college in history to repeat as baseball national champions. Their current goal was to earn their way back to the series next summer, and to win.

William decided to continue working out with the team instead of joining. That way, he could avoid problems from things like more medical exams or his unusually high batting average. He didn't think the 'Canes really needed him to join. They were a great team and, even if they missed the College World Series last year, they hadn't had a losing season since 1957.

He loved practicing with such a fine group of players and coaches. After work, Janna usually came to the field to watch. They went to games together and she also became a Hurricanes' fan. Their daily lives fit as easily and beautifully as their nights together.

Jim was pleasantly surprised at his return, and eager to welcome him as a full-time student and future colleague. He occasionally practiced with Jim's rec team, and those players tolerated his perfect switch-hitting, as long as he didn't join a team. Jim also got him involved as a volunteer coach for his Little League team, and he introduced him to his wife, Mary, and their four year old daughter, Michelle.

There was much to enjoy in South Florida. Janna bought William a bicycle, and they often went biking across the steep bridge to Key Biscayne in the bright, summer afternoons, when it didn't get dark until late. They went sailing along the bay in their sailboat, kite boarding in the ocean, and kayaking and paddle boarding around the mangrove forests in the quiet waters of Biscayne National Park, and they took wonderful walks around Coconut Grove.

William gradually became more accustomed to Earth. He avoided violence on television and in the news, but he had learned from his studies that violence was deeply ingrained in the whole story and history of Earth. He could never accept it, but he read everything he could to try to understand.

One evening when he and Janna were reading in bed, she heard him sigh, and she looked up from her book to ask what was the matter.

"Engagement parties, wedding invitations, bridal registry, reception, I don't see how we can do all this, but I do want to marry you, Janna."

"What on earth are you reading?"

He showed her the cover of *Amy Vanderbilt's Complete Book of Etiquette*.

She laughed, "you'd read anything, wouldn't you?"

"Of course, but how can we have this wedding?"

"Keep reading, I'm sure there's a short paragraph on quiet civil ceremonies in the back."

He flipped some pages. "You're right, but don't you want something nice?"

She grinned. "Is this a proposal?"

"Definitely not, I need to get a diamond ring and talk to your father, would you marry me?"

"This is a proposal!"

"Not until I get a ring."

She leaned against the smooth skin of his chest. "You've already given me diamonds and I don't need a ring, I just need you."

"You already have me, and buying diamonds seems like the only thing in the book I know how to do."

They laughed and he put his arms around her and held her against him. "It seems so complicated."

"Do people get married in Abidan?"

"Yeah, but it's just a big family party at home. We make promises to each other and a Prayer Guide participates, but we don't have all this ceremony."

"Hmm, that sounds nice. You probably have fewer family fights and stressed out people during your weddings. Do they have churches in Abidan?"

"Not like here. We worship in the main hall of our warehouse neighborhoods where all of our meetings are held. We always follow worship with a big picnic. Usually it's in the neighborhood park. In summer, we picnic outdoors. It's still very cold, but we dress warmly and we have outdoor heaters. It's about the only time we go outdoors, so it's nice. I have happy memories as a child from those worship day picnics."

"That is nice," she said, "but I can't picture the warehouse neighborhoods. If they have a park and a town hall they must be a lot bigger than I thought."

"They are fairly big, about the size of a neighborhood like Coconut Grove."

"Really?"

"Yeah, there's blue sky and filtered sunshine, plants and small trees, houses and city blocks. They're linked with other domed neighborhoods and centers. It's nice, but I was always aware I was under a dome. It's kind of hard to describe, but I've never known anything quite like being outside in Florida."

"I thought you lived in domes because of the oxygen, but apparently you can go outside?" she asked.

"Yeah, Abidan has a thin atmosphere, so you can be outside, you just can't stay out there for a long time. We mainly have domes because it's such a frigid environment, with hardly any plant and animal life outside."

"Everything's so different," she said, "do you have premarital sex in Abidan?"

He smiled, "Couples in serious relationships have sex as long as they've had their annual birth control implants."

"Do they have divorce?"

He touched the tip of her nose. "As they say on Earth, don't even think about it. We do have it, but it's rare, counseling usually works."

"And your implant's good for another two months?"

"Yes," he looked thoughtful, "How do you feel about having my children?"

She paused, "if it were just the two of us in a good world, I'd like nothing better than to have your children, but, as it is, I have some deep concerns. Should we have a child knowing its death date? That is, of course, is if he survives in this dangerous world until 2070. I guess that's the death date for all of us."

"Undoubtedly, a huge concern, but we have time to plan. Scientists are advancing in worlds of discoveries. By that time, we should know the genetic causes of human violence and be able to mediate or cure it through mutagenesis and other gene therapies."

"So you think science will rescue us."

"I do, not only with gene therapy but in other ways as well. There may be colonies on Mars, the space station, a giant space elevator. I'll have a plan to protect us."

"One of the many reasons I love you so much," she smiled, "and what about the differences in our DNA?"

"As far as I know from what I've studied, it should be fine. A sonogram would be a good indicator if there are any problems."

"And better than genetic testing."

"Yes."

She looked thoughtful, "so our child would be half alien. Maybe he or she could go to Abidan?"

He shook his head, "Universal law forbids halflings from inhabiting planets of peace."

She rolled her eyes, "I'm beginning to really dislike Universal law."

"Even though you're a lawyer and presumably like laws?" he teased.

She smiled, "I think your child would be really amazing, but I don't know, I'm not ready now, I'd like to enjoy things as they are for now, is that okay?"

"Whatever you want."

"Maybe I'd better get on the pill," she rested her head on his shoulder. "I'm glad we had this conversation."

"Me too, and I do want us to be married, so when can I talk to your father?"

"Hmm, you've been back a month and haven't met my brother and he lives here now. I'm seriously overdue for a visit. Would you like to meet my family? We could go see my brother in Aventura, and then fly to Tallahassee to meet my parents."

"I'd love that, but first I'll get you the ring so we can announce our engagement." He returned to his book.

"You can stop reading now. I'd be very happy with a simple ceremony, and no engagement ring, but it would be nice for you to meet my family first."

She kissed him gently, then suggestively, "can we stop talking now, Superman?"

"Yes, dear." He put his book down.

"You're a fast learner, I like that," she teased.

Chapter 36

THE FOLLOWING WEEK, WILLIAM BOUGHT HIS LOVE AN engagement ring, took her to dinner at the Biltmore Hotel, and asked her to marry him. Janna happily said yes.

She took him to her brother's house in Aventura to meet him and his family. Her brother Zack was a large teddy bear of a man with brown eyes and black thinning hair. His wife Carol was tall and blonde, with a sweet face and a wonderfully kind demeanor.

William felt anxious, and tried to keep the questions on his side, "Janna tells me you have two little boys?"

"Yeah, they sure keep us busy too," Carol chuckled. "They're asleep now. You'll have to come back and meet 'em. I probably won't tell 'em they missed Janna, they adore her."

"We have that in common," William smiled at her. He looked around the living room decorated in soft blue colors with lots of kids' toys in one corner, "you have a beautiful home."

"Thanks. Some day we'll get our living room back, but we've pretty much given up trying to keep the toys out of the living room," Carol explained. "We have a pool fence so Andy can play with his stuff on the patio, but somehow it still ends up in here, and it's easier for Bobby, he's the baby, to crawl around on the carpet."

"I'd love to meet your children. Janna's told me all about them." He was aware of Zack scrutinizing him with skeptical thoughts.

"Forgive me, but this really is a surprise," Zack said. "I'm sorry to act so dumbfounded. We're happy for you, of course, but we didn't even know Janna was seeing anyone, seems like all she does is work. We don't see her for a month and all of a sudden she's engaged," he laughed, "but now that I think about it, my little sis always has been her own person."

Janna showed them her ring.

"Wow!" Carol said. "If you don't mind my asking, how big is it?"

"Three carats, from Tiffany's." She couldn't resist showing off a little and she hoped it would help them accept William.

"It's gorgeous," Carol said.

"That etiquette book did give good advice," he teased.

Janna smiled back, "maybe, but we still want a private civil ceremony, instead of a big wedding."

"What do you do?" Zack asked.

"I'm a student at the University of Miami."

"Oh, what'cha studying?"

"I'm double majoring in Biochemistry & Molecular Biology and Criminology. I'm an undergrad student now, but I'm planning to do grad work in Human Genomics."

When Janna saw Zack look concerned, she said, "he already has a Ph.D. in Sociology from the University of Belgium," Janna added, "well almost, he just finished writing his dissertation."

"You're not one of those perennial students, are ya?" Zack asked.

"He's very intelligent so he likes to study," Janna said.

"You and my sister definitely have that in common," Zack laughed, "but there comes a time when you have to get out in the real world and make your way, make some money so you can support a family."

"He can afford school, so don't worry," Janna said.

"Where'rd'ya come from?" Zack asked.

"Belgium," William said.

"Oh yeah," Zack said, "I guess that's why your doctorate's from there. You don't look like you're from Belgium."

"Everyone says that." William felt relieved to get a comment he expected. "I guess it's my Florida tan that fools them."

"Your family there?"

"Just a few cousins, my parents are deceased and I'm an only child." Blake felt keenly aware of Zack's skepticism and of the awkwardness of the situation.

"I forgot to tell you," Janna said, "William plays baseball with the University of Miami team, I mean he's not on the team, but he works out with them."

"Wow, that's impressive. How'd ya get that?" Zack asked.

"A professor friend of mine set it up."

"You must be pretty good. They're a helluva team. Of course, they got shut out of the College World Series last summer by my old alma mater Florida State University, but Miami's been to Omaha a bunch. They won it the year before didn't they?"

"Yeah, and their goal's to win it again in 2001," William said.

"They might just do it, too, think you could introduce me to some of the players?" Zack asked.

"Sure, any time," William shifted his position on the couch. "I practice with them every afternoon."

"That'd be great. Maybe I'll become a 'Canes fan. That'd be a switch, wouldn't it," Zack laughed.

"I'll look forward to introducing you to the team. Janna tells me you have a car dealership."

"Yeah, Lexus dealership," Zack took a sip of Diet Coke, "I got a degree in marketing from FSU and was in the foreign car business with Dad in Tallahassee. I decided to try a bigger market, and since my sister's here and Aventura's a pretty affluent area, I thought this'd be a good place, and so far, so good. The first month's sales have been outstanding. You should bring him by, Janna. Give you a discount if you're in the market for a new car. What d'ya drive now?"

"Actually I drive a rental Lexus SUV, I had one before and I liked it," Blake said.

"Good man," Zack said, "when's your lease up?"

"In eleven months."

"Well, keep me in mind."

"I will."

"Back to baseball, you gonna watch the Olympics?" Zack asked. "I think the U.S. team's got a good shot at the gold."

William paused.

"Oh yeah, it starts tomorrow night," Janna said, "thanks for reminding us."

"I love the Olympics," Zack said. "You gonna take him to meet Mom and Dad?"

"Yeah, we're going Saturday," Janna said.

Zack chuckled. "They're great people, but if you think I ask a lot of questions, you oughta' see our dad. I'm sure he'll like you fine, though," Zack added in a reassuring tone.

"Are you really thinking of not having a wedding?" Carol asked.

"Yeah, especially with William not having any immediate family and all," Janna said.

"Mom's not gonna like that," Zack warned.

"I know, but I'm sure she'll like William."

William felt good when it was time to go, and sorry that he was eager to leave. These were good people, but it was hard to lie to them.

"I'm so happy to meet you both," he said. "It means so much to be with a family again, since I...lost my family. Please don't worry, I love your sister very much. I'll do everything I can to make her happy."

"I'm sure you will," Zack said kindly, "she seems very happy now." He kissed Janna and shook hands with William. "I hope you'll come back soon, maybe watch some of the Olympics with us."

"Thanks, I'd like that."

Chapter 37

WILLIAM LOOKED ANXIOUS AS HE STARTED THE CAR, "Zack had some pretty skeptical thoughts."

"You did fine. He's always been a very protective brother," Janna patted his leg, "and the baseball was a real hit, I really appreciate how hard you tried, it's just difficult to lie."

"Yeah, even harder to tell the truth," he smiled.

Janna nodded, "I was thinking maybe we should take our honeymoon in Europe, see Belgium, so you can have a past you can talk about."

"What's a honeymoon?"

"I can't believe you didn't see that in your etiquette book," she teased, "but don't worry you'll love it," she leaned against his shoulder. "So, what did you think of Zack and Carol?"

"I liked them of lot, and I hope I can become a real part of your family. Do you think your dad will ask a lot of questions I can't answer?"

"Like when Zack asked about the Olympics?"

"Yeah," he said, "thanks for helping out. I assume they're about sports."

"Yeah, they're amazing, every two years they alternate between summer and winter sports, and the best athletes in the world compete. The opening ceremonies are tomorrow night, in Sydney, Australia, which was why Zack was asking, Sydney's a beautiful city. I've been there."

"Sounds exciting."

"It really is, but like all stuff on Earth it hasn't been without problems, years ago there was this ice skater named Tonya Harding whose friends intentionally injured the girl she was competing against, a beautiful skater named Nancy Kerrigan, they actually clubbed her in the legs. Fortunately, she managed to skate in spite of her injuries and won a silver medal." They both sighed, and Janna continued, "The Olympics started in ancient Greece as a way to promote peace through competitive games. They'd actually stop wars in order to have the Olympics."

"I've wondered if competition in sports could replace war."

"Doesn't seem like it," she said, "but the Olympics are still great, finally something good to watch on TV."

"I'd love to watch them with you."

She leaned against him happily.

"What else do I need to know before visiting your parents?"

"I think we'd better tell them about Irina," Janna said, "it'll worry them but it'd be worse if they just found out, and with the trial being in October they'll hear about it."

"We'll have to tell enough lies about my past," William said, "at least we should be truthful about what happened to her."

"Yeah, that's the least we can do. They'll likely assume it was a romance since their generation thinks you live with a woman only for that reason, so they might think you're a little unstable wanting to get married so soon after, but I'll just have to do the best I can."

"You always do, anything else?"

"Can you talk football?" Janna asked, "my dad's not a fanatic, but he really likes football."

"I work out in the weight room with the Miami football team; I know quite a few players."

"Not good, my dad's a Florida State fan, Miami's a big rival. I think it'd be good to read up on football, especially Florida State Seminole football."

"Got it," he smiled. "What about the presidential election? Is that a good thing to talk about? I've been reading a lot about Al Gore and George Bush."

"Yeah, but sometimes that's not a good subject to discuss because people can feel strongly about politics and that can create bad feelings. I'd stick to sports, family, the weather..."

"Sounds good. I want your parents to like me."
"All they really want is for us to be happy," she smiled.
"That's easy," he smiled back at her.

Chapter 38

Janna's dad did not ask questions. He sat quietly staring at Blake and gave short answers as they struggled to make conversation in her parent's living room.

"Did you watch the opening ceremonies of the Olympics last night?" William asked.

"Some, Zack's the one who really follows it," her dad answered. "He says you play baseball for Miami?" He was skeptical.

"Actually, I just work out with them. They're a great team, but your Florida State team beat them in the Super Regionals last summer."

"Yep," Mr. Anderson said.

"Zack's so happy you know the baseball team," Madge Anderson contributed gently, "and the opening ceremony was beautiful, wasn't it? The Olympics are always quite a spectacle."

"I thought Sydney did a great job," Janna added.

"I was very impressed," William said. "Mr. Anderson, Janna said you like football, how do you think the Seminoles will do this season?"

"They're gonna be okay," he said.

"They play North Carolina State tonight," William said.

"I hope it's not a home game and we're keeping you from going," Janna felt concern.

"No," her dad answered, "It's away, but we wouldn't have gone. It should be an easy win, we can watch it if you want. Maybe your boyfriend can see his first football game tonight." His tone was partly teasing but mostly challenging.

Even if things felt uncomfortable, William liked meeting Janna's parents and seeing the stately brick home with white columns where Janna spent her childhood. It was near downtown Tallahassee in a hilly neighborhood of beautifully-maintained houses, small fenced yards and big shady trees. The inside of their home was formal, but warm, with dark mahogany furniture and dainty china figurines and crystal on display. He pictured Janna as a little girl there.

Her parents were friendly, but much more formal than Zack and Carol. When Janna showed them her engagement ring, her dad looked at it suspiciously and her mother admired it.

"But, don't you want a wedding?" she asked.

"I'm sorry, Mom, but we want something small and private, and you know how hard that'd be."

"Well, how about a reception?" Madge asked, "William, what do you want?"

"Whatever you and Janna and Mr. Anderson want," he smiled.

Her father spoke. "Son, can we talk in private?"

"Yes, sir," Blake felt his chest pounding. He looked at Janna.

"It's okay, he won't bite," she tried to be lighthearted.

They went into the den and closed the door.

"I hope I'm right," Janna said.

She looked at her mom. "What do you think, isn't he wonderful?"

"Well, yes, he seems very nice and he is the most handsome man I've ever seen, but it's all so sudden, and you are our youngest, and no wedding, and that business about living with a woman who was murdered, and he is old to be a freshman in college. We were really surprised when we got Zack's call."

"What'd Zack say?" Janna asked.

"He said you are very happy and he likes him, especially the baseball, he just thought there was something different about him."

"He is different," Janna said. "He's from a European background, and he's very sweet and considerate, which makes him different from most guys I've dated. And the woman was sharing a rental house with him and they had a platonic friendship. Her murder was a real tragedy. Three thugs killed her for no other reason than the money in her purse and savage cruelty. At least one of them raped her. I'm preparing for the trial now."

"Well, it was a terrible thing, very unfortunate, and I wish you didn't have to deal with such awful people. But, Janna, no wedding, really?"

"We can have a wedding if you really want one, Mom. It's just that William doesn't have any family, except a few cousins in Belgium who wouldn't come to a wedding in Tallahassee. He doesn't know many people in Florida so he wouldn't have many friends to invite. I wouldn't want to embarrass him, or make it look strange for you and Dad either. His best friend's an African American professor and my office friends are a pretty multi-cultural bunch too. Would that be a problem?"

Madge hesitated, "I don't think so. I'd like to think prejudice is a thing of the past."

"Me too. Another problem's the timing. I've already got the first part of November off work for our honeymoon, and we've bought our airline tickets. That'd be awful soon for you."

"November is awfully soon, but I could manage, I'm good at parties, you know."

She smiled at her wonderful mother. "You are very good at parties, Mom. We can have a wedding if you really want one, but let's keep it small."

"How about a private wedding at home and a reception at the club? I saw one written up in a magazine somewhere. Now where was that article?"

Janna helped her look. "That might be a good idea, Mom."

Her mother wanted a wedding and was even willing to put it together on short notice. Her mom was so sweet, she really deserved a wedding, and it would be nice for William too. She wondered how the father of the bride and the groom were doing. It seemed like they'd been out of the room for a long time.

"Does he belong to a church?" her mother asked, "if we can't get a priest on short notice, maybe we can get one of our minister friends."

As he sat on a leather couch across from a stern Bob Anderson, Blake felt anxious. He read deep skepticism in the man's thoughts. The longer they sat without saying anything, the more uncomfortable he felt. The older man sat on a matching leather chair, staring at him.

"Mr. Anderson, sir, Zack said you would want to ask me a lot of questions," William cleared his throat, "so far, you haven't asked me anything. I'd be glad to answer any questions, if I can."

Janna's dad cleared his throat. His complexion was ruddy and his lips were set, which added to his stern appearance. "Son, I don't want to sound unkind, but you come into town, with no family, no friends, you say you're 25 years old, but you're a freshman in college. You meet my daughter, who's a successful attorney, though she's working for the government now and not making too much money, she could make a lot in private practice some day. You're living with some woman who was murdered. Janna told me about that, I understand it was a tragedy and they caught the guys who did it, but it doesn't make me feel any easier. You buy her a big, showy ring, which may or may not be a real diamond, and you say you have money, but how do I know that? And if you do, how do I know you know how to be careful with your money? And you don't look like you're from northern Europe. I was there with the United States Military for a time and I never saw anyone in northern Europe who looked like you. So, if I'm not real talkative, that's why."

Blake felt like a fraud. Truthfully, he was a fraud, but not in the way this man thought. If he were to tell the real truth, it would be much worse. He wished Janna were there, but she wasn't, it was up to him. He spoke carefully, "My people were originally from southern Europe, I understand. I'm afraid I didn't pay much attention to my family history. It's not that interesting when you're younger. My parents moved to Belgium when I was a child, went into the textile business and were very successful. They were killed in a plane crash when I was 22 and, since I was their only child, I was their sole heir. I studied at a university in Belgium, and worked in my parents' business, but I sold the business last year and moved to South Florida to study disciplines like sociology, criminology and genetics. That is where I met your daughter." He felt relieved to get through the story of his past, and miserable that he had to lie.

"I shared a rental house with a woman studying genetics. It was a platonic friendship, not a love interest. My major professor had recommended her because she was also from Belgium and needed a place to stay. Janna told you how terrible it was when she was murdered. Janna is prosecuting the criminals." Mr. Anderson still did not say anything, so he kept talking; it was better than silence.

"Sir, I know you may not like everything about me or my background, and you are concerned for your daughter, but I do love your daughter with all my heart and soul. She's a wonderful person, she is so intelligent and beautiful and sweet and I would honestly do anything for her. I would protect her with my life. I had a girl friend in Belgium, but I can truthfully say that I have never really been in love before. And I do have enough money to take care of her, even though I'm not working now." William noticed that Mr. Anderson's thoughts started to soften as he spoke about his love for Janna.

"Do you think you have enough money?" He was embarrassed to ask the question. "I mean, if you don't mind my asking."

"Not at all, sir, I appreciate all the concern you have about your daughter. My dad would do the same thing, I mean, if he were in your place. I'm not superrich, but I have approximately five million dollars in savings in Switzerland, which is also in Janna's name. I have a checking account in Miami. I can send you statements. I live off the interest, but I want to buy a house for Janna so I'll have to spend some of the principle. Would you like to see my bank statements?"

Mr. Anderson cleared his throat again, hesitated, and nodded yes. "Have you been to immigration?" he asked.

"Yes, I have a student visa and I hope to become a citizen when we marry," William said.

Janna's father nodded. "Don't forget, you'll have to file income tax now that you're living here."

"Yes, sir."

"Janna or Zack will know an accountant if you don't have one. It's a good idea to have an accountant prepare your taxes. I think it's a good idea to keep your money in Switzerland in the bank. You don't want to let someone talk you into making investments you don't know anything about. You really can't trust people, unless you know them well, real well. Always remember, if anything regarding money sounds too good to be true, it probably is. And don't forget the bank statements."

"I won't."

Mr. Anderson stood and offered his hand. "Now, shall we go see how the wedding plans are coming along?" Blake thought he saw the serious man come close to a smile.

William gratefully shook hands, and the two men, soon to become family to each other left the room.

Her mother started dinner in the kitchen while her father lit the charcoal grill on their patio in the back yard. A domestic calm settled upon the two couples as they went about the mundane tasks of grilling steaks, boiling corn, chopping salad and heating French fries. Blake felt more at ease now that the conversation with her father was over. Janna's dad had accepted enough of what he said to accept him.

After dinner they checked the score of the football game and since it wasn't close, they decided to have their pecan pie and decaf on the porch. Dusk faded into night. An occasional firefly blinked to light the dark. Unseen locusts buzzing high in the trees yielded to the sweet twittering of nighttime crickets, a pleasant background for their gentle conversation.

Janna treasured the evening. She knew that William loved family, and he was beginning to become a part of hers. It was too bad they had to tell so many lies, but she assumed it would get easier as time passed.

Her parents stayed up later than usual to hold onto the sweetness of the evening. Tomorrow they would worry again about the pending marriage. But in that soft, quiet night they were re-living all of their precious past that can never be brought back again, which made it all the more perfect and valuable.

As William listened, he saw Janna as a sweet child, an excellent student, a determined athlete. He pictured her winning awards, adopting stray animals, putting on neighborhood shows, biking all over town, jumping on their trampoline, playing capture the flag with the other kids, or launching some money-making scheme with her brother and sister. He felt closer to her than ever.

They watched the last quarter of the football game. Florida State won by 49 points. Janna's dad seemed to enjoy talking to William about the game. When they turned in, Janna stayed in her childhood room and William slept in Zack's old room.

The next morning, they went to church and afterwards to the country club for a champagne brunch. Her mom loved the excitement she caused by introducing Janna's exceptionally handsome fiancé to their many friends.

When they met their friends, the Thompsons, Jack Thompson, a jeweler, focused on Janna's ring. "It's a good diamond, all right," he said, "and that star pin is exquisite, Tiffany's, isn't it?"

Janna nodded as she saw her mother give her dad a satisfied glance.

"He's so gorgeous," Fran Thompson said to Janna's mother. "I didn't know Janna was engaged. How long has she known him? Where's he from?"

"It was a surprise for us too," Madge said, "but a good one. She met him in Miami, he's from Europe."

"Well, he's really handsome. When's the wedding?" Fran asked. "Maybe our book club can have a party for them."

"That'd be lovely," Madge smiled at her friend. "They're flying back today and we're on our way back to the house. It was William's idea to rent a car to save us airport duty, he brought us a beautiful gift too, Godiva chocolate."

Fran nodded approval.

William put the luggage in their car while Janna hugged her parents. She treasured the comforting feel of her mother and father. William kissed her mother and shook hands with her dad.

As they backed down the driveway, Janna looked at her parents standing there waving. They had always been there with their strength, their warmth, their values, their simplicity, their solidness, their love. Tears filled her eyes as she thought of her wonderful childhood and wonderful parents. It had been a great visit.

"I know they had plenty of concerns," William said. "They're such nice people, I really want their blessing."

"You'll have it" she said, "first meetings are just awkward."

"I hate lying."

"I know, but can you imagine if we told them you're from another planet?" she smiled. "This is one of those times when a lie is good for everyone."

"People on Earth have no concept of life on other planets."

"True. You know what a hard time I had. We just don't have any experience that helps us accept it."

"I'm glad you did," he kissed her cheek.

Chapter 39

THEY HAD A GREAT TIME AT ZACK'S WATCHING THE U.S. Baseball team beat Cuba 4-0 to win the Olympic Gold Medal. William was beginning to understand that winning on Earth could be fun.

Not long after that, the trial of Irina's murderers began. As Janna prepared for trial, she tried to consider William's feelings and not discuss it, but the memories associated with Irina's murder made it a difficult time. He thought of Irina many times, as he observed Janna conscientiously marshalling her skills to ensure that the terrible evil doers would be punished.

William tried to focus on his research, even as he found it ironic that he was studying the genetic causes of human violence. One of the things he studied was the MAO-A gene. The 2R allele of the VTNR region of this gene appeared to increase the likelihood of serious crime or violence in humans. He was able to link aggression with several genes influencing brain structure and chemistry, serotonin, dopamine and neurotransmitter density.

He also conducted research with drosophila melanogaster, fruit flies. By experimenting with these flies, he sought to identify ensembles of genes that mediate aggression. By analyzing inbred lines of their genes, he found 266 transcripts associated with aggression. He also found evidence for extensive epistasis, suppression of gene expression by one or more genes, which could have implications in the mediation or elimination of aggressor genes. His research also made him think of Irina.

William did not attend the trial. Janna thought the deliberations would be too difficult for him. He kept himself busy, as Janna did all she could to achieve guilty verdicts.

One Saturday afternoon, he encouraged her to take a break from work to drive with him along South Bayshore Drive. Several miles north of her condo he turned into a driveway surrounded by lush tropical plants. The drive lead to a very large, two story Mediterranean style home of tan stucco and an orange barrel tile roof.

"This is the house I want to buy for you, if you like it," he unlocked the front door with a key he had borrowed from the Realtor. "I talked to Zack and your dad about it. Zack said it sounded like a good deal, your dad said houses in Miami are way too expensive."

She smiled. "It's beautiful, you did such a good job."

They walked through the large living area of Mexican tile, white walls, high ceilings made of cypress wood. It looked onto a pool and waterfall spa, beautifully landscaped with tropical flowers, shade trees, and a strip of open grass next to a high stucco wall.

"And all new, I really feel like a bride, no wonder people get so excited about weddings."

"Your mother's excited about our wedding."

"I know, it's been so wonderful of you to talk to her on the phone so much, while I've been busy."

"It's a good way to get to know your mom, she's as sweet as my own mother, and she likes me a lot, I've researched weddings pretty thoroughly."

"I'm sure you have," she put her arms around him and kissed him, "you probably know more than her friends."

"That's what she said."

She grinned. "You haven't shown me the bedroom yet."

"Which one? There're five."

"Planning a big family?" she teased, "I think I'd like to see our bedroom first."

They walked across the living room to the master bedroom.

"This is fabulous, look at the size of those closets, and bathroom, is this an exercise room?"

"If you want."

"I seem to be getting plenty of exercise trying to keep up with you, you have some pretty amazing stamina."

He felt concern, "I hope you know I can do as little or as much as you want."

"No complaints," she grinned, "and you're always so considerate, like these past two weeks I've been so busy, let's go back to our condo, and I promise not to do any more work until tomorrow."

"How's the trial progressing?"

"I think we're only going to be able to get the maximum penalty for one of them. I guess he's the worst of the three, but they're all despicable."

"Why is it so hard to prove?" William asked, "isn't it obvious what they did?"

She shook her head. "It's not that easy for lots of reasons. First, we have to prove their guilt beyond and to the exclusion of any reasonable doubt. If any juror has a doubt that the defendant actually committed the act, then that defendant won't be convicted. Second, we have rules of evidence and that means certain evidence we gather can't be discussed at trial because of procedural rules. For example, we can't mention that all three defendants were convicted of other crimes prior to this trial, so the jury doesn't get the whole story. Third, these defendants don't go into court looking like thugs, the Public Defender cleans them up and dresses them to look like businessmen. And fourth, they're not required to testify. The law allows them to sit quietly and the judge will instruct the jury to make no assumption of guilt or innocence because they didn't testify on their own behalf. And finally, it's a 12 person jury with no prior knowledge of the case; that's okay because you want them to be impartial, but the verdict has to be unanimous. If one person on the jury doesn't want to convict them, they walk free. That juror might have a good reason, like a reasonable doubt, but they could also be motivated by race or prejudice or their own personal likes or dislikes. Have you read about the O.J. Simpson trial in 1994?"

"The former football star?"

"Yes, most people were pretty certain he was guilty of killing his wife and her friend, but Simpson was acquitted. Simpson's defense team was able to convince jurors that there was reasonable doubt about the DNA evidence and that the L.A. Police were racists and prejudiced against Simpson."

She continued, "a civil trial is quite different. There are only six jurors and they make a decision based on the preponderance of the evidence. They can have reasonable doubts, but still reach a decision. Three years after the O.J. Simpson murder trial, Simpson was sued and convicted of wrongful death and battery in civil court."

"I assume they have these criminal rules, so they don't make a mistake?" he asked.

"Yes, these protections are built in to safeguard the innocent," Janna said, "which is, of course, a good thing in itself. We learned in law school that it's better for 100 guilty to go free than for one person to be wrongly convicted, but that's unfortunately about the way it works. There's not much chance of a truly innocent person being convicted, but hundreds walk out free largely because of the rules that protect them. That's why it's extremely hard to get a conviction. And even if you get one, the district court of appeal at the next level can overturn it."

"It's like other good concepts," he said, "it's a good idea to protect the innocent, but I see how it can be manipulated. I also see why it's such hard work."

She sighed, "and I really want to see that justice is carried out for Irina."

He nodded. "All you can do is your best. Nothing will change what happened."

"You're right, but we've got to get these bad people off the streets. Maybe I'll think of something, but where were we? It'll do me good to take a break, and spend time with my wonderful husband." She gave him his favorite little smile.

Chapter 40

THE TRIAL CONCLUDED AS JANNA PREDICTED. THE JURY recommended the death penalty for one criminal, and life imprisonment for the other two.

"The jury knew they were all guilty but didn't want to give the death penalty to the two others," Janna explained to William, "it's really hard to tell exactly what happened the night of the murder. The evidence shows that the guy that got the death penalty was the one who actually killed her. The other two were accessories and were clearly a part of it, but the jury didn't want to give them the maximum penalty. Our juries are so used to crime it's pretty hard to get a jury to recommend the death penalty if there's any doubt as to exactly who did what."

He looked sad. "What happens next?"

"The judge will sentence them a few weeks from now. She can overrule the jury and give the death penalty for all three, but what will probably happen is that she'll go with the jury's recommendations and only one will be executed. Then, there will be appeals on top of appeals and maybe 10 or 20 years from now the murderer will get the death penalty. For the other two, the judge will probably sentence them to life in prison or less. In a few years, with the possibility of shortened sentences for good behavior, and because of overcrowded prisons, they could be out on the streets, again. We refer to it as the 'revolving door of justice' because so many criminals get out and commit more crimes, and that's a big frustration. At least we have the three strikes rule, so if they get convicted of another felony crime, they'll be in prison for good. I hate to think of them committing more crime, but I don't know what else I could've done. I gave it my all. Moira and K.J. said the same thing."

"At least it's over," William said, "which I think is a good thing for you."

"I guess," she said, "and I do have time to think about our wedding now," she smiled.

They moved out of Janna's condo and into their new home. Janna thought how easy William made things and odd that it took an alien to handily accomplish what could be a big task for others. He educated himself about interior design, drew a plan, budget and time schedule. She was happy with everything he did and thought he had the perfect balance of traditional and casual. And it had been easy enough that they also had time to enjoy their beautiful pool and spa before the cooler evenings of late October.

The week before the wedding, they flew to Tallahassee for an elegant party given in their honor by her mother's book club friends. While they were there, they bought their wedding rings from Jack Thompson. It pleased her parents that William had remembered their friend. William met many of the people who would soon attend their wedding. Bob Anderson was friendly to him, and thanked him quietly for the bank information.

Janna and William were apologetic that their wedding day was the same day as an FSU home game against Clemson, but Bob Anderson assured them that it would be another easy victory, and the club would have plenty of TV's available for anyone who wanted to watch football.

They spent a last hectic week in Miami getting ready to be away for their wedding and European honeymoon. There was little time for anything else, except to feel happy.

Chapter 41

As she dressed for her wedding in a sweet daze of emotions and memories, it seemed to Janna that November 4 had arrived suddenly. She was in her childhood room with her mother, her sister-in-law Carol, and her older sister Lauren. Janna wore her mother's wedding gown, a simple, fitted dress of white satin, and a long, handmade lace veil that was her maternal grandmother's. Her mother arranged orange blossoms across the tiara of the veil. Janna loved their sweet smell and wondered where her mother found orange blossoms in November.

"You look so beautiful," her mother said. "I hope you'll be very happy. Oh, I've got to stop crying, my makeup will run. It reminds me of my own wedding, except you're so much prettier." Madge glanced over at Lauren and Carol who were standing by the window talking.

"I can't get too excited about today," Lauren was saying, "for one thing, people always think I'm beautiful until Janna shows up, and then they hardly notice me. It's always been that way, but I guess I shouldn't mind so much today. It is her day. But marriage, ugh, you have such high hopes on your wedding day and everything seems like it's going to be so happy, and then you get home and some time passes and you realize you're married to a son-of-a-bitch. I guess marriage to a politician is the worst. John thinks he's so important being a senator, he's started to believe his own bullshit. And he chases every skirt in Washington and no telling how many bimbos he gets in bed with. I hate him for it. And he wants me to get pregnant, probably because it would look good on his campaign posters to look like the perfect family man. I don't know whether to get pregnant or divorce him."

"Well, Zack's an awfully nice guy," Carol said, "but marriage is such an awful lot of work, especially with kids, and he thinks he's helping, but he never does the things I need done, and just the very time the kids are sick or have some big program, he's out of town or has some civic club meeting. Things are never as nice as the day of your wedding, that's for sure."

"For heaven's sake, you two," Madge interjected. "This is Janna's wedding day. To listen to the two of you, you'd think there's no such thing as a happy marriage. Now go on downstairs and mingle, it'll be time for the ceremony soon." Madge hurried them out.

"Oh I'll go mingle, Mom," Lauren said, "but I'm sure all I'll get to do is watch John chase some of our young, pretty cousins who've never seen a senator up close," she turned to Janna, "I'm sorry, Janna, I've just been having a hard time lately. You really are gorgeous and I really hope you're happy, and don't let William ever go into politics, at least he's born in Europe. That's a help." Janna smiled weakly. She felt sorry for her sister.

"I guess I'd better go too," Carol said. "Zack's probably lettin' the kids run all over the house, knocking down Grandma's expensive rose vases."

"Yeah," Lauren said as they walked down the stairs, "if I smell any more roses, I think I'm going to be sick."

Madge turned to her daughter. "Don't let them spoil your day. Imagine, those two standing around talking like that while you're getting dressed. This should be a perfect day for you, you look so beautiful, and there is such a thing as true love. Your father and I may not be a wildly exciting couple, but we really are happy together, we hardly ever disagree on anything, anymore. And William is a prince, and he's been so helpful to me, I've got to stop crying. I hope you'll be very happy, my precious daughter."

"Thanks, Mom. You're the greatest." She kissed her mother.

Madge dabbed her eyes with a dainty lace handkerchief and said, "Well, I guess I'd better go downstairs, and check on the musicians."

"Thank you so much for everything, it really is lovely, and I've never seen so many beautiful roses, it makes the living room look heavenly."

"William bought them. He said get as many as I wanted. Lauren said I got way too many but I don't think so, we're going to re-use them at the reception."

"Roses, music, my family and William. It really is a perfect day for me." Janna's smile was radiant.

"And William's professor friend, the best man, is such a gentleman and his wife is lovely," Madge continued. "And your friends Moira and K.J. are great."

"Thanks, I can't tell you how much I appreciate everything." Janna dabbed her eyes with her grandma's lace handkerchief. "Now, I've got to stop crying."

"I really do need to go downstairs. Bob, you can come in now and see your gorgeous daughter." Madge called to her husband who was waiting near the bottom of the stairs.

When Mr. Anderson walked into the room, he stared at his daughter and did not say anything. He grunted and cleared his throat and finally was able to tell her she looked beautiful and to wish her happiness, but his voice sounded raspy and tight.

The photographer took pictures of her and her dad. Then they heard the musicians downstairs and the wonderful notes of the wedding march. Her dad extended his arm to her, pressed his lips tightly together and they walked down the stairs.

The family stood as Janna and her father reached the living room. William, Jim, Moira and the minister waited at the hearth.

William was afraid he would cry. Having all these kind, nicely-dressed people around him in this lovely home made him miss his family. He could not help thinking how much they would enjoy being there with him. Zack was videotaping. With the many thoughts swirling through his mind, he wondered if somehow he could send them a letter, or pictures, or a video?

He read the thoughts of the guests assembled there. He felt touched how they had put their personal concerns aside to celebrate the presence of his true love and marriage. Janna's dad set aside his skepticism, Lauren put her own problems in the background. Jim and Mary set aside their awkward feelings at being the only blacks there. Moira shelved her worries about her friend's new husband being an alien. They had all come to be there to enjoy the beautiful moments of his marriage to Janna.

When he saw his bride, his scattered thoughts flew off like blown bubbles on a windy day. He saw and felt only for Janna, who was so lovely and exquisite appearing on her father's arm. When they touched hands and looked at each other he felt that he was not on Earth or Abidan, but in some place where time and space were suspended and the time was perfect and golden and as pure as the stars on a perfectly clear night. When they exchanged the words that were so beautifully written, and the shiny gold rings, he was only aware of the pulsing touch of her, the look, the feel of her, her wonderful presence. "And a man shall leave his mother and father and cleave unto his wife."

The reception afterwards was the greatest celebration he had known. He did not distract himself by reading thoughts then, but chose to enjoy the present. As he stood in the receiving line with his bride and her parents, he was touched that so many people came from Miami to be there, Moira and K.J. and so many others from the State Attorney's office, Jim and Mary, and the University of Miami baseball team and coaching staff. The players looked so different from when they were on the field, and slightly uncomfortable with arm and chest muscles bulging in their new or borrowed suits. He recognized many of the Anderson's friends. It was fantastic, a wonderful celebration of a wonderful marriage. He felt very grateful to everyone on this strange planet for being so happy for him.

Zack and Carol stopped by.

"Hey, when you get released from the receiving line, you really should come join your party," Zack said. "I can't believe the whole University of Miami baseball team is here. How great is that?" He looked at William, "you must be a real baseball stud to have the whole team here, and the band, the food, it's all really good, Mom's even got the club to do fireworks later. This's a helluva party, can we bring you some more champagne? We're way ahead of you."

Janna looked at her parents. "Mom, it looks like most people are here. Can we go party now?"

Madge looked around, "Sure, let's all go party."

Carol laughed. "We're way ahead of you on champagne, and Mom, thanks so much for getting a baby sitter. Zack and I haven't been out together with a sitter in such a long time, it's awesome."

Madge smiled. "You work hard, you deserve some fun."

William raised a glass of champagne to Janna. "To my wife." He smiled at her. "That sounds so good. To my wonderful, brilliant and exquisite wife."

She gazed into his sparkling blue-green eyes, "to my wonderful, brilliant and exquisite husband. It does sound really good."

"Shall we dance?" William asked his wife.

When they moved together the room grew quiet. The guests were mesmerized by the stirring image of this beautiful young couple dancing together in perfect rhythm with each other.

Madge found Lauren sitting alone at one of the dinner tables, watching her newly married sister and husband like everyone else in the room.

"Oh hi, Mom," she said. "Have a seat. They really are a handsome couple, aren't they, like movie stars, wouldn't you know Janna would find the perfect man? If John ever looked at me once the way he looks at Janna, I'm not sure what I'd do, but I wouldn't hate him the way I do now, I'd give anything for him to look at me like that, but, look at my husband, over there talking to Cindy, he'll probably try to hit on Janna before the evening's through."

Madge observed the party. "I wouldn't worry about Cindy and your other pretty cousins. It looks like the senator's about to be upstaged by the baseball team," she laughed. "Do you want to divorce him?" Madge asked.

"Well, I do and I don't. I guess that's part of my problem. In my own way, I'm caught up in the Washington scene too, it's exciting to be so close to where everything's happening. Although being a wife to a senator is not as good as being a senator myself, I have my law career, and I love Washington, and John's not really a bad person deep down. I don't really hate him. He works very hard and is a good public servant, it's just that the power has gotten to his ego a little bit, and the girls are part of it."

"Maybe you should sweeten things up at home for him," her mother said.

Lauren made a face. "He's never home anyway and if he is, I usually have to work late."

"You know, politicians don't really want a divorce even in these times where it's more acceptable. Maybe if you don't want a divorce you should think about starting a family. You're 30, you know. If you're really going to divorce him, of course, you don't want children, but men with big egos, as you say John has, can get a lot of enjoyment out of having their own child. It might change him. Of course, children can put a strain on a marriage, and they can't really fix a bad marriage, but in your case, it might give you both a reason to come home together. And a lot of time the strain of children is brought on by not having enough help or money to take care of them, but you have plenty of both."

"Well, I don't know, Mom, it'd be tough on my career," Lauren said. "You know you have to work long hours in a corporate law firm, it's not like the State Attorney's Office where Janna works. And even if they say they don't discriminate, you know they do, because if you're not there to do the work, you're not gonna get the promotions."

"I'm not suggesting you would have to quit. You can get help. You could decide that if you have the child, how much time you want to be home."

"You might be right, John really does want a child. I always thought it was just for the campaign posters, but he does like kids. Did you see him at the wedding with Zack's kids? Probably the only time he wasn't thinking about skirt-chasing all day." She patted her mother's hand. "It's good to be home, Mom."

"And a child is something his mistresses can't give him, hopefully."

Lauren laughed. She looked up. "I think your new son-in-law wants you to dance." She smiled at William. He was so nice it was hard not to like him. He smiled back at her. He loved the sisterly resemblance in her. "Now don't run off," he said to Lauren, "I want to dance with you next."

She was still smiling when John appeared to ask her to dance. He assumed that the smile was for him. He had not seen her smile in a long time and it made him feel good. He felt almost surprised to notice that his own wife was a very attractive woman. He had not really looked at her for a while. "Would you like to dance?"

Lauren stopped herself from making a sarcastic remark about him asking her to dance for appearances and kept her smile as she stood up to dance.

Maybe it was being home, maybe it was being in the presence of newly married love, but Lauren felt happier than she had in a long time.

"I should bring you home more often," John said. "You're a beautiful woman and you are so much prettier when you smile. Yes, it's good to get out of Washington for a while and back to our roots. It's really important to get out and be among ordinary people."

Lauren decided to ignore his slightly pompous tone and give him the benefit of possibly being sincere. She was enjoying his attention too much to spoil the moment.

The room filled with dancing couples, William and her mother, Lauren and John, Jim and Mary, and Zack and Carol.

Janna was dancing with K.J. "You really are the most gorgeous bride I've ever seen," he said, "but then, you always were the most beautiful and classy woman I've ever known. I was disappointed we never hit it off, but I guess things work out for the best."

"Thanks, K.J."

"Well, I decided if I couldn't have you, I'd have your legal assistant, so Moira and I are going to get married," he announced.

"You and Moira? That's wonderful."

"Yep," he smiled. Janna thought he looked almost shy as he continued, "sometimes it's the most obvious things you miss, she and I are really suited for each other, we get along great and she's such a wonderful person, she's funny, pretty, nice, she puts up with me."

"Yes, and she's probably too good for you," Janna teased.

"Don't tell her," he whispered, "that'll be our secret."

She smiled, "I'm very happy for you, I can't believe you all didn't tell me."

"We just decided on this trip, this marriage stuff must be catching."

"That's wonderful, when's the happy occasion?"

"As soon as you can cover the office for us," he said.

"Anytime, except the next few weeks, of course, you sure you don't mind that we'll be gone for three weeks?"

He shook his head, "you deserve it, especially after the Vega trial. Go ahead and have a great time. He's really the right person for you, isn't he?"

"Yes."

"I suspected as much when you went to New York together, but then he left so I figured it was over, but I guess my instincts were right all along." K.J. looked across the dance floor. "Hey, it looks like the baseball team's starting a conga line, let's go find Moira and William."

Janna smiled happily.

Chapter 42

William looked at his precious wife in the half-light of the afternoon sun. They lay in bed together at the White Swan Hotel in Stratford-upon-Avon in England.

"It's like the fireworks at our wedding," she said, "only the fireworks were inside me, how do you create all that pleasure? It's good to be married for many reasons, one being that I can feel less sinful."

He kissed her breasts, and quoted from *Romeo and Juliet*, "Oh give me my sin again."

"I like that, quoting Shakespeare in his hometown, here's one for you, Juliet's nurse said it, 'God's lady dear, are you so hot?'" They laughed.

"Then 'Let lips do what hands do,'" he covered her body with kisses and gently levitated her as he made love to her again.

Later, they went to dinner at the English pub in the hotel.

"It's so fun to be here with you," she said, "I studied Shakespeare in college, but I haven't read everything like you have."

"I've learned a lot about human nature reading him, but I think it's hard for people to understand the original text."

" 'When he himself might his quietus make with a bare bodkin, who would fardels bear?' "

He nodded, "to be or not to be, that is the question."

"Strange that probably the most famous soliloquy and greatest love story are both about suicide. I'm glad you're certain of an afterlife, even though 'no traveler returns,'" she mused, "too much to think about for a honeymoon."

"Yeah," he said, "I look forward to sightseeing tomorrow, there's so much still here from Shakespeare's day, like this hotel's been here for 500 years, even before Shakespeare. He may have come here for his last drink before he died in 1616."

"Think how Earth has changed since then, and think how it's going to change," she sighed, "so what happened after his last drink here?"

"According to the vicar, Shakespeare contracted a fever after a merry drinking party with Ben Jonson and John Drayton, his writer friends, who came from London for a visit, but no one really knows. Would you like to see Trinity Church where he's buried?" he asked.

"Sure," she answered, "I remember the epitaph he wrote, 'Curst be he who moves my bones.'"

"It worked, didn't it? He's still there, but the bones are one thing I wonder where his soul is."

"Aye, there's the rub."

He laughed.

She grinned suggestively, "let's go back to our room."

"Welcome to Belgium," he announced a few days later as he returned to their hotel room with coffee and pastries.

She sat up, "what time is it?"

"Afternoon, you needed some sleep, you were looking a little tired yesterday."

"I was tired," she yawned, "it's awfully hard to keep up with you, and you don't even sleep much either."

"I try to get six hours, though I only need three," he said, "but I do sleep."

"No wonder it's hard to keep up," she smiled, "I feel great now, thanks for letting me sleep in."

"Like Shakespeare said, 'Even love itself must pause to rest.'"

"Apparently," she took a bite of pastry, "so, what are we doing today?"

"I thought I'd show you around my adopted hometown, I've checked it out and it's a beautiful place, I'm relieved to report."

She smiled at him, "I hope we'll visit your birthplace, like we did Shakespeare's."

"That can be arranged," he kissed her, "but eat your breakfast."
"Yes, dear," she smiled.

"It all looks the same as when I was here in college!" she said as they took a taxi from the train station to their hotel, it's so good to be in Florence again, Firenze bella! I can't wait to show you everything, and where's that pizzeria where they throw the dough in the air just for the Americans?"

"I'm sure we'll find it," he laughed, "I truly couldn't be happier to be here with you."

"Anch'io, tutti va bene," she said, "by the way, your Italian's perfect, it must be nice to learn a language so easily, I have to work at it."

"Grazie, tanto," he said.

She took his hand, "We've been to Brussels and seen where you spent your 'childhood,' let's go see where I spent one of the best parts of mine."

William was astounded at the beauty of Michelangelo's David, probably the greatest sculpture on Earth. They marveled at it from every angle, amazed that the statue was almost 500 years old.

"I wonder what a new Renaissance era would bring?" he said.

"Like your thesis," she smiled, "I have to say, in spite of all the bad things here, you make a good case for Earth's creativity, especially from our current viewpoint of David. Look at the expression on his face; he was the definitive symbol of the Renaissance. Of course, his expression is so tense because he was planning to kill, but at least Goliath was a bad guy."

"Yes," said William, "and it's a spectacular work of art."

She stifled a yawn, "I hate to leave, but we've been here for a long time."

"Yeah, and I believe my love is tired," he stroked the back of her neck, "let's have dinner and then I'd like to suggest you go to bed early and get some rest. I'll give you a massage."

"With your strong, beautiful hands all over me, I'd love that," she grinned.

"A sleep massage, Jannie."

"I love those too," she yawned, "I always thought I had a lot of energy, until I met you."

In Rome, they had time to catch up on the political news from home. The presidential election between George Bush and Al Gore was extremely close and had not been decided. The issue was over voting in Florida and its 25 electoral votes. A hand recount of ballots had been ordered in four Florida counties, including Miami-Dade. In Palm Beach County there was controversy over the "butterfly ballot," where the candidates' names had been listed on both the right and left columns of the ballot, and did not line up, which caused confusion at the polls. Another problem was that many of the punch card ballots were poorly marked. The Florida Supreme Court had ruled that the hand counts should continue, and the counties had five days to complete them.

The issue was far from settled. The Italians were very entertained by the controversy, and philosophical, as they always were about any government matters. They also enjoyed the fact that the Florida Governor was George Bush's brother. Janna and William were not sure what to think. It was a mess, but they eventually became philosophical like the Italians and continued their wonderful honeymoon tour.

"It's strange, isn't it," Janna said, as they stood before the Colosseum, "we're having the time of our lives on a fabulous honeymoon, and people died here for the entertainment of others."

"The theme of good and evil is so pervasive," William said, "at least there are no gladiators and persecution of Christians here anymore."

"True, but guess what the winner of the Academy Award for best picture this year was?" Janna asked.

"*Gladiator*?"

"Yep," she answered, "at least we're making movies about it and not actually doing it any more, I guess you could say that's progress. She took his hand, "You know what I'd like to do now? Let's go say some prayers in St. Peter's on our way to the Sistine Chapel."

"Buon idea." He held her hand.

They knelt near Michelangelo's Pieta inside St. Peter's Basilica. The beautiful marble statue was so sacred and impressive, even as it depicted Mary's great sadness as she held her dead Son in her lap. Janna hoped William didn't know about the deranged man named Lazlo Toth who broke this beautiful statue with a hammer. It was years ago, and it was possible that he had missed it. She wouldn't tell him. He deserved his moment of peace.

From Rome, they drove south to Brindisi, a pretty town at the end of the Appian Way. That was where they boarded a ship for Greece.

"The Adriatic is so calm," she said "but I feel seasick."

"I'm sorry," he said, "let me get you something for it."

"Thanks."

"I think I've enjoyed Greece best of all, probably 'cause it's our last stop before home," she linked arms with him as they stood watching the Parthenon at sunset, "it's one of life's great moments to be here with you."

"I'll treasure this always," he gazed at the ruins, "I imagine this place in its original state, with the 40 foot statue of Athena in gold and ivory and a reflecting pool inside."

"Yeah, that would have been great to see, when I first saw the Parthenon I was surprised at the ruins all over the ground," she said, "then I read how the Ottoman Turks used it as a gunpowder magazine and how the Venetians fired shells on it."

"1687," he said, "that explosion destroyed much of the structure and killed 300 people."

She shook her head, "hard to get away from the examples of good and evil."

He sighed, "but the examples of Earth's creativity, not just here but the British Museum and Louvre, are amazing nevertheless, and our honeymoon has been truly wonderful."

"Yeah it has, what a lovely night this is."

"Travel's an amazing concept" he said, "we don't really travel on Abidan."

"Yeah, I guess, one domed city looks like another?" she asked.

"Pretty much," he said, "and with so little curiosity people rarely travel to other planets."

"Lucky for me you came here," she grinned.

"Yeah," he also smiled, "can we have another honeymoon again soon?"

"Great idea," she said.

She was airsick on the trip home. The flight was not rough, and it was unusual for her.

"Do you think you could be pregnant?" he asked.

"I hadn't thought of that," she said. "I have a friend at work who got pregnant on her honeymoon, and she was also on the pill, so I guess it's possible, but not likely, probably just all the different food we've eaten. I'm sorry it's over, it was such a fabulous trip."

"Yeah, where to next?" he asked.

"Africa would be nice."

"I'd love that, just like I love being anywhere with my dear wife."

"I like the way you say that, no regrets?" she asked.

"Only that our worlds are arranged this way in the first place, never about choosing to be with you, don't worry, Jannie," he touched the tip of her nose.

"Well, I can't help it, but I'm so happy that you're here with me."

"Me too," he said.

Chapter 43

"So how's married life, Jan-An, uh, Blake?" Moira asked when she returned to the office.

"Fantastic. I highly recommend it."

"And Europe?"

"Wonderful."

"You look great, marriage really agrees with you."

"I think I'm pregnant."

"You've got to be kidding? Was it planned?" Moira asked.

"Definitely not, I was on the pill."

Moira chuckled, "your new husband must be pretty potent, you sure you're pregnant?"

"I've had two positive E.P.T.'s and they say you can't have a false positive. I'm seeing my doctor this afternoon."

"What about being, you know," Moira lowered her voice, "half alien, will that cause any problems?"

"He's pretty sure it won't be a problem, but I think we're both looking forward to having a sonogram just to be certain."

"Are you happy about it?"

"Yeah," Janna paused, "except I can't help thinking about what a terrible world our baby will grow up in. We see examples of it every day in this office."

"Yeah, but not a reason not to have children," Moira sighed, "but we do need to do a much better job of protecting them, we just can't have another Columbine."

Janna thought about the horrible shootings at Columbine High School April 20, 1999: 12 students and 1 teacher killed, 21 injured, 3 others injured, 2 suicides. Moira was right. That should never happen again. She thought about the destruction of Earth in 2070, and that she should warn Moira. They should probably tell K.J. about William being an alien, now that he and Moira were getting married. A lot to consider. Let it go, for now. "You're so right," Janna said.

"How do you feel?" Moira asked.

"A lot of anxiety about being a mommy after being so wrapped up in my career, and I feel nauseous most of the time, morning has nothing to do with it, it's supposed to be a healthy sign and it usually only lasts the first trimester, so I have only nine more weeks of feeling like I'm going to throw up all the time. I need to get busy and quit complaining."

"Yuck, nine weeks of puking doesn't sound like much fun, but I guess you've already had your fun," Moira chuckled, "is William excited?"

"Yes, very, he's great about everything," she looked out of the window in her office. "He really is my prince, my knight in shining armor."

Moira smiled fondly.

"So what have I missed," Janna asked, "do you think we're going to have a president anytime soon? What a mess this election is."

"Really, and the irony, to think our presidential election might be decided by a hanging chad or a butterfly ballot."

Janna shook her head, "on a much better subject, tell me about your wedding plans."

Moira beamed, "we're getting married January 27 by the pool at the Sheraton Bal Harbour, they don't do beach weddings, which I always thought would be so cool, but you can see the beach so that's good enough, we'll have the reception inside, I'm still trying to find a priest, but if not, we'll get Frank to do it, he's a notary."

"That's a good idea, Frank would do a great job."

"Yeah, we didn't want to get any judges in case of conflicts, but Frank works for K.J."

"That would definitely work, what else have you planned?"

"We're going on a Caribbean cruise for our honeymoon, I'm so excited, and I found a dress in a wedding shop on Calle Ocho, it's really pretty and wasn't even too expensive, although K.J. said to get what I wanted, I think all five of my sisters are going to be in it. I hope you'll be my maid of honor."

"I'd love to, Moira, I feel really, well, honored."

"Thanks, that takes the pressure off, I won't have to pick one of my sisters over the other, and you're like my sister anyway," Moira said, "for the bridesmaids dresses, I'm choosing black, strapless cocktail dresses and each bridesmaid will have a bouquet of flowers in a different color with matching shoes."

"What a great idea! And everyone can use a black cocktail dress later," Janna said.

"Yeah, I saw it in a magazine, it looked really neat and I thought it was such a good idea."

"It is. I can't believe you and K.J. will be married in a short time," Janna said, "we've certainly been through a lot, haven't we?"

"Yep, like another world!" Moira laughed.

"You and K.J. will do well together, for an earthling he's a great guy, and he seems very happy."

Moira laughed.

"How was your Thanksgiving?" Janna asked.

"Good, I cooked a turkey, want some leftovers?"

"Thanks, but I need to quit overeating, I've already gained five pounds."

Moira shrugged, "like you ever need to worry, you always look good, so did you have Thanksgiving?"

"Zack and Carol had a late Thanksgiving for us yesterday. William had never had a Thanksgiving before; he loved it."

"Oh yeah, that's right, I guess they have different holidays," Moira lowered her voice, "anyone in your family suspect he's not from here?"

"So far, so good, thanks to having a trustworthy friend."

"They probably don't have Christmas or Hanukkah either."

"No, they don't."

"Wow, imagine having your first Christmas as an adult."

"Yeah, it should be fun, and interesting, well, I guess I'd better go put January 27 on my calendar and get back to work."

"Yep, there's never a shortage of criminals to prosecute, that's for sure," Moira said, "it's called job security."

"Yeah, we might as well get to it, what've I missed?"

Moira shook her head, "there were 17 violent crimes since you've been gone, and the number of repeaters is so disheartening, but you're pregnant, we should be focusing on happier news."

With each passing week, Janna's nausea subsided, and she and William continued their gentle routine of work, study, and outdoor sports. They spent time with Zack and his family, and William became more comfortable with them. They often met for happy hour on Fridays with Moira, K.J. and other work friends, and Janna was their designated driver. Her sonogram showed that they were expecting a normal son, by all appearances.

William's first Christmas came and went in a beautiful way, and Moira's wedding was all that she and K.J. had wanted it to be. The Miami Hurricanes' baseball team even won the College World Series by beating Stanford 12-1 on June 16.

Life was full and they loved it.

Chapter 44

Janna breathed deeply, "it seems so amazing that we're going to have a baby today. Do you think everything will be okay? Will he appear normal enough?"

"Everything will be fine." William caressed her neck and shoulders with his strong, smooth hands.

"Thank you, that feels so good, I love you."

"And I love you," he said, "I've never heard of pain in childbirth, I'm so sorry it hurts you."

"It's okay." She took a deep breath, "I hope the baby's not going to be too much for us to handle, I worry about losing us as a couple, do you think we'll ever be the same?"

"It won't be the same, but nothing ever is, the only true constant in life is change. I think it'll be better, and we'll never lose the two of us and what we mean to each other."

"Thanks for saying that, and I worry how I'm going to do as a mom."

"You'll be wonderful," he said, "and I'll help you all I can, I've been doing a lot of reading."

"One of the many things I love about you." She took another long breath. "I guess I shouldn't worry, I know he'll have a great dad, but I still worry, a new life is such a responsibility, especially knowing what we know about our world. Our son will be 69 when the world ends, if he has children, they could be in their 40's and they could have children in their teens."

William massaged her shoulders, "sweetheart, one thing at a time, you're getting too far ahead of yourself, and I'll protect you and our baby as much as I can."

"You're right," she agreed, "but we're bringing an alien child into an evil world. What do you think will happen to him? Will he look the same? Will he fit in? Will he have anomalies? Will they be obvious? Will he be bullied? Will he be happy?"

"All in good time, darling." He tenderly put his arms around his love.

Several hours later, Janna and William sat in the big comfortable chairs of their birthplace suite and looked lovingly at their baby. Janna gently held their son in her lap. Their new little boy had attracted the attention of the doctor who examined him. He had called him extraordinary, but checked him off in the normal range, to the relief of his parents.

They gazed into his tiny face. He was very extraordinary. He was the product of their love. He had beautiful blue green eyes that sparkled at his loving parents and his little lips curved in the suggestion of a smile, even though he was a newborn. They named him David because they liked the name and Robert became his middle name, for her father.

"I'm grateful that he looks normal," Janna smiled, "and he's very beautiful like his father. I wonder what his future will be. I hope he'll have a wonderful life and be very happy."

Her thoughts drifted away while William sat contentedly in the wonderful presence of his beloved wife and baby. "Truly remarkable," he said, "but you must be exhausted, darling, why don't you sleep now? David and I will be right here with you."

"Thanks, I think I will, oh, and could you please call Zack? He said not to worry about calling in the middle of the night and he'll call everyone for us, and we may have a lot of company tomorrow, so we need to get some sleep, even you, Dad," she smiled. "What time is it?"

"11:50."

"So July 31 is his birthday, I was born on a Tuesday, too, what a wonderful day."

William smiled happily, "yes it is, now let's get some sleep while we can."

"Is that couch going to be okay?"

"I'll be fine," he said, "good night, sweetheart, you make a wonderful mother, like everything."

By the time he retrieved his phone to call Zack, he was glad to see that Janna was already asleep.

The first six weeks of David's life were idyllic. Janna and William felt that each day with their precious baby was like a newly discovered treasure. Their baby's room was a haven of childhood sweetness and boyishness, painted in blue and decorated with baseballs and bats.

William made everything easy. He took care of Janna as lovingly as he took care of their new baby. He made sure she had good food, clean laundry and plenty of sleep. It was as Moira had said during one of her visits, "he's definitely from another planet."

They had lots of company, but William was careful with that too, as he did not want to tire Janna. The rest and nutritious food speeded her postpartum recovery. She would likely go back to work part-time in the future, but she was not ready to return yet. It was all too new and wonderful.

Having healed so quickly, it seemed as though their lovemaking had continued almost without interruption. As William had predicted, everything was better than ever. He made sure this time Janna would not get pregnant again until she wanted to. She needed time. They needed time to love their new son.

Janna felt that life could not be more perfect than when she was inside the wonder and safety of their baby's room, with her beloved husband and her beloved child. She felt that nothing bad could ever happen.

Then one day, the world changed.

Chapter 45

Janna was in the grocery store contemplating her baby's smile. David's blue-green eyes sparkled and his sweet lips curved as he kicked his feet and waved his arms from his position on his back in his infant carrier. She was thinking of the power of a baby's smile and the incredible bond of emotions that it created, probably part of nature's plan to ensure survival. She adjusted the carrier inside the grocery cart, held his little arm and spoke some baby talk with her own big smile. How could anyone see a baby smile and not want to take care of him?

She became aware of people talking loudly and with a lot of animation. Two men near the deli department spoke of jets crashing. She caught snatches of other conversations of shock and fear and airplanes. At the checkout counter an older man spoke excitedly to the cashier. Janna asked them what happened. They told her that terrorists had flown a jet into the World Trade Center in New York and another into the Pentagon. Another jet might be headed for the White House. She was as stunned as everyone else in line. The Korean check out lady said that this Country was too nice to foreigners. She said she was a foreigner herself, and she knows that other countries are not as nice. The man who carried her groceries to the car told her about an Arab who had worked at this store, who said he hated the United States. The man told her how he had said to the Arab that this was America, and he should either love it or leave it.

She turned on the car radio. The news was full of horror. An American Airlines jet had been hijacked by suspected Arab terrorists on suicide missions. It crashed into the north tower of the World Trade Center. A hijacked United Airlines flight hit the south tower.

Another American jet had crashed into the Pentagon. Another United jet had also been hijacked and was in the Pennsylvania area. She telephoned William. The University of Miami had closed and he was on his way home.

She arrived in time to see the television pictures of the towers burning, and the horrible replay of the second airplane crashing into the south tower. Her heart ached. She was thinking what an awful repair job it would be for the tops of the towers when the south tower came down. It looked like there was an explosion first near the crash site and then the majestic building collapsed one story at a time, falling in on itself. People were leaping to their deaths. The sound of them hitting the ground was horrible. It was all too horrible. "O my God" was all she could say. David was still sitting in his carrier where she had placed him on the floor near the television. He started to cry. She picked him up. She was still hugging her baby when the north tower came down.

At first she felt shock and grief for the loss of the beautiful buildings, the Windows on the World where she and William had dined. Her thoughts quickly turned to the people there. It was unbearable. All those beautiful, productive people whose only sin was getting to work on time that day. People with families, people with heartbreaking stories, people frantic to learn about their loved ones. People hurting, people missing. Productive people. Innocent people.

"Oh my God," was all she could say. The world is truly coming to an end, she thought. She knew from her reading and William's research that scenes like this were inevitable, but the reality was so much more horrible. The culture of hate and violence had a terrible path to take before the year 2070. Like cutting off a hand one finger at a time, or killing a people one baby at a time. Did it have to be so painfully long? The hate, the horror, the slaughter of innocents. It would almost be better to be annihilated now than to take us one tower at a time, one beautiful, productive building at a time, one symbol of America at a time.

She was still holding David and watching the damage to the Pentagon when William came into the room. He put his arms around them both. Janna and William cried for the first of many times. David took a nap on a fluffy quilt on the floor next to them, while they watched and watched and watched. They could not do anything else.

"The world is over," she said.

"No it's not," he reminded her. "We have a six week old baby."

She looked at their sleeping son. He had grown so much already. And she knew that William was right.

Chapter 46

William opened the door for Janna to Tap Tap Haitian, a restaurant in South Beach.

"Date night, what a great concept," she looked around at the colorful Haitian murals. "I hope you like Haitian food," he said, as they were seated, "the review described it as part restaurant and part cultural center."

"It's such an interesting place," she smiled at him.

He reached across the colorful table to hold her hand, "shall we try a Soley, it's one of their specialty drinks, aged Barbancourt rum with fresh passion fruit juice."

"Sounds very good," she held his hand, "and thanks for getting Mary's niece to babysit so we don't have to worry about David. There's so much to worry about, especially since 9/11," she looked around, "you certainly can't tell that we're at war in Afghanistan, can you?"

He sighed, "you wonder what this war will accomplish when all is said and done. Did you see the public opinion poll that 88% of Americans back military action in Afghanistan in response to the 9/11 attack?"

She nodded, "A lot of other countries in the survey, including the UK, favored extradition and trial of Osama bin Laden over military action. I do too, war is so terrible…so are guns, I was reading a criminology report that the 1990's had the highest number of mass public shootings ever, more than four each year. Columbine is just one of them."

"And I still hope that we can find a cure."

"You're certainly doing your part with your research," she sipped her Soley, "this is good."

"I like it too," he set his drink down. "I'm seeing more and more evidence that genes play a significant role in aggressiveness in humans. Comparative genomic studies also show genetic networks associated with aggression across phyla, like mice, monkeys, dogs, zebrafish, and birds. I see it in the fruit flies I'm researching."

She looked thoughtful, "so what does research show in humans?"

"In humans, the promoter region of the MAO-A gene has been linked to increased aggressiveness, involving the breakdown of neurotransmitters like serotonin, dopamine and norepinephrine in synapses. An allele of the DRD2 gene and the DAT1 gene, the dopamine receptor and transporter, are definite contributors, and they're inherited, but gene-environment interaction is huge. The aggressor genes exert in particular environmental conditions, that is, the genes increase the risk of aggression only when combined with environmental risk factors, such as abuse and neglect. They even see a difference when parents do not have regular meals with their adolescents, or when there is only one biological parent raising the child."

"And how would you fix the environment?" she put her drink down.

He paused, "with enough time and education, a culture can change. I guess we're getting too serious for a date night."

"So hard not to," she said.

"We know what's going to happen, ultimately. The question for us is how can we treasure what we have, while we have it?"

"Yes," she glanced at her menu. "I like it here. The Haitian people have certainly had their share of tragedy, this place's a wonderful tribute to their spirit."

He opened his menu and smiled at his beautiful wife. A folk-jazz trio began to play.

"Nice," she smiled. "So, what do you recommend, Griyot, Creole prawns, or whole steamed fish in lime sauce?"

Chapter 47

"What should we do?" William whispered to Janna. It was August 2, 2003, the Saturday after David had turned two. Six little two-year olds from David's pre-school had come to a party at their home. Zack and Carol and their two boys, Andy and Bobby, were also there, along with Jim and Mary and their daughter, Michelle, and Moira and K.J. and their newborn daughter, J'Anna.

David was opening his presents and had just received a toy gun.

"We'll just ignore it and put it away later." Janna whispered back. "She knows we don't want David to have guns, so if I say something she might make a fuss, she seems to be looking for one."

William nodded.

"Just don't video it," she said.

He smiled. "You always know what to do."

"I'm not sure about that, but thanks for saying so, and we have more videos of David than we can ever have time to watch anyway," she laughed, "but it's all so special, isn't it?"

William put the camera down. "Our son is already two, like the metaphor of time rushing by like a river."

"It really does rush by."

"And it's all so very dear and wonderful," he said.

"Yes, that's why we won't let the toy gun ruin the party."

David looked at the toy gun thoughtfully. He did not touch it or play with it, but it was not long before several of his little friends were fighting over who could play with it.

Janna winced. Mary and Jim rolled their eyes.

"Something wrong?" Alicia approached Janna. It felt like challenge almost radiated from the woman.

"No, it's just that David seems too young for such a realistic looking gun," Janna answered.

"Well, really, Janna, in your line of work, I can't expect you to object to a gun," Alicia said.

"I suppose not, but William and I don't favor guns for children," Janna ventured.

"Do you want me to take it back?" Alicia quizzed.

Janna paused.

"Well, it would be hard to do that, anyway," Alicia continued, "I'd say it's the most popular toy here, wouldn't you?"

Janna felt that Alicia seemed a little too pleased with herself as she walked off to join a group of moms across the room.

"Bitch!" whispered Janna's brother Zack who had witnessed the scene. "I think I'd take her off the party list."

Janna smiled. "I'm afraid I was thinking the same thing."

"Look, David," William said, "let's see what's in this package. It's from your cousins."

"Soccer stuff!" David said excitedly as William helped him unwrap a large box and pull out a small soccer ball and shin guards, frame parts and a big net. David strapped the shin guards to his little legs.

"Carol and I know how to give appropriate gifts," Zack chuckled, "and he's already so coordinated, we figured he'd be a natural."

Janna looked at her brother, "thanks so much, and thanks for always being there."

"Wouldn't miss it, can't believe your baby's two, and Andy's six and Bobby's three already, they grow up too fast."

"They really do," Janna said.

"I'm sorry Mom and Dad couldn't be here," Zack said.

Janna felt concern, "yeah, everything all right? They usually don't miss birthdays."

"Yeah, I know. I think Dad's been under the weather, but they'd have said if it was anything serious."

"Hope they're okay," Janna said.

Zack looked around. "Well, it looks like people are starting to take off, want us to stick around and help you clean up?"

"We'll be glad to help too," Mary said.

"You're welcome to stay, but there's not that much to do. We can get it."

"If you're sure, I guess we'll go then, thanks so much," Jim said.

"Yeah, thanks" said Mary. Their daughter Michelle thanked them too.

"Us too," said Zack, "we'll take our two rowdy boys home, great party, Janna."

"Thanks," she smiled happily at her brother.

"Yeah, thanks very much," said Carol, "always fun to be together." She nudged Andy.

"Thanks Aunt Janna, Uncle William" said Andy.

"Yeah, awesome goody bags!" said little Bobby.

Everyone laughed.

"Yeah," Zack added, "who would've thought the best prosecutor in Miami would turn out to be such a great mom?"

"Shh, K.J. might not like that," Janna said.

"Actually he'd be the first to admit it, on both counts," K.J.'s black eyes twinkled, "and Moira's right there with her." He put his arm around Moira who held their baby girl.

"Janna and Moira are great at everything," William added.

"And a great little boy too, real sweet and real smart," Zack said as he walked down the front walk, "I got some great pictures of David, he was smiling in every one of 'em."

William hugged Janna after the last guest had left. "You really are a wonderful mother to our little boy."

"Thanks, but you're the one who makes it all work."

"Let's play with my toys!" David said.

They smiled at their wonderful child.

"Oh, yeah, I need to stash the toy gun," she said quietly to William, "strange how some people like Alicia seem to be looking for an argument, she must be living proof of aggressor genes," she grinned, "but life's too short to dwell on it, and it looks like we have a soccer game to play."

David pulled at William's hand, "come on guys, let's play."

"Good idea," William said, "first let's finish picking up from the party, then we'll put the soccer net together and you, Mommy and I can play soccer.

"Cool!" David smiled.

Chapter 48

Janna was pensive as William turned their car into the drive to the Boca Hotel and Club. "Nice!" she said as she looked at the stunning pink façade ahead of them.

"Thought it'd be a nice place for a weekend together."

She smiled quietly.

The beautiful waterway view from the large windows of their tower suite added to the elegance of the setting. Janna sat tentatively on the edge of the king sized bed facing the windows. William sat next to her and looked into her lovely face, "you don't need to feel shy, there's no pressure."

"I know, but if I had to guess you've read my thoughts and know I've been giving serious thought to having another baby, and you brought me here for a lovely, romantic weekend to make a baby."

It was his turn to feel shy, "look who's reading thoughts now, I hope you've also read my thoughts that it's up to you. Either way, it should be a wonderful weekend."

She gazed at the beautiful blue water, "kind of a win-win situation."

"Which is true of every day, and night, I spend with you."

She leaned her head again his chest, "and a great weekend for David since he gets to stay with Zack and his cousins, and for Zack and Carol, since we told them we'd give them a weekend alone too. For a guy who grew up without competition, you're pretty good at setting up win-win."

He smiled at his love. "I hope you're ready for dinner now, the only reservations I could get at Cielo are in a few minutes."

"The top of the tower, that's great and I'm actually kind of hungry."

Janna looked at the view of beautiful blue sky, neat white buildings along the Intracoastal Waterway and the bright blue Atlantic Ocean. "This is so beautiful, thank you."

"Champagne? They have a 1996 Grand Siecle."

She smiled, "you think of everything."

They enjoyed an elegant dinner and did not address the subject of a baby until coffee and dessert. She took a sip of coffee, "a child we conceive now would be 66 when the world ends."

"With David, we already have those worries," he said.

"And David needs a brother or sister."

H smiled. "The main thing is that if we do decide to make a baby, I thought it would be special for us to be able to remember the experience, since we kind of missed it the first time."

She laughed, "yes, it kind of caught us both by surprise, me being on the pill and all, but I certainly have no regrets, it's great having David, and you make everything about taking care of a baby so easy," she gazed into his eyes, "yes, I think I would like to make a baby with you tonight."

He reached across the table and held her hand.

"It makes me excited to think about it," she stroked his hand.

He glanced away from her flushed face only for as long as it took to get the server's attention and say, "check, please."

Chapter 49

Time passed like a river, sometimes rippling, sometimes meandering or rushing, but always moving forward, never pausing, never stopping, relentlessly pressing to its destination.

They spent Christmas 2003 in Tallahassee. David was almost 2 ½ and she was pregnant with a second son who was due in April. Zack and Carol and their kids, Andy, 7, and Bobby, 4, also came from Miami for the holidays. Janna's older sister Lauren and her husband, Senator John, had traveled from Washington with their baby girl. Lauren and John were completely absorbed with their six month old daughter, Courtney Alexandra, a rather large name for such a tiny child, or so their dad, Bob Anderson, teasingly said.

Bob had prostate surgery last summer for a malignant tumor, and although he had recovered, the health scare gave them all even more reason to celebrate their time together as a family.

On New Year's Eve, Bob stayed up with his family to see the year 2004 begin. They made dinner at home and watched the TV coverage at Time's Square. Andy, Bobby and David tried to stay awake until midnight, but David was the only one who made it. That surprised everyone, since he was the youngest, except for his parents who knew that David was like his father and did not need much sleep.

Although William would always be aware that he was different, he felt comfortable to be with the family. He no longer had to struggle to make conversation or constantly worry about hiding his past. He was building a past with his new family. When he read their thoughts, he knew they liked him, which made him feel very good.

There was always plenty to talk about and new memories to be made. The next night would be another late evening for Bob, when they watched FSU face the University of Miami in the Orange Bowl football game. The UM baseball team had made the College World Series last summer, although they were eliminated by Texas in the second round. And their children were a wonderful topic of conversation. William was grateful to be a part of it.

He had never had any contact from Abidan, although one day he received a letter advising him that there was an agent in New York City. He sent a letter to his family through the agent, but never received a reply. He would always miss his family in Abidan, that was unavoidable, but he also loved his family on Earth.

The New Year made him think about the year 2070 and his growing family. He and Janna followed media coverage of the space station with special interest, but they often put their thoughts of the future in the background so they could live in the present.

After their visit to Tallahassee, they took an extra week of vacation to take David to Disney World to give him some attention before his world changed with a new baby brother. William was a genetics professor at the University of Miami, with a few more days of winter break, and Janna was still working several days a week at the State Attorney's office. She liked working part-time, and William made it easy for her.

"Look at David hug Winnie the Pooh, isn't that the most precious thing you've ever seen?" Janna's eyes filled with tears.

"Adorable," William smiled, "you had a great idea for us to come here."

"We have to take advantage of your time off, professor, and it's good for David." She placed her hand against her belly. "I'm scared. I can't imagine that I can ever love another child as much as I love David. I'm worried about how I'll handle a second one, are you?"

"Not at all," he put his arm around her, "you're only afraid now because you haven't seen him yet. Once our child is here, I'm sure it'll be as natural for you to love him as it has been natural for you to be such a good mother to David, don't worry, sweetheart, when we see our new little one's face, we'll find it easy to love him, after all, he's also a product of our love for each other, and of our love for David."

She took a deep breath, "you're right, of course, you always have such a good perspective on things, I'm probably worrying unnecessarily, it's just that I want to be perfect at this."

"You are perfect," he said.

"Thanks, but I'm far from it," Janna responded.

"Daddy, I know these characters are genetically absurd but they're fuzzy and I like them, especially Pooh," David said.

"I like them too, son," William smiled at his boy.

"Mommy and Daddy, look there's Tigger! Let's go see him bounce, then can we go on the big slide?"

"Okay," said Janna, "but how about I watch you and Daddy go on the slide? My tummy's a little big right now with your brother inside."

"Okay, you can watch Daddy and me."

Chapter 50

THREE MONTHS LATER, JANNA WAS IN LABOR AT THE hospital, with William by her side.

Jim and Mary appeared at the door to their room with their two week old son they had named James Blake.

"Just stopped in to say hi," Mary said, "we won't stay, we know you're pretty occupied, but we were here for a little follow-up blood work for J.B. and heard you were in labor, couldn't leave without seeing you, and we wanted you to see J.B. in his little outfit you gave him."

Jim proudly showed off his son to Janna and William.

"He's a beautiful baby," said Janna, "I'm so glad you dropped by, everything okay with J.B.?"

"Apparently he has a touch of jaundice," Mary said, "they say it's nothing serious, he should be fine."

"Good," Janna said, "so, what's it like having a second baby? I'm a little worried about loving the second one the same."

"It's a bit of an adjustment, Michelle's eight so she was used to being the one and only for quite a while," Mary touched her wrist, "don't worry it's just as easy to love the second one, it will all be fine."

Janna smiled at her, "that's what William says."

"How do you feel?" Mary asked.

"Not bad," Janna answered, "about like last time."

Mary nodded with empathy, "yeah, at least this time you know for sure the contractions do let up and the whole thing's temporary. It's not just gratuitous pain."

"Thanks," Janna winced with another contraction.

Jim said, "we'll be on our way now but be sure to give us a call when your boy is born."

"Can't wait to see him," said Mary, "it'll be so nice to have baby boys the same age."

"Definitely," Janna nodded, "thanks so much for stopping by."

"Yes, thanks," William added, "we look forward to seeing you soon."

Several hours later, Adam William was born, and it was love at first sight.

For the first few days David was a model big brother. He enjoyed the excitement as much as the rest of their friends and family. He was inspired by the role of big brother, since people made it sound important and actually gave him presents for being a big brother.

Janna and William were overjoyed by the birth of their new son, and the fact that David was taking it so well. But several days after they were home with the new baby, it became clear that the adjustment was not complete.

"You know, guys," he said to his parents one morning at breakfast, "we made a big mistake having this new baby, all it does is cry and sleep and poop. I know what we should do."

"What's that, honey?" Janna asked.

"Give it to Dr. Rodriguez. She's nice and she'll know what to do with it, and we won't have to bother with it anymore."

She did not dare look at William. It was so cute she was afraid she would laugh, and that would not be the right thing to do for David.

"We really can't do that, honey," she said gently. "First of all Adam is ours so we can't just give him to your pediatrician, and Dr. Rodriguez already has enough babies to take care of, but maybe we should get someone to stay with Adam while you and Daddy and I go to the park this afternoon. What do you think about that?"

"Awesome, can we go now?"

"Let me make a phone call," Janna said, "would you like to take a picnic?"

"Yeah! And my soccer ball too!" David said happily.

Janna was glad that she and William were both working light schedules. Although they often took turns focusing attention on David, he liked it best when they got a baby sitter and left Adam at home. In that way, the time passed and David was content.

Things changed when Adam began walking and talking. David started to appreciate his little brother, who clearly worshipped him.

Always, always they were surrounded by the good and bad of Earth. There was constant grim evidence of a culture given over to violence, and heartwarming tales of wonderful people who continued to do the right thing.

The movie *Hotel Rwanda* was released. It portrayed a powerful true story of the Rwandan genocide in which over 800,000, mainly Tutsi people, were killed by a militia of extremist Hutus, and an ordinary hotel manager who showed tremendous personal courage. He risked his own life to save the lives of his family and more than 1,000 refugees by granting shelter in the hotel where he worked.

They did not see the movie. Although William had grown more accustomed to the culture of violence on Earth, it was still very hard for them both. They tried to focus their time and attention on their children, their extended family and their friends, even as they worried about the horrible state of the world where these children were growing up and the end that was coming.

As David and Adam grew, the two boys became best buddies. Janna and William tried to remember each joyful day of their precious family life together.

Chapter 51

"Hi Jannie, what brings you to campus...everything okay?" William asked.

"Yeah, it's about David, he's fine, nothing wrong, I just want to get your advice. If I remember your schedule correctly, your next class isn't until 1:30, can I buy you lunch?"

"Sure, cafeteria okay?"

"Fine."

"So what's up?" William asked.

"I got a call from David's Little League coach, some of the parents are upset that David hits so many home runs and want him tested for performance enhancing drugs. I wasn't quite sure what to say, he's six! Of course, he can pass a drug test, but I think parents are talking and they'll keep talking, and I'm afraid all this will hurt David."

"What did you say to the coach?"

"That I'd ask you," Janna smiled.

"Good answer, except I don't know what to say, I usually defer to your expertise for parenting issues."

"I guess we both saw this coming," Janna said, "that's why we didn't put him on Jim's team so we wouldn't put Jim on the spot. What do you think we should do?"

"I remember my experiences," William said. "People want you to do well and hit home runs, but they don't want you to do too well. I think we should talk to David."

"And?" she asked.

"See how he feels, what he's already observed, give him some insight, see what he seems to be able to handle. I think we still agree not to tell him he's a halfling, but he knows he's different."

"Yeah, I've always thought parents looked so silly letting their kids decide everything," Janna said, "but I think you're right, we should talk to David and see what he wants to do. I think our goal's still for him to have a normal childhood."

"As much as possible," William said.

"I'll get Zack or Carol to pick up Adam, so I can talk to David when I take him to baseball," she said.

"You want me to come?" William asked.

"You've got class, we can talk at dinner, I just wanted you to know what's going on, and to get your thoughts, professor, I love you."

"I love you too."

"Call me sometime when you have no class," she grinned, and William laughed.

"Hey kid, how was school?" Janna asked as David got in their car.

"Good. I'm getting used to being teased for good grades," David kissed her, "they used to tease you too, didn't they, Mom?"

"Yeah they did, and it hurt my feelings, until I got used to it, like you have. Do you get teased at baseball too?"

"Yeah," he hesitated, "it's kind of like they want me to be good, but not too good, cuz if you're too good you make everyone else look bad, and they get jealous."

"Have you experienced that?" Janna asked.

"Oh yeah. That's why I strike out sometimes, on purpose, is that bad?"

"Probably not in this case, how do you feel about it?"

"It seems like a lie, like I'm not doing my best like everyone's supposed to do, but it works. I do the same thing in school, I mean miss stuff on purpose, so I don't get teased for being perfect."

"Does it make you happy?" Janna asked.

"Kind of," the boy said, "do you know why I'm different?"

"As your dad would say, good genes."

"Yeah, I guess," he grinned.

"Are you happy?" Janna asked.

"Yeah, baseball makes me happy."

"What would you say if I told you some of the parents want you to be tested for performance enhancing drugs?"

David laughed, "like the pros?"

Janna laughed too, "yeah."

"As long as I can still play baseball," David smiled.

"Okay, dude, here you are, want me to stay for practice?"

"No, I think I'm gonna strike out a lot," David got his baseball bag from the back seat and slung it over his shoulder, "it could get ugly."

"Love you."

"Love you, too."

"So how was baseball?" William asked David at dinner.

"He sucks," said Adam, "when Mom and I were picking him up from practice, he struck out three times, I never strike out."

David laughed, "that's cool, bro, give me five."

Adam laughed and gave him five. "You don't really suck," he added.

"I know," David said, "just don't let anybody tease you for being too good when you get older, ok?"

"Ok, bro," Adam laughed.

"Hey, did you hear they want me to get a drug test, Daddy?" David asked.

"Yes, son, and your mom says you're okay with it?"

"Yep, you had to have one too, didn't you?" David asked.

"Yes, I did," William answered.

"Good genes, huh?" David smiled.

"Yeah," William said to David. He turned to Janna, "everything okay?"

"Fine," she said. "We all love it when David smiles."

Chapter 52

WHEN JANNA AND WILLIAM HEARD ABOUT THE SHOOTings at Virginia Tech in April of 2007, they thought of Steve. Their friend was a professor there, and the news reports were horrible. Janna made the phone call with trembling hands, and was greatly relieved when Steve answered the phone. She gave William a thumbs up sign. Steve had just returned from Nepal and had not been on campus that day, but the news was terrible.

A student named Seung-Hui Cho made two separate attacks about two hours apart on the Virginia Tech campus. He killed 32 people and wounded many more before committing suicide. It was the deadliest school shooting in U.S. history.

They held hands as they watched the tragic TV news coverage. Their first thought was that their boys were at school and they were safe there. Then they wondered if they were safe there, or anywhere.

"What are we doing to keep our children safe?" Janna asked, but it was a rhetorical question.

"In 1996 in the Scottish town of Dunblane," William said, "a deranged unemployed shopkeeper took four handguns and killed sixteen children and one teacher. The outcry in the U.K. was overwhelming. They wanted to avoid becoming like America before it was too late. They banned handguns and automatic weapons, and they instituted an onerous system of gun ownership rules involving hours of paperwork, criminal reference checks and mandatory references."

Janna nodded, "that same year in Australia a shooter in Tasmania killed 35 people, and Australia banned the sale and possession of all automatic and semiautomatic rifles and other weapons. They instituted a mandatory buyback program that retrieved some

700,000 guns. I know from experience, and in my heart too, that those measures would help, even though changes take time, but I don't see that happening here."

"Gene therapy could be further along," he said, "but embryonic stem cell research has been banned for many years. I believe God gave us science to take care of each other and make things better. It may not make a difference, adult stem cell therapy seems promising, but embryonic stem cells are pluripotent, and we have so little time in terms of developing a cure, we need to do all we can."

"We definitely need a cure, even now, it would help, but I don't hold out much hope," she said. "What's the warrior gene? I've been hearing criminal defense lawyers talk about using it as a defense."

"It dates back to the early 1990's when they discovered a Dutch family of very violent men who carried a mutation that suppressed their MAO-A gene, so it's been around a while, but the term 'warrior gene' wasn't coined until 2004. Apparently everyone has the warrior gene, but it can come in at least two very slightly different versions or alleles. Early studies found that people who had a low version allele, about 1/3 of the population, were statistically more aggressive and the MAOA-2R allele doubles the rate of serious and violent delinquency."

He continued. "The warrior gene is a variant of gene MAO-A on the X chromosome which is why it is much more likely in men. It doesn't show up in women unless it's on both X chromosomes, which is rare. It's also linked to testosterone. However, whether or not the warrior gene exerts depends very much on the environment and other factors. In other words there's no simple answer. The warrior gene is criticized as a pseudo-discovery because it's an either-or fallacy. You either have it or you don't, so you're violent or you're not, as if only one gene controls violence. That would be like saying there's one gay gene, or one gene for art, alcohol abuse, high IQ, or gambling, and so on. It takes much more than one stray allele to produce a violent person, and even more to cure that person."

She squeezed his hand. "It's great you're still trying, but I believe God is right, Earth is a mistake. The evidence is overwhelming. Think about this, we don't even know how many guns there are in this country. I tried to find out, but researchers don't know for sure with all the sales and re-sales. Their best guess is there are at least 270 million guns in the U.S., and you know many of them are in the wrong hands, like at Virginia Tech. That's why some people feel they need to own guns to protect themselves in a dangerous society. I mean everyone in the State Attorney's office owns a gun."

They did not know what to do about the latest atrocity. The truth was no one really knew what to do. They sat in silent thought until it was time to pick up their boys. It was not the end of the world yet, it only felt like it was.

Janna did not pray. God was not listening.

Chapter 53

It was not long before the memory of the mass shooting at Virginia Tech faded from the world's consciousness. William had written in his dissertation that the protective mechanism in the brain was a healthy reaction to tragedy. It allowed people to carry on with their lives and their work, but the collective amnesia also seemed to prevent action to change things.

William continued his research to find a cure for aggression and Janna worked to prosecute criminals, but for them it was much the same. They could not fix Earth, so they did their best to focus on all of the good things.

They took two months off work in the summer to spend time with their boys. That summer, David would turn seven and Adam was already three, and there were many things for them to enjoy. The two boys swam and played baseball and read books. They went to the beach, and played on their bikes in their neighborhood.

Learning new things came as easily for them as hitting a baseball. They learned to play tennis, golf, sail board, kite board, and to sail their parents' boat. They were curious, extraordinary children, with extraordinary thoughts and questions.

Janna was glad for William to answer many of their boys' questions, especially the ones about religion. Janna had come to accept the reality that although God had turned against Earth, He was still very present in the Universe. Since her college years, she had been ambivalent about her religious beliefs, but knowing that God had rejected Earth created a void. She did not blame God for turning away, she agreed with Him, but she missed Him, nevertheless.

Janna and William watched their boys' accomplishments with

pride. At the same time, they tried to make sure their children's lives as halflings were as normal as possible. They were aware of the jealousy from others that existed, the teasing, the mean remarks, people like Alicia who were aggressive with their envy.

David and Adam did not have many school friends, but it did not seem to bother them. They had each other and their parents. They had their extended family and friends, and the UM baseball team, who were all as proud of them as though they were their parents.

They did many things together as a family. They loved their three-week trip to Yellowstone and the Grand Canyon, where they went hiking and horseback riding and whitewater rafting. They enjoyed their soccer and baseball teams, and they all had great fun at David's baseball tournaments at Disney's Wide World of Sports in Orlando.

Life was as full and happy as Janna and William could make it for them.

It was before the last baseball tournament of the summer that David asked his mother, "are my drug test, birth certificate and all that team paperwork in order?"

"Yeah, why're you asking?"

David smiled, "I just wanted to make sure, I'm thinking I won't hold back in this last tournament, I think I'd like to be an MVP."

"I think that's a great idea," Janna smiled, "and you may be on a different team next year anyway, go for it!"

He did. David won the tournament for his team and was MVP, and everyone was happy. William learned more about the elation of winning.

It was a perfect summer. They would always be glad that David had that.

Chapter 54

It was in the next year, in 2008, that the river of their lives stopped. That day could never be forgotten and it would never blend sweetly or gently into anything.

The day started gently, around bowls of cereal at the kitchen table. Janna was looking forward to a successful final argument in her trial. She was optimistic that she would get capital punishment or at least a life sentence for a repeat offender who had kidnapped a little boy from the playground and murdered him. She did not tell her children about her work. She would not have had much of a chance to talk that morning, because Adam and David were so involved in debating about whose Transformer had the most power.

Janna hugged and kissed her precious sons. She loved the young, strong feel of them. She paused a moment to tuck in David's shirt and say, "See you at your baseball game tonight!" She kissed her beloved husband and she was off to work.

It was William's turn to be out of the door. He would take the kids to their different schools before his teaching day began. Later, he would get Adam and they would join Janna at David's Little League game.

He and Adam walked David to his second grade class where an animated, portly teacher wearing a Tyrannosaurus Rex tee shirt greeted them. The kids in her class were clearly excited about the field trip they would take that day to see the dinosaur exhibit at the science museum.

"I want to go too. I know a whole lot about dinosaurs," said Adam.

"I'm sure you do," the teacher responded, "if you're anything like your brother. He's practically memorized the encyclopedia, and seems to know every dinosaur that has ever been discovered."

"Me too," said Adam.

The teacher turned to William. "Have you talked to your wife about David?"

"Yes, we're content for him to be in your class."

"But he's got an IQ over 200 and he's reading on a high school level," the teacher said.

"We know, but what about his socialization?" Blake asked.

"Honestly, it kind of comes and goes," she said, "they like him when it's time to pick teams, but they usually don't include him in things, and the Hispanic kids don't know what to make of him, he speaks Spanish as well as they do, but with his light eyes and hair, he doesn't look like them. He considers Dr. Harmon to be his best friend."

"We want him to have a normal childhood as much as possible," Blake said.

"I appreciate that, Dr. Blake, it's just that he's so extraordinary. It's not that I don't want him in my class, he's the model student in every way, but he misses questions on purpose so they'll accept him. As a teacher, that's hard to see."

"I know. There aren't any easy answers, but he really likes your class, and we can't put him in high school."

"Well, we'll talk some more," she said as she returned to her noisy students.

William waved to David as he and Adam departed. In the years to come William would always remember the sweet smile David gave him as he waved goodbye that day. He would carry it with him for all time.

The river stopped for William when the two policemen appeared in the back of his classroom. He knew it must be something terrible. He remembered Irina. He thought of Janna. He thought of his boys. He deliberately finished his sentence to give him one last second before he must know why they came. They dismissed his class. He felt his chest pounding, his whole being poised in terror. It was David.

There was a mass shooting at the science museum. A deranged man had come to the museum with a semiautomatic weapon and killed twenty children and six adults, before killing himself. David and his teacher were among those who were killed.

The police were very sorry. They would go with him to tell his wife. The thought of Janna jolted him to force his paralyzed mind to think. He called Zack. Carol would pick up Adam at preschool.

Zack met them in the back of Judge Akeeno's courtroom. Janna was speaking. The secretary sent a note to the bailiff. When the bailiff read it, he reeled and sat hard into his chair. He passed the note to the judge. Judge Akeeno started to speak, but he hesitated. Mrs. Blake was about to finish her closing statement.

"And so, ladies and gentlemen of the jury, I submit to you that you have heard the testimony of the witnesses," Janna's voice stated clearly. "I have reviewed the testimony of each witness for you; and that testimony proves beyond a reasonable doubt that the defendant committed this unspeakable crime."

"Ladies and gentlemen, this is not just a crime against the State of Florida or the people of the State of Florida, this is a crime against Jesse, whose little life was just beginning. This is a crime against Jesse's parents, his family and friends. This is a crime against Jesse's little brother who will never get to play catch with him. This is a crime against Jesse's mother and father who will never see him play Little League, or be a Cub Scout or spend holidays with him, or go to his graduation, or wedding or hold his children in their arms. Jesse's family must live with the consequences of this crime for the rest of their lives. The defendant has ruined their lives and has caused them pain that will never go away. It is up to you to make this defendant pay for this terrible crime."

"Therefore, I ask you, ladies and gentlemen of the jury, to find this defendant guilty of murder in the first degree, not just on behalf of the State of Florida, not just on behalf of the people of Florida, but on behalf of Jesse's little brother, and his mother and his father and all of the people whom his young life touched or would have touched. I ask you to do the right thing for Jesse. Thank you."

It did not matter for Janna that she was able to finish her closing argument, and that she got a first degree verdict. It did not matter that William and Zack were there to share her grief. It did not matter that Lauren and John and Jim and Mary and Moira and K.J. all tried to help. It did not matter that there was an outpouring of sympathy from their friends and the entire legal community. It did not matter that the other victims' families shared her grief. It was over for Janna. The river had stopped.

In all of the days that followed, William knew that no matter how pulverized by the weight of his loss he felt, it was worse for Janna. Her soul, her life, her sparkle were destroyed. He hoped that time would repair her.

But time did not pass gently. The days did not flow. It was as though each day had to be chiseled from granite and forced to happen. Sleep was no comfort. She had to wake back up to it. There was nothing else for Janna to think about but David. He was in every part of her mind.

The funeral was in Tallahassee. David was buried in a family plot near the graves of Janna's grandparents and some aunts and uncles. William understood why they were called survivors. This was so much harder than losing Irina. He did not know how to help Janna. The only word she spoke during the funeral as they sat with the family at the front of the church; the only life at all she showed that day was when she turned to him and said, "I want to go to Abidan." He was glad that she passed out before they got to the cemetery, but then, without her, even though the whole family and friends like K.J. and Moira, Jim and Mary, and many of the baseball players were there, he had never felt so alone.

Chapter 55

IN THE GRANITE DAYS THAT FOLLOWED, THE PAIN OF their loss dominated the household. The days limped by. They were all so filled with sadness they did not stand out, only the day when David had been killed.

Janna quit working and spent most of her time sitting quietly and staring into space. Or she would spend hours going through David's pictures and videos. William continued to teach part time so he could further his genetics research, and Adam spent as much time as he could at his Uncle Zack's house where life seemed almost normal.

William remembered the day when he checked to see if Janna's gun was still in their closet. It was there. He wondered if it was on a high enough shelf. He did not want to mention the gun to Janna because her state of mind was so fragile. He did not touch it. Something about the old commandments he had been given by the Great Creator stopped him. He was not sure how the gun worked, but he guessed it was a small comfort to know the weapon was there if he had to try to protect the rest of his family. He reflected at how far he had come from his Planet of Peace to feel that way.

He kept a light schedule so that he could spend most of his time at home trying to help Janna and be with his son. Adam was so quiet it was hard to find things to talk about. He had the same problem with Janna. Zack, Carol, Lauren, John and their mother, all tried to help. Mary, Jim, Moira, K.J. and numerous other friends tried to help. He tried to renew her interest in the presidential campaign. Nothing made any difference.

It frightened him to see her sit for hours and stare at David's pictures or at nothing. He had stopped reading her thoughts. They were too sad.

"Where's Adam?" he asked one afternoon when he found her sitting in a black tee shirt and shorts by the pool.

"He's with my brother for the day," she said.

He sat quietly next to her.

"I'm sorry, it's just that Zack and Carol are able to give him some normal home life and he loves his cousins, he has fun there." She sighed. "Mom called. Dad's prostate cancer has come back, they're going to run some more tests. I guess we should go up there, but I just can't deal with my father being sick. I don't know what to do."

"I'm very sorry to hear that." He touched her thin hand.

"They think they can treat it. They'll know more when they run more tests. Poor Dad, if we lived on Abidan, he would never have had cancer."

"Maybe they can treat it," he said, "some of the research is very promising, if you decide to go, it's no problem for me to get off work. It might be good for you to see him, think you should try some more counseling or try the support group again?"

"I've had a year of counseling," she shook her head, "and you know the support group with the other victims' families only makes me feel worse, and I'm the one who used to hand out grief literature as though it was possible to heal. I'm so sorry but I'll never be able to accept it. I feel so awful that I can't carry on, and I know I've been a terrible wife to you," she put her hand on her forehead. "It's as if the life was taken out of me that day and I can't get it back, and I feel so terribly guilty that you ever came to this place. You should be on your Planet of Peace and we should have never had children only to lose them."

"But we still have Adam. We can have another child. The souls of the just are transmuted. I have faith that David is leading a good life in another world. Adam needs so much. There's so much we need to teach him. He's growing up. He needs you. He needs a sister or a brother too. He needs a family back. Please don't cry, Janna. It won't help. You've cried too much. Think of Adam and me. We need you."

"I do think of Adam and you. I know I've abandoned my little child to my brother. Do you think that makes me feel any better?

And you, my darling, the most wonderful, incredible person I've ever known. I love you so much and you've come to this horrible place for me. And that makes me feel even worse. It's like I have an incurable illness, but I can't cure myself, honey, I can't. And all the help you've been so wonderful to get for me hasn't cured me either. Remember what you wrote in your dissertation about that protective mechanism in the brain that allows people to have tragedy in their lives and still be able move on, and even manage to laugh and have fun? I don't have it. And you concluded that that mechanism is healthy, otherwise no one would want to live. Something's wrong with me because I can't turn it off. I can't forget. I can't move on. I can't cure myself. I need David. I want my baby son who was killed," she sobbed.

"But your son who's alive needs you," he said. "Remember how you felt just before Adam was born? You were worried that you could never love him as much as David, and remember the way that feeling went away as soon as you saw his little face? Well, you need to do that again, sweetheart. You need to look into Adam's little face and love him."

"I know. You're right. I do, but I can't turn it off" she said. "I love you both so much. It's not a lack of love that I feel. I'm too afraid. I'm afraid to let Adam out of his room for fear something will happen to him. I can't do that to a five year old boy, and I'm overwhelmed by guilt that you live on this terrible planet because of me."

"You've always been such a fighter. You wanted to rid the world of crime. You can't give up," he said.

"But I have given up, there's no hope for the future, nothing I did in this world to fight crime made any difference, I couldn't keep my own son from being murdered. The culture of violence has won here. Our world is wrong, horribly wrong. God has judged this planet as a mistake. I'm not a very religious person, but I know this to be true. We cannot save the Earth without God. If God can give up on us, why can't I?"

He looked at his love, but this vacant, frail little girl seemed so far away, "because I haven't given up."

Tears filled her eyes, "oh my darling, I love you so much, but I don't want this life for us, I want to be transmuted, I want to find David. I could go to Abidan, and bring David there, then you can come too. There's an agent in New York. If you can't take Adam, he can live with Zack and come to us later."

"But how do you think you could be transmuted?" he asked.

"I could give myself a lethal injection. Similar to what they give in assisted suicides or capital punishment, only it's a single dose."

"Darling, Jannie, listen to what're you saying. You're talking about killing yourself like it's a choice. You're such a smart woman, how can you possibly think it's a viable option? You have a child, and me. We couldn't live without you. You can't think this way. I don't even know how transmutation works. There're undoubtedly rules against suicide. You'd probably never see David or Abidan. We have no idea where his spirit has gone. Honey, you can't think like that."

"I want you to help me," she said, "then it wouldn't be suicide and you can return to Abidan. They'll take you, I know they will. Remember when you got that letter from the agent in New York? You could contact him. I know they'll take you, and David and I will join you there. I have a wonderful brother and sister-in-law and Adam can have a happy life with them, and you can leave instructions in your journal that, before World War III, he can join us then, and David. Earth will continue its downward spiral. Nuclear destruction is in 62 years. It will not get better here."

"This is madness," he said. "It won't work. Transmuted souls take another form, they begin new lives as infants, and even if you somehow got to Abidan, I don't know for certain if I'd be allowed to return after all the commandments I've broken, and our ages would likely be out of synch, and Adam's a halfling, he wouldn't be allowed to come. You can't ask me to choose between my wife and my son. I already chose you and Earth. That decision was made a long time ago. We still have 62 years, that's enough time to develop a plan to save our family. There is much we need to do here, now, much we need to teach our son, more children we should have. You can't commit suicide because of some idea that we have no basis to believe would work. We need you. You have to face your problems here on Earth. That's our only real chance."

"Adam is happy with Zack's family," she persisted. "He's afraid of me. He'll be better off with Zack, but if you want to stay with him, my darling, until he grows older you could come later. I will always love you. That will never change. They'll take you in Abidan. I know they will. You still have your Universal passport. I've seen it in your drawer. It will work, I know it will work. If I have to transmute as a child and if you want to come later after Adam is older, it would still work. The Great Creator of Life will know what it's like to lose a son and He will help me."

"No! We must start over here. Our son's a halfling, with extraordinary skills for an Earth child, that's an awful lot to ask of your brother. There are things that only we can teach Adam, and we need to be here to do that. We need to raise our own son. We can move to a more peaceful country like New Zealand or Switzerland. We can have brothers and sisters for Adam. We'll start over. We can put our lives back together. That's what we must do. Please give up this insane idea," he pleaded.

"It's too late, I want my baby who was killed. I want my father to be well."

It began again, the uncontrollable crying and sobbing that would go on and on and on and never seem to stop. He reached for the portable phone, his friend that would summon the rescue vehicle that would administer a sedative and take her to the hospital, where she would stay until the doctors would say that it was safe for her to go home again, and then she would come home and stare at nothing or at David's pictures and probably speak of transmutation again.

He had taken her and Adam to New Zealand for a month to see if a new life in a more peaceful country would help her overcome her depression. But she only sat and stared. The striking beauty of the peaceful country did nothing to raise her spirits. Adam was as quiet as always. Janna was right, he was afraid of her. He had little to say and missed his cousins badly.

Now she was in for another stay in the psychiatric floor of the hospital.

He tried to talk to Adam about it. He struggled to find the words, "your mommy's sick again. I had to take her to the hospital to get well."

"It's a bad hospital," Adam said. "She never gets better there."

"Maybe she'll get better this time. I miss her."

"Yeah. Can I go to Uncle Zack's today?"

"If you want to, but I thought maybe you and I could do something together. Want to go to the park and hit some baseballs or go fishin'?"

"I don't know," Adam said. "I like being at Uncle Zack's. Andy and Bobby always do fun stuff. Our house's too sad."

"I know it is, Son. We need to make it happy again."

"But we can't do that 'cause David died. It's better to go to Uncle Zack's."

"Well, you go to Uncle Zack's a lot. You can go tomorrow. Let's do something together today, just you and me."

"Okay, but promise we won't go to the hospital to see Mommy. I don't ever want to see her again unless she gets well." Adam started to cry.

William hugged his dark-haired son while the little boy cried. He hoped that crying would help him heal. It felt so good to hold his boy and kiss the bushy little head of hair that had a faint woodsy smell to it. Adam looked so much like his mother. William felt overwhelmed by his love for him. At the same time he was aware of his own awkwardness at being a dad on Earth. He remembered the way Janna had wanted to be the perfect parent. He felt that way now, and he wished with all his heart that Janna still did too. He was strongly aware of his own inadequacy, both to help his son and to help his wife. "It's okay, honey. I know you don't really mean anything bad about your mommy. It's just been very hard for you. Very hard for such a little boy. Hard for all of us."

"Is it my fault?" the child asked.

"No, darling, it's not your fault at all. Not at all. Don't ever think that, honey," William said emphatically.

Adam wiped his eyes, "okay."

"Now, let's go have some fun together and not worry about anything today, okay?"

"Okay, can we go fishin' and to the park too?" Adam asked.

"Sure, let's go."

Chapter 56

WILLIAM VISITED JANNA FAITHFULLY, BUT HE NO LONGER brought Adam with him. She would ask about him and then turn silent. The conversation was much the same. She looked so helpless in her hospital room. She often lay in bed though she was usually dressed. She wore black jeans and a black tee shirt, and had a heparin lock on top of her wrist, ready to deliver drugs that would maintain her in a tearless state. The drugs did that, but they also seemed to increase her ability to sit and stare.

When Janna's father passed away, William delayed telling her. She had known that he was very ill and had refused any more chemotherapy. She did not ask. Zack came and told her and she cried and cried, but when she quit crying it was worse, because she only sat and stared. Her doctors felt that she was not well enough to attend the funeral. Zack, Carol, Andy, Bobby and Adam all traveled to Tallahassee without Janna. William did not think that Adam should attend the funeral. He was not sure what effect it would have on him to be near David's grave. Zack agreed, so they left Bobby and Adam with a sitter when they went to the funeral. William stayed in Miami to do what he could for Janna.

Several months passed until one day, while Janna was still in the hospital, she seemed to improve. A man whom no one knew had been to visit her in the hospital. Doctors could not explain the reason for the change. Her medication levels were the same, but her doctors felt that she could go home, if she would continue outpatient treatment. They told William that she was eager to return home and they felt that was a good indication that she had improved.

Janna seemed content to be home. She made sandwiches for

them and they ate by the pool and she talked more than she had in a long time. Adam had turned six while she had been in the hospital. Zack and Carol had given him a party. Janna seemed out of touch as she struggled to converse. She did not even know that it was the year 2,010, but she was different. There was a shining excitement about her. Adam wiggled in his seat and would not look at his mother. He kept looking toward the glass sliding door where Uncle Zack would come to pick him up.

When Zack arrived, Adam looked like he could hardly wait to go. But on that day, he glanced back at his mother for a moment and said, "You look pretty today, Mommy. I hope you're going to be better now." He moved toward the front door to wait for Zack to talk with his sister and brother-in-law, as they came inside the house.

"You look good, Sis," Zack said.

"How's Mom?" Janna asked.

"She's doing pretty well," Zack said. "Lauren and John have been great. They've spent a lot of time with her, even invited her to live with them in Washington to help with Courtney and the new baby, supervise all the day care and stuff. She may do it. It'd be good for her. Carol and I'd like to have her here too."

Zack looked at Adam who had appeared at the door to the pool. "Got all your stuff?"

"Yeah."

She stood up, "Adam, please give Mommy a hug."

The little boy gave a pained look and moved sideways into her.

She turned him toward her and hugged him hard. He started to squirm away, but she held on. Then she looked into his dark eyes in his little face, so much like hers. "I love you so much, sweetheart, always remember that. I wish with all my heart I could be a better mommy to you. Please don't ever think that I loved David more than you. It's just that after we lost David, it was like I didn't know how to be a good mommy anymore. I was too afraid of everything and it's like I've been sick in my head, and I didn't want to hurt you by making you watch me be sick. It's why I'm happy for you to be at Uncle Zack's. Always be a good boy and do the right thing. And always remember that your mommy loves you very, very much."

"Yeah, I know, you're hurting me. Let's go, Uncle Zack," the child anxiously moved toward the front door, but then turned to wave his small hand. "I love you, Mommy," he said.

Tears sparkled in her eyes, "and I'll always love you." She gave Zack a hug. "Thank you so much, Zack, for everything. I'm sorry, I'm really sorry I wasn't able to cope." She blinked back the tears. "Take good care of Adam, please."

"Sure, don't worry, we always do," Zack answered.

"Thank you," she took a deep breath.

"Now you take care, Sis."

They were gone. She pulled William by the arm into the house. She appeared flushed and excited.

"What is it?" he asked, with fear in his heart.

It was there in the bedroom in her dresser drawer. The lethal injection she had talked so much about. To her, it was her vehicle to the planets of peace, to David.

"No! Sweetheart, you've gotta give up this crazy obsession. There are many planets of peace. We don't know where David would be and what host his transmuted soul inhabits. It won't work. You'll never find him."

"It will work. I'm his mother. I will find him. Please help me. I'm going to do it anyway, but if it's not a suicide my chances will be better. I'm so sorry, my darling, but it's over for me. It was over the day David was killed. I can't cure myself and I can't turn it off. It's been two years and nothing works, the counseling, the doctors, the drugs, the support group, moving to New Zealand. Nothing works. It's over. I can't be cured. I have to try to find David. My darling, it will work, and you can come to Abidan. We can live there and when we find David we can bring him there, and later Adam. It will work. Even if we are different ages or you don't come until later, it can still work, and we can live a long time because there will be peace. Please, darling, I want this more than anything. My life here is over. Earth has no future. I cannot give up this idea, and I cannot go on like normal."

Through his heavy tears, he could see her filling the hypodermic.

His darling love was begging his help. He knew that he would do anything for her, but he could not do this. What could he think of to stop her?

"But, you seem so much better, you're getting better," he said.

"No, I'm not, it's just that I've made my decision and I've got the drug to carry it out. Earth is wrong. God has given up on us. I want us to leave. Please, please help me. What's the alternative, call 911 again and sedate me and send me though counseling and keep me locked up in the hospital on stupefying medication?" She reached for the needle. "I love you, my darling, now and always. I love you forever, with every particle of my being. I love you. I will find you and our child, and Adam later. I will wait for you. Forever. Until we meet again, my darling."

He felt frozen, and exhausted and panicked all at once. He fumbled for the portable phone, dialed the familiar numbers. He tried to stop her, but the look on her face made him hesitate for one fatal moment.

"Darling, please," she begged. He succumbed. Holding her in his arms he helped her finish what she began, he helped her finish what she had begged of him for two years. He held her closely until she was limp. He wrapped her in his tears.

He was startled by the sound of Adam's voice and frightened expression.

The child had returned to the house to get his new video game while Zack waited in the car in the driveway. "You hurt Mommy!" he cried.

"Adam, wait." The boy ran down the hall toward the closet. William gently laid Janna's body on the floor, hastily kissed her cheek and pulled a blanket around her. She was still so beautiful. Adam appeared from the closet door. He had his mother's gun in both hands and was pointing it at his father.

"Adam, you know your mommy was sick. She begged me to help her so she can find David in heaven and we could all be together again some day." He moved toward his son who was pointing the gun at him. "Adam, give me the gun. This is not a video game or a toy. It's real." William started to take the gun. They struggled. The gun fired. It struck William in the chest. He fell to the floor near Janna's body. Adam was six years old.

William pulled Adam close to him as he knelt over him.

"Daddy, did I hurt you? I didn't mean it. Daddy, you're bleeding a lot. Are you gonna die?"

"Sweet boy, listen to me, it's not your fault. Put the gun in my hand. I already called 911. When they come and Uncle Zack comes, tell everyone I shot the gun. Zack and Carol and Bobby and Andy are your family now, my darling boy. Be a good boy and always work hard and do what you're told. And always remember, none of this is your fault. It is not your fault. You had nothing to do with this. Only remember that there is a heaven and Mommy and Daddy will always look out for you from heaven. None of this could have been stopped by you. It is not your fault. Some day, my child, you'll understand. Daddy has a journal book that you can read when you're older. Remember, Mommy and Daddy will always love you and watch out for you from heaven. None of this is your fault. I love you, son."

"I love you too, Daddy. Daddy, there's blood everywhere. Is this what it was like for David? You won't die will you? Please don't die," the little boy pleaded.

"Say it, Adam, buddy, say it, say it's not my fault," William insisted.

"It's not my fault."

William smiled. They were the last words he heard as a being of the Earth.

Zack and the rescue people reached the bedroom at about the same time. "Oh my God," was all Zack could say before he had to attend to all of the many details of the tragedies. He knew that his biggest job was to protect Adam from having still more tragedy ruin his life.

The river of time had stopped for Janna and William but it rushed forward for Zack, and even though he felt like drowning, he knew that he had to survive for the people depending on him.

Chapter 57

Soul Processing Center-Earth

The following has been translated into words to conform to this text.

And so it was in the Earth year of 2010 that the souls of William Aaron Blake and Janna Anderson Blake left the Planet of Evil Earth and entered the Soul Processing Center. Their suspended spirits rested side by side in Cluster Batch #122097/2861371/AA1 in rows of translucent containers. The entire warehouse was so large the ends of the place were not visible and the entire unit glowed in a white light. Ministering Angel Apprentice Joachim, clad in radiant white, reported for duty to the instructor, Ministering Angel Elizabeth.

Angel Elizabeth knew that the first questions of the new apprentice would be about the Soul Processing Center. Many other questions typical of new apprentices could follow if unchecked, and the task was to teach the trade with all possible speed.

"This place is so huge, you cannot see how far it extends. Where is it, is it in the clouds?"

To which the Angel Elizabeth patiently responded. "The time for questions will come. You must apply yourself to learn your trade as quickly as possible. Our role is to deliver God's judgment and consequences. It is not a hard task as long as you obey the rules with no exceptions. That is the most important thing for you to learn. The skills will come with practice."

"I will. I already know how to perform transmutations."

"We will take one process at a time," said the Angel Elizabeth. "We will begin with something basic - a cluster-batch of murderers and suicides. None of these will be transmuted. Transmutation is applicable only for the just. These must all be ionized. You see before you an enormous row of translucent tubes containing suspended souls. To each individual container there is attached a missive explaining the pertinent record of the soul's identification, the image from its most recent life, its status and planned disposition. It is a safeguard to make certain that the souls have been sorted properly. We will address sorting skills at a later time."

Angel Elizabeth continued. "The individual images are for additional identification. We want to be correct but remember that if you are ever in doubt, always ionize. Always. Only the truly just can be transmuted. There is space on the missive for you to show that your work has been completed."

"What happens in the Ion Chamber?"

"The souls are disintegrated into charged particles that repel each other so completely, and are scattered across the Universe so thoroughly that they can never reassemble."

"But what is the difference between that and transmutation, where you strip all the memory and environmental influences?" the Apprentice Joachim asked.

"A significant difference. In transmutation, we are required to obliterate all contamination with environmental factors, but the soul's being remains intact. The emotions, the personalities endure. Timing is also a consideration in transmutation. It is sometimes necessary to hold a soul until it can be properly synchronized in its next life. That is why the place is so large, so we can hold souls for their next lives, if need be. No more questions. Your first soul is ready for processing. Remember all that you have studied. Until you use the Ion Chamber several times you cannot know its exact procedure. Always review the missive first, and complete it afterward. There are no exceptions in this cluster batch. You must ionize them all."

The Apprentice did as instructed, and processed the murderers and suicides one by one. When the Apprentice had learned the Ion Chamber operations, the Angel Elizabeth was free to supervise the other new apprentices in that period of time.

The Apprentice Joachim was most surprised that the souls

remained in a suspended state for processing. It was best. There was never any resistance, no last sigh of protest when the souls were dissolved forever in the Ion Chamber.

The next two souls ready for processing seemed unusual. Angel Joachim summoned the Angel Elizabeth for query. The Angel Elizabeth verified the report on the missive.

"There should be no question about these two, ionize them both."

"But he's from Abidan, a Planet of Peace."

"Read further. He chose to live on a planet of evil and has been corrupted by his environment. The other one convinced him to assist in her suicide/murder. A man of peace involved in murder can never be transmuted. Ionize them both. We have work to do. I still have much to teach you about sorting and transmutation. I would not deal with evil planets at all, but the Creator insists on transmutation of the just. These are not the just."

"But their son was murdered on Earth, and his soul was transmuted. She believed in transmutation and is trying to find her son, and he is a citizen of Abidan."

"No exceptions. Do you want me to ionize them? I have other apprentices to review. Remember that it is always better to be too careful. Your job is to never risk contaminating the Universe with the knowledge of evil."

"Yes, I will do it." The Apprentice readied the chamber. "Can I ionize them together?"

"No, individually is the most effective technique. Never risk peace in the Universe for sentimentality. The mall shooting victims are arriving. There will be much confusion among the victims, and there will be many angels and spirit guides involved to help them cross over. Finish this cluster batch and report to sorting 3 unit."

"Yes."

Angel Joachim was weary and could feel the sway of the dangerous influences of sentimentality. The job must be done. Peace in the Universe was paramount. Joachim could almost feel the tiny charged particles of these two souls tearing apart and scattering into the vast Universe. It did not seem right.

Chapter 58

A DECADE HAD PASSED SINCE THE FAMILY TRAGEDIES, as the rushing river of time continued its relentless move forward for Zack. He was pleased with all he and Carol had been able to do to help bring the family into the calmer waters of peace and healing.

Following the tragedies, Zack and Carol had moved their family back to Tallahassee. They felt they had to leave Miami because they needed a new environment for their boys, especially Adam. It was also good for them to be near their grandparents. Zack's mother Madge, who turned 80 that year, had decided to stay in Tallahassee, and Carol's parents also lived there.

Zack had sold his dealership in Aventura for a good profit and bought a large home in a newer neighborhood north of Tallahassee. He assumed responsibility for the family business, Anderson's European Imports, and their business was very successful.

Zack and Carol considered themselves fortunate to have three wonderful sons, Andy, Bobby, and their nephew, Adam. All three boys lived at home, although the two older boys attended college in town at FSU. Andy was a junior studying marketing and Bobby was a freshman planning to major in finance. They both enjoyed their share of partying at their fraternity house, but they kept it in balance, with good grades and helping out at home. They considered their cousin Adam to be their brother.

At 16, Adam was remarkable. His IQ was over 200 and he was almost perfect at both academics and sports. His family knew that he sometimes intentionally missed things like test questions and batting baseballs, so he could fit in better. He was interested in everything, especially science and astronomy, and he was strikingly handsome. He had inherited his good looks from both his parents, but he looked mostly like his mother, with her dark hair and dark eyes. His brothers were not jealous of him. They were proud of his accomplishments, and they were especially protective of him because the family tragedies had affected Adam most of all.

Zack and Carol became Adam's legal guardians. Since he was family, they did not feel the need to officially adopt him, although they considered him their son in every way. At first, Adam used to call them Uncle-Dad and Aunt-Mom, but gradually they were just Mom and Dad. Zack made sure that Adam's inheritance was put in trust for him until he was 25. Adam didn't need the money. Zack was able to provide handsomely for all his family.

The authorities had listed the deaths of Janna and William as a double suicide. Although it was generally accepted that the loss of their son David had been the cause, the stigma of self-inflicted death lingered in the quiet conversations of people who whispered about it. They described the tragedy as a Romeo and Juliet story, but the suicides were never mentioned in Adam's presence.

Zack privately thought that the death of his sister and her husband might be more than a double suicide. He intuitively felt that somehow Adam may have been involved, but little Adam never spoke of it and Zack never mentioned it.

When Adam first came to live with them permanently, he had many nightmares and long fits of almost uncontrollable crying. As Zack would hold the little boy in his arms for hours, it would seem that the crying would never stop. With sobbing and tears, the child would make incoherent utterances about blood, and guns, and his mother's suicide. The phrase that was most intelligible was the one he repeated over and over, "it is not my fault," but Adam never spoke openly about it or explained it. Zack did not press him, but held him closely, as if trying to extract all of the sadness from the child that he possibly could, trying to absorb it for himself, anything that would take it away from Adam. As sad as Zack felt over the loss of his lovely sister, and her remarkable husband, helping Adam to heal was like a curative for both father and son. There was nothing else to do that was more important.

As the years passed, Adam's mind gradually let go of the terrible memories. He had been four when David died and he had not seen it happen, but he could still see the scene of his mother dying in his father's arms and of himself struggling with his father over the gun that fired and killed his dad. He would never forget all the blood, but each time the painful memories came to him, the memory of his father telling him that it was not his fault gave him comfort.

The move from Miami had helped Adam most of all. Except for the cemetery in town, it could almost be as though the awful things that were now past had happened to someone else.

Adam's 16th birthday coincided with the Easter holidays and Lauren, Senator John, and their daughters, Courtney and Victoria, traveled from Washington D.C. to be there with the rest of the family. Adam's girl friend, Susan, and his grandparents, both Grandma Madge and Carol's parents, also joined them.

Adam was glad of the opportunity over dinner to ask his uncle, the senator, about the fate of the International Space Station.

"Thanks for inquiring, Adam, I'm real proud of that one," Senator John responded. "We plan to refurbish and reconfigure it so it will be practically a new station. That should extend its life until the year 2040. It's been a great success, not only in technological advances, but in diplomacy. We've got 16 countries working together on a common project in space, and the U.S. is still the leader. I feel fortunate to have been involved with the project."

Lauren smiled. "We're all proud of you."

John looked at his wife and smiled back.

"Hey, congratulations on winning the National High School Debate Competition," Lauren said.

"Thanks," Adam responded.

"What was your topic?" John asked.

"Gun Control."

The senator nodded with understanding. "I'd like to hear that, maybe Congress should hear it too," the senator added.

Their conversation was interrupted by laughter and singing. Adam's brothers carried in the cake glowing with 16 candles and everyone placed wrapped gifts on the table.

"I'm not frequently at a loss for words," Adam said, "but I don't know if any words exist that can express my deepest feelings of gratitude to the most wonderful family on Earth."

When Bobby saw Adam start to choke up, he lightened the mood, "blow out the candles, bro, I want some of Grandma Madge's cake."

Everyone laughed and Adam did as directed.

"Speaking of not usually being at a loss for words, I'm fascinated by your paper on your idea for a 'thoughtcrime' detector" Aunt Lauren said, "I want to hear more about it later, but right now, I guess you need to open your gifts."

Courtney rolled her eyes. "You know Adam's gift from us was your idea, Mom, I'm not claiming credit, Adam might not like it."

"Oh cool," Adam said, "a thought texter."

"We thought you might like to have one since they're new," Vick said, "but they don't really work that well, they're kind of slow."

Adam read the package. "'Convert your brain waves into digital text with this latest brain-machine interface headset,' I like it," he said, "thanks!"

The last gift he opened was a set of keys to a new car.

"It's in the driveway," Andy said. "We kept it hidden at Grandma's for the last two days. Thought about keeping it at the frat house, but thought better of it."

The new car was a beautiful silver color hybrid with collision warning, pedestrian detection, video, electrification and a street view map system.

"This's great!" Adam said. "Thanks so much!"

After rides in the new car, the family spent the rest of the evening at home. The holographic video game from Andy and Bobby was a big hit.

Lauren kissed John on the cheek, "you want to play too, don't you?"

The senator looked sheepish. "If it's okay, I don't get much chance to play video games," he smiled, "especially holographic ones."

"Have fun," Lauren grinned, "I want to have a chat with Zack anyway."

Carol, her parents and Madge insisted that Lauren and Zack have coffee together on the terrace while they cleaned the kitchen.

"This is such a pretty place, Zack, you've done so well by everyone," Lauren said, as she looked at the illuminated back yard pool and combination basketball and tennis court against a night view of the prairie preserve.

"I hope you're comfortable," Zack said.

"Of course, I love the guest room. I feel like it's our room we use it so much, and Court and Vick are fine with the Murphy beds in the guest study.

"It made sense for Carol to have one of the bedrooms as an office, she does so much volunteer work," Zack took another drink of coffee, "this six bedroom house on five acres was definitely a stretch when I bought it, but it's worked out good."

"You've done well with the business too. Dad would be proud. You've done well with everything."

Zack chuckled, "not bad for the 'B student' of the family."

"You're the heart and soul of this family," Lauren said fervently, "I don't know what we would've done without you, after everything that happened, and Adam's such a great kid, they're all great kids."

"Yeah, can you imagine Adam winning ten grand in that contest?" Zack said. "He came up with this thoughtcrime detector idea all on his own; and the good thing is, I even understand it, it's got all kinds of practical applications like airports, sports stadiums and other events that attract big crowds, imagine using computers to predict who's gonna commit a crime."

"What intrigued me was using it in the courtroom. What a great idea. I bet the colleges are all over him, National Merit Scholar and a three-sport wonder."

"Yeah, not just Harvard, but everyone, Yale, Princeton, Brown, Duke, Cal Tech, MIT, University of Chicago, you name it. It's overwhelming. The University of Florida is really after him, gave him a great offer too, for both sports and academics," said Zack. "They've got some new grant to build a spectrograph on the world's largest telescope they own with Spain in the Canary Islands, and they're all over him to join their astrophysics department, and of course, they've got a great athletic program, Southeastern Conference and all that."

"Where do you think he'll go?" Lauren asked.

"I'm not sure what he'll do, but I'm pretty sure it will be some place close to home or near family. Georgetown could be an option cuz it's close to you all, or he'd probably consider Harvard if Court goes there, and, of course, Gainesville's close," Zack said.

"Do you think he'd be a University of Florida Gator since his brothers are Florida State Seminoles, or is the rivalry that big of a deal?" Lauren asked.

"Not really, he might get a little teasing from his brothers, but all in good fun, nothing serious," Zack said. "At one time, we were all University of Miami baseball fans, so we're pretty open minded."

"I'd forgotten, do you hear from any Miami friends?"

"The Harmons usually visit once or twice a year and we always get holiday cards. Moira and K.J. have five kids."

"Wow, times change, didn't the Harmons have a boy Adam's age?" Lauren asked.

"Yeah, J.B. and Adam are the same age, they keep in touch, apparently J.B.'s really good at baseball too, maybe they'll end up together in college."

"That's cool," Lauren sipped her coffee thoughtfully, "still seems hard to believe, all that happened, doesn't it?"

"Yeah, it sure does," Zack said, "you've been a big help throughout the years, you and John both, we really appreciate how close to the family you've stayed, you're so good about visiting, and your girls are a joy, we always love your visits."

"Thanks," said Lauren, "I think I was always a little jealous of Janna cuz things seemed so easy for her, but I had no idea, of course, I hope I can make it up to Adam."

"Nothing to make up, really, but I know what you mean," Zack said, "and we really appreciate all you've done for Adam, for all the family."

"That reminds me, I'm taking Court and Vick on a college tour over spring break, do you think Adam would like to come?" Lauren asked.

"More than likely, he loves spending time with his pretty cousins, and that'd be a good way for him to see some colleges, I think it'd be great if you could take him, I'm a little overwhelmed to have a genius for a son, to think he can go anywhere and it won't cost him a dime. I still think he'll probably end up closer to home, but we'll see."

Lauren laughed. "They may never leave the upstairs here."

Zack laughed too, "yeah, Carol calls it 'Guy's World.'"

"Well, whatever Adam does, he's pretty amazing. I just hope he'll be happy," Lauren said.

"Me too," added Zack, "he really deserves it."

Chapter 59

After Adam's 16th birthday, Zack finally decided to ask him if he wanted to see his father's journal. He had not read the journal himself but kept it carefully put away. There never seemed to be a good time to mention it to Adam, but Zack had often worried about it. Carol agreed that it was probably the right thing to do, even though it also worried her. She suggested a night when she had a meeting, so it would be easier for the two of them to talk.

"Hi, Dad, how's it going?" Adam sat down on the large, comfortable family room couch with a sports drink and granola bar in hand.

"Real good," Zack switched off the television. He gazed at the handsome boy who looked so much like Janna. "There's a helluva lotta junk on TV, even with all the new channels, it's still a lot of junk."

"Yeah, there sure is, even the History Channel, I try to stick to sports and documentaries," he sipped his sports drink, "where's Mom?"

"Literacy Coalition meeting, she left dinner, want to have it in here?"

"Kitchen's ok, that's easier isn't it?"

Zack heated and served their penne pasta with chicken while Adam tossed the fresh salad.

"How's the new car?" Zack asked.

"Great! The safety stuff just keeps getting better and better," Adam said, "thanks again, I really love it."

"You're entirely welcome, Son, how was football practice?"

"Good, I think we're heading to the playoffs."

"With you as QB, I don't doubt it at all," Zack took a bite of pasta, "hard to believe you're 16, kid, except, of course, for the car and driver's license."

"You know, Dad, I know I don't thank you enough, but I really appreciate all you've done for me," Adam said. "I could've had a really bad life if it hadn't been for you and Mom."

"You're a great kid. I'm just glad we were able to be there for you," Zack took a drink of water, "do you ever think about your first parents?"

"Yeah, sometimes, I wonder about everything that happened, but it always seems like it happened to somebody else, which is good, I guess," Adam paused to eat some pasta, "but turning 16 and feeling older has made me think about it some, I wonder what it would have been like if my first parents had lived, or if my dad had lived, but you're really my dad, so it's confusing."

"I was thinking about your father's journal. Would you be interested in seeing it?" Zack asked tentatively.

"I remember him telling me about it, I never knew where it was or what it was. Have you ever read it?" Adam asked.

"No, maybe I should have, but I always felt like it was your property, and it'd be like prying if I read it."

"I think I'd like to see it. You think I should?" Adam asked.

"I don't know, Son, I've worried about it a lot, on the one hand I think maybe your parents would've wanted you to read it, but on the other it may be best to let it be forgotten."

They ate quietly, letting their thoughts roam.

"This pasta's delicious," Adam took his last bite, "Mom does such a good job."

"Want some more?"

"I'm okay for now."

Zack finished the pasta on his plate. "This journal thing's up to you, hate to open up old wounds," Zack said, "but it's yours to do what you want."

"Yeah, I'd like to see it," Adam started picking up their dishes, "I think."

"Okay, I'll go get it," Zack took a deep breath.

He returned in a few minutes with a red leather volume with the gold letters inscribed on it, "Journal of William Aaron Blake." The book was slightly faded and the spine was loose. "Why don't you read it and we can talk about it after," Zack handed him the volume, "I'll be glad to talk about it with you."

"Thanks," Adam opened the book and let out a slight gasp, "I don't think I've ever seen a picture of my first parents."

Adam looked at the two photos, one of his mother and the one of his parents. He shared them with Zack.

Zack sighed, "after the tragedies, I put all the photos of your parents away, I just thought it'd be too sad, actually, I asked your Aunt Lauren to safeguard them for the family. They're part of our family history, so I couldn't just get rid of 'em, I just didn't think having them out would help us heal, under the circumstances."

"That was a good idea," Adam nodded, "I have such a flood of emotions seeing these photos now. I think this one of the two of them was in front of the old World Trade Center, before it was destroyed."

"Yeah, looks like it was in front of that fountain that used to be there on the plaza."

"Yeah," Adam nodded, "they were good looking, weren't they?"

"They were the most gorgeous couple I've ever seen, like movie stars, everyone said so, your mother was always so beautiful."

Adam saw his dad start to choke up, "maybe Aunt Lauren could keep these too?"

Zack nodded and held onto the photos.

"I think I'll get this done," Adam started up the stairs with the book, "I'll talk to you after, wish me luck."

"I do, Son, let me know when you wanna talk, I'm here for you."

"Thanks."

Zack looked at the pictures he was still holding. I was right, he thought, it is too sad. He wiped some tears from his cheeks and went to the office to find an envelope. He remembered the day he last saw Janna. He hadn't realized at the time that she was saying goodbye to him and giving him Adam. It was the loss of David, of course, that she never got over, but it was all too sad. He sighed, he had to keep helping Adam, that was all he could do. "Thank you for trusting me with Adam," Zack whispered to his deceased sister.

Zack gave Adam some time and then climbed the stairs. He cracked the door open to Adam's large, comfortable room, sparkling with images of success, academic awards and sports trophies.

"Hi Dad," Adam said. "This stuff's pretty strange. Listen to this *'I wish with all my being that I could take Janna with me to live in Abidan, but the Great Creator forbids it. No one from a planet of evil is allowed to go to a planet of peace...*

"And listen to this,*'...God has judged Earth as a mistaken experiment of bad genetic composition fatally flawed by a culture of hate and violence. God will allow Earth to be annihilated in the year 2070 by nuclear destruction in World War III...*

"And this, *'...She cannot go to Abidan. She would never be able to get past the Genetic Code Scanner in the Milky Way Transport Station...*

"*'...But to leave my family on Abidan, to never see them again, is an unthinkable thing for me, yet I must think about it. I must decide..'"*

"I don't think I get it," said Zack.

"Apparently, at least, according to this, my dad was an alien from a peaceful planet in the Milky Way Galaxy called Abidan," Adam said.

"Good God!" Zack was dumbfounded.

"Yeah, and this explains why my mom committed suicide," Adam read from the journal, "*Janna is obsessed with the idea of transmutation of the soul and I fear the worst. She thinks that her soul can find David's soul if she kills herself. She thinks that I would be allowed to return to Abidan, and that Adam's soul can join us after he has lead a normal life on Earth with her wonderful brother and sister-in-law. They are wonderful people, but we need to raise our own son, who is a halfling. I wish I had never told her the little I know about transmutation of the souls in the afterlife. There is an afterlife and I know David's soul has been transmuted to a new life, as all just people on Earth are, but how she could ever find him, I do not know. I know too little. I fear very much that 'a little learning is a dangerous thing' and I am very afraid of what will become of Janna. She is clearly unable to function normally. She says she cannot be cured and cannot turn off her grief. She has rejected Earth, as well, because God has rejected it. The help we have tried to get for her does not seem adequate, and I do not know what else to do. Adam and I need her so much, we could not live without her...'"*

"Oh my gosh," said Zack as Adam shut the book, "what do you make of this?"

"I have different feelings on different levels," Adam began. "As a student of science, I accept there's life in the Universe, and I can even accept that people from other planets would look like us, given an equivalent or similar chemical base, so that isn't a problem for me, but accepting that my biological father was an alien is a completely different thing, the main concern being that it would make me one-half alien, a 'halfling' as his book says. I am different, we've all known that, but do you think that's why I'm different?' Adam asked.

"I don't know, Son, I'm a little out of my league here," Zack said.

"Well, at the very least it's a little deflating," Adam said with a slight smile, "I thought I was just special, now it turns out, I'm kind of a freak, it's a little disappointing to say the least."

Zack smiled, "you're never disappointing, no matter what."

"I appreciate that," Adam said, "but I really don't want anyone to know about this, like Andy and Bobby and Mom, or Susan, or the football team. I think they'd feel differently about me and treat me differently."

"What do you think we should do with it?" Zack asked.

"Put the thing away," said Adam. "I think I'm more fragile than I thought, mentally. My first family's gone and there's nothing I can do about that, and I have the greatest dad and mom and brothers and family in the world and a really great life. I'm just not ready to deal with past tragedies I can't change, or World War III or bad genetics or the afterlife, or any of these issues. Is that wrong?"

"Not at all," said Zack. "We really can't control any of it, and it brings up more questions than answers, that's for sure."

"I remember the day David died, I was four, and I remember seeing my parents die when I was six and I just don't want to relive it; and WWIII is 50 years off, and I can't really do anything about that either, at least not now, can I ask you to hide it for now?" Adam asked.

"Sure," said Zack.

"Thanks," said Adam. "Is it okay to just wanta be a teenager in denial?"

"You bet," said Zack.

Adam gave Zack a hug, "You've built such a secure, happy life for me Dad, is it wrong to just want to enjoy it?"

"No, Son, not at all." There were tears in Zack's eyes. "Well, at least I've done my duty."

"You've done way more than that, Dad," Adam had tears in his eyes as he looked into his uncle-dad's kind face, "you saved me, and I love you so much for it. I'll never be able to thank you enough."

"Your happiness is more than enough thanks," said Zack.

They hugged each other again.

Downstairs later, Zack squeezed the covers of the journal together as if to make them fit more tightly and hide the strange information within. "My brother-in-law was an alien!" Zack whispered, shaking his head, "Adam's right, let's just be in denial, I'm not gonna' say anything." He put the photos back in the front cover of the journal, no point in opening up old wounds for Lauren, since he was putting the journal away anyway. He squeezed the covers again and put the journal away. He would not tell Carol, or anyone. That was what Adam wanted.

Chapter 60

As the years passed, the red color of the cover of the journal faded to brown, and the gold letters on the front lost their shine as dust gathered on it where it lay hidden on a high shelf. The spine cracked open further.

Grandma Anderson passed away at the age of 91. The visit to the cemetery for her funeral brought many memories. Zack was glad that the green carpet and tent covered many of the family graves. He reflected that as sad as it was to lose his mother, it felt almost like a blessing. She was the first family member he had buried who had died of old age. He and Adam had talked about it. They both thought that it made them feel more peaceful about her passing.

Zack also thought the biblical quote that the priest read at his mother's graveside had a special irony.

"One generation passes away, and another generation comes; But the earth abides forever. The sun also rises, and the sun goes down. And hastens to the place where it arose... That which has been is what will be. That which is done is what will be done. And there is nothing new under the sun."

Zack thought that if William's journal was correct there may well be new things under the sun, but he guessed the Bible may be right, the Earth will endure, just not the people. Denial, denial, Zack repeated to himself. He glanced at Adam and was pleased to see Adam holding up well.

Zack and his family continued to prosper and change. Andy married first and then Bobby. Andy and his wife bought a house in Zack's neighborhood, and Bobby and his wife remodeled the home of his grandparents Anderson. Vick and Court both married and settled in the Washington D.C. area. And then, another generation came as wonderful new babies began to appear.

Adam completed his undergraduate degree at the University of Florida, summa cum laude, and continued to be the "three sport wonder," as his Aunt Lauren described him. He enjoyed his tenure as a Florida Gator. He roomed with his childhood friend J.B., and they played on the baseball team together. He also loved the fact that UF was close to home. With safer and faster cars, it was easy for him to spend Sundays in Tallahassee with his family. He could also travel to Cape Canaveral to the Kennedy Space Center to collaborate with the scientists on the Solar Probe Plus mission.

After earning his Ph.D. at Georgetown University, Adam became a distinguished author and lecturer. He did not like moving away from his family in Tallahassee to join the faculty at Georgetown, but he visited home frequently, as his Aunt Lauren and Uncle John, the senator, had always done and continued to do. He was grateful to be near his aunt and uncle and their growing family, and he enjoyed the unique discipline of Science, Technology and International Affairs that he taught at Georgetown. Adam also advised for NASA, private initiative space projects and the Goddard Space Center. His NASA advisory position enabled numerous trips to Florida, as he continued his work on space exploration using ground and space telescopes. He had identified hundreds of planets, as the list of new planets changed almost daily.

Adam married Susan, his high school sweetheart. He remained, as always, a well loved member of his family. He was successful, fulfilled and happy.

Chapter 61

THE DAYS, WEEKS, MONTHS AND YEARS MOVED FORWARD like the water of a river, sometimes rushing, meandering, flooding, slowing, but never backward, forever moving forward.

Twenty years later, in the year 2051, Adam's oldest son, Noah, was ready to graduate from high school. Noah was the oldest of three sons. Adam was terribly worried by the proximity of the year 2070, and the prediction in his father's journal that 2070 was the year when World War III would bring about the nuclear annihilation of the people on Earth. When Adam had been 16, he had wanted to avoid his biological father's journal. Now, he had a wife, three growing sons, and extended family, and the threat of nuclear annihilation was only 19 years away.

As far as Adam knew, the journal was hidden. Adam had never looked at it again after he asked Zack to put it away, but in subtle ways, the journal had shaped his life. He had come to believe that he probably was a halfling. He had advanced cognitive skills, extra chromosomes, no vestigial organs, superior vision, an excellent immune system and extraordinary gifts, even in the age of designer babies. While none of those characteristics were proof he was half alien, he felt that it was likely true.

He also believed that life on other planets was certain and inevitable, although he had not yet witnessed it. He had always believed that planets that had similar chemical composition to Earth, or had been terraformed, would produce life similar to inhabitants on Earth. Adam was deeply involved in studies of astronomy from the space-based telescopes. These advanced telescopes directly viewed extrasolar planets in detail and established facts about their geology and climate. He had discovered over 10,000 planets, many of them in what scientists once referred to as the Goldilocks Zone, from the children's story, meaning just right. There were many planets that met this criterion range. He believed that the planet Abidan, in the Perseus Arm of the Milky Way Galaxy, may be one of them.

There were other compelling reasons for Adam to believe that his first father's journal was true. The world situation was so precarious that the date of annihilation seemed very real, threatening and inevitable. Evidence of the Great Decline pervaded the world. Wars, atrocities, genocides and mass shootings were almost commonplace. Gas and germ warfare had killed hundreds of thousands of innocent people. The nuclear arsenal of the world was greater than it had ever been at any time in history. Dirty bombs and limited nuclear wars had wrought devastation and destruction in many parts of the world. The Cold War, which had a brief respite at the end of the last millennium, festered with increasing tension between the United States and Russia. China was an even greater threat with its cruel leadership and territorial ambitions. Peace in the Middle East was as elusive as it had ever been. Civil wars raged in Venezuela, Iraq, Syria, Kenya and Korea. The culture of violence in the environment was worse than at any time in history. Individual crimes were worse and more frequent than ever: child molesters, serial murderers, suicide bombers, murderers of children, murderers who were children, drive-by shooters, mass shooters, school shooters.

And yet, the terrible political, criminal and social situation existed alongside remarkable advances in science, medicine and technology.

Carbon emissions had decreased exponentially due to advanced nanotechnology, improvements in energy efficiency and power conservation, solar, wind and wave power and fourth generation nuclear power. Fusion power was also becoming available. Advances in nuclear pulse propulsion were bringing unmanned exploration to the outer solar system and a space elevator was under construction in Australia.

Cars were computer-controlled and the use of artificial

intelligence had eliminated virtually all road management issues. Cars traveled at over 200 mph, and car crashes and traffic fatalities no longer occurred. Hovering/flying vehicles were currently being developed. Femtoengineering had become practical, leading to significant breakthroughs in anti-grav, force field generation and teleportation.

DNA scanning and instantaneous decoding of genetic material had improved crime scene analysis and forensic science, although gene therapy in the treatment of human violence had thus far met with only limited success. Synthetic genomics continued to greatly advance. The number of cells able to be synthesized in a single organism had reached 100 trillion, the total number of cells in the human body. It was possible to merge AI and human intelligence, although it was heavily restricted, as the number of available brain-computer links continued to increase.

Medicine and diagnostic technology had kept pace. Tiny cameras provided 3D imaging of internal structures and brain activity yielding significant advances in MRI scans. Organ failure was a thing of the past because new organs were grown from a person's own stem cells. The need for organ donors was obsolete. In recent years, 98% of all cancers had been cured through the medical use of nanobots inside the human body.

Adam appreciated the technological advances just as he deplored the fact that the culture of hate and violence on Earth had grown worse. At the age of 47, as a father of three sons, and as a person blessed with a wonderful extended family, Adam felt responsible. He knew he should review the information in his first father's journal and formulate a plan to ensure their safety. He thought he should involve his oldest son, Noah. The boy was brilliant, and, after all, this journal was written by his grandfather. Noah could read the book without the memory of that distant, upsetting nightmare of the indelible sight of his mother and father dying on the floor of their home in Miami. Noah was 16, the same age Adam had been when he had read his father's journal. He asked Zack to bring it when he came to visit for Noah's high school graduation.

The graduation ceremony in Washington D.C. was a family

reunion. Zack and Carol came to visit for a week. Andy and Bobby also arrived with their families. Adam's Aunt Lauren and Uncle John, who had been a United States senator for over 50 years, still lived in town. Their daughters Vick and Court also lived in D.C. with their families. Susan, Adam's wife of many years, also had numerous family members attending, mostly from Tallahassee.

Adam was grateful for the opportunity to visit with all his family, especially his dad. At 79, Zack was still very active. He was in good health and kept a full schedule, but Adam knew that even with medical advances, he could not last forever. For that matter, Adam thought, if the date of the Earth's demise was accurate, there would not be much time for any of them.

Adam treasured his visits with his dad in the evenings after dinner.

"We're all proud of Noah," Zack would say, "of course, all your boys are talented and you were the star of your generation, but you must be awful pleased to see your sons doing so well, and without the tragedies you had to deal with. Your boy Noah's got some real leadership skills and charisma from what I hear, and he's a gifted speaker too."

"Yeah," Adam nodded happily, "I'm very grateful."

Zack continued, "and there doesn't seem to be any jealousy among them, either, always a good thing not to have."

Adam loved the time with his wonderful dad. They had shared so much tragedy and joy and good times. They also shared an amazing extraterrestrial secret that Adam had put aside when he was 16.

"I think I found Abidan," Adam told Zack, when they were alone for an after dinner chat.

"You mean the planet your first father's from?" Zack asked.

"Yeah," Adam said.

"Really. How do you know?"

"I remembered a few clues from the journal and then I supplemented that with some information on the Internet, and I think it may be the right planet," Adam explained.

"What'd you get from the journal?" Zack asked.

"Well, you know I haven't seen it since I turned 16, but I

remember it," Adam said. "It's mainly sad stuff, about my poor mom and David and all, but there's a neat description of a trip we took out west. I kind of remember the trip; I was three at the time. My father wrote a beautiful description of the national parks we saw, and how different they were from anything on his home planet of Abidan. The comparisons are the only clues I've discovered. He wrote that he'd never seen anything like Yellowstone and the Grand Canyon, because he lived on a planet of frozen lakes and rivers, a chilly ocean, snowy plains and sparse vegetation with a thin oxygen atmosphere. He also wrote that most of life on his planet was lived in warehouse cities and towns, beneath huge domes. I combined that description with some climate, geology and location facts I found on the Internet, and then I looked for the planet through our mega-telescopes. I found one in the Mar's position, with the right chemical and temperature profile and I think it may be Abidan," Adam said.

"That's amazing," Zack said thoughtfully. "So, if you accept you're a halfling and there's an Abidan, like the journal says, does that mean Earth's going to be destroyed in the year 2070?"

"I have to think so," Adam said, "which is why I wanted you to bring the journal."

"Well, here it is," Zack said. He produced the faded volume wrapped in a clear plastic bag. Zack had recently sent the photos of Janna and William to Lauren, as Adam had requested long ago, even though he didn't think it would be a problem for Adam, now. Lauren was glad to have the photos after all these years.

"Thanks for remembering, I'd never forgive myself if I didn't take action," Adam said, "we have a lot of wonderful family members to protect, and we definitely need a plan. I'd like Noah to be involved."

"You think Noah should read this?" Zack handed the journal to Adam.

"I was 16 when I read it," Adam said.

"Yeah, and you wanted me to hide it afterwards, and we both chose to be in denial."

"True," Adam said, "but the time's getting close. We need to prepare, and I think reading the journal will be easier on Noah, because he doesn't have the bad memories," Adam said. "I'll be 66 in 2070, and I know that's not old, but the boys'll have so much of their lives ahead of them. We need to get the next generation involved, and I think Noah's the most likely candidate to provide some strategies and the leadership to carry them out. We have the space stations and colonies on the moon and Mars, so there are some options."

"Well, I see the wisdom of what you're saying and I'm glad to have the brightest minds in the family working on it," Zack smiled, "I'll be pretty old, 98 to be exact, but I'll more than likely be around and I'll support whatever you do."

"Thanks Dad," Adam grinned.

"So what do you think about all that afterlife stuff in the Journal?" Zack asked, "maybe I should be thinking about that too."

"I believe very strongly in an afterlife," Adam said, "even though I'm not certain how it works. My first father wrote about transmutation of the souls of the just people on planets of evil, and didn't know exactly how it worked either. On planets of peace, they cap your life at 130, at least on Abidan, and have a peaceful, beautiful ceremony to recycle your soul. It does sound similar to reincarnation, but it seems like it may occur in another dimension," Adam said. "So, even though I don't comprehend the entire process, I believe it happens. The soul is the connector. It can inhabit the body or the spirit, and when it quits transmuting to new lives, it becomes the spirit, apparently we live on in the spirit."

"So, you're really sure it happens," Zack stated.

"Absolutely, and I think it's peaceful, even here on a planet like Earth. Your spirit guide helps you cross over and your loved ones are there too, angels, music, and the beautiful light of God," Adam said.

"Well, that sounds okay," Zack said hesitantly.

"I believe that it's nothing to fear, and that souls find peace in the Universe," Adam said.

"I like that," Zack said.

They both sat in quiet thought until Zack spoke, "I think I'll turn in, but I sure enjoyed talking with you like I always do, and I sure am looking forward to hearing Noah's speech tomorrow, need to get my beauty sleep for it."

"Sure," Adam said, "good night, see you tomorrow, and thanks for bringing the journal."

"Sure, no problem," said Zack. "Good night."

"Hope you sleep well," Adam said with a fond smile.

Chapter 62

CEREMONIES OFTEN BRING WITH THEM A SHARP reminder of the swift passage of time. The joyful, traditional graduation was no exception. Yesterday's children were moving forward. The graduation ceremony itself also seemed to pass as quickly as the graduates in their caps and gowns leaving the auditorium. It seemed like such a brief time before Noah was off to his grad party and dance, and the family members were in various stages of settling in for the evening. Zack and Adam took the opportunity for another visit.

"Didn't I tell you? Great speech," Zack said, leaning back comfortably on the tan leather couch. "I was so proud of him, I don't think I've ever heard a more inspirational speech, when he talked about peace and all the beautiful things he said, I thought Carol was going to have to leave she was crying so hard, and all that about 'the future, what if?' Why it brought tears to my eyes. Where'd he get those ideas?"

"All over, he's interested in everything, he even got some of the ideas from my father's journal."

"What'd he think of it?" Zack asked.

"He was intrigued by it, didn't say too much, but I can tell it had an impact on him from his speech, especially 'the future, what if?' part."

"Well we were always worried by that journal, but this boy made something good out of it, sure was a great speech. What a kid, just think what he'll do at Harvard."

Adam smiled. It was the last night of Zack's visit and Adam cherished their time together. Tomorrow, he would worry again about the year 2070, and each of his family members would return to their homes, having had their perfect day.

But the family did not return the next day. Because the river stopped for Noah in the early hours of the morning of June 7, 2051.

Noah was talking with friends in the parking lot of the school auditorium. An old car hurried through the parking lot and opened fire on the boys. The three drive-by shooters were boys aged 15, 16, and 17. They were "bored" and wanted to kill someone for the "fun of it." They shot Noah in the back.

Noah lived long enough to be taken to the emergency room, but not long enough to see his family on Earth. The ER team that could not save him retrieved a solid gold St. Christopher medal from his pocket, to return to his family, as they wished the beautiful young man, "Godspeed."

Chapter 63

SOUL PROCESSING CENTER-EARTH, ENGLISH TRANSLATION

And so it was in the Earth year 2051 that the soul of Noah William Blake in Cluster Batch 8315101-748474-8337566CR3 at Soul Processing Center-Earth was made ready for transmutation. Ministering Angel Joachim was explaining to Apprentice Angel Ephraim the complex process of arranging transmutation of the souls.

The Apprentice Ephraim studied the missive. "It says here that his last words were a request that his soul be transmuted to the Planet of Peace Abidan, in the Perseus Arm of the Milky Way Galaxy. His grandfather was a citizen of Abidan and many of his family members are still there. What a handsome child he was, look at that image."

"Yes," Angel Joachim stated, "I...processed his grandparents in a past time."

"Are there any rules against honoring a request for a specific planet for transmutation?"

"No." Angel Joachim's aura seemed to glow more brightly.

The Apprentice reviewed the host locator. "Imagine, we could actually send him to his ancestors."

"This is irregular, but there is an opportunity. There is no Universal Law against it," Angel Joachim said. "Ready the tunnel of transmutation. Let us proceed with haste."

Angel Joachim thought of the souls of the grandparents of this splendid boy. Joachim had known they were good and just people.

And it came to pass that in that time the immortal soul of Noah William Blake, citizen of Earth, was aware of the extraordinary passage in the tunnel of transmutation.

The journey in the tunnel of light was swift and long, joyful and painful. The swirling, tumbling, rushing carried him like the sometimes rough current of the river of time. He felt the stripping of history, memory, environment, and, at the same time, the loving presence of a spirit guide, exquisite music, and the rushing, tumbling, swirling tunnel of blue and white light.

On and on, past memory, past history, past all knowledge of evil, past all touch with life in the olden days, past anger at his shooting, past the loss and separation from his family, past pain and hope and joy and suffering until there was little that remained of the Earth being.

Only life as it had been in the tunnel of light. Only life miraculously transformed into light in the loving Presence of a Being. Rushing, swirling, tumbling on and on until his soul became the tunnel of light.

And then it stopped.

Chapter 64

ABIDAN

On Abidan, the gentle life continued in the years after William Aaron Blake had departed for Earth and never returned. In the year that compared with Earth year 2051, William's younger brother Isaac became a grandfather. Isaac's son, John William Blake, and his wife Rachel gave birth to an infant son on Abidan.

The family had gathered at Isaac's home for the Celebration of Birth. It was a large family convocation of many generations. Isaac's parents as well as his sisters, Margaret and Ruth, who had also been William's sisters, attended the celebration with their families.

The spacious room was filled with the laughter and happiness of the adults. The large, back yard was overflowing with the joy of the children playing among the rounded shade trees and perfect green grass. The sun shone brightly in the blue sky above the huge dome that covered their neighborhood.

Little Noah William Blake slept peacefully through the party that had been given in his honor, but he was still the center of attention. Ruth was comparing him with pictures in an old family album.

Ruth had never outgrown the title of "family philosopher" that her older brother, William, had given her when she was a child. Her brother, William, had left many years ago to travel to Planet of Evil Earth to conduct research for his dissertation for his Ph.D. in Sociology. He never returned, although he had signaled them from the Milky Way Transport Station to tell them that he had fallen in love and would marry a wonderful girl on Earth. He said that he would try to contact them again, if possible. He had also sent each of them beautiful and thoughtful gifts.

After all this time, Ruth often felt William's strong presence, especially at family gatherings. She had been 13 when he left and she was now 64. In several years, she would begin her middle age.

"Look," she said holding the album near the sleeping child, "he looks very much like his great uncle William."

John looked at his baby son, then at the likeness of William as a baby, then back at his child. "You are right, there is a family resemblance, but people look similar on Abidan. Was William the one who went to the Planet of Evil?"

"Yes."

"I never met him," said John.

"No," said Ruth. "He was gone before you were born. It is too bad you never had a chance to know him. You would have loved him as we all did."

The doorbell rang. Their family friend, Irina, was at the door. She brought a thick envelope from the University.

"That is odd," said Ruth as she showed their friend Irina into the living room to see everyone. Ruth opened the package. "It looks like a scholarly work and it is very old. How did you happen to bring it here?" Ruth asked Irina.

"I was at my job at University and they asked me to bring this to your family since they knew I was attending the Celebration of Birth," Irina explained. "I do not know the contents, but I believe they are significant."

Ruth handed the package to Isaac. He looked surprised. "It is my brother William's dissertation, the one about whom we were speaking. And there is a large spiral notebook. Oh, I see, there is a letter here. It says Professor Shem's soul has been recycled and these papers were found among the professor's effects. They are being returned to the Blake family."

Ruth smiled, "Imagine, to have something from William at this happy time in our lives. We are twice blessed." She looked at Isaac who was still holding the bound work and asked, "What is the title?"

Isaac looked surprised, "The Next Generation of Noah."

Rachel took a breath. John looked at his wife and then at his sleeping baby.

"I thought you named him Noah because you liked the name, but how strange that it would turn up this way in my brother's dissertation." Isaac had a question in his voice.

"We do like the name," Rachel responded. "We did not know anything about this."

Before Isaac could read further, the dissertation and blue spiral notebook were put aside. Noah William Blake had opened his bright blue-green eyes and announced loudly to the world that he was awake.

"Oh look," Ruth said, "he is beautiful!" Everyone stood aside so the great grandparents and grandparents could approach the crib first, according to the traditions of the Celebration. As the family assembled, Irina stood in the background, staring at the blue spiral notebook and dissertation on the side table where Isaac had put them.

Ruth walked to the back door and opened it onto the yard where the young members of the family were playing. Two adults stood near the children, watching carefully over them. Ruth called to the children, "John, Edward, Mary, Edith, Rachel, David...everyone, come and see your new cousin. He is awake!"

The happy, tawny skinned children with pink cheeks, hazel eyes and brown hair clustered by the back door. They rushed through the door in a flurry of excitement to meet their newest cousin, except for David who stayed behind to wait for his parents who were in the yard.

Ruth looked lovingly at her beautiful daughter and her daughter's husband, the young adults who had been watching the children. She said to them, "Come and see your new cousin!"

To everyone who knew them, this couple was like the definition of love. They met as babies at a worship day picnic and had grown up together with a special friendship and devotion that had matured as they had. When they married young, no one questioned that it was the perfect union. Their deep connection and consuming passion for each other stirred everyone around them, and inspired them to learn the deeper meaning of love. This remarkable couple influenced citizens in many ways. Some even copied the way they had modified the jumpsuits that they wore.

Ruth looked at the handsome couple. Their arms were entwined as they lovingly held each other and kissed.

Ruth called to them, "Come Janna, come William, I feel sure you want to see your cousin." Still holding hands, Janna and William joined their son, David, who smiled at them, the sweet smile they had always loved. Together, the three of them followed their cousins inside.

"This is such a loving family," said Rachel. "It is so wonderful. Everyone always socializes so well with each other. And look how happy the children are to see their new cousin. They love each other so much. It is as though our family members have known each other before, in different lives across the Universe."

"Maybe they have," smiled Ruth. Her gaze rested on William and Janna linking hands with David, who was between them, as they approached the crib of Noah William Blake. Ruth's eyes twinkled. "Maybe they have."

Janna's eyes sparkled with tears as she squeezed the hand of her beloved son, and looked into the bright, beautiful eyes of her dearest husband.

"I have the most extraordinary feeling," she said, "it may be this wonderful new baby, this blessed child of Adam, or our success with the Curiosity Center we founded, but somehow, in some way, in a world devoid of competition, I feel we have won a great victory."

At that moment, baby Noah looked at his family and held out his arms to them.

William looked at the exquisite profile of his wonderful wife as she leaned forward to pick up baby Noah. He looked at his son, David, whose sweet smile had been the memory he had carried with him for all time. William's eyes also sparkled with tears.

"Yes we have won, darling Jannie," he said, "and it is our mission to continue."

End

CPSIA information can be obtained at www.ICGtesting.com
Printed in the USA
LVOW06s0016180415

435080LV00001B/3/P

The Nut that Changed my Life

Bruce Hayman

© Bruce Hayman, 2007

J B Hayman,
Tasman Downs Station
Box 17
Tekapo Postal Centre,
Lake Tekapo

ISBN 978-0-473-12551-6

Designer: George Hook,

Publisher: GH, Wellington

Printer: Astra Print, Wellington

Contents

Acknowledgements	2
Part One	
Family Background, 1859 - 1920	3
Part Two	
Life at 'Tasman Downs', 1920 - 1941	33
Part Three	
War Service, 1941 - 1945	87
Part Four	
Life Since the War, 1945 - 2003	201
Appendix One	
Journal of Jean de Carteret	229
Appendix Two	
Excerpts from the 150 Squadron Operational Record Book	259

Acknowledgements

I would like to thank the following for their help in making the publication of my memoirs possible:
- Sue Hornsey, who typed up a large portion of the manuscript and made it all available in electronic form;
- Nicola Hornsey, who did so much to get the photos scanned and onto disc;
- David Gunby, who edited my memoirs, and supplied Appendix Two, detailing my operational flying;
- Karen Simpson and Justin Wills, who most patiently read the book to me in proof;
- and others too numerous to mention, who encouraged me to work up my recollections into book form;
- but above all, my thanks to Linda, Jane and Ian, who have throughout supported me in what turned out to be a much bigger and longer task than I had ever expected it to be.

Part One

Family Background, 1859 - 1920

What is it that makes a person's life interesting? I have lived a seemingly pretty ordinary farming life, embracing eighty years of the twentieth and twenty-first centuries. I went away to boarding school for a few years in the 1930's, then in the 1939–1945 War trained as a pilot and ended up flying Wellington bombers in the Italian Campaign until late December '43, when a crash on Mount Etna put me in hospital till May 1945, when the war in Europe ended. Not much in that to grab the imagination; but over the years when recalling incidents and events round the fire of an evening to friends and relatives, it has been suggested on numerous occasions that I should write a book. Now in my eightieth year, where should I begin?

Thomas and Ann Hayman

I'll go back nearly one hundred and fifty years to the 26th of July 1859 when my great grandfather, Thomas Hayman, married Ann Kingsbury in the 'Parish Church of Holy Trinity, Saint Philip's, in the County and City of Bristol, England, according to the Rites and Ceremonies of the Established Church after Banns by me, - C. Godfrey Ashwin, Minister.' So runs the record.

Thomas signed the register by making his mark, which I feel perhaps calls for a bit of explanation. Born in the year of Queen Victoria's accession, 1837, he was a bright lad, but very much spoiled by his indulgent father. Early in his life Tom played truant, going to the coalmines instead of to school. This was not discovered for quite a while, and when it was, his father did nothing effective to correct it. So Tom continued at the mines, quite out of hand! He refused any schooling, preferring to become skilled in the miners' craft, and to box and wrestle, at which he became proficient.

His father, originally a Devonshire man and owning a small farm and butchery business in Somerset, was a noted strongman in his day. Unfortunately, I didn't seem to inherit much of that strong man stuff though I was reasonably athletic; but Tom's father once won a wager by carrying a ten hundredweight (500 kg) bale of hay, lowered on to his back by winch gear, from his neighbour's barn to his own, three chains (60 metres) away. No doubt something of a record!

Tom, though slightly under average height, inherited his father's toughness, and in the miners' Saturday athletic and boxing contests was only beaten once, and that was by his elder brother, Henry. This came about when the regular scheduled bouts were interrupted for independent contestants; a hat would be tossed into the arena, to be followed by the hat of anyone accepting the challenge. Unbeknown to Tom, Henry's hat was thrown in, followed by his own. Tom had to take a beating, and seemed quite bucked by Henry's prowess.

From his youth on, Tom showed an independent spirit, a great sense of fair play, and a detestation of humbug and insincerity. Such was the man who at twenty-two, married Ann Kingsbury, aged nineteen. She was a girl of great strength of character and was, from all the tales told by her many children, the heart and centre of the family. As the record of the years unfolds, from many sources come tributes to Ann's qualities of heart and mind, her wisdom, her business ability, and the thoughtfulness and care for others that made her so greatly loved.

Emigration to Australia and New Zealand

No particular reason can be found why the young couple left England. Certainly it was a period when the tide of emigration was flowing strongly towards the colonies and the New World. So November 1862 found them with their two children, James and Walter (who became my grandfather), aboard the good ship *Ivanhoe* out of Plymouth bound for Australia. The *Ivanhoe* was an iron screw steamer of 64 h.p. 263 tons burden, length 161 feet, breadth 21 feet, built in 1850 at Newcastle on Tyne. It doesn't appear to be what one would call a luxury liner for the young couple's 113 day voyage to Melbourne. Moreover, the young mother's plight was added to by the arrival on Christmas Eve of their third son, John Ivanhoe. The Captain marked the occasion by presenting him with a silver christening mug.

Early in February 1863 they sailed into Port Phillip Bay, anchoring at Geelong. After a stay at the settlers' staging camp, Tom was offered a job on a new station property in Gippsland, about sixty miles up country from Melbourne. His farming ability and general knowledge suggested a good future on the land, and so the family was soon established in a three-roomed slab house built with some help from his employer. For the storage of foodstuffs there was a cellar with a heavy trapdoor. Tom was engaged in fencing, tree felling, and generally clearing the bush for grazing and cultivation.

About eighteen months later, by which time their first daughter had arrived, Tom and the other men returned in the late afternoon from working on a boundary fence to find the house a smouldering heap, and no sign of wife or children. It was quite evident what had happened. Tom had fenced in the nearby spring in the creek to prevent kangaroos and aborigines from fouling the water there. 'Walkabout' natives, resenting his interference with the waterhole which they regarded as their hereditary property, had in revenge burnt down the white man's 'gunyah', and, so it seemed, murdered his family! Frantically raking through the still burning debris, Tom heard faint cries from the cellar, and throwing up the heavy-beamed trapdoor found Ann and the children terrified, choking with fumes, but otherwise unhurt. No one had told Tom that the natives might resent his action, but so incensed was he at this calamity that he immediately packed everyone on to the dray, and driving through the night and all next day returned to Melbourne. He swore he would not remain in such a 'Dang inhospitable country' with wild and murderous natives on the rampage. He would try New Zealand, where the natives were said to be more civilised and friendly. They had lost almost everything, but the sale of horse and dray gave them a passage to New Zealand in the *Blue Jacket*, one of the American-built fast Clipper sailing ships built at East Boston.

Early Days in New Zealand

Tom and Ann landed at Lyttelton early in March 1865 and to all intents and purposes stony-broke. Legend puts their cash at 2/6 (about 60 cents)!, which Tom spent on castor oil for a tummy upset in one of the children. According to his robust reasoning, this was a cure for most ills!

About the time that Tom and Ann had left England, Ann's brothers and sisters had also left, but had come to New Zealand. And so after trudging up over the Port Hills on the Bridle Path with their meagre possessions, they found their way to where Henry Kingsbury and his family had gone to live at Saltwater Creek, near Leithfield. Things were a bit crowded at the not over-large house at Saltwater Creek with the influx of Tom and Ann and their four children, so shortly after the Hayman family moved to Rangiora.

There, Tom worked for Mr Dampier-Crossley at 'Mount Grey Downs', and with a companion drove the first cattle that went by land over to the West Coast gold diggings. Their route lay up the Hurunui River, over the Harper Pass and down the Taramakau. It was here that Tom nearly lost his life in the flooded river, being washed off his horse, breaking three ribs and nearly drowning. Jim, his eldest son, recalls in his memoirs:

> *I remember Mother's anxiety about Father's long, long absence, no telegraph in those days! It was one night after dark that I sighted Father's face in the window of our home in Ashley Street, Rangiora, to which place Mother had taken us from Saltwater Creek. I was then old enough to attend Miss Dudley's Infant School.*

Cust

In 1867 the family moved to the Cust district, where Tom Hayman had bought a small farm of thirty-seven acres from Thomas Grey Conway, the holder of the original Crown Grant. It was there at North Moeraki Downs that they built a sod house of the type still preserved by the Ferrymead bridge on the road from Christchurch to Sumner, (circa 1865) with thick walls, thatched roof, and a huge fireplace which the children remembered ablaze with manuka sticks. There the family grew up under pioneering conditions, baking their own bread in a colonial oven, making their own butter and cheese, keeping hens and ducks for eggs, butchering their own animals for meat, and curing their own bacon. This last recalls a near tragedy. John was only a little fellow at the time; his mother, hearing terrified cries from the yard, rushed outside to find the family sow beginning to make a meal of the child! With a front leg on John's back, the sow had attacked his head, which was bleeding profusely. Tom came home: 'Drat you' he said, and that was the end of the pig!

Conditions were hard in the 1860's and 70's and theirs was the kind of life common to most early Canterbury settlers, and preserved in the memoirs of many families. Tom Hayman was one of those who built the first Cust School of sun-dried bricks, around which centred the community life of the district, in which the family took a full share. Tom was an excellent worker, ditching, fencing, building sod banks, ploughing, harvesting etc. Few could equal him in the handling of a scythe. There is a story told which illustrates this, as well as exhibiting his puckish humour and love of a contest. The scythe men used to work as a team, each cutting a swathe of the standing grain crops as they circled the paddock. This day Tom was in the lead. His mates thought it would be a good joke to gang upon little Tommy, as he was called, and 'drive' him. Little Tommy, soon seeing what was afoot and tough as whipcord, cracked on the pace round the field, came up behind the team and 'drove' them with a 'Get on, get on or I'll chop your heels off!' Among other jobs the boys became skilled at binding sheaves with a handful of stalks of the grain, a twist, another twist, a deft tuck in with the thumb, and the job was done. Indeed they soon were able to work like men, with the consequent loss of schooling.

Many were the stories told in the family of the days at Cust. Of the great flood of 1868, filling the whole valley between the Cust and the North Moeraki Downs. Of the whole family (eleven children then) off to Church in the dray. Of the time (speaking of drays) they were on their way to a tea meeting at Cust in the tip dray when the pin came out, and ham, chicken, salads, cakes, dishes, plates, cutlery everything and everybody cascaded onto the muddy road! Tom was no doubt in his own way a pioneer, but Ann, coping with a large family in what we now would call extremely primitive conditions, was even more of a pioneer. There are stories of going to school across the swamp, jumping from niggerhead to niggerhead. Their first teacher was John Dobson, a brother of the Dobson who was murdered on the West Coast by the Burgess, Sullivan and Kelly gang.

Willowby

After about ten years at Cust, the family moved in 1877 to Willowby, near Ashburton. By then there were twelve children, though little Thomas Ernest, born in 1872, lived only three months. Their father, autocratic by nature, was a strict disciplinarian, but it was to their mother they gave the devotion of their hearts. She was an excellent manager, wise, of great natural dignity, and her Christian teaching and example were reflected in the lives of her children, and also in fact in the community, where neighbours received many a kindness. With no modern aids to housekeeping, the girls learned the value of hard work as the basis of cheerfulness, cooking, washing, sewing, knitting, mending etc, as did the boys in the outside world and on the farm.

The move to Willowby must have seemed like a patriarchal progress, with the bearded father in the dray with the mother and younger children, and Walter and John driving the stock. They lived first in a rented house at Winslow while Tom and the elder boys built a sod house of the familiar pattern at the new farm. Six weeks after their arrival, Florence was born at Winslow. Here we might spare a thought for Ann, six weeks from her delivery, travelling ninety miles in a springless dray on the roads of 1877 and also having to ford some of the rivers!

Tom had bought 250 acres on Chatmos Road between Boundary and Main South Road, 100 acres in the homestead block, and 150 acres in the 'top section' about a mile nearer the railway. The homestead, 'Ashfield', was three and a half miles from Willowby School and Church.

The sod house became the dairy when the permanent house was built. This was a well and sturdily constructed timber house of two storeys and eight rooms. Walter and John had a hand in the building of it. Grounds were spaciously laid out with a large orchard in front planted with many types of apples, plums and cherries. Shelter trees and hedges were planted, as the whole county was tussock in those days. A stable, loft and implement shed were also built.

The farm was a good one with light to medium soil, excellent for sheep and oats but hardly heavy enough for the sustained growing of wheat.

This was to be home for the next twenty-one years. Jim was the only one who did not come to live at Willowby, so that Walter, John, Jinny, Fanny, Sally, Emily, Charlie, Harry, Tom, Sam and Florence, made up the family. There, Rosa, Hubert (stillborn), Ernest, Arthur and Eva were born. It was there six years later that Ann their mother died at the age of fifty-one.

The Haymans were a high-spirited lot by all accounts and made plenty of fun for themselves. To grow up in such a numerous family was surely a rare experience. They were a community in their own right and also an integral part of that large community that centred round school and Church, and indeed they put down deep roots in the Willowby district. Sally, Jinny and Rosa married local farmers, Sam a farmer's daughter, and John and Harry daughters of the schoolhouse.

Centred round Willowby Methodist Church was a virile religious and social life, whose depth and reality has been demonstrated through the years, and no appraisal of the Willowby scene would be either adequate or true, which did not take this into account. Names could be given of a number of stalwarts of those days to whom the Hayman family owe a debt of gratitude.

Another pillar of what must surely have been a unique community was the Schoolhouse. There, Benjamin and Susannah Low, cultured, dedicated and of lovely character, taught the children of the Willowby School for many years. From the time they came to this country until their retirement, they had a profound influence, not only on generations of children, but also on the life of the district as a whole. Of their talented family, Susie and Flo married John and Harry Hayman. Ben (BA, BSc.) and Elsie (MA.) were teachers, and Daisy the youngest, became the mainstay of Corso in Whangarei. In her ninetieth year, Daisy (Mrs W Roberts) recalled how she enjoyed invitations to get into the crowded big four wheeler and go home with the Haymans after church, to lunch and tea and back to evening service. She too wrote lovingly of Ann their mother and of her grief at her death.

The Hayman Clan was very fond of choral music and part-singing. Tom himself had a fine baritone voice, and so supported the large and flourishing church choir, which under the guidance of the Wheeler family attained a high degree of excellence.

As the family grew up, the Hayman boys, when not working the home farm, went out contracting, ploughing, reaping, threshing, chaff cutting, stripping grass seed etc. Much grain was grown on the plains in those days, especially on John Grigg's estate at Longbeach, with some of the larger fields of crop stretching beyond the horizon! There were times though, before the shelter belts had reached an effective height, when the raging nor-westers, tearing down out of the mouths of the gorges, piling up the worked ground and burying the fences, allowing the stock to roam at will!

With the extensive plantations that cover the plains now, it is hard to realise that firewood was very difficult to get back then, and coal was dear to buy. It became a regular trek for some of the boys to go to Peel Forest with drays to bring back the winter's firing, and many were the stories told of this fifty mile round trip. Their adventures and mishaps were often connected with crossing the Rangitata River. Later, picnics at Peel Forest became an annual event, with an occasional week's camp there; perhaps this accounts for the family's delight in later years in camping holidays.

Tom was always the genial host, at his best carving the large roast, entertaining the 20 or more round the table at Sunday dinner, and watching out for the needs of the numerous small fry clustered around. It may have been on one of these occasions that small Emily, her plate of food having been cut up too finely for her liking, announced to the world at large that it was 'All momstered to pom!' It has been a family saying ever since.

Another philosophical remark came from Tom's laconic acceptance of the loss of a new ten-guinea ram, which he put in the same paddock with the original occupier. After mutual inspection, old and new backed off twenty or thirty yards and charged like mediaeval knights in a tourney, meeting head on with a crack like a gunshot. New fell dead with a broken neck, 'Howsumever, there 'tis. Let be how shalt.' was all he said. An equable man was Tom, and Ann was certainly a wonderful woman, sewing, and baking, washing and mending for her family, teaching Sunday School with a baby on her knee, catering for a table at Church tea meetings and at School. It was on one of these occasions that Rosa the baby was with her mother in the dray when the horse bolted. As the wheel went into the ditch and the dray tipped over, Ann tossed Rosa to safety on to a nigger-head.

Life at 'Ashfield' was not without its difficulties. Tom Hayman, though a great worker, was not a good manager, so that Ann was the real business head of the family. She was highly thought of for her ability by the business people in Ashburton. Both Mr Bullock and Mr Ferriman, wealthy merchants of that time, spoke with deep respect and admiration of her wisdom and strength of character. Her brother, Sam Kingsbury, had a shrewd business head, and Ann used to get his backing for her judgement on many matters. He recounted with some heat an instance when this was over-ruled. Soon after its establishment most of the Willowby farm was put into wheat. There was a bumper crop, which at the local price of 2/6 a bushel would have cleared off the mortgage. Walter persuaded his father to go for a killing and ship the wheat to England where at the time the price was double! Against the mother's strenuous opposition this was done. In the event they lost the lot, even having to pay something extra to square the account for the freight!

But by and large, contentment reigned in the home, thanks to that unique personality, Ann the beloved. Here is a tale told by an old couple about the days when they were young. They had newly come from Ireland, he willing to tackle anything, though both were poorly equipped for colonial life. His gently nurtured little wife had no training in household duties and Ann took the girl under her wing, teaching her how to cook and manage her affairs, mothering her in every way and giving her wise counsel. Many years after they still spoke of her with fervour. One of Ann's children wrote:

> *What a record! Only the initiated can hope to comprehend the unceasing drain on the physical strength and vitality of the mother who bears and rears such a very large family [Between the ages of nineteen and forty-five she had eighteen children with never an interval of more than twenty-six months between their births!] Yet Mother never allowed the strain of family affairs, endless duties, the weariness of the body, to break through her magnificent self-control, or cause her to complain.*

Is it any wonder her family almost worshipped her? How she made time to befriend, counsel and care for neighbours and all who needed help is beyond me. Truly Love is the supreme gift.

Ann Hayman's Death

In April 1891 Ann Hayman took ill with peritonitis following acute appendicitis. She was taken to hospital protesting that she could not be spared yet, but on the 12th of April she died. On her headstone in the Ashburton cemetery are the words: 'If to me one thought of Heaven be more bright than another, it is of Rest'. She had confided that that was her idea of heaven. Surely she had now found her rest!

The desolation of the family to whom she meant so much can be imagined, as also the profound sense of loss amongst her many friends in the district. Emily had to come home from Training College to nurse her Mother and look after the family. After she left Willowby the onus of running the household fell on the next two daughters, Florence and Rosa, fourteen and twelve at the time of their Mother's death. It was a heavy burden, there being nine in the family home at that time: the Father, Harry, Thomas and Sam, the two girls, Em, Arthur, and little Betty. Washing, ironing, mending, garment-making, scrubbing and cleaning, besides preparing the meals, taxed their strength; but it was all cheerfully undertaken and capably carried through. They baked all their own bread, churned their own butter, and pumped and carried all the water for their chores. Sundays brought numerous visitors for dinner and tea, as of yore, for they were resolved as far as they were able to fill their Mother's place.

In after years Arthur wrote a set of recollections, and some of them may be quoted here. He writes:

> Swaggers often turned up to be fed and watered and maybe bedded down for the night in the hayloft. Father attended to that of course. One afternoon when Rosa was about seventeen years old, a swagger called asking for food. The men were not at home, and Florence was upstairs. Rosa told him to wait on the porch while she rustled up something, but with a leering look and manner he pushed into the kitchen and started a line of palaver. Without hesitation Rosa got a chair and reached for one of the two shotguns over another door. The swagger let out a startled yelp, shot out of the door and away at high speed 'till he reached the road. Brother Tom, riding home from the top section, saw this and came home at a hard gallop to look into the matter. I may say that Rosa had never handled a gun in her life, but 'his nibs' didn't know that.

> To hark back to the days when I was just a little chap. Father and I were going home from the top section in the dray, when a very heavy hailstorm suddenly broke upon us. Dad was wearing only a jumper over his shirt, and this he gave to me, and so there I sat safe from hailstones as large as walnuts. Dad had difficulty controlling the horse, and I well remember the sight of his wrists and hands, bleeding from the battering of the hailstones.

At home family worship was routine every morning after breakfast with a Bible reading and a short prayer. In the evening, Dad liked to have the newspaper read to him, and when I was old enough that became my pleasant duty. He also liked a good novel, or a racy biography, and this I coveted too. It meant an extra hour out of bed, and besides, it was great fun reading to Dad. He had a keen appreciation of a good author and a well-told tale, and when I stuck on the meaning of a difficult word or situation, could be counted on to come up with its sense.

It has been told how Ann had to be manager and financial controller as well as mother, housewife and all the rest. Now that her guiding hand was gone, despite all his hard work, Tom fell into a morass of difficulties. Perhaps his lack of education was a heavy handicap; on the other hand, literacy does not necessarily confer sound judgement on anyone. Be that as it may, it fell to Sam, who eventually took over 'Ashfield', to carry his responsibilities and rescue him from his financial troubles. Though he survived Ann by forty years, that last half of Tom's life must represent a gradual decline from the plateau of those spacious Willowby days.

Tom's Later Years at Willowbridge

In 1897 Tom Hayman, then aged 60, sold 'Ashfield' to Sam, his twelfth son, and moved to a house at Willowbridge, which he had bought with half an acre in a corner of Walter's 'Opiro' property, which had until recently been part of the Studholme Estate at Waimate. A year later Tom married Louisa Jane Moore, a widow with six children. Louisa was a quiet, delicate woman, who after several years succumbed to T.B., and Tom eventually married Jane Hodgkinson, with whom he went for a trip 'Home'. They soon returned, saddened by the conditions of abject poverty they encountered in England. He said he would never have a shilling in his pocket if he remained there. He was fortunate in both his later marriages. Jane, who survived him, had a delightful sense of humour, was deeply religious, and despite the handicap of partial blindness, loved and looked after her man wonderfully well. Their mutual fund of jolly humour and fellowship of mind, their identity of interests, and her lively intelligence, made for them a very happy home.

As the result of two misadventures, and the onset of severe rheumatism, Tom became increasingly crippled during the last twenty years of his life. While he was working in a deep shingle pit, there was a premature fall, partly burying several men. Both of Tom's legs were broken, and a pick pierced one of them. While he was recovering in hospital, he declared that he 'wasn't going to stay in that toody show' and walked home eight miles. He was in such bad shape when he arrived that he was taken straight back to hospital.

On another occasion, while Tom was working on his punt it fell from its trestles and broke one of his legs. However he never complained and sturdily wrestled with his disability. While he could hobble along on his two sticks, he loved to go fishing in that same punt on the Waihao River. He was an expert at handling it, and knowing the river like the palm of his hand, could judge the best spots in which to find fish. He was also an expert with an eel spear at night. He was also a keen gardener, possessed of green fingers. While he was able to work it, the shallow gully in front of the house was a picture. It has been suggested that since his ability lay in this direction, the flair for tools, the inventiveness and very considerable practical and engineering strains which have developed in their descendants, probably came from the Mother's side. Who knows?

Here is a further picture from Arthur's pen.

> *Several years before his death, Dad then quite blind, wanted a weatherproof washhouse built for dear old Grandma, and asked me if I would undertake the job. So I borrowed Harold's truck, lifted Dad on board and we set off for Waimate to get the timber, iron etc. He had a lot of fun chaffing and playing verbal ball with the businessmen we contacted. After we had gone some distance on the way home, Dad asked, 'Where are we now, Art?' I told*

him we were nearing John Manchester's hill. 'Good' says he, 'I've got past that old cemetery again!' He enjoyed every minute of that trip, though the jolting of the truck must have been painful.

Toward the end of his life Tom was both blind and bedridden, but any comparison to the last of Shakespeare's Seven Ages would be quite false. He kept his lively interest to the end, and was always good for a joke and a shrewd sally. On the 7th July 1931 he died, full of years, at the age of ninety-four. He was buried in the Ashburton cemetery beside his Ann. It was impossible to mourn his passing. 'After life's fitful fever he sleeps well.'

'The Four Generations', 1924. Front: Tom Hayman, seated, with author on his knee. Rear: Jack and Walter Hayman (author's father & grandfather).

Walter Hayman

Of the eighteen children that were born to Tom and Ann, the second son, Walter (who in late 1919 became my grandfather), was born in England, and was four years old when his parents came to New Zealand. He also had very little schooling when he was a child and about six months when he was nineteen, under the tutorship of Mr Low at the Willowby School. He worked an early model portable steam engine and threshing mill, and owned one of the first self-propelled traction engines and threshing plants in the Ashburton district. In 1883 he took up land at 'Whatstone', and in 1886 married Elizabeth Frampton. In February 1888 my father John (Jack) Edgar Hayman was born. Walter sold out in 1896 and bought 'Opiro', a 360 acre property of the Studholme's 'Willowbridge' estate which he had won in a land ballot. He later increased his holding to 540 acres. The 'Opiro' homestead, a large brick structure, was begun in 1901, his brother John being the architect.

Aerial photo of 'Opiro' Homestead, late 1960's.

My father, Jack, was about thirteen years old then, and he carted most of the bricks for the new house from the kiln eight miles away, doing two trips a day with horse and dray carrying 320 bricks per trip. No wonder my Dad's hands were tough and gnarled! In all he carted 83,000 bricks from Quinn's kiln at Makikihi.

Before moving to Willowbridge, Walter was for many years an enthusiastic volunteer in the Ashburton Guards, then later he became a foundation member of the Studholme Mounted Rifles, with the rank of sergeant. This squadron had the honour to be chosen as bodyguard to the Duke of

York at Christchurch in 1901.

Walter did a considerable business dealing in sheep. In 1906, a dry year in Hawkes Bay, sheep were shipped from Napier to Timaru. On one occasion when driving a couple of thousand from Timaru to Studholme with a single dog, he nearly lost control of the very hungry ewes in the Pareora riverbed. He was also a successful exhibitor of Shropshire sheep, Shorthorn cattle, and also of his favourite horse, 'Kruger', in the fifteen-stone hack class.

Walter was prominent in Waimate and South Canterbury local body affairs. He was 25 years on the Hannaton School Committee, being Chairman most of that time, and also Chairman of the Waimate branch of the South Canterbury War Relief Society, a member of the A&P Association from 1899 and Chairman in 1922. He was also a Director of the Studholme Saleyards Company, an early member of the Farmers Union, and a member of the Timaru Harbour Board from 1907 till his death in 1934, being Chairman from 1924 to 1928. As a child I was intrigued with the telescope he had upstairs at 'Opiro', where he could read the names of coastal ships and then drive the thirty odd miles to Timaru in his Crossley car to assist attending to their arrival at Timaru. I spent many happy times when on holiday down at 'Opiro', inspecting the surrounding area from the balconies and upstairs windows with that telescope.

My Father, Jack Hayman

My Father was about eight when he accompanied his father on to the block of land at 'Opiro', making the journey down to Studholme by train, and then walking the three miles out to where the block of land was on the coast just north of the Waihao River. To mark the spot where a house was to be built, my Dad pushed his walking stick (actually a weeping willow stick) into the ground, which later grew into a lovely tree, remaining there for ninety-odd years.

Author's father, John Edgar 'Jack' Hayman

Times were hard in the early days at 'Opiro', so my Dad's education was pretty sketchy, but about the turn of the century, 1900, he spent six months at the Burkes Pass School where his Uncle James was teacher. He would have been about twelve at the time. At holiday times there were trout to be tickled and caught in the surrounding streams, and birds' egg collecting, some types of which, such as sparrows', thrushes' and blackbirds' eggs, were worth I think, from memory, a penny (2 cents) a dozen at the County Council office. Starlings were a useful bird for the farmers, so their blue eggs were not saleable. However by carefully putting a few ink spots on the large end, they could easily be passed off as thrushes' eggs! It was perhaps white-collar crime, but could you blame a twelve-year-old boy? Thirty years after I could also be accused of the same trickery.

Solid-tyred bicycles at this time had largely replaced the traditional 'Penny Farthing' cycles and Dad and another twelve-year-old took on the task of biking to the Hermitage and back to Burkes Pass one weekend: not a bad effort in those days of bullock wagon and horse cart roads. The Tekapo and Pukaki Rivers were bridged but lesser rivers had to be forded. No doubt it was a challenge for young boys. One thing they didn't have to worry about was punctures with their solid rubber tyres. On the return, after the slog up to the top of the Pass from Dog Kennel Corner (now

Haldon Corner), the bike being fixed pedal drive, the lads put their feet up on the handle bars and let gravity take them back down to the Burkes Pass township. My Dad used to say he never attained a speed like that again until the acquisition of a Harley Davidson motor cycle seven or eight years later. Dad's short sojourn at Burkes Pass ended when he had to return to 'Opiro' to work on building the new homestead.

The First Car

The Hayman Clan had its first association with motor vehicles in the early 1900's when Dr. Pitts of Waimate started doing his rounds in a horseless carriage, the first seen in South Canterbury. Not to be outdone, my grandfather, Walter, ordered a vehicle from England. A few months later, in 1906, a message came to the 'Opiro' homestead at Studholme, that a large packing case was on the wharf at Timaru consigned to 'Walter Hayman, 'Opiro,' Studholme Junction, South Canterbury, New Zealand'.

The following day Walter, and 18-year-old Jack, the eldest of Walter and Elizabeth's four boys and two girls, took the horse and gig to catch the train at Studholme for Timaru. They were well equipped with appropriate tools and soon had the packing case dismantled to reveal the shiny new Humber car. Petrol, oil and water were poured into the appropriate places according to the instruction book. Tyres were pumped up by the hand pump supplied, to sufficient pressure to take most of the bulge out where the weight was on them. With the petrol turned on and the controls set as indicated, the starting handle between the front wheels was pulled to swing the engine over a few times and the engine chuff -chuffed into life.

It was agreed my father should drive, so off they went, off the wharf, across the railway tracks and up Strathallan Street and turned south down Stafford Street where a local constable stopped them, saying: 'Halt! You can't have that infernal machine careering down the road! You're frightening all the horses. Someone will have to go ahead to warn of its approach.'

Humber car being driven by Jack Hayman, with family members, 1906.

So Walter got out and walked ahead with my father following with the Humber in low gear. This slow progress continued until they considered they were clear of the constable on his bicycle, and Walter then hopped in and they continued on their way to Studholme, no doubt frightening a few horses on the way.

Trains and steam traction engines had of course been around for many years, so the first motor vehicles should not have been too terribly unusual. But motor vehicles, which we now, in the 21st Century, take for granted, were not common 90 odd years ago, and it would be with great pride that Walter and Elizabeth would take the family to the Nukuroa Methodist Church a few miles distant, near the Hannaton School. Incidentally, my father usually drove, having a natural aptitude for mechanical things. Not that his father hadn't also, since by the time he was twenty, Walter had his own portable steam engine and threshing plant. Soon after this, he acquired one of the first self-propelled steam traction engines, chaff-cutter and threshing mills in the Ashburton District.

My Father followed in like manner, from the age of eighteen being in charge of and driving the Burrell traction engines and running the chaff-cutters and threshing plants, plus the ten or a dozen men that were required to run the operations in those 'Good old days!' Were they 'Good old days'? The work was physically hard and the days were long. The only comparison today that I can relate to out on the farms is shearing, where it still costs a lot of sweat per dollar! I always think it feels much more rewarding to know one has earned one's pay rather than receiving it on pay day whether one has done much or not. One thing in favour of those 'Good old days' of physical effort was, of course, that there was little unemployment!

Threshing Mill at 'Opiro', 1920's–1930's.

A Near Miss in the Crossley

The Humber served Walter's family well for many years until it was replaced by Crossleys, and I am reminded now of an incident that occurred round 1919–20, when the threshing was going in full swing down on one of the bottom paddocks at the home place, 'Opiro'. To keep the whole operation running smoothly and apart from the numerous other things that could cause hold ups and financial loss, an adequate supply of corn sacks was necessary to contain the grain that was being threshed.

To alert them back at the homestead that the supply of bags was getting low, Dad gave the customary three loud blasts on the steam engine's whistle. This signal immediately alerted Walter, his father, who hopped into the Crossley and shot off to Waimate to replenish the supply.

Returning shortly with a few bundles of bags in the car and some on the carrier at the rear of the car, but completely forgetting about the afternoon Boat Train Express, he drove straight over the level crossing at Studholme with a more than usual rip and a roar and hurried back to the field of operations. Low and behold, he had neither bundle of bags or carrier at the rear of the car. All had been swiped off by the train's engine!! How close can you get to a major accident? I might add that Walter was too shaken to go back to retrieve the needed bags. Someone else went and collected them from where they had been scattered. Walter never again took chances at the numerous level crossings in existence in those days.

Jack Hayman's Harley-Davidson

About 1910 my Dad purchased a Harley Davidson motorcycle from Andy McLaughlan, the cycle dealer in Waimate at that time, and he put that machine to good use during the next sixteen years, specially during the harvest season, to commute from home base at 'Opiro' to areas round the Waimate district, where he was operating the harvesting plant. This consisted of the Burrell traction engine, Clayton and Shuttleworth mill and Andrews and Beaven chaff cutter. There were, as well, a couple of bunkhouses on wheels, plus of course the cookhouse, commonly called 'The Stink': no doubt for obvious reasons!

Coming along also, somewhere in the vicinity, was the 'Water Joey', a horse-drawn dray containing a 200 gallon tank, which the Water Joey had to fill two or three times a day, usually pumping the water by hand pump from the nearest stream or water race. It was quite a laborious operation, and a lonely unpopular job, but the engines were thirsty coal burning machines that required a steady supply of water and coal to convert to steam power for their various uses. Occasionally the Water Joey would get access to a piped water supply to fill the 200-gallon tank. This was sheer luxury!

When moving from farm to farm as the various jobs were completed, the Harley would be lifted up through the rear door of the cook shop (stink) while my Dad drove the whole outfit to the next farmer's field of operation.

Cars and motorcycles back then had rubber tyres, but practically everything else travelled on iron wheels, which actually crushed the shingle roads of the time down to a pretty smooth surface. This great crushing and ironing effect on the roads was manifest up to the 1920's with the traction engines and large wagons that they hauled, carting the huge loads of merchandise that required moving in a developing country, such as timber, coal, fencing material, fertiliser, seeds, grain, chaff and of course wool, to the nearest railhead. I know up here in the Mackenzie Country, the engine driving contractor would be given an extra 80 kg bag of coal if he would drive his engine and following wagons a foot or so left of road centre on his journey to and from the different back country stations. This resulted in a much broader ironed-out surface for the early motor vehicles, and of course horse drawn gigs and buggies etc. By the 1920's, motor trucks with their solid rubber tyres and later pneumatic ones brought the demise of the traction engines. Steam power inevitably had to give way to the more convenient and faster transport, as we know it today.

But to get back to my Dad and his Harley Davidson twin cylinder motor bike. Land had been leased on the south side of the Waitaki River at Hilderthorpe, which required him to visit frequently to tend the sheep and monitor the crops he had growing there. The bridge across the Waitaki River over which he had to cross was at that time and indeed until the 1950's shared by both road and rail traffic. It spanned a distance of one mile! Not many vehicles back in the early days of motoring had speedometers, and least of all, Harley motor bikes. My Dad had naturally estimated that if one could travel one mile in one minute, you would be attaining the breakneck speed of 60 miles per hour, a hair-raising speed for those days of usually rutted, corrugated and pot-holed shingle roads on a top heavy narrow tyred motor cycle which was also sharing the highway with mainly horse drawn traffic, and of course, while crossing the bridge, trains! But an advertisement for Harley Davidson motorcycles had stated once that it was 'the fastest thing on two wheels' and that a top speed of 60 miles per hour could be achieved. And so on several occasions, with his cycle salesman friend, Andy McLaughlan, as pillion passenger, with watch gripped firmly and the second hand accurately counting off the seconds, Dad would roar round off the road and down along the planking by the rails at full throttle. With heads down and peaked caps turned rearwards they would thunder over the planking. It was a race against time! They didn't always reach the optimum speed; but with a bit of minor adjustment and tuning and good conditions, they frequently achieved the one-mile in one minute! As many roads were measured off in miles from the nearest Post Office with numbers attached to the roadside telephone poles in those times, you might wonder why the bridge was chosen for these bursts of speed; but the wooden bridge which was in good order at that time would have no gig, dray or wagon wheel ruts or pot-holes, and of course was straight. Other slow traffic was always a possible hazard, and the train timetables always needed to be kept in mind!

During his early motorcycling days Dad added a sidecar to the Harley. This proved invaluable for getting spare workers from their homes, or off the train, or taking injured men in for treatment etc, or getting spare parts for machines or taking worn equipment home for repairs in the evenings.

From the Harley to the Maxwell

The sidecar on the Harley was a very much-envied means of transport at a time when the train or horse transport were the usual ways to get about. Dad never had any trouble getting someone to accompany him on his short excursions, whether younger brothers or sisters or friends, one of whom was Lilian de Carteret Griffin, a friend and fellow student of Dad's sister Daisy at Canterbury College in Christchurch about 1908–1910. Lilian came down on the train from Christchurch on occasions to visit Daisy at 'Opiro'. My dad, Jack Hayman, then in his early twenties and the owner of the Harley and sidecar, was no doubt a bit of a heart throb for Lilian, the youngest of the family of four girls. Gallivanting about the Waimate district over a few summer holidays, the couple became engaged.

Then came the occasion when he was returning from the train station at Studholme with his future bride in the sidecar and the wheels of the Harley got into the winding and deep ruts of a farm dray, with the bike and sidecar ending up on its side with the occupants thrown over on to the grassy roadside. This event didn't go unnoticed by Walter, who had been observing their progress through his telescope from the homestead's upstairs balcony. As there was no apparent movement after the accident, he popped into the Crossley and hurried down the drive a half mile, to where the Harley was on its side with the sidecar in the air. The vehicle's occupants were not in the least bit injured, but were simply lying in the sunshine on the grass, laughing. Walter didn't, I might add, see the joke, and vowed that motorbikes were not suitable machines for his future daughter-in-law to be travelling in. He immediately ordered a Maxwell two-seater car, with a dickey seat at the rear for passengers or luggage etc.

The young couple were thrilled with their new car with its windscreen and fold down hood until, that is, they were presented with the account for its purchase price! That little Maxwell, though, served them well from their wedding in 1914 until 1923, by which time they were well established up here at 'Tasman Downs', where a more robust and larger vehicle would be better suited to the rough roads, flooded and unbridged streams, snow and greater distances to travel.

My Mother and her Family

Dad married the then Lilian Olivia de Carteret Griffin in 1914 in Morrinsville, where her father, the Reverend Thomas Griffin, was minister of the Methodist Church.

Griffin Family – Thomas & Lydia (author's maternal grandmother), Lilian Griffin (baby) the author's mother, & her sisters, Maud, Ella & Adelaide.

She was the youngest of four daughters. Her sisters were Ella (Mrs Charlie Schneider), Maud, a missionary and school teacher in India and later Fiji, and Adelaide, who took up nursing and later became Matron of the Cashmere Sanatorium in Christchurch. Their mother, Lydia de Carteret Griffin, came to New Zealand as a seven-year-old child with her parents, Jean and Rachael de Carteret (née Le Gros). Jean had become disenchanted with his occupation as a teacher in the Channel Island of Jersey, and so he and his wife Rachael decided it would be better to emigrate to New Zealand where land was becoming available. The possibility of getting his sons settled on farms was a great attraction.

The family, Samuel a teenager, Stephen twelve, Annie nine or ten, Lydia seven, Emma, and Matilda who was just a baby, left Jersey on 30th May 1859. They were delayed in England for a month or so due to Lydia developing what appeared to be chicken pox. They had to disembark from the *Natoka* just prior to her sailing for New Zealand, but apart from the cabin baggage, all their other worldly possessions had to remain in that ship's hold. The family stayed in lodgings at Gravesend 'till the next boat to New Zealand left on the 20th of August. This ship, the *Nourmahal*, got them to Auckland three and a half months later on the 6th of December 1859. Appendix 1 is the diary of that journey written by Jean de Carteret. This journal was translated from French to English by my cousin's husband Oliver Mourant (a Jersey lawyer), a number of years ago. The original French diary is preserved in the Alexander Turnbull Library in Wellington.

Three births and a Death

For five years my mother and father, John Edgar and Lilian Hayman, lived in the Cottage at the front entrance to Walter's 'Opiro' property, and here their three children were born: Pat, Betty and I, Bruce.

The Author's mother with daughters Pat (standing) and Betty, 1918.

Unfortunately Pat (Patricia) died in 1919 of a burst appendix just a few months before I was born. She was just three and a half years old. She could have been saved if Mother's bossy sister Adelaide, a qualified nurse, had kept her nose out of things and let the child be taken to the Waimate Hospital only ten or eleven miles away, where Dr. Pitts would have easily removed the offending object and saved Pat's life. Adelaide's treatment with 'Dinnefords' was a narrow-minded, tunnel visioned idea of a cure for a child's lower abdomen pain by an inexperienced nurse! My father wouldn't speak to that sister of my Mother's for years after that! Mother of course was terribly distressed, but I wasn't going to be concerned by events in the troubled world outside, and unwontedly arrived on Boxing Day 1919, six months later.

'Tasman Downs'

'Tasman Downs' was originally taken off 'Balmoral' station in 1878 by a Mr Newlands, a Christchurch gentleman and an absentee owner. The property being 500 feet lower and only 18 miles distant from Andrew Cowan's 'Tekapo' station, was acquired by him and used for wintering his younger sheep on turnips etc. and for the growing of oats for chaff for horses etc.

About 1900 'Tasman Downs' changed hands again when Emil Schlaepfer, a Swiss, took it on for twelve or thirteen years, during which time a land swap was transacted with the neighbouring runholder of 'Braemar', 'Tasman Downs' getting 180 odd acres on the north side of the Braemar Road in exchange for a more sloping block down towards the Tasman River. Emil Schlaepfer sold out in 1914 to Mr Herbert Elworthy, the prosperous owner of 'Craigmore' station near the Pareora Gorge in South Canterbury. He had 'Tasman Downs' stocked with 2000 two tooth Romney ewes from his property down there.

But Mr Elworthy only owned 'Tasman Downs' for a year before putting it on the market again and my grandfather, Walter, bought it. He did so because my Dad's sister Daisy suffered from T.B. and was advised to get up to the higher drier atmosphere of the back country in preference to the damp conditions near the sea coast. Sadly, she only got as far as Fairlie, where her condition deteriorated and she was forced to return to the hospital at Waipiata, out of Dunedin, where she died.

The cold snowy wintery conditions of the Mackenzie Country with no grass and practically no hay were more than the Romneys on the station could endure, and more than half of them died that first winter! However the prices for wheat, oats and chaff were good in the war years and the Clydesdale horse teams were kept busy working all the arable land on the 1800 acre property to keep up with the mortgage repayments. Walter was, like most of the previous occupiers, an absentee owner, just motoring up from 'Opiro' on the odd occasion for a night or two. Managers were employed to attend to the day-to-day operations.

The buildings consisted of a four-stand blade shearing shed with night space for barely 100 sheep, and a chaff house and stable with about 8 spaces for feeding chaff to the horse teams and riding hacks. It contained room for storage of 250-300 sacks of chaff and also a 16ft. square room for harness, saddles, horse covers etc. (This room became the schoolroom in February 1923, when my Mother started the 'Tasman Downs School'.) Accommodation was limited to a 14ft. by 16ft. kitchen dining area and a 14ft. by 12ft. bedroom. A single bed, lean-to room had been added at some time, and this was known as the Boss's Room, for his occupation when visiting. There were also a couple of former mobile huts that were of the type pulled behind the steam driven traction engines and haulage plants and thrashing machines. These were the abode of the single men employed, and could accommodate quite a number in bunks and stretchers. Sleeping bags were not around then and comfort was achieved by covering oneself with blankets over whatever you had available or chosen as a mattress, which in the times of low prosperity often consisted of sacks containing straw or chaff. One's personal comfort was not a priority for many then, when to be indoors and to be fed and have enough cash for tobacco and an occasional binge was luxury. (I should mention here that alcohol was not to my knowledge ever in any Hayman household. I brought back the habit from my experiences in the 1939–45 War. However I kept the insidious habit under wraps until after my mother's death in the 1960's.)

Cooking was done on the old black Orion stove, which incorporated on the opposite side of the firebox and ash drawer an eight gallon water tank, which of course had to be replenished through a lid on the stove top as the hot water was drawn off through the top at the front of the stove. The firing of the stove was basically coal, as wood was scarce and hard to chop up to the small size required to fit the firebox. Water was carried in buckets from a spring about 100 yards away from the house. Why it hadn't been piped over nearer I don't know. Those sort of luxurious improvements didn't come 'till my Dad arrived in 1920.

Part Two

Life at 'Tasman Downs', 1920-1941

When in June 1920 my parents took over the 2000 acre high country property from my grandfather, 'Tasman Downs' was only marginally economic. All neighbouring stations averaged 25 to 30 thousand acres, with our nearest neighbour having 65,000 acres. My parents moved up there when Thomas Wheeler, the manager of 'Tasman Downs', gave his notice of departure and Dad was told by his father: 'Johnnie my boy, you had better go up and look after the godforsaken place 'till we can get rid of the bloody thing!'

Panorama of the Tasman Valley, c 1925. 'Tasman Downs' (left side of bottom photo connects with right side of top photo). Homestead to the right.

'Tasman Downs' may not have been godforsaken, but it was certainly remote. It was 45 miles to the nearest town and railhead at Fairlie, 84 miles to Timaru, and 18 miles to the Tekapo Hotel, where the mail and papers were delivered by the Mount Cook bus three times a week. Even in these modern times we still have to go the 18 miles to Tekapo for papers, mail, etc. I might add that we seldom go just for mail, unless it is for something urgent such as machinery parts, registered mail etc.

First Memories

It was in July of 1920 that we as a family arrived at 'Tasman Downs' in the little Maxwell. I would have been seven months old. Now this is hard to believe, but I often reminded my mother of going through the gate between Tekapo and Balmoral and proceeding up the much bumpier and narrower Braemar Road. The only glimpse that stuck in my memory was being in a pram with tassels round the hood and seeing about 200 yards of road back to that gate from where the pram was in the Dicky seat at the back of the Maxwell. I must have been propped up enough for that glimpse of the world to become imprinted in my memory. Mother always rejected the idea that I could remember that scene back in July 1920 when I would have been less than seven months old, but as she said, that was the only time that the Hyde Park wicker basket style pram with me in it was ever in the back of the Maxwell.

I also recall was when I was three years old and Mother was starting the Tasman Downs School with the eight or nine local children on the 6th of February 1923. I guess I also wanted to join my sister and the other children going into what had been the harness room of the stable, but which the Education Board had refurbished with desks, maps, a blackboard, storage cupboard, wind-up clock, inkwells and a kerosene heater. An Aunt who was here at the time was called over to take me away, as my vociferous protestations on the Schoolhouse steps were a noise distraction for Mother's new pupils. I recall screaming and kicking my Aunt as I was being carried back to our house.

My next vivid memory is of my sixth birthday, when after apparently being reasonably well enough behaved, I received a tricycle. Prior to that my most prized possession was a home knitted Gollywog, black of course with red lips, white eyes and black curly hair. I no doubt eventually loved him to death! Poor old Sambo.

Since the 1980's the purists or whatever they call themselves have banned the use of words describing dark-skinned people, like Niggers or Wogs, Redskins etc. One of the best musical groups of the mid-1900's on radio and TV unequalled for melodious harmony, swinging beat and easy listening were what they called themselves 'The Nigger Minstrels,' later known as 'The Black and White Minstrel Show'. 'The Ink Spots' were another small group of four American Negroes who produced some beautifully harmonious recordings in the 1940's on the 78 rpm records of the era. I have tried to get hold of some of their reproductions on tapes on CD without success.

The Reo
In 1923 the Maxwell was changed for a largish six cylinder Reo with the customary side curtains and fold down hood. It was also of 1914 vintage. It had, seemingly, plenty of power and was up on 25-inch wheels. The tyres were 35 x 5 inch. It was a bit thirsty, like most cars then, but 18 to 20 miles to the gallon wasn't, I guess, too bad. After all even today in our 4WD ute we only get 26 mpg; but then of course we usually travel twice as fast.

That old Reo served us well for the next 12 years, when Dad changed it for a Straight 8 Hudson sedan that had been used by a Mr. Scott of the Texaco Oil Company and had done about 100,000 miles. Incidentally 'Texaco Scott' as he was commonly known as, reputedly always drove at 60 mph., a good speed for the mostly corrugated shingle roads of those days. He was apparently quite a character back in the early 1930's as he travelled round from service station to service station, selling and displaying his oil company products, which he carried in the back of the Hudson.

There are one or two incidents involving the Reo car that I can recall that are worth mentioning. The furrow legs of the plough had become badly bent, and it was beyond Dad's capability to get them set back right again, on our little forge. My Father was an excellent blacksmith, but a complete plough was a bit too heavy to handle. So the wheels etc were removed and it was hoisted up with endless chain gear to a large tree branch. Then the Reo with hood folded down, and rear seats removed, was backed underneath; and the plough and was lowered aboard with the plough beam ends protruding two or three feet either side.

When it was securely roped on, I and my sister Betty, 18 months older than I, got in amongst the plough and went with Mum and Dad to Timaru, where the plough was straightened at Wallace and Coopers with the aid of their powerful steam hammer. It was apparently a fine day as I don't recall having any problems keeping the day's groceries and purchases dry that we were sitting amongst with the plough in the back. There were no plastic bags back then. Brown paper was the norm. I think I was about six or seven at the time.

1914 Reo car with the author and his father, c.1928.

Punctures were an accepted feature of motoring in the early decades of the twentieth century, and most careful motorists carried at least two spare tyres, plus a tyre repair kit and of course a tyre pump. Flat headed fruit box and packing case nails, worn out horse shoes, horse shoe nails, bits of metal brushed off the rims of cart or wagon wheels etc. were the main cause of punctures. Small nail holes in the inner tube could be pumped up enough to get you the last few miles to home, or repeat pumping every 10 or 15 minutes was sometimes better than grovelling round in the muddy or dusty shingle in one's Sunday best clothes. Dad always wore knee high gumboots on most journeys and took his shoes under the seat. Of course his trouser legs would be carefully folded inside the gumboots to preserve the neatly ironed creases.

The monthly, or whenever, journeys to Timaru and beyond always had to start at 6 am. Dad's day would start at 4.30 am, with the house cows to be milked, separating to be done, pigs, dogs, horses etc to be attended to. Then came breakfast, and if wintertime, when all water-cooled engines were drained, two three-gallon buckets of hot water had to be taken to the garaged car and the radiator and engine block filled. Anti-freeze cooling systems didn't seemingly come into popular use 'till well into the 1950's. However the cars were easily started with warm water already in them.

I don't know why we never cottoned on the anti-freeze up here in the Mackenzie Country till about 1955. After all, the liquid-cooled aircraft engines used in the 1939–45 war were cooled with a glycol mixture. I first tried an anti-freeze product that came on the market about 1955, in a 1949 Chevrolet Fleetmaster I had purchased second hand the year before, from Dr. Charles Halstead. By that time it had done just on one hundred thousand miles, but was in pristine condition. However the introduction of the anti- freeze mixture to its internal organs resulted in the softening and or loosening of the rubber hose connections, resulting in a spectacular boil up of rusty liquid splashing out and about the engine compartment on its first journey with the new coolant! I've never had any trouble with anti-freeze since and wonder why it hadn't been more readily available before.

But to get back to the 1920's and our 1914 model Reo car. It had not been converted to be driven on the left side of the road and so had the steering wheel on the left side, which was the norm for America. Four wheel brakes hadn't come into vogue then, but the Reo's rear wheels, apart from brake shoes on the inside of the brake drums, also had brake bands externally on the outside of the drums. The outside band, apart from being applied by the hand brake, also was operated by the clutch pedal when depressed practically to the floor.

This arrangement made it ideal when stopping or starting off again on a hill! However Mother hated it as she always operated anything mechanical in a forceful manner, and so when changing gears, in her way of thinking, the clutch required pushing right to the floor. Half way down would have been sufficient. It had quite a long movement; but when pushed right down the car would come almost to, and sometimes right to, a stop and so stalling the motor and then having to get going again in low gear. It was a crash box but withstood the moaning and groaning and gnashing of teeth remarkably well. I don't recall anything ever having to be done to the gearbox. Automatic and synchromesh gearboxes came later, and today changing gears is a practically effortless movement and done almost without thinking.

Most warning device horn buttons are and were located on the centre of the steering wheel; but the Reo had its horn button located on the side of the driver's door at about knee height. In this position it could be operated without taking ones hands off the steering wheel. Dad invariably made a feature of this with strangers, especially children, by telling them that the car was equipped with a sixth sense, and could warn birds or animals and people or other vehicles of its approach. So at the appropriate instant the Klaxon type horn would sound, with its distinctive sound announcing the vehicle's approach. All very mysterious to the uninitiated.

Another tricky idea Reo had was a device on the exhaust system supposedly to increase the power when ascending steep hills. This device was a hinged metal flap arrangement situated on the exhaust pipe at its forty five-degree bend from the manifold down pipe to the underfloor section to the muffler. This device, operated by a small handle on the floorboards, enabled the driver to open the flap and enable the exhaust gases to be discharged directly down towards the road. This of course resulted in the exhaust note increasing to aircraft engine proportions and road dust being blown up in large clouds. When used, this was immensely enjoyed by me as a small boy as you could well imagine. Whether it had any beneficial effect on the vehicle's progress is doubtful, but it certainly sounded impressive. It made conversation in the car difficult, however, and so in spite of the numerous hills on our roads was not used much, despite my pleas. Carbon monoxide poisoning had not been thought of much I guess back then. Anyhow the canvas hood and floppy side curtains let in enough draft to dispel the danger of poisoning.

Another gadget that came with that car, and which was most useful when on the road at night, was, as Dad called it, the 'Trouble light'. This light on about ten feet of flexy wire could be plugged into a socket on the dashboard, as we do these days with electrical gear into the cigarette lighter socket. They hadn't cottoned on to cigarette lighters in cars in the early 1900's with their 6-volt electrical systems. When switched on, the base of the assembly, which shielded the bulb and held it in place, became magnetized, enabling it to be held in any desired position on the metal body of the car. This was immensely useful when attending to any problems at night and especially for changing tyres etc.

From about the mid 1930's punctures became less and less frequent. One thing which helped considerably was the introduction of a vehicle with a large magnet energized by a motor, which picked up most of, if not all the loose scraps of metal nails etc. A couple of trips over the major roads were probably sufficient to clear the offensive metal bits from the surface.

The Roads

Having the roads sealed of course made a big difference to the motorist. The first section on State Highway 1 in the South Island was the 10 or 11 miles from Christchurch to Rolleston, which was concreted in 1932. By the beginning of the Second World War most of S.H.1 in the South Island, had been tar-sealed, to a large extent by the Contractors known as

British Pavements. By that time the Timaru to Pleasant Point section of S.H.8 had also been sealed.

No more sealing was done then 'till after the War, 1945–6. I guess all towns and villages are now connected by sealed roads, and with the advent of vastly superior tyres, punctures are extremely rare.

Some other glimpses of motoring I think are worth recalling. For instance bridges were not always considered necessary except for crossing the major rivers. Lesser streams were bridged with fairly lightweight materials considered strong enough to carry light traffic, up to 30 hundredweight (one and a half tons). These structures were quite OK for cars, horse drawn gigs and drays, but trucks, buses etc had to ford the streams. A problem would also arise after a flood, when the river had changed its course and no longer flowed beneath the bridge. There were no bulldozers then. They didn't appear 'till the late 1930's. Horse drawn implements and picks and shovels etc could take weeks to repair the damage and so fording streams was all part of motoring especially in the back country.

A classic example was the 11 miles from here at 'Tasman Downs' to visit the Burnetts at 'Mount Cook' Station. I decided on one visit in the late 1920's to count the number of streams on the journey. During the hour the 11 miles took, we went through 43 streams, some only trickles but two or three up to the axles. And remember there were no four wheel drive vehicles back then! Also I counted, as I had to open and shut them, 12 gates. Visiting one's neighbours was an interesting exercise, and if possible accomplished on a fine day!

The weather was, however, not always fine and dry on other journeys we had to make, and flash floods with heavy rain and or quickly melting snow were always a possibility. There were three or four bad places on the Braemar Road between Tekapo and home here where we were held up at times. If the floodwaters looked menacingly deep, Dad would get the five-foot by eight-foot canvas cover out from under the back seat where Betty and I would be sitting. The cover would be clamped down tight under the bonnet and the other end pulled well back between the front wheels as far as it would go under the engine compartment. It was then a case of going through the floodwaters at about 10 to 12 miles an hour. It nearly always worked. The only times it didn't was when the rear wheels lost traction on the wet gravel on the slope up on the far side. This would result in having to attach short lengths of chain to the rear wheels. There would be no show of putting on a full set of chains when nearly up to your waist in water. We always seemed to get home and then of course, for Dad it was the cows to be milked etc. Were those the good old days? I suppose the chains should have been put on first before entering the flooded ford; but of course 99 times out of a 100 the faithful old Reo would scratch her way through on her big wheels.

Dodge truck stuck in snow: author's father shovelling: 1937

On one occasion we were stuck in the flooded Maryburn Stream. We had with us a distant relation, Freda Williams, who with Betty and me was up on the back seat nursing items of groceries etc that had to be kept up out of the water swirling round on the floor. The front wheels were nearly up the far slope of the ford and so the engine was clear of the water. We had been stationary for a few minutes while Dad was clearing rocks and loose shingle from round the rear wheels with the shovel, a necessary part of equipment back then. In fact I still carry a shortened shovel in the

4WD vehicles today. At this stage Freda called out to Dad, 'How far is it to 'Tasman Downs' from here?' The reply was 'About six miles'. After another burst of noise from the motor and a bit of backwardsing and forwardsing, Dad was again asked how far it was to Tasman now. To which he replied, 'About six inches less than it was the last time you bloody well asked.' Dad was not given to swearing; but on an occasion like this when he was up to his waist in freezing cold water and struggling to get us going again, I think it was justified! However we got going again on the next attempt. I would have been about seven at the time.

It was not long after this that traffic was held up at Edwards Creek, half a dozen miles south of Tekapo. We were returning from town in the late afternoon and cars were being towed through the floodwaters, which as usual were not going under the little bridge. An enterprising fellow with two Clydesdales would yoke a chain round the front axle or on to one of the front spring and chassis dumb irons, then sit up on the bonnet and for ten shillings, pull you through. If however you gave it a go and stopped in midstream the price was two pounds: four times as much. We hadn't any cash on us apparently, and Dad wasn't going to get the cheque book out, so he rugged up the front of the car as usual, and in spite of Mother's protests that it would cost us four pounds if we got stuck, we drove successfully through. I guess we were lucky, or at least enterprising.

On another occasion coming back from Timaru in the late 1920's the stream at Mawaro, between Cave and Albury, was in high flood. There was no bridge there then but the nearby farmer, Mr. Wreford of 'Clanaborough', could see the opportunity to make a few quid and so was there with horses pulling stuck vehicles out for five pounds or pulling you through for one pound. I remember Dad saying, 'Well he is not getting any of my money' and Mother replying, 'Surely you're not going to try driving through there. It looks pretty deep.' 'We'll use the railway bridge, it's just there,' said Dad. So we backed back about fifty yards to where the road to Mawaro crossed the Fairlie railway line and straddling the rails, with the car wheels on the sleepers either side, went bumpity bumpity all the way across to the level crossing at the farm driveway on the other side. I can still remember well giving a cheeky wave to the people in the dozen or so vehicles waiting their turn to be pulled through.

We didn't wait to see if any other enterprising motorists followed our idea of using the railway bridge, but the one foot gap between the sleepers was no problem to the faithful old Reo on its 35x5inch tyres.

As mentioned previously, tyre tube punctures and blowouts were the accepted hazards of early motoring days with the beaded edge and cotton type rubber impregnated tyres of the times. What wonderful improvements have been made to motoring these days with the advent of nylon and tubeless tyres. I think that the better tyres on vehicles are the single most important advance in motoring as we know it. In the 21st Century one would be unlucky to get a flat tyre in a hundred thousand kilometres!

One evening in the late 1920's after getting back into the Reo after shutting the last gate on the way back from Timaru, Dad remarked, 'Well that old rear tyre is going to get us home again.' That remark must have put an idea into my head. So getting a paper bag which had held bananas or such like from the large cardboard carton of groceries on the rear floor, I carefully blew it up and when the car was bumping over a rough and rocky patch down our mile long drive, I banged it down on my knee, creating a loud shot-like explosion, and then by swaying from side to side, created the impression that we were travelling on a flat tyre. Dad wasn't impressed at having to get out and prepare to change the tyre when so near to home. However on discovering all was well and realizing that it was only a paper bag that had burst, merely remarked, 'You young devil!' Some time later on another journey when I tried the same trick again with a bursting paper bag, the response was not at all hilarious. I was about six or seven at the time.

The Dunedin Exhibition

In December–January 1924–5, Dunedin hosted a quite extensive exhibition and we got all excited about going way down there and staying with friends, and apart from what ever the exhibition held in store for us, there was the added prospect of riding on trams, cable cars etc. I was nearly five when we went. On the morning of departure we took off pretty early. The last few hundred yards of our drive to the mail box and front gate was very rough at the time, so Dad chose to go on the nearby grass, which was much smoother. Then suddenly. Bang! The front wheel had dropped into a large rabbit hole, unseen in the long grass. The hole had no doubt been considerably enlarged by the energies of an enthusiastic dog. Be that as it may, the Reo had broken the left-hand front spring, and the axle was holding on by the front half of the top spring leaf. The chassis had dropped down about seven or eight inches on to the axle and remains of the spring.

'Well that's it,' said Dad. 'We'll have to go back. We can't go down to Dunedin with the car all lopsided like this.' So down to the yard we went with considerable sobbing and anguish. However, Dad wasn't going to be beaten, and in about an hour had jacked up the car and clamped a block of wood and half a dozen short sections of old car tyre for the chassis to rest on and we were on our way again. You didn't have to worry about Warrants of Fitness in those days. I gather that another front spring was fitted while we were at Dunedin for the week.

I think we went most days to the exhibition and on one occasion on going through the turnstiles I was held back for a minute or so while someone checked the numbers. Apparently a gold watch and chain was to be presented to the one-millionth visitor. As it has turned out in my life I wasn't destined to be lucky. On this occasion I was the 999,999th. visitor. A middle-aged man received the watch. There was no second prize!

I can't recall much of what was exhibited. I had a ride or two on some of the things in the amusement park; but the highlight of it all that I remember most, was my first introduction to a form of ice cream. This was a small block of ice cream about the size of an oblong chocolate biscuit wrapped in silver paper. It was probably sporting a vanilla flavour and was enclosed in a silver paper wrapper and was known as an Eskimo Pie. I was allowed one or maybe two per visit and ever since have been addicted to ice cream in its many shapes and forms. Is it fattening? It hasn't had that effect on me; but then perhaps I don't get as much as I would wish if I had lived nearer the shops. However my wife Linda makes a very desirable ice cream mixture which I enjoy once or twice a week.

On the morning of Christmas Eve 1924, we left our friends the Blakes in Dunedin and set off for my Grandfather's farm at 'Opiro' near Studholme Junction, where we were going for Christmas. As we journeyed along at our usual 35–40 miles per hour and were negotiating some of the winding road through the farmland south of Palmerston, there was lying on the side of the road a neatly wrapped boot box sized, interesting parcel. We had better pick it up. After all it was Christmas Eve and no doubt someone's present had fallen off a previous vehicle. The brakes were applied and we stopped about 50 yards past the intriguing looking parcel. Dad ran back while we watched him bend down to pick it up. He didn't quite get his hands on to it before it suddenly shot off the road, up the bank and under the hedge accompanied by gleeful laughter from the children on the end of the retrieving string. Dad was told, 'You are the 15th car that has stopped this morning'. No doubt it was a harmless and healthy amusement for those country children. I know we have laughed about the incident many times since; but I guess this was only one of many times that sort of trick has been played.

An Epic Journey

In the winter of 1923 the good old Reo was forced to make an epic journey. Most of the 18 miles from here to Tekapo, apart from a few cuttings and sunny slopes, was virtually a narrow sunken rocky track about eight or nine feet wide and averaging two feet deep. This was the way the earlier bullock wagon teams, horse drawn carts and wagons and steam traction engines had, with the help of the rain, pounded the tussock covered soil, sand and shingle down to the old glacial rocky moraine deposits. It was no racetrack! The average time for the 18 miles was about an hour, but winter conditions were a different thing altogether, mainly due to drifting snow. With the reformed road conditions, frequently graded fine shingle surface, concrete bridges and gates replaced with cattle stops, 25 minutes is about the norm now for the 18 miles to Tekapo.

That winter back then had been a long one, with many falls of snow and nor-west winds which had piled the snow in deep drifts in the lee of the south sloping terrain, not forgetting the fact that the road was filled at least to the surrounding surface or more in many places. No wheeled vehicles had been along the road from 'Guide Hill' Station to the Forks Bridge near the main road for sixteen weeks!

I had started complaining of earache during August of that year. I was three and a half years old. The single wire earth-return telephone line was still working OK and could be maintained in adverse conditions from horseback. Dr. Talbot, the ENT (Ears, Eyes, Nose and throat) bloke in Timaru was contacted, and Mother was advised to watch my temperature and also told that a few drops of olive oil in the ear might soothe the pain. My temperature was well over 100 F. but the olive oil did seem to soothe it a bit. Getting the olive oil to drop in my ear was a problem as the temperature was down to zero Farenheit: minus 32 degrees. I remember the teaspoon of oil being heated over a candle to get the warmed oil to pour.

Conditions at Tasman back then were pretty basic. There was no electricity, and only a basic weatherboard-clad timber-framed iron-roofed, four-roomed dwelling lined with paper, patterned according to one's choice, and pasted on to hessian scrim tacked to the walls. This may have been O.K. in average conditions but in the severe winters of the early 1900's did little to keep our bedroom warm. It was part of our getting up in the morning requirements for my sister and I to empty our hot water bags and hang them up again on the nail back in the kitchen. This could be difficult, as on many winter mornings the water would be frozen solid! The woollen covered rubber bottle would of course have been pushed well down the bed away from our little curled up but warm bodies under our woolly blankets and duck feather-filled eiderdowns.

The tank was of course kept full to overflowing by the constant pumping of the hydraulic Ram operating by the spring water 170 feet lower down the slope near the Tasman River. A kettle of hot water or the heat from a kerosene blowlamp could usually persuade the water to flow from the tap at the tank before covering it up again. The long drop dunny (loo) down the path caused no problems except the discomfort to the user!

Anyway, by morning a trip to hospital was considered urgent. So the car was prepared with chains fitted and another sack full of horse harness chains was put on board along with a full kit of tools, picks, shovels, crowbars, axes, lengths of timber, jacks, wire, water cans, petrol etc.

It was a fine enough day when we left about 9am, after another −30° overnight temperature. Betty was dressed for the occasion and directed to walk over to 'Braemar' Station, about one and a half miles following the school children's track through the five to six inches of snow that was about all we had down here by then. One of the Murray girls was coming over to meet her.

The first three and a half miles to the Cassie's place at 'Guide Hill' Station, we reached with a few minor problems with iced or half iced-over creeks and some snow drifts which required only two or three bashes at, to get through. But from there on the snow was deeper and the sunken road and its numerous twists and turns round hummocks and cuttings on hillsides had trapped snowdrifts to alarming proportions.

The nor-west winds had shifted a lot of snow into the lower areas and the treeless Mackenzie countryside was like a Siberian wilderness. A few northerly facing steep slopes showed a few tussocks and rocks, but the road in most places of course was well filled with wind-blown snow. Some fences were showing in places and of course the phone line poles could be clearly seen as they stitched their way over the hill. The line did not necessarily follow the road and in many places was up to half a mile away. As Dad had assisted in erecting the phone line many years previously and had done his fair share of its maintenance he had a rough idea of the terrain it followed.

The road line up through 'Guide Hill' had to be followed in many places and this required an hour or so of snow shoveling, backwardsing and forwardsing and bashing one's way through the drifts and prodding with the shovel handle to ascertain the most suitable path to follow amongst the rocks and creeks etc, of the open country. We had to get back onto the road for a bit to get through the Maryburn stream where Dad changed from digging snow with the shovel to breaking a track through the ice in the ford, with a pick and crowbar. When he considered it was sufficiently broken up the old Reo was forced to gnaw its way through the water and ice up the slope on the far side with the aid of its chain clad wheels. At this stage the normal car tyre chains had been ripped to pieces and replaced by wrapping draught horse harness chains round the tyres and between the spokes of the wheels.

One wonders how the cars back then stood the strain of the abuse they were subject to endure, on the ill-formed roads and open terrain where was considered that if a horse could get over it then surely a bloody motor vehicle could also!

I might add here, that the four wheel drive vehicles as we know them now, at the beginning of the 21st century, wouldn't have made as good a fist of it as the old 1914 Reo did seventy-five years ago, the main reason being that they are built too low. Have you ever had one stuck in a foot or so of hard packed snow with all four wheels spinning in mid air? You either need a winch or else do a lot of digging or wait till the snow melts.

However our old car did succumb to its treatment another hour or so later near the top of the 3,000 foot high Irishman Hill, where we were bashing our way through two to three feet of snow along by the phone line. Upon backing off and having another bash at it, there was a terrific commotion and clattering at the rear and I saw the floor boards at the back being thrown about from where I was peeping out over Mother's shoulder from under her big black rabbit fur coat. The car was at a complete standstill. The damage was inspected.

The rear flexible fibre universal joint on the drive shaft had finally given up the struggle and disintegrated leaving the three short arms on either ends of the drive shaft simply holding shattered remnants of fibre bolted to them. We didn't have a spare one of them. Later on we always carried one but for the next eight or nine years that we had the car we never needed it even though the one on the front end of the shaft would have been in use for over twenty years!

So there we were immobilized, not even half way to Tekapo yet and well into the afternoon. Cold water in one of my hot water bottles was replaced with hot from the engine. Then Dad went to work on repairs. The split pins, nut and bolts were removed from the three spider legs on the shaft ends, the front piece put back on the splinted shaft end at the front and the three spider legs were then bolted loosely together and we were mobile again, forcing our way up and over Irishman Hill and following the phone line down to the Irishman Creek bridge and hut, where there was a phone. Our progress was reported and my condition was to be relayed to Doctor Talbot in Timaru. At that stage my earache was severe and my temperature nearly 104° F.

Some olive oil was warmed and soothingly dropped in my ear. Hot water bags were filled with hot water from the engine and replaced with creek water. The car had boiled quite a bit at times due to the cooling effect of the radiator being blocked at times when the car was virtually being used like a snowplough forcing its way through the drifts. At those times some of the water was replaced by packing snow into the radiator with the cap removed. It is a tedious job to get much in when the engine is boiling and trying to blow it back out again.

However, we were now about half way to Tekapo and an open road, and from here on it was mostly flattish to downhill. We achieved that eight to nine mile section in not much more than one and a half hours, arriving at the Tekapo Hotel as the sun set at about 5 p.m. Eight hours for eighteen miles. I guess it might be classed as a slow speed record!

It is only right to say here that the Mackenzie County Council had earlier on tried clearing the Braemar Road with the horse-drawn equipment available at that time; but with a six or eight team of horses tramping on the snow and packing it down a snow plough being pulled behind did little

49

in the way of clearing a road and horse drawn graders were equally ineffective, unless on freshly-fallen snow. Crawler type and Caterpillar tractors started appearing about the late 1920's and snowploughs could then be pushed and roads cleared more effectively.

There was a hard winter I recall in 1938 when the area up here received nineteen falls of snow and the Braemar Road was cleared twenty three times! During the latter part of that winter, when intending to go out or return it was necessary to phone one's intentions as the snow was piled up from six to ten feet on either side leaving no room to pass other vehicles.

However, to get back to our snowy journey when I had to be taken down for a mastoid op on my left ear.

Upon our arrival at Tekapo, Dr. Talbot was contacted again and as my temperature was bordering on 105° F., dangerously high, the time factor was now critical. He brought the necessary equipment with him and journeyed the forty miles to Fairlie where we were met at the Fairlie Maternity Cottage Hospital (now the Moray Home for the elderly). The twenty-seven mile journey from Tekapo to Fairlie took us nearly two hours on the icy, snowy rutted road, but apparently we were in time for the successful completion of the minor but critical operation, which, it was stated, saved my life.

The universal coupling on the car was repaired and Dad returned home a day or two later. It was blowing a warm Nor'wester by then and though the road was still mostly choked with snow, the surrounding tussock land was negotiable through the softened snow with a new set of chains on.

One of the men from 'Braemar' Station had been attending to the hens, cows and dogs during our absence, but on entering the house we found the warmer atmosphere had thawed the frozen pipes, which had been burst and so the water was pouring out under the kitchen door. What a welcome home!

Dad, what an effort and struggle you went through with the old Reo to enable me to enjoy life for another seventy-five or so years. All I can say now in your absence is 'Thank you.'

Hare and Rabbit Shooting

A distinctive feature of the Reo, as with many American cars of the fold-down hood type, was the windscreen, which was divided horizontally, enabling it to be also folded in half. This feature was ideally suited for night shooting rabbits and hares, which have always been abundant up in these areas, though with the introduction of R.C.D. (Rabbit Calicivirus Disease) in the late 1990's the rabbit population has been reduced dramatically, thank goodness. There are, though, still quite a number of hares around.

Dad's Uncle Arthur (my great uncle) who was actually only four years older than Dad, had been badly gassed in Flanders during the First World War, and found the dry Mackenzie Country air was beneficial in helping his wheezing and restricted breathing. He used to stay up here quite frequently whenever the opportunity offered. Dad and he were great mates and I in my youth always looked forward to his visits. He was a crack shot as was my Dad also, with the double barrelled 12 gauge. Arthur had come back from the war with a five shot Browning Automatic.

From the time I was seven or eight, I was allowed out with them on these night shoots, my job being opening and shutting gates, picking up the shot hares and rabbits, breaking the necks of the wounded ones, etc. What fun it was. Dad was driving on the left hand side, of course, in the Reo and keeping the prey dazzled with the moveable spotlight clamped to the side frame of the windscreen, while Uncle Art blasted away with the screen folded and the spent shells being ejected out over the front door. It was really deluxe shooting while sitting in the front seat. Oh yes. There was some fun to be had back in the 1920's.

I of course also thoroughly enjoyed these nocturnal excursions standing up, hanging on to the back of the front seat and standing up to my knees in bleeding furry corpses. The back seat would have been removed but the car's rear compartment always took a bit of cleaning out. That was sometimes my job, while the rabbits were being skinned in the morning before school. Good undamaged buck rabbit skins could be worth almost the price of a gallon of petrol, but shot damaged ones were worth only a few pence. Hare skins didn't appear to be worth anything.

On the subject of hares, though, they do a lot of damage to pasture and crops, and especially winter-feed turnip crops for the sheep. Consequently these crops had to be ring-fenced with rabbit proof netting, temporarily tied to the existing fences with binder twine. Naturally, of course, when there was some snow on the ground, hares would come down off the surrounding native tussock country to feast on these succulent delicacies. The odd one would push its way under the netting where it was a bit insecure from the rocks and clods of turf placed to hold the netting down. These odd ones would be shot next day before putting the sheep back on.

One year, about 1929 or 30, when the hare tracks could be seen spreading out for miles around like the spokes of a spider's web, and converging onto a beaten track round our 40 acre paddock of turnips, it was decided to have another go at eliminating some of the greedy sods. So late one cold moonlight night, Uncle Art, Dad and I converged on the paddock and at the half dozen places where we had, the afternoon before, tied the netting up sufficiently for the hares easy entry, we quietly cut the string and securely closed the netting down again, with the rocks and spade sized turf clods. What hares were still on the turnips we trapped! We didn't get them all, as I can remember the odd one getting out while I was shutting the netting section I had been allocated. There was even the odd one getting out between my legs as I was cutting the retaining string over the opening.

Next morning after breakfast on Saturday, we went back up to the turnip paddock where we meet up with Mr. Jack Cassie, who had been asked down to join in the fun. What a sight met our eyes. The paddock was alive with hares standing, hopping, running, eating and squatting everywhere. A shot or two were fired at the nearest ones and then what a commotion. They took off in a rush like an avalanche, heading for the far corner where they piled up in a tangled heap, feet deep. In fact some of the ones on top, in the confusion, were literally being pushed or falling over the top of the three-foot high fence. In a few seconds the living heap of hares dispersed and scattered back over the paddock.

In an hour, the supply of shotgun cartridges was exhausted and so a supply was borrowed from George Murray at 'Braemar'. Even I, with a supply of plump grape-sized stones for my shanghai, was in need of a few more pocketfuls. I got quite a few with my homemade fork-stick rubber bands from old car tyre tubes and boot leather pouched shanghai (catapult).

Hares don't appear to have very good vision straight ahead. You may have noticed that as they flee from potential danger, and if not being closely pursued, they will stop occasionally and look back sideways with one eye, before continuing on their way. This trait enabled me to get a good shot with the shanghai, as the odd one came hopping along by the netting, looking for a place to escape. I had acquired the use of a shanghai at a pretty early age, having been shown how to make one by Dad's younger brother Jim, and so at the age of nine or ten, was no mean marksman! Even now, 70 odd years later, an unruly farm dog cannot be entirely free from getting a bit of a tickle up at anything under 25 yards. But no dog has ever come to any harm by my hand, and they respect you for the discipline. An irregular-shaped pebble whizzing past nearby is all that is required to bring an over-exuberant dog to heel.

Eventually, with the help of a few sheepdogs, we got the turnip paddock cleared of live hares. When we had counted them all up, there was the easy to remember number of 365! I don't know what happened to them all but no doubt the neighbours' dogs and ours had a hare diet for a week or two. After all they would keep well for a while in the frosty winter conditions.

Rabbits? I can't recall anything about rabbits being included in the bag that day. You would think that there would have been an odd one; but if so, they would no doubt have found a burrow to lie low in and with the task of getting all the hares that the dogs were keeping on the go, the odd rabbit burrow would have been overlooked.

After the 1939–45 War, hare carcasses acquired a value when frozen and shipped to European markets. The eastern side of the Tasman Valley, where the terrain sloped down the old glacier moraine bed towards the Tasman River, was apparently ideal hare country. During the 1950's numerous hare drives were conducted in the area. Fifty or sixty enthusiastic shooters would be invited to bring their shotguns and with ammunition supplied, be instructed by the Drive organizers to spread out in a line about 60 yards apart along the terrace top, three miles or so east of the rabbit proof fence near the Tasman River. These drives would usually start about 10am. And with plenty of talk and shouting to one another and the odd good, well-trained foxy or similar rabbiting dog along the line and the odd shot to be heard, the hares would be lifted from their squats and get in range of the shooters. In not much more than a couple of hours they would converge in a semicircle down at the rabbit fence and the last victims be put in the saddle bags of the packhorses which had been following behind in the hands of some of the local shepherds or non shooters.

The copper would be boiling, full of steaming hot saveloys, and with plenty of buttered bread and mugs of tea, lunch would be had at the nearby homestead, here at 'Tasman Downs'. The hares would be counted and then the buses and other transport would get everyone back up to another five or six square mile block ready for the afternoon drive, over on 'Braemar' Station, after which refreshments would be served etc, and the day's hares counted to be taken away and frozen. The proceeds would be going to local schools, football clubs, Salvation Army or some such worthy cause. The number bagged was always many hundreds. These drives were a welcome social event where many folk could see one another and have a good day out. I think everyone enjoyed themselves, except of course the hares!

We haven't had hare drives up in this area now since the early 1960's. Different neighbours these days have different ideas about some things. It's a pity. In some ways, life in the isolated areas was more sociable in those days; but better roads and vehicles make people more independent and of course television has cut out the get–togethers with evening card and board games, and community singing round the piano.

Communications

One of the most useful amenities of the 1900's had been being connected to the national reticulated network in the form of a party telephone line, privately owned and maintained by the station owners to which it was connected. This phone system enabled the people on the six properties of our party line to converse with one another, but getting connected to the outside world depended on the proprietor of the Tekapo Hotel answering your call and plugging you into the other party lines or the main one that went on up to the Hermitage at Mount Cook. It wasn't always possible to get connected through the Tekapo exchange if the proprietor or staff were busy with meals, pumping petrol, sorting mail, milking cows or whatever.

The line consisted of number 9 gauge galvanized wire attached to an insulator on top of hardwood sawn poles spaced 40 to 50 yards apart and sufficiently high above the ground to eliminate the possibility of horse riders being decapitated.

The system worked on just a single wire with an earthed return. This could result in poor reception in very dry conditions if an adequate earth had not been established. I recall our earth wire was connected to a copper radiator from an old truck. This was buried deep in the garden, beneath the downspout from the house roof guttering. Not scientifically designed by today's standards, but it worked pretty satisfactorily for just on 50 years. The system was operated by a pair of one and a half volt dry cell batteries in each telephone apparatus fastened to a wall in the house. To make a call you had to first lift the handpiece off its hook and enquire if others were using the line by saying "Working?". If you recognized the voices on the line you could sometimes join in the conversation or as some people did, just quietly listen in, or as usual wait for the line to clear when the "ring off" would be heard.

To make a call the generator handle on the side of the machine would be turned to send the appropriate call sign to the person you wished to make contact with. The numbers were basically morse code, one turn of the handle being a short and three turns a long. One turn also indicated a ring off. It was most annoying if people forgot to ring off and you were waiting to put a call through!

The calls on our line were:

Mount Cook Station	D
Braemar	T
Tasman Downs	A
Guide Hill	S
Godley Peaks	M
Glenmore	R
Exchange	L

We put in a double copper coated line in the early 1960's which enabled us to have dial phones, and then in the 1990's we were hooked to the world network through radio translator link from the top of Mt Mary to a dish type aerial on a pole in our yard. No more fear of people listening in to your conversation now I think. We now have a fax machine, internet, walkie telephone and cellphone reception.

What enormous strides communications have taken in the last century. TV has also been available here since the late 1960's.

Mileage Markers

Another interesting innovation that was added to the network of telephone poles in the early 1900's was that the Mackenzie County Council thought it was a worthwhile expense to have the mileage marked off along the roadside, starting at the Post Office in Fairlie. The numbers were cast onto half inch thick cast iron plates 8 inch by 10 inch and fastened to the phone poles about 6 feet from the ground and at 1 mile spacings.

My memory has it that a Jack Small was one of the 2 or 3 council staff assigned to do the job of putting the numbers up the poles. They were required to measure the miles accurately with a one chain (22 yards) steel measuring tape, 80 of which represented a mile. Progress would not have been particularly fast, but on reaching the Burkes Pass Hotel (13 miles from Fairlie) and settling in for the night and some liquid refreshment they agreed that a better method of counting off the miles was required. Many years later I heard Jack Small telling my dad how they simply measured the circumference of the dray wheel, tied a rag to a spoke and counted the number of revolutions it took to traverse a measured mile. Progress was much improved from then on and the miles were marked off all the way to the Hermitage (about 94 miles) at Mount Cook, down to Black Forest on the Haldon Road, through to 'Godley Peaks' Station on the Glenmore Road and up past our place on the Braemar Road to 'Mount Cook' Station. The 43 on the pole near our front gate indicated a distance of 43 miles from Fairlie. The mile pegs were a very useful method of directing travellers on back country roads. I guess all those markers are gone now as the poles have been removed for better and more modern telephone systems.

Back in the horse era, and slow not always reliable motor vehicles, to know how far you had travelled and how much further you had to go was some sort of comfort. Now distance seems irrelevant and is just measured in the time it is estimated for the journey!

Our Water Supply

About 1918 a water supply was established at the Tasman homestead for the Wheelers (cousins of my dad) who were then managing the property. This water supply system operated through the workings of an hydraulic ram situated adjacent to an adequate natural spring down near the Tasman River and 150 vertical feet and half a mile distant from the homestead.

These rams operated on a principal whereby 90% of the water required to operate the valve mechanism was wasted and only about 10% was pumped up the 3/4in galvanized pipe to the 600 gallon tank at the house. It worked with very little attention for 35 years. It was then that Lake Pukaki was first dammed and raised 300 odd feet, thus drowning the ram and spring.

At the time of establishing the ram pumping water supply, my grandfather Walter and my dad, who were getting it established finally got it going and then waited for the supply pipe to fill and start filling the tank. It finally started trickling in and at the sight of which Walter remarked, "I could keep that up myself on a cold day"! However, it did pump about 200 gallons a day which, with careful use, kept the house supplied.

We were encouraged to use the "long drop" loo whenever possible, and the flush toilet only sparingly.

When the raising of Lake Pukaki caused our water supply spring ram etc to be submerged the Ministry of Works gave us £50 to get ourselves an alternative water supply from the spring nearer the homestead. This proved to be unsatisfactory as its supply dwindled considerably in dry summers. I, however, established a gravity flow supply from another spring half a mile further back up the valley in the horse paddock which was fairly trouble free apart from occasional air locks, supplying us for the next 20 years. In the mid 1970's, when the lake was raised 150 feet, the complete homesteading of house, yards, buildings etc had to be moved to higher ground. This resulted in a completely different source of water having to be located, the result being that a 2 inch alkathene pipe was pulled in by a MOW D8 bulldozer from a spring-fed stream three miles distant in the neighbouring property, 'Braemar' Station. As a road was eventually constructed along the eastern side of the then-to-be-filled Lake Pukaki and this road being fenced on the property owners' side, the lower paddocks of 'Tasman Downs' Station were denied access to water which had previously been available. The new piped supply therefore, besides providing the homesteading location with adequate new water, was also destined to provide stock water to that area now virtually dry. We now have about ten ball cock controlled water troughs to check and maintain, and they have served us reasonably well but natural running water is hard to beat. We have had to pave an area extending a couple of metres around all the troughs with boulders and paving stone rocks. When the frosts start in the winter months all the troughs have to be drained and the ball cock shut-off valves removed and the supply lines turned off. Supplementary feeding of stock can only be carried out in paddocks that have natural running water. This is not too much of a hassle as with the water races that I have made about two thirds of the farm has running water of some sort.

'Tasman Downs' homestead prior to the dormitory wing being added in 1938. Lake Pukaki was distant in those days!

    I picked up the basics of water race surveying and forming back in 1932 as a 12 year old. Mr George Murray of the neighbouring 'Braemar' Station employed a surveyor to measure off paddock acreages and design water races around hillsides etc. During the Christmas holidays and probably other odd weekends Ken Meson (one of Wattie Meson the teamster's sons about my age) and I were commandeered to assist in these operations. I won't say we were employed as no monetary reward was offered, as back in those depression day there was very little about, an example of which could be illustrated by the occasion of the annual Tekapo sheep sale. About that time whole mobs of sheep were being knocked down for 10 shillings per mob. George Murray simply took some of his sheep that hadn't raised a bid over to the Tekapo lakeside and cut their throats. The expense of taking them back to Braemar or elsewhere was more than they were worth. No-one lived at Tekapo back in the 30's except the "Dry" hotel proprietor, the Hunter-Westons, Gould and Joan at Mount John Station and Lucy Wills of 'Tekapo' Station. As many sheep perished during the more severe winters of the times back then, a few more along the lakeshore only added to the carnage for the gulls, hawks and other carnivorous predators.

But to get back to surveying. Ken and I were loosely known as the "chainmen" for Jock Nansen the surveyor. We had to measure off the distances surveyed with the use of the surveyor's chain, a number of links which measured exactly 22 yards or what was known as one chain. When taking the levels for water races to be established we went ahead with the chain measure and a pole about 12 feet long, clearly marked in feet and fractions of an inch, which could be clearly seen by the surveyor through his magnifying and levelling theodolite tripod mounted instrument.

When the correct levels had been established we had to mark the places where the water races were to go with either a stick or by turning up a spade full of turf for the teamster to follow with the first furrow of the plough, coming along later with the horse team pulling a "Martin ditcher". A few times up and down the length of the excavation usually enabled the water from a creek's source to be let in at the top end and the finishing touches to be completed with picks and shovels.

I might add here, that neither Ken nor I, even as 12 year olds, were strangers to the use of these implements. It was interesting and exciting to see water flowing along hillsides and unusual places where in nature's plan of things it had never been planned to go!

One of these diversions on the neighbouring 'Braemar' property, under the watchful eye of George Murray, after supplying water to stock in half a dozen Braemar paddocks, was also able to get water into 2 or 3 paddocks at the north west corner of our property, and eventually flowing on down and boosting the meagre flow in the creek near our homestead. This stream is still flowing well 70 years later, with the help of more up-to-date machines to keep the embankments in place and clear the weeds and sediment build-ups.

Twenty five years later, in the late 1950's, when after the loss of 500 acres of 'Tasman Downs' to power development with the raising of Lake Pukaki, it became evident that more use should be made of paddocks on the northern eastern side of the property. This land was OK for cropping but grazing was limited due to having no water unless after a period of heavy rain. If a water race could be designed to get water out of the north east branch of Boltons Gully Creek and traverse the rolling contours for a mile or so to the lowest saddle in the next ridge it would put water to a large area of my now 1300 odd acres. Surveyors were expensive, married life with 4 small children didn't encourage saving and I was endeavouring to pay off the mortgage, which incidentally I did achieve after a further 25 years.

There was a 30 inch long wooden spirit level on the place that Dad or I had used for house and shed building that could be used for getting levels no doubt. I made a wooden tripod about 40 inches high with a couple of adjustable legs and a swivelled top attachment, also adjustable. At each end of the level I attached a 1.5 inch long aluminium strip to be used as sights. One was filed down a 64th of an inch lower than the other end. This I figured would give a water flow of about 1.5 inches to 25 yards. I took my apparatus up to the low part of the ridge and sighted back up to where the creek crossed the road near the boundary fence. It appeared possible that the water could be made to flow down to that place: but the world is round and a spirit level shows a straight flat surface.

I got a 2 x 1 batten about 6 foot long, found a black rubber ring that fitted around it but could be moved and enlisted the help of John Hogg ('Guide Hill' neighbour) to hold the baton at the 20 to 25 yard intervals when I had sighted the level of the rubber band and he would then push a short length of willow stick in the ground at that place. I always had the exact height from the last stick in the ground to the top of the spirit level sight edge. In this way we moved along the proposed water race. We then with the International M tractor pulled a single furrow along centred on the line of willow sticks and made the first cut, followed after with a Martin ditcher. My primitive surveying turned out to be surprisingly accurate and the water followed our excavations extremely well with only a very small amount of hand work around large boulders or difficult ridges. That water race services a dozen or so paddocks and adds a considerable amount to the life blood of the farm.

Boarders at 'Tasman Downs'

In 1936 Mother started taking in boarders to supplement the number of pupils at the Tasman Downs School. The Tekapo School didn't come into being 'till 12 or 14 years later, and one of the first two children who came to board was Joan Trott from the Tekapo Hotel. The other early boarding pupil was Jean Keen from Timaru. Her father, John, was supervising the running of the Timaru Woollen Mills at the time. Jean was a wheezy, delicate seven or eight-year-old at the time and the high dry Mackenzie Country air was thought to be beneficial for her condition. Four years later, when she left as a 12 year old, she was as healthy and fit as any young girl could wish to be. The number of boarders that Mother took in rapidly increased to 12 primary school-aged girls, and along with a cook and a matron, there were 17 of us at 'Tasman Downs' in those days. She kept the boarding establishment going until 1945.

Pupils exercising in the snow outside the 'Tasman Downs School', 1940's. (Photo accompanying a newspaper article.)

The Hudson

In 1934 our faithful 20 year old Reo had served us faithfully for 12 years, and had done countless thousands of miles, so Dad upgraded from the canvas hood and flappy side curtains. We got a two-year-old straight eight Hudson Sedan. It had already travelled sixty odd thousand miles under the hands of the Texaco Oil Company's agent, a Mr. Scott, commonly known as 'Texaco

Scott.' He reputedly did his rounds between service stations on the almost entirely shingle roads of those times, at an average speed of 60 miles per hour. That Hudson was well run in when we got it! I was a 14 year old boarder at Timaru Boys High School at the time and felt very proud when Dad and Mum first came with the Hudson. My sister Betty would have been a daygirl at Craighead Diocesan School then and boarding out privately.

Bruce and Betty Hayman, off to Timaru Boys High School and Timaru Girls High School boarding establishments, 1933

The Hudson was called on to transport boarders to and from the bus as it passed through Tekapo, or the train at Timaru and always with a trailer load of luggage and masses of groceries, farm requisites etc. It also had to endure, often, chains on the rear wheels to cope with the snowy and boggy conditions on the Braemar Road before the 1950's. Even so, the Hudson only let us down once, when a rear axle broke on the way home, just as we pulled up at our mail box only a mile and a quarter from home! It of course also had to face the numerous inadequately bridged and often flooded streams that had to be negotiated then; but with a good sized rug or the cover off the trailer tucked under the front of the bonnet and left to trail back under the motor, we always seemed to be able to get back home. I sometimes wonder really how we coped with those conditions, and the car engines with carburettors and ignition distributors mounted so low down on those old side valve engines. Those so-called 'Good old days' were not always that good. Not if you still had the house cows to milk when you returned from a not always uneventful journey.

Author and his father setting out on a camping trip around Nelson and West coast, 1940, in their 1932 Hudson car.

'Beach'

We had got to know the Keen family through the home spinning knitting and weaving hobby that had developed in the area through the inspiration of Lieutenant Commander Richard Beauchamp RNVR, who had walked up into the valley here in the mid 1920's looking for a job. They were fully stocked with men at 'Braemar' so we, who didn't normally employ anyone, gave him a job here. Dick Beauchamp or 'Beach' as he was commonly called had quite an influence on our little community. He had ice skates from England and as skates here seemed unprocurable, my Dad got to work and made up six or eight pairs of skates for some of the school children. Dad had only hand tools back then in 1926, apart from a smallish blacksmith's forge, cold chisels, punches, hand drills, hand emery wheel, hammers, rivets etc. There were no gas torches, welders, metal shears, power hacksaws, electric grinders, sanders, drills etc, that we take for granted these days. But skates were made out of old files forged to shape with the fire and anvil and riveted to shaped scrap metal sheet salvaged from discarded implements, rusty water tanks etc. These skated were screwed on to the soles of suitable old boots etc. We all learned to skate on these early models. It was not 'til the late 1920's that better designs of skates became available at the sports goods stores.

We were snowed in that winter for months. Dad rode on horseback out to Tekapo a time or two for mail etc, and Beach suggested that if he had a pair of skis he would ski out to Tekapo. So Dad selected a couple of Australian hardwood three-by-one inch battens that were set aside for making gates. With Beach's directions and assistance with planing and shaping, a pair of skis was made in the next few days. Bindings were improvised from horse harness straps, dog collars etc. Suitable lengths of Macrocarpa branches were shaped up for poles. Beach went off to Tekapo where he stayed the night and returned the following day with a pack-full of essentials. I can still visualize the occasion on that beautiful clear sunny winter's day, with Beach, standing on the sky line ridge nearly a mile away and 200 feet higher than our homestead, yodelling at the top of his voice to capture our attention. Then when he observed a few of us out in the snowy yard, he started his descent. None of us had ever seen anyone on a downhill ski run before. The snow here would have been not much more than five or six inches down here at that time and well crusted, and I guess it would have been not much more than a minute before he arrived before us at the yard gate, with a snow-bronzed look of exuberance on his 29 year-old face.

Those skis are still here along with a pair my Mother bought about that time. Wooden of course and no edges as we know them now.

Beach was the son of Sir Harold and Lady Beauchamp of London, Sir Harold being a Harley Street Specialist and Physician to King George V. When mail was seen to be posted to Lady Beauchamp and letters coming back to our mailbox, addressed to Lieutenant Commander R R Beauchamp RNVR, it was too much for George and Mrs Murray at 'Braemar', next door, to resist. Beach had to go over there. Apart from Bruce and Gerald, then in their twenties, there were also a couple of eligible daughters fast growing up! I might add that there wasn't much privacy in our local mail then, as we all depended on one another to get mail etc from the Mount Cook Bus drop-off depot at the Tekapo Hotel on Tuesdays, Thursdays and Saturdays. But we depended on one another on this road, for neighbours to put papers, mail etc in our boxes, a mile up the drive at our front gate.

There is still no delivery in much of the back country; but with much improved roads and more comfortable vehicles we mostly get our own mail, papers etc from the Post Shop at Tekapo, 18 miles distant. I might add that it is often a week or so sometimes before the occasion arises for a journey out, but two or three times a week, it seems now, one or other of the family are on the road.

Getting back to Beach; he was at 'Braemar' for a year or so, and married Molly Murray. Lady Beauchamp came out to New Zealand a time or two and brought out Beach's daughter Elizabeth, whose mother had died just after her daughter had been born. It was the loss of his wife that persuaded Beach to get as far away from England as possible. Coming up here to the back country of New Zealand did just that.

Beach took on running the Tekapo Hotel for a while before building 'Penscroft', the first house in the now Tekapo township, that is, apart from the Black's and then Hunter-Weston's 'Mount John' Station homestead.

While Molly and he and their young children were at 'Penscroft' in the early 1930's, Beach took on the 'Mount Edward' block, the mountainous area of Lucy Wills's 'Tekapo Station'. I don't think this proved to be a particularly lucrative enterprise, and what with heavy snow losses amongst the sheep, and low wool prices in the depression years, 'Mount Edward' was sold and a home spinning and weaving industry was carried on back at 'Braemar' for a year or two, with Elizabeth riding her pony over here for her primary schooling, along with the children of the married couples from

'Braemar', the Greens and Inesons.

Author spinning, 1932.

Beach and Molly, with a number of children, went on teaching and school administering, mainly at Maori and underprivileged children's schools – a far cry from commanding a destroyer at the Battle of Jutland in the First World War. He was a great fellow whom we all admired very much, and I was especially fond of him.

Childhood Toys, Interests and Hobbies

Beach made me, as a six year old, model yachts and aeroplanes etc and had his early 1900's Meccano set sent out from England and given to me. It was a very comprehensive set with hundreds of pieces, wheels, axles, metal girders, plates, strips, angles, windup motors etc, along with hundreds of nuts and bolts etc. I used to spend evening after evening making three or four foot high models of the Eiffel Tower or Sydney Harbour Bridge, as it was being built in the 1930's, as well as Kingsford-Smith's 'Southern

Cross' aeroplane, Sir Henry Seagrave's racing car, the 'Golden Arrow', and many other things that a mechanically-minded boy could think of, such as trucks, traction engines, trains, tractors, ploughs, grubbers, hay rakes, bulldozers, snowploughs etc. It seems a pity that those sorts of leisurely, time-consuming construction sets are no longer popular. Children today I guess just haven't the time to spend fitting hundreds of metal bits together with hundreds and hundreds of nuts and bolts. Plastic Lego type construction sets can of course train an imaginative mind to construct all sorts of wonderful and colourful creations so much more quickly and easily.

I have still got most of that 'Meccano' set but over the 75 years since I had it given to me many pieces have been lost by my growing children, and I must admit that some of those Meccano pieces can be very useful on repairs or construction of some jobs round the home or workshop.

My first encounter with aircraft was in 1926, when a little De Havilland biplane landed about a mile away on the neighbour's place. The pilot, Ken Hall, a North Canterbury farmer, was at that time interested in George Murray's daughter, Molly. Nothing ever came of that, but my interest in aeroplanes was certainly aroused. So it was back home to the farm workshop, making wooden aircraft replicas with propellers that whizzed round in our prevailing nor'west winds. There was no shortage of winds in this area, down the Tasman Valley and just a few miles from Mount Cook.

During the late 20's and early 30's there were many epic aircraft flights to enhance the excitement of a young country lad, including Kingsford Smith's crossing of the Pacific in the Southern Cross, and then the Tasman Sea and on down here to Christchurch, and the epic flights of Amy Johnson as well as Jim Mollison's. There was also our own New Zealander, Jean Batten, and then of course, not to be overlooked, Charles Lindberg's epic Atlantic crossing. Then there were the Schneider Trophy world speed record aircraft races, won by the Supermarine seaplanes, forerunners of the Spitfire. Also round about that time Sir Henry Seagrave set a new world land speed record of 232 mph in the 'Golden Arrow', powered by a V12 Rolls Royce aircraft engine. It was all heady stuff for a hands-on, mechanically-oriented lad.

About that time there was a wind-up tin model of the 'Golden Arrow' in a shop in Timaru. I would dearly have liked to have that model toy, but the price of 17/6 (seventeen shillings and sixpence) was way out of our league in those depression times of 1932. However my Mother came up with the brilliant idea that if I placed rocks round all the edges between the paths and the rose gardens in an area adjacent to our homestead, known as Dobson Park, I could have the Golden Arrow! This area had been cleared and laid out by a lambing shepherd, Les Dobson, in his spare time the previous year. So with old Dolly, a semi-retired Clydesdale draught horse, and a 6ft by 3ft sledge, I completed this task in a week or two, working after school and at weekends, and so I duly acquired the wind-up 'Golden Arrow', which incidentally, I still have, and it continues to go like a rocket! I saw on TV a while ago an identical model, sold at Sothebys for £2,000!

At that time I was in my last year at my mother's Tasman Downs Primary School, the schoolroom of which had been the harness room of the stable! The elevation here is 1800ft and so close to the mountains that snow is a regular occurrence, with quite severe frosts during winter months, and I never envied the day children's half hour journey to and from school on their ponies during those wintry days.

Children arriving by horse at 'Tasman Downs' school, 1939. Boarders seated.

School days, though, could be flexible and if the weather was too abominable, a phone call would keep the children at home, and that day would be caught up at the weekend. During the 23 years Mother taught at 'Tasman', she never missed a day through illness or whatever! Some teachers and others today don't seem to have that same dedication to duty.

Author's mother, Lillian Hayman

In my spare time off from farm work we all had great entertainment, with swimming, rabbiting, bird-nesting, tickling trout, ice skating, tobogganing etc. We are pretty isolated out here; mail and papers only get to a Post Depot 18 miles away, and the nearest town, Timaru, 25,000 population, is 84 miles distant. We made our own amusements and it was great fun.

Recycling

I had always considered myself able to get things going again that had ceased to function or needed modification to make them work better, but with the advances in the electronic fields of recent years I leave those areas to the experts. It seems that we have been forced into a society where many of our household and workplace appliances are not designed to be repaired or to last for more than a few years, but to be discarded when they become unreliable or cease to function. We have become a very wasteful throwaway society. Were the 'Good Old Days' that much different? We didn't perhaps throw much away, with of course a few exceptions such as bottles and tins and cans.

Fuels were bulky things back in the 1920's and 1930's. Petrol and lighting and heating kerosene came in four-gallon tins ten inches square by fifteen inches high, completely soldered up and leak-proof. These tins were packed in pairs in wooden boxes, the complete package weighing about seventy pounds. There must have been millions and millions of these tins and boxes made up till the introduction of what we know as the 44 gallon fuel drum. (It is actually a 50 gallon drum in the United States, theirs being about seven eighths of the British Imperial gallon.) Where have all those tins gone now? They were I recall, put to many uses as buckets and handy storage receptacles for other commodities; but the vast majority of them would have just been discarded to rust away. The throwaway society as we now know it is not just a recent trend of the Western World. It has been going on for years.

I adopted my Dad's trait of being skilful with my hands and during the 1920's and early 1930's, when masses of these tins and packing cases were about, I acquired the ability to make use of the tin by cutting it into all sorts of desired shapes with the dextrous use of tin-snips. Before I was ten, the skills of using the soldering iron and tin rivets (no pop rivets back then) always kept me occupied in any spare time I might have had on wet days or after homework. Buckets of varying sizes, lunch baskets, feed and water receptacles for chickens, hens or pets, funnels, tin mugs etc were all items on the agenda with some useful purpose in those days and the cost was virtually nothing, which during the depression of the 1930's was a significant factor. Of course for me, windmills, waterwheels, model boats and aeroplanes and intricate metal shapes to add to my Meccano Set were very important.

The discarded packing cases made from beautiful knot-free North American timbers were also put to good use whenever they were available.

The half-inch timber sides, tops and bottoms, plus the seven-eighths inch thick ends all nicely planed smooth and cut in nine or ten inch widths were great pieces of timber for making shelves, small cabinets, wood or coal boxes or anything the mind could think of.

As a small boy I made numerous sledges, dobbins [go karts], wheelbarrows, birdcages, rabbit hutches, tree houses etc. The other bonus with these packing cases was the fact that each packing case was held together with 44 one and a half-inch flat head nails. What more could a boy with an active mind and a workshop wish for? The workshop had saws, hammers, planes, chisels, rasps, drills, braces and bits and a 1880 model lathe, which had the power supplied by a treadle which you operated with one foot while working it. Dad got it in the early 1900's after it got burnt in a fire that had partially destroyed the Waimate flourmill buildings. I think he paid two pounds for it. We still use it for average work as the fire warped it a bit. I have now supplied it with an electric motor, more expensive but a damned sight easier!

Author's 'windcharger' for batteries, Tasman downs, 1936.

This brings to mind a quote in a *Popular Mechanics* magazine 50 years ago stating that 'If you are doing a job that a quarter horsepower electric motor could do, you are working for ten cents an hour!' Food for thought isn't it?

These days of course electricity is the basis of most activities, and hand tools are becoming less and less necessary; but for many jobs out here on the farms hammers and nails and staples, nuts and bolts, screws and rivets are in use almost daily. Spades, picks, shovels, crowbars, sledgehammers and mauls are still necessary on the odd occasion. Mostly though, as the saying goes these days, 'If there isn't a machine to do the job, you don't do it!' I don't think that people are getting lazy really, but perhaps more efficient and in many cases skilful. However, there is still lots of hard work to be done out there. Computers give us immense information but basically only manipulate other people's money, produce the answers to most of our difficult problems and masses of paper.

We had radio from 1927, and also about that time we acquired a second-hand 32 Volt petrol-motored Delco lighting plant and batteries. That old plant, which had originally started service in 1914, supplied our establishment with illumination until we were linked up to the National Grid in 1961. With Mother playing the piano and self a ukulele, we had wonderful sing-songs, dances, party games etc. Picnics down on the shores of Lake Pukaki, which adjoins our property, were always a welcome diversion, and usually the neighbours would join us there. Our three-ton truck would carry a large number.

Bill Hamilton's Bentley

When I was about 12 years old, I was to go to stay with a friend in Christchurch during the Christmas holidays. I was told I could go by bus and train or I could ride the 160 odd miles there in the Bentley with Bill Hamilton (later Sir William Hamilton, after his invention of the Jet Boat in the 1950's), a near neighbour. Naturally I chose the ride in the Bentley. What boy wouldn't! Bill had purchased the car a few months previously while on a trip to England, and before returning, had raced it at Brooklands against none other than Malcolm Campbell in a similar car, whom he beat! Roads out here were all shingle in those days, but for Bill 70mph was the normal cruising speed, and all other vehicles were left in our dust. The first section of hard-surfaced road in the South Island, back then in 1932, was from Rolleston to Christchurch, about 10 or 11 miles; we hit 100mph on this stretch. It was pretty exciting for me, not having ever been more than 60mph in our 1914 Reo, with 35 to 40mph being the norm in those days.

Betty's Death

My sister Betty went off to board at Timaru Girls High in 1931, and I went to Timaru Boys High School boarding in 1933. Two and a half years was enough for me, though, and I persuaded my parents that I would be much better occupied helping Dad (who had recently suffered a bit of heart flutter) on the farm. So in August 1935 I left high school and started work at home. Betty, though, having moved subsequently to Craighead Diocesan School, went off to study at Otago University and had just completed her training as a teacher when, in November 1938, our family was struck a terrible blow. A bout of measles led to complications and Betty died of spinal meningitis. She was 21. What a waste it was of a potentially excellent teacher if she had been privileged to follow her Mother's example.

Author's sister, Betty, 'Tasman Downs', 1938.

The Horses at 'Tasman Downs'

Very few farmers these days still have to use horses on their properties. The trusty old horse has mostly been replaced by motor cycles, quad bikes, four wheel drive, utilities, and in some of the more inaccessible hill country, helicopters. The last pony the children had on this place was put down twenty years ago and it was back many years when the last occasion occurred of anyone arriving in the yard on horseback and that was the rabbiter who was employed in the district.

I of course was familiar with horses from the time I could walk, and can well remember being hoisted up on to the sweaty back of the draught horses and with legs spread out across their broad shoulders, hanging on to the cold steel harness that protruded above their padded leather working harness collars. One quarter hour ride about once round the paddock near home would be my allowance for the day then Dad would get on with the job of whatever the team was working at cultivating or whatever at the time. I would have been about three years old at the time.

Horse-drawn plough, 'Tasman Downs' early 1920's.

It was about that time in the early 1920's that Dad bought a well-proportioned hack for use here on the Station. He was a good easy-riding gelding named Jap. On riding him up from Fairlie where he had got new shoes fitted at Miles's Blacksmiths, the journey to Tekapo was uneventful; but by then a nor'west wind of gale force proportions was blowing, and with the waves of the nearby lake thrashing about underneath and the spray splashing over the sides of the bridge, Jap decided he didn't like the look of it at all and refused to go any further.

Dad had on previous occasions experienced draught horses jibbing and not getting a loaded dray moving again. A small branch of prickly gorse put up under the animal's tail was usually all it took, though, to change its mind. I recall Dad citing the time the Water Joe's horse refused to budge past the cook shop once during the threshing mill engine and huts era. The Cook was quick to size up the situation and as it was near mealtime, a hot boiled potato under the jibber's tail quickly moved him and his cartload of two hundred gallons of water along to the steam engine, where it was needed. However, a more gentle approach was called for to get Jap across a strange bridge on a very windy day. The under-blanket was removed from beneath the saddle and tucked under the horse's bridle straps to securely hold it over Jap's eyes as a blindfold. Then getting a good grip on a ring of the bridle, and holding his head close by his shoulder, and talking comfortingly to him, Dad led Jap across the storm-swept bridge without further trouble, and the remaining eighteen miles of the journey on to 'Tasman Downs' was completed in an hour or two.

Jap was an excellent station hack and served out his time on the farm for many years. I never rode by myself on Jap, but learnt the rudiments of horseback transport on a retired station hack we had acquired from next-door 'Braemar' Station. Maria was a biggish mare, probably about seventeen hands high and seemingly enjoyed her semi-retired life after her years of strenuous mustering of both sheep and cattle, rounding up unruly other horses, packing heavy loads out to mustering huts etc, and having to get used to enduring many different-styled riders on her back. She had developed an affinity for children. They were lighter, and didn't usually want to go too far from home. Most children in the district had their first rides on Maria, including many visiting children who had come out to the country for the holidays, and she didn't mind one or two extra on her back at a time. She lived to the ripe old age, for horses, of thirty-two, and would have been about twenty-six or twenty-seven when her arrival here at 'Tasman' enabled my sister Betty and I to go solo on horseback and hold the reins ourselves. Being a large animal she had become accustomed to being led over to a handy wooden gate to enable children to climb up on her back and get positioned on the normal farm hack saddle, there being no special riding equipment supplied for kids back then.

There were of course occasions when we had dismounted for some reason or another well away from a gate, bank, or large rock, when other ways of remounting were called for. If both Betty and I were out on Maria we could usually assist one another to get back up on Maria's lofty back; but there were occasions when I resorted to climbing up her legs by grasping her tail until up sufficiently for Betty to help me scramble over her rump and get seated behind the saddle. Old Maria apparently didn't seem to mind and I used this method of mounting on a few other occasions until big and agile enough to get mounted in a more conventional manner. Why the old mare didn't lash out at me and hurl me halfway across the paddock with her heels I don't know. Of course, at our young age we would not have been much of a burden to her, compared to the loads she would have carried in her younger days.

When Maria died, we graduated to a bumble-footed ex-polo pony named Class, and she served our needs 'till our teenage years saw us away to boarding school in the early 1930's. I would have been coming on to sixteen years old when I came away from Timaru Boys High to help Dad on the farm and another ex-polo pony called Lady Gay came under my hand. She was a nimble little mare, which suited me well but had proved a bit light for the weights of some of the polo players she had been required to carry. For the next three or four years I became involved in the Polo scene a bit in the summer season. My main requirement seemed to be to get some of the horses to where the polo games were going to be played round the Tekapo area.

The players that I can recall participating in the late 1930's were: Bruce Murray from 'Godley Peaks' Station; Gerald Murray from 'Glenmore' Station; Hunter-Weston from 'Mt John' Station; Bill Hamilton (later Sir William) from 'Irishman's Creek' Station; Ron Hoskins from 'Simons Hill'

Station; Charlie Parker and his son Tim from 'Halbrook' Station; and sometimes Mrs. George Murray's nephew Harry Major, would be down next-door from the North Island.

Polo was played from time to time within a ten-mile radius of Tekapo. As no-one had a horse-float to tow behind their car, or they hadn't been thought of in the mid 1930's, it seemed to be my lot to get the horses over to the most suitable flat area for the Saturday afternoon or Sunday's game. I often rode one or led two or three others across country for these events.

Lady Gay had obviously enjoyed the polo games and expected me to hit various grey to whitish objects in the paddocks as I rode round the sheep and lambing ewes with my shepherd's crook. If she spotted a grayish lump of dung, or better still a mushroom or toadstool, she would quicken her gait and place herself in a position where I could get a good hit at it on her right side. If, as happened occasionally, I missed the object she would whip round for me to get another crack at it. Of course the handle of a shepherd's crook has nowhere near the striking surface as a polo mallet. These interesting diversions from the usual pattern of riding round the sheep made the job a bit more interesting I guess but it was short-lived. Little Lady Gay hated water!

She was practically useless for mustering the sheep off the low-lying land at the head of Lake Pukaki and out across the braided streams of the Tasman River, as it was back in the 1930's and 40's before the Upper Waitaki Hydro Development of the 1950's flooded the area with the building of the first Pukaki Dam.

Lady Gay went no doubt to a drier area somewhere and Pinto, a skewbald bay and white gelding, was the next hack. He was agile, sure-footed and gutsy. He enjoyed the rough going creeks and river crossings but had a great respect and rightly so, for quicksand, of which there were many areas near where the silty glacial waters of the Tasman River slowed down as they neared the lake. You quickly learned to avoid suspicious- looking areas by trying them with the mustering stick, which was always part of your riding equipment.

Author on his favourite pony, 'Pinto', with 'Moss', the dog.

There was of course the odd sheep which inevitably got caught and usually perished, although occasionally you would be lucky enough to be able to get one out. There was one occasion when a woolly hogget near some water, but on the dry sandy edge, apparently down to get a drink, had puddled around too much and the quicksand had pulverized and caught the animal by the fore legs. I was able to get its back legs and by slowly pulling with all my strength get the woolly little hogget back out on dry land. Then to my horror I realized that one of its fore legs had simply been pulled off, shoulder blade and all! To cut the animal's throat was the quickest way to put the poor creature out of its misery. Once you are embedded in those sands it is almost like being set in concrete!

Fortunately we didn't lose more than perhaps half a dozen sheep embedded in the quicksand, and to my knowledge only one person and his horse perished in this way, that being Jimmy Grindell, the local rabbit and Stock Inspector of the early 1900's. We did lose three hundred hoggets though on one occasion when a quick overnight torrential nor'west rain unexpectedly caused a major flood in the Tasman River and the complete valley floor was inundated to a depth of two feet or so with swirling flood waters. The bodies were washed up on the beach near our boundary with 'Guide Hill' Station. Dad employed a man to come and help him get the skins off before they got too decayed. I know it was a stinking job, but at least some value was recovered from this substantial loss in our stock numbers.

However, the five hundred odd acres of river flats and islands were a seemingly vital part of our two thousand odd acres in those days. For one thing in the dry summers grass and clover always were abundant on account of the high water table of that area. Also the winter snows didn't remain on the ground for long due to the microclimate at the lake and river level. This of course enabled stock to be grazed out on those lower flats when the remainder of the farm was under snow.

The moment of truth of course would come when the spells of frosty weather changed to warm nor'west rain and the consequent rapid snow melt at Mount Cook, the Tasman Valley and surrounding areas, caused flash flooding of the Tasman River. Stock, especially sheep, had to be removed quickly when these weather changes appeared imminent. It was at these times that sure-footed Pinto would carry me out over the swampy and flood threatened areas adjacent to Lake Pukaki and the river. There was a backwash area of the lake terminating near the exit of the Boltons Gully Stream. This had to be forded at a belly-deep crossing that, over the years, cattle had used. Once through there, the dogs who had swam across were then called upon to do what they liked doing best – start barking intermittently, to get the sheep 'lifted' and heading off into the nor'west and along the river bank which by then was quite often starting to lop over with its milky, silty, glacial water. Though it was fifteen miles down from the foot of the glacier there would be, at times, large chunks of glacial ice being carried along with the floodwaters. Luckily most of the sheep knew their way along and up to the previously-opened gate. And though splashing along near the riverbank, where the water would be shallowest, the sense of urgency kept them on the move with the dogs barking and my occasional 'ha-hoos'. Pinto mostly followed his own instinct and though on occasions I would urge him to go a bit more to left or right near deep guts or swampy places he would shake his head to my bridle urgings and take me to a better and safer crossing. He never put a foot wrong before it was too late! No doubt it is from these sorts of situations that the phrase 'horse sense!' originated.

It would quite often be dark by the time the last few stragglers were coaxed through the gate and up on to higher ground where, though in teeming nor'west rain they wouldn't be drowned or have to stand in ice-cold water. I might add that neither Pinto or I were by this time overburdened with bodily warmth, but a quick trot across the cow paddock and into the shelter of the stable would get the blood circulating again. Pinto would get a feed box of chaff, a drying rub-down and his cover put on. The dogs were tied up and fed and hopefully the two or three house cows would have been milked etc. and then it'd be into a hot bath and a meal, satisfied that another unsavoury task had been completed.

A few years later when in hospital in England in 1944–5, a letter from home brought the sad news that Pinto had been put down on account of his deteriorating feet. Men are not supposed to cry, but that news from home brought tears to my eyes. The war in Europe at that time was close to ending and I was starting to look forward to returning home again and enjoying Pinto's friendly company and easy riding gait. Horses I've been associated with since then, never impressed themselves much on me, and memories of them are now forgotten.

The Farm Routine

Life carried on back up here on the farm in the 30's, with skating, a bit of golf, even less polo, fishing (not necessarily legally), rabbiting, and of course farm and tractor work. We ran about 2,000 sheep then, and two or three house cows, which I milked twice daily, and also separated the cream from the milk by putting it through a separator turned by hand. Once or twice a week the cream would be hand-churned into butter. The surplus skim milk and whey from the butter, with other household scraps, was fed to the pigs, which ended up on the table as home-cured ham and bacon.

Author on the Fairway tractor, feeding out hay with his father, winter 1940.

The Outbreak of War

The Second World War brought the rationing of many imported commodities, not the least of which was petrol. The straight eight Hudson was big and comfortable, but a bit thirsty and our allocated ration of petrol only permitted us to go to Timaru, 84 miles distant, once a fortnight with the 20 miles to the gallon that was about par for American cars of the era.

As petrol was rationed per vehicle, not per engine capacity, my mother purchased a 13 or 14 year-old Austin Seven, which allowed us an extra couple of gallons per week. If the journey didn't require the transport of too heavy a load and time was not at a premium the little Austin was very useful and economical with its 50 odd miles to the gallon and leisurely 35 miles per hour on the predominately shingle roads back then. It was a two-door glassed-in little box and, with comfort not high on the priority list, buzzed along somewhat reminiscent of a fly under a sheet of paper! However the Hudson did its job admirably on the snowy, boggy and often flooded roads of the war years and after. The little Austin Seven shivered its time away down in one of the count out pens of the shearing shed, being called on occasionally to do an economical light-hearted trip to Fairlie or

Timaru, and even to Christchurch if the journey was warranted.

When the war started we young fellows flocked to the cause. I was needed on the farm, so didn't offer my services, but was called up by the Army. My parents appealed the call-up, and so I had about a year in the Home Guard. That was an interesting diversion from farm life on the weekends etc., but I didn't consider I was contributing much to the war effort, apart of course from the produce we were exporting from the farm. So on the first working day in January 1941, when I had just turned 21, I hopped on the Harley and off down to the Recruiting Office in Timaru and offered my services in the Royal New Zealand Air Force, hoping to be a pilot. I needed to have a University Entrance Certificate in Mathematics to qualify for pilot training. So after passing the medical and physical tests, and being pronounced fit enough to become a pilot, and qualify for training, they put me on a Correspondence Educational Course.

Author: taken just prior to leaving for war, 1940.

Having been away from school since I was 15, six years before, it was a bit of a culture shock to that part of my brain box. However, after four months study in the seclusion of my bedroom, I duly went to sit the entrance exam back at Timaru Boys High. I even managed to sit at my old desk with my name that I had carved under the lid 6 or 7 years before still showing amongst dozens of others. The exam results came by mail a while later, and joy of joys, I had passed with a creditable 78%! Also during that learning period I had constructed myself a Morse Key with parts of old Ford Model T coils and Ericsson telephones, learnt the Morse Code, and had got well on the way towards the eight words a minute that had been indicated would be required later, before receiving my wings.

Ice Hockey

During that last winter here at home, our Lake Tekapo ice hockey team played in the knock-out competition and won the Erewhon Cup, the top ice hockey trophy in New Zealand at that time. I never played again after the war due to injuries; but at least I retired undefeated, having scored the winning goal! George Cassie from 'Guide Hill' Station was also in the team, and on one night's journey back from hockey practice on my old 1918 Harley Davidson motor-bike and sidecar we chased a hare for seven or eight miles before it found an outlet to escape, at the Maryburn Creek.

*Author on his 1917 Harley-Davidson motorcycle,
with ice skaters on a pond at 'Guide Hill' Station, 1938.*

I might add our speed in those conditions was well within the realm of what a hare was capable of and there would have been times when we would have been hanging on to the bike and sidecar and running alongside, or, in George's case, behind, to keep the circulation going in those sub-zero conditions. Nowadays one would think twice about going out at night in a well-heated four wheel drive vehicle in snow conditions as they were then; but we thought it was fun and I don't think we ever missed a hockey practice on Thursday nights and certainly never a hockey match.

Part Three

War Service, 1941-1945

Call up for the RNZAF

Having volunteered for aircrew training in the RNZAF on the first working day in January 1941, I finally received, at the end of September, instructions to report to the RNZAF Initial Training Wing at Levin, about 90 miles north of Wellington. A bunch of us raw recruits were Course 21. We were assigned billets in groups of five and in alphabetical order, so we were all H's in our wooden-floored tent. We were kitted out in Air Force blues, all the same size, which we took back to our billet to exchange later for articles of a better fit. We were called over the Tannoy system to the parade ground, where somehow or other the drill sergeant got us lined up in threes. Some of us had some bits of experience with military training perhaps at school, or the Home Guard. For others it was literally basic training. All airmen received their air force number at the time they had passed their entrance exam. The first two numbers were for the year, the next the month, and the others the numerical order of allocation that month. My number, NZ 415318, indicated my enrolment as being the 318th person in May 1941 to volunteer for aircrew duties in the RNZAF. (Incidentally, all aircrew were volunteers).

We were knocked into shape at Levin, and between square bashing and route marches etc, had intensive lectures and practical hands on experiences with basic aero engines, carburettors, airframes, machine guns etc. and of course lectures, medical and dental inspections, kit and hut inspections, and generally getting used to obeying orders, and respecting senior ranks, learning to salute correctly, and generally getting into condition to be responsible members of the RNZAF. That basic training lasted about a month.

I can still vividly recall a time when a class of us were all working on a Browning machine gun each on tables in front of us, and at that stage had the guns completely in pieces. The Sergeant in charge of us then put the lights out, and instructed us to get our guns back in working order again in the dark! I know I was very pleased with myself, having been able to complete the task in double quick time. The lecturer was quite surprised that I had fitted all the firing mechanism, sears dogs springs etc, the right way round, and that indeed the machine gun would be capable of firing! Perhaps I should have been a gunner? I guess that was about the last time I was ever involved with the intricacies of Browning machine guns. Later on operational training, and later on Ops (i.e. Operations), I left the guns to the crew members who had been trained extensively on their use. However, at the time I was fascinated by the way they worked.

Prior to my entering the Air Force, my experience with guns had been confined to my Father's double-barrelled 12 gauge shot gun, and a Remington 15 shot bolt action 22 repeating rifle. I had shot many thousands of rabbits with this rifle as they were incredibly thick on the ground in those days. It was no trouble to shoot 20 an hour on a stroll along the hilly parts of our farm. Thank goodness we have got on top of the pestiferous little sods now. You would be lucky to find 20 on the whole farm now! Apart from the 10 shillings a week I was paid, and my keep, my main source of income was from rabbit skins, the best of which could be worth as much as a gallon of petrol, about two shillings and fourpence; but only the best winter buck-skins ever reached that price. Most skins were worth less than half that. However, so much for guns.

Pilot Training in New Zealand

After basic training we were split up, and I didn't see much of Harkness, Harrison, Higgins, and Henderson, the LAC (Leading Aircraftsmen) pupil pilots I had shared the tent with at Levin. Some of us went to the Elementary Flying Training School at Harewood, Christchurch, now the International Airport, while others went to the other training bases round the country. I started my flying training on DH.82 Tiger Moths in late November 1941. What a thrill it was to be up in the air flying. I had never been up in an aeroplane before! But after about 5 hours dual, an epidemic of mumps went through the establishment, so those of us who were afflicted were taken out to nearby Burwood Hospital to recover. I got back into flying again in mid-December on Course 23 and after another 4 or 5 hours dual, went solo. I finished basic flying training at the end of January 1942 with 36 hrs dual instruction and 25 hrs solo. My rating says I was 'above average'! One man's opinion? Yes I sure was going to be a Spitfire pilot. I could throw a Tiger Moth all over the sky, and had only nearly killed myself once or twice. Oh yes. It was another case of local boy makes good! But ah ha, Spitfire pilot it wasn't to be!

Author training at Harewood airfield, ear Christchurch, December 1941. The aircraft is a DH82 'Tiger Moth'.

I went on final leave from Harewood in early February 1942. I well remember getting out of camp that morning. As my Flight Commander hadn't been available to sign my leave pass the night before, I had to wait for his return to duty at 7.30 am. Things were desperate. He arrived late, and I had to catch the boat train due to leave Christchurch Railway Station at 8.20. This train would get me to Timaru in time to catch the Mount Cook bus, which ran every second day. Up one day and down the next!

I eventually got my leave pass signed, which permitted me to get out past the guardhouse at the gate, where I had a taxi waiting. If I missed the train and consequently the bus, I would lose two days of precious final leave. It was nearly train departure time.

'Where to?', the driver enquired. 'The express train', I replied. 'It will have left by now', he answered. 'Well, catch it', I replied, and so the driver stoked up the nippy Ford V8 and we made it to Rakaia, the train's first stop. It was an exciting trip, about as fast as a Tiger Moth! We easily caught the train. The Wellington–Lyttelton ferry had been delayed by a rough crossing and so the train was an hour late. The bus waited in Timaru for the train's late arrival, and so I got home OK that night.

After nearly a month at home, I was directed to assemble with 50 or so other pupil pilots at the Manning Pool, Wellington. We were housed in the now disused 1940's Exhibition buildings in the suburb of Rongotai. We were there for about a week, while we were finally checked over for diseases and rashes, coughs and colds, and all orifices were duly inspected by worthy medics! We stayed at Rongotai 'till a suitable boat became available to transport us for further flying training in Canada with the Empire Air Training Scheme.

The *Titjalengka*

The suitable boat for our transport across the Pacific turned out to be a fairly new Dutch ship of ten to twelve thousand tons, the *Titjalengka*, which had formerly plied round the East Indies. She was a diesel-powered vessel under the command of a Dutch Captain.

The *Titjalengka* had been to Singapore to pick up fleeing wives and children of the beleaguered garrison there, under threat of the advancing Japanese. Unfortunately the Japs arrived sooner than expected, and with shooting to be heard and tanks to be seen not far from the wharf, the captain apparently blew three short blasts from the ship's horn to summons absent crew members back on board. There was no time to delay the ship's departure. The chief engineer was ordered to start the huge diesel engine, the bosun cut the ropes to the wharf with an axe and they got to hell out of there! There was just a scratch crew of only half a dozen or so plus a Chinese cook on board, along with two lucky women and five children who had managed to get aboard before the Japanese took over the city of Singapore. It has been well documented by a few of the survivors as to what fates befell those who did not manage to escape from the brutal treatment meted out by the Japs.

The *Titjalengka* with its scratch crew meanwhile headed for Wellington. In the Coral Sea ten or a dozen survivors of a sunken American submarine were rescued from their rubber dinghy. The crew of the *Titjalengka* was now more than doubled.

We were allowed out of Camp one afternoon, and went down to the Wellington harbour and saw our ship at the wharf. They were fitting a 4 inch gun to the deck at the stern. It has always amazed me as to where New Zealand would have acquired a spare gun and ammunition to be placed on this vessel. The Captain did not wish to go with other boats in an escorted convoy, but preferred to sail full speed across the Pacific, and take his chances with Jap submarines. No doubt the New Zealand hierarchy must have thought that a high-powered gun would have been some protection for the dozen or so of us budding airmen, and others on board. Also being loaded aboard were large quantities of stores and victuals for our voyage. As we watched crates of beer, scotch, Coke and other beverages being slung up off the wharf, someone mentioned that there was a case of jaundice on board. One of the Americans standing nearby remarked, 'Well with a dash of Coke, I guess we'll drink that too!'

The following day, Tuesday the 17th of March 1942, we went by tram down to the Wellington railway station at 10am and marched from there to the ship's side, claimed our named and numbered kit-bags from the pile deposited there, paraded, answered to roll-call, were allocated a cabin number, and climbed on board.

We left Wellington harbour at 5pm and had lost all sight of New Zealand by 9pm. It would be almost three and a half years before I would return.

Vern Ashbolt from Christchurch, a brilliant pianist, and I, a fair to middling but not so brilliant tenor, discovered to our disappointment that there were no musical instruments on board. Surely a piano was more important to have on board for a long voyage than a ruddy great gun!

Boat drill, roll-call etc, were part of life on board. The NCO in charge of us said that there had developed a slight problem, and asked whether there was anybody experienced in bird nesting. That had been in my more youthful days, a customary country occupation, when the local Council, paid us kids a penny or two a dozen for certain types of birds' eggs! I immediately declared my ability in this regard. 'OK Hayman', he replied, 'you will be on watch duty up in the Crow's Nest'.

The ship, being short of regular crew, actually required us all to do four hours on duty of some sort, every day: cleaning, polishing, kitchen and mess duties, or on lookout or watch. It certainly helped to pass the time. Three weeks from Wellington to Panama at 22 knots. It was easy to realise that there is an awful lot of water in this world! The only other thing we saw was one Albatross, which followed, about 100 yards behind the ship, for ten days. It never appeared to flap its wings or pick up any scraps off the sea; but just floated along about ten feet above our wake.

Our gun was tried out a day or so out of Wellington, and before the advent of the Albatross. An empty 44 gal drum was thrown overboard, and when about 400yds to the rear, the order to fire was given. A resounding cheer went up from all who were watching when the target was blown clean out of the water. I'm sure we all felt a false sense of security knowing we had a weapon and gun crew capable of at least shooting back at an aggressive enemy. Luckily we never encountered one!

And so the days passed with sunbathing, one or two stints of being on watch, playing cards, whittling bits of wood, playing table tennis, singing, reading, yarning etc, and later on after the pool had been filled, having the odd swim. The pool wasn't filled till we had been at sea for a couple of weeks. The weather was a bit cool, as we sailed on a curved route well south of the normal shipping lanes.

Towards the end of March we spent a bit of spare time rehearsing for a concert, which was an interesting diversion from routine for a few days. The concert was held on April 2nd. Vern and I did a Shadow play, took part in a Maori Haka, and sang a song or two. There were some excellent items performed, and it made for a wonderful night's entertainment.

The pool, filled with seawater, was the centre piece for the crossing of the Equator ceremony, when 'His Marine Majesty, Neptune', King of all the watery Realm, came on board and granted us individually 'His Clemency'. The ceremony mostly consisted of being pelted with eggs and tomatoes etc, and having your head plastered with a watery custard powder mixture, and then being thrown into the swimming pool. I might add we spent a considerable time later sluicing down the deck and pool, but it was all great fun.

On Easter Monday, 6th April, as the grey mists of morning cleared, I happened to be on watch from 4am up in the Crow's Nest, and perceived the dark shape of a vessel quite close on our port side. I informed the Bridge through the speaking tube of the presence of an unidentified ship on port side. Immediately the warning bells sounded all over our ship, and the Tannoy instructed people to assemble at action stations; but as visibility increased and the mist cleared, it was revealed that the vessel was nothing other than a rusty old collier under an allied flag. It certainly had been unidentifiable, as its unreadable name was almost entirely obliterated by rust, but no doubt it was still doing a worthy task in those difficult times.

As dawn finally broke, we realised that we were now right off Panama. I give full marks to our Dutch Captain and his skeleton crew for excellent navigation. There was no GPS (Global Positioning System) in those days.

We were allowed off at 6.30 and had a hilarious time in town with some local USAAF chaps, who showed us round till 9.30 pm. This included a hair-raising ride in a Panamanian-driven V8 taxi. It was all the more exciting as it was our first experience of any life beyond New Zealand shores, apart of course the brainwashing that Hollywood movies had given us in previous years.

The following morning it was our turn to ascend the locks, motor through the canal, and descend at the other end to Colon. It had been a very interesting day, with Catalinas and other types of military aircraft, all new to us, overhead continuously.

From Colon it was up through the Caribbean and Gulf of Mexico, for the next four or five days. It was very hot, and we slept on deck at night, and were in and out of the pool the rest of the day, between watches.

New Orleans

We reached the mouth of the Mississippi River on the 11th of April 1942, the entrance being defined by two parallel rows of piles about a mile apart, and about a foot between each one in the row. This caused the river to flow along between the two rows of piles, and allow sediment to drift out between them, at the sides. We picked up the pilot out near the entrance to this channel, which was at that time 80 to 90 miles down from New Orleans, and far out to sea from sight of land! As we proceeded up river, mud flats started appearing beyond the pile-marked channel, and gradually vegetation and habitation, with formed levees defining the river banks. It was unusual to be travelling along in a large ship, with habitation and farm work progressing on either side, and below us!

We eventually arrived in the harbour pool at New Orleans in the afternoon, and were allowed off for a few hours. Four of us were greeted at a street corner by a very pleasant lady, who in a delightful southern drawl enquired if we would like to be shown round the town. We of course accepted, and were ushered into a magnificent Cadillac convertible, driven by an equally magnificent 20 year-old, the daughter of our first acquaintance. We were shown round no doubt the better parts of New Orleans, with beautiful homes, pillared porch entrance ways glistening in their paint, and folded back window shutters. We glided into the drive of one of these mansions, and were invited in for coke and cookies. Immediately the phone was in operation, and in a few minutes, three other delightful damsels arrived, to make up the foursome for us lads. Great southern hospitality!

After a wonderful afternoon, we were taken down to the Illinois Central railway station, had roll-call, said goodbye to our hostesses and boarded the train for Chicago at about 9pm. We had meals in the dining car, bedded down in the Pullman Sleepers, and arrived at Chicago at 9.30pm the following day. We weren't permitted off the station, so had a hair cut and shoe shine, then boarded another train for Canada about midnight. We had breakfast next morning at Detroit, then crossed under the Detroit River to Windsor, Canada. We had lunch on the train, and arrived at Toronto about 3.30pm.

Toronto

In Toronto we went straight out to the Manning Pool, escorted by a Guard of Honour and the local Brass Band, which was all heady stuff. We had another thorough Medical, were fingerprinted, issued with blankets, and allocated a bunk number under the grandstand of the now disused Exhibition buildings, with about a thousand other budding airmen. We had some difficulty locating our bunks again after being down town for a few hours. The area was laid out in sections with alphabetical lanes and numbered rows. Not easy in the dark!

There was a Barber's Parade next day, and we all had a haircut. I had had one the day before, but in those days we all were required to be of similar appearance in the hair department anyway! We were issued with tags for our blankets, and our 'New Zealand' shoulder pieces, which we had put on, and then went to town for a while.

We were at Toronto Manning Pool for ten days, and it was very pleasant. Maybe the dental inspections and teeth repairs were not so pleasant, and I recall the guy who was attacking my teeth remarking, after inspecting the work that had been done back home, that New Zealanders must have about the worst teeth in the world but the best dentists!

There was morning parade and roll call daily, ended with a route march for the 25 or so of us in our group. The destination was usually the Downyflake Donut Shop on the waterfront, where the girl friend of the Corporal in charge of us worked. The rest of the days at Toronto were occupied visiting homes we were invited to, and going to see films. We also spent a day at Niagara Falls, shooting ground hogs with an Elinor Gooderham, a budding Annie Oakley! She was even shooting them from 50yds, with a Winchester 22 pointing over her shoulder, and sighting it with a make up mirror!

Vern and I had a hilarious evening at the Icelandia Skating Rink, where we had been taken by Elinor and Ruth (somebody), to be shown how to ice skate. Vern was no mean skater, and I had up to that time played on the wing of the undefeated champion New Zealand ice hockey team, Tekapo. I also did quite a bit of figure skating. So after having our hired skates put on for us, and being half carried on to the ice by our escorts, we proceeded to put on a pretty spectacular display of a person's first experience on ice. I think Ruth and Elinor were lucky to survive with little more than a few bruises, after we had fallen with them, and on them, numerous times, and being helped up again by several willing bystanders, who were of course also on skates. After about half an hour of this stupidity, we started to show some signs of getting the hang of things in this supposedly Canadian sporting pastime. Within an hour, Vern and I put on a pretty reasonable demonstration of the intricacies and delights of fun on the ice. Not quite Torvill and Dean standard, but a lot of fun.

Pilot Training in Saskatchewan

The ten days of this wonderful Canadian hospitality all too soon came to an end, and we boarded a Pullman Sleeper on a Canadian National

Railway train at 11pm on the 24th of April 1942, heading for Saskatoon, Saskatchewan.

Our Flight, now about fifty of us, were allocated two sleepers, so we had a bed each. After a couple of days heading west on the train we left the spruce and birch forests behind, and came out onto the Prairies, arriving at Winnipeg an hour or two later. We had a quick look round in a taxi before going on to arrive at Saskatoon about 9.30pm in a light snowstorm. There we went the three miles out to the RCAF's No 4 Service Flying Training School of the British Commonwealth Air Training Plan, in open trucks, had a hot shower, and hot meal, and got to bed at midnight.

Training base: Saskatoon, Canada, 1942.

We had a few lectures the next day, and I looked over the planes with my instructor, and filled in about a dozen forms, cards etc. The following day involved more parades and lectures, at one of which, in a rich Canadian accent, the instructor said, 'We've got you guys out here to teach you how to fly. You can go a thousand miles in any direction, and you won't hit anything higher than ten feet'! How right he was. Even from 20,000ft over Saskatoon you still couldn't see the Rockies.

I started flying in the twin Jacobs radial-engined Cessna Crane aircraft at the end of April. I did 3hrs dual, and some taxiing practice with my instructor over at the auxiliary field of Vanscoy. While I practised taxiing, Flying Officer Leith shot gophers out of the window. I didn't question his actions at the time. Who ever did question their instructor? After all he was a Flying Officer and I was just an LAC. But looking in later life at photos of the Cessna Crane, I don't know how he ever shot any gophers out the window without shattering the port propeller! However, he did get a few of the little sods. They didn't take as much notice of an aeroplane as they did of a man with a gun walking, but they had to be controlled, or the whole field would be dug up as if roughly cultivated.

Cessna Crane. Photographed by the author, 1942.

Days were divided between lectures and flying. I went solo after seven and a half hours dual, in early May.

(By the way, at that time we had no choice about going on to Fighters, in spite of one's aptitude in that direction, as the Allies had virtual aerial domination and more multi-engine pilots were required, so hence we all went on to the twin-engined Cessna.)

As more than half our time was to be spent on the ground with lectures etc., we were required to purchase certain equipment to record what we learnt. So down to Woolworths I went on a tram. The lass behind the counter helped me sort out black ink, red ink, (no ball-point pens in those days) pencils, ruler, set square, protractor, compass, notebooks, lecture pads etc. Then before she started to wrap it all up, she asked, 'Is there anything else you may want?' To which I replied, 'Oh! Perhaps you could put in a couple of rubbers?' She appeared to blush a bit, and went along the counter to where another shop assistant was. They whispered to one another, and glanced in my direction a few times, before she came back to say, 'No. I'm afraid we can't sell them in this shop.' At which I pointed to a compartment, to the rear of where she was, and said, 'But there are some over there.' To which she replied, 'Oh! You mean erasers.' Then I blushed. After all I was (according to my parson's daughter mother) a polite, well brought-up lad.

The girl was named Dot Hanson and I made a date with her shortly after this incident, and we got on well for the duration of my stay at Saskatoon. But that subject was never mentioned. She and I were like sister and brother. The comfort of the opposite sex was a necessary ingredient for a boy far from home. A touch of homesickness I guess.

There were numerous incidents worth mentioning during our flying days at Number 4 SFTS. One gruesome task we were required to complete soon after our arrival on the Station was to gather up the disembowelled remains of a recently graduated Sergeant Pilot who had, in his youthful exuberance attempted a low-level flight along the winding Saskatchewan River. He didn't see the heavy ferry cable stretched from bank to bank. We gathered most of his remains to put in a body bag from amongst the remains of the aircraft or strewn along the river bank, but a section of innards was still to be seen, draped round the ferry cable, near the middle of the river. A gymnastic member of our bunch was directed to proceed, hand over hand, the 60 to 70 yards to where the offending item was, and drop it down to where some of us were standing waist deep in the river. This exercise naturally didn't go unnoticed by quite a group of citizens from the nearby town, and the whole exercise certainly brought home to all those involved the stupidity of low flying, and most definitely in an unfamiliar area.

We all duly got the message, but a bit of below 2,000ft flying slowly crept back into our hopefully unnoticed activities. It was risky, though, because the Canadian Mounties could report you if you were down low enough for them to read the identification numbers of the aircraft. I guess they must have turned a blind eye to some of our less than orthodox activities. However, beating up girl friends' houses and the like could lead to severe penalties, or even grounding. The Air Force didn't appreciate telegrams having to be sent to bereaved families stating that 'The Air Ministry regret to inform you that your Son so and so has been killed while on active service.' They didn't all die as a result of enemy action!

I know of one fellow being greeted by his Instructor after landing with 'Been doing a bit of low flying, George?', and replying, with a surprised look, 'No Sir.' 'Well it's unusual how you have got green wheat straw trailing from the tail wheel. Don't push your luck too far!'

One enterprising pupil pilot, low on fuel and lost, put down on a suitable flat area and phoned up from a nearby farmhouse to let his C.O. know where he was. A tanker was sent out to refuel the Cessna, with instructions that he was to stay with the aircraft until a senior pilot came to fly him back to base. By the time the plane had been refuelled, quite a number of the local country folk had assembled round the Cessna, as it was well away north of the usual flying area. And so, the question was asked, 'What is it like to fly?' To which he replied, 'O.K. then, come on two or three of you and I'll give you a ride.' So off they went, had a bit of a fly round, and landed again. Then of course more young and some not so young wanted a flight too, so off he goes again. The Cessna Crane had a seating capacity, all up, of five. So with a bit of money changing hands, the pupil pilot was doing quite nicely thank you! However, after an hour or two of this exciting exercise, the fuel was getting low again. So the plane was parked near the homestead and tied down. Guards were arranged to keep watch on it during the night.

Next morning, the Chief Flying Instructor arrived, and they got all set up for take off, when the Instructor said, 'I thought this plane had been refuelled.' 'Well a tanker did come out, and it seemed as if he put some fuel in it,' said the now apprehensive pupil pilot. 'Well I think we had better wait for a bit more,' said the CFI. So they did that, and nothing more was said. The pupil pilot certainly was lucky.

Another lad wasn't quite so fortunate, but nevertheless enterprising. He got low on fuel, landed near a country garage, opened the gate out on to the road, and taxied down to the pumps, where he got some fuel, if of considerably less octane rating than the usual aviation gas. He told the proprietor to charge it up to the Air Force, and then proceeded to taxi back out to the area where he had landed. Unfortunately when turning through the gateway, a wheel dropped into a ditch, and a wing impaled itself on a fence post! It had been a nice try, but that was the last of his flying career as a pilot.

The Canadian Prairie was undoubtedly a wonderful area to teach a large number of young fellows to fly, but by Jove it was easy for us inexperienced pilots to get lost when flying over this featureless area, the whole countryside being laid out in a grid pattern, with fully-formed roads every six miles, running east and west and north and south, and lesser roads inbetween. The only variations on this were the railway lines, and of course rivers, which in our area was limited to only the Saskatchewan River.

Cessna Crane photographed over the Saskatchewan prairie from the Crane the author was flying.

On a couple of occasions, like many others, I resorted to flying along about 20ft above a railway line until a settlement came in sight, then reading the name on the end of the railway station. It was then a routine matter to climb back up to 2,000ft, find that place on the map we always had with us, and head off back to our familiar flying area. Naturally on pre-planned cross country navigation flights we didn't get lost, as we would have prominent towns or locations at turning points, and compass headings to adhere to. It was when you had been asked to go well away from the normal flying circuit, and practice for an hour or so some of the flying manoeuvres that you had previously been shown, that disorientation seemed to occur; but I guess it was all part of our training.

Cessna Crane cockpit layout, 1942. Photo by the author.

A somewhat nerve-wracking experience happened to me when returning from a normal hour's flying practice at our auxiliary field at Vanscoy; upon my depressing the switch to lower the undercarriage, the red warning light came on indicating a malfunction in the landing gear. It could be seen from the cockpit that though the port wheel was down, the starboard one wasn't! Try as I may, I couldn't alter the situation. The lowered one could not be raised nor the raised one lowered. There was nothing else for it, but a one-wheel landing! I thought, 'By Jove this could be a bit messy', and with a dozen or so other trainees crowding the main airfield, I realised a landing there could be quite dangerous not only to mine, but also to some other person's health!

I buzzed the control tower and my problem was immediately noticed. A red 'OK' was being flashed to me by Aldis Lamp, and a red warning rocket was fired to clear all other aircraft from the landing field. Two fire engines came out and parked on the grass beyond the runway, while I kept circling above. Finally the ambulance came out and parked by the fire engines. The thought raced through my head: they must think I'm going to get hurt!

They gave me a green light to come on in. I did a normal approach onto the grass. After all, that was how I had been taught. As the one wheel touched the grass I cut the motors and held the starboard wing up as much as possible with the aileron. The starboard motor had stopped with the prop horizontal, but as our landing speed decreased and the wing dropped to grass cutting level (the retracted wheel was actually keeping it just clear of the ground) the prop moved back off compression, struck the ground, and we swung round 180deg and came to a stop. I was helped out and congratulated on a fine effort, given a medical check over, told to get in a serviceable plane and do a couple of circuits and bumps (take offs and landings), just to keep my hand in. The undercarriage of the Crane operated by a bicycle type chain out to the mechanism in the engine nacelles, and was driven by an electric motor under the rear seat. The frightening episode that occurred was because one chain had come off and jammed, locking one wheel up and the other down!

About half way through our course, the previous Flight had their Wings Parade. The whole establishment was made spick and span for the occasion, when relatives and friends were invited to witness the presenting and pinning on of the hard-earned and coveted Wings. We were confined to Barracks during this event, but could witness proceedings through the windows.

The Station tabby cat, a tom, had joined us in our temporary confinement, and was on this occasion being particularly annoying, jumping from bunk to bunk and yowling etc. Lofty Dunlop, a cow cocky from Taranaki, announced, 'I'll nut you, you bastard. That'll quieten you down!' So with a bit of assistance, the offending animal was put head first in a flying boot, a razor blade was produced, and quick as a flash the job was done, and with a slightly higher tone of yowl, the offending creature was released out on to the parade ground. Escape was obviously in the animal's mind, so straight through the stiffly standing airmen on parade it streaked, under the seated visitors' legs in the viewing area, and up the flagpole, to their rear, where it proceeded to lick its wounds. The Wings Parade continued, basically unruffled, but the incident certainly broke the monotony of our uninteresting afternoon.

Our training continued, and as the summer temperature increased, flying started at 4 am and ended at 8 am to avoid the disturbing thermals that formed over the landing area as the temperature rose. Then it was lectures from 12.30 to 4.30 pm and sometimes more flying again in the evening. They were full but wonderful days.

Quite a considerable amount of time was spent on the Link Trainer, which consisted of an enclosed mock aircraft cockpit on a stand. You climbed in, shut the door, and 'flew' the machine entirely by instruments. An Instructor followed your progress from a seat outside, nearby. This simulated instrument flying allowed the trainee to inadvertently crash the machine without causing any damage to one of His Majesty's aircraft, though a bit, perhaps, to his own ego! Certainly these Link Trainers were a very valuable addition to the Empire Air Training Scheme.

These were exciting, but pressured times in a young person's life. However, the wonderful hospitality and generosity shown to us by the Canadians always bring back happy memories. We could get down to town fairly regularly to the movies, roller skating, dining at the Besborough Hotel, Sunday dinners out at people's homes, pancakes and maple syrup, strawberry shortcake etc. There were bike rides near the river, and the surrounding countryside, plus community singing round the bandstand in the park by the river on balmy evenings, the music being supplied by the Big Band style local musicians. The war seemed, and in fact was, a long way away: just something you read about, or heard on the News.

Besborough Hotel, Saskatoon, Canada.

After our uneventful Wings Parade on the 14th of August, when our Wings were pinned on by none other than our own NZ Air Commodore Tiny White, we also then became Sergeant Pilots, which was a great boost to our ego, as we no longer needed to wear the white flash in the front of our caps, denoting a pupil pilot.

Some of the more academic types also got their commission then, to be Pilot Officers. I never envied them. I much preferred to be just one of the boys. Some of my friends received their commissions early in their careers, but often preferred the company of non-commissioned airmen. Later, on active service, both my navigator and bomb aimer, who had their pilot officer stripes, tried to spend much of their time with us in our less institutionalised and relaxed off-duty hours.

With our Wings and Chevrons lovingly sewn on by our respective girlfriends, we celebrated with the Wings Dinner at the Besborough Hotel.

'Wings at Last': *the author in uniform, Canada 1942.*

George Helm and I then took 48 hours leave, and went by Greyhound bus to Lake Waskesiu in the Prince Albert National Park, about 130 miles north of Saskatoon. We hired a couple of horses next morning, and set off along a trail through the spruce and birch trees. Then we stopped and George handed me the reins of his horse while he dismounted to pick wild raspberries. Suddenly I was almost thrown over the head of the little mare upon which I was sitting by the stallion, which moments before, George had been quietly riding. When our mounts had finished their courting, we smartly rode them back, and hired a canoe instead. In this we paddled out to an island, where the RCMP had a floatplane base. The log cabin style Police Station was locked up. No doubt the Mounties were away 'Getting their Man,' so we set off the mile or so back to shore. The wind freshened, and the lake became quite rough. However we made it back, sopping wet, and thrown up on the beach. After returning the canoe, we continued our sightseeing round the Park, on a couple of hired bicycles. At least we had almost full control of them.

Leave in New York

After doing a few more flights, and having a total of 230 hours flying behind us, we said goodbye to Saskatoon, and boarded a CPR train about midnight, heading East for a week or two's leave.

We crossed the border between Canada and the United States at Niagara, where we had to go through the Border guard station and declare our identity etc. The limit of Canadian currency for an individual to take out of Canada at that time was, I think, $50. So we all dutifully declared that was what we had, showed our appropriate documents and proceeded on our way walking over the Rainbow Bridge to the United States. About half way across the Bridge, one of the Canadian Border Guards came running to catch us up, and asked who was Bob Cotton? Upon being identified, Bob was handed his wallet back, which he had inadvertently left on the Guard Station counter. The guard had no doubt rummaged through Bob's wallet to find who it belonged to, couldn't help noticing the four hundred or so dollars that was there, as it was in all our wallets. But all the Guard said was, 'Enjoy your leave, boys': which we did. The Guard could probably have been officious and searched us all for the limit money, but he must have been a good sort. We made sure that we didn't bring much back. In fact Bob and I were down to only a few cents on our return to Canada a couple of weeks later.

We had to give a contact address while away, so picked the Piccadilly Hotel, 5th Avenue, New York. We arrived at Central Station, New York, on the 31st August at 7.30 am. The five of us then took a taxi to the hotel. There were George Helm, Barry Vernazoni, Bill Dunn, Bob Cotton and I in our group. (Of these, only Bill Dunn and I would survive the war.)

While our suits were away being pressed, we had a shave and shower etc, then went out to La Guardia Airport, saw a few late model planes, and made a date for the next day with some girls we met there. The New Zealand flashes on our shoulders and our Wings insignia were an immediate talking point. An exceedingly generous gentleman, Herbert S. Ogden (a Wall Street banker) took us in tow, and out to dinner and a Vaudeville

Show, and then to drinks (a Tom Collins, my first alcoholic beverage) at the Harvard Club, which also had a swimming pool on the 5th floor.

We quickly realised the Piccadilly Hotel was a bit out of our league on our limited cash reserves, what with Tommy Dorsey and his band there playing dinner music, and Edward G. Robinson and Heidi Lamar at a table next to ours for breakfast. So we booked into the ANZAC with accommodation for servicemen. It was known as the Phi-Gamma-Delta Club, at 106 West 56 Street, and cost about a dollar a night, which included a blanket or two and numerous bed bugs! However we were not figuring on spending too much time in bed.

On leave in New York, September 1942. From left to right, Bob Cotton, George Helm, Barry Vernazoni, author, Bill Dunne

When leaving the Piccadilly, the Cashier informed us there would be no charge. Herbert Ogden had paid, and would have paid for as long as we wished to stay there! Phenomenal American hospitality! We did accept his offer, though, to make use of the facilities at the Harvard Club, where we would have swims and drinks most days. I had very fast cottoned on to the joyous benefits of alcoholic beverages!

We had a wonderful ten days in New York. Herbert wangled permission through the Naval Academy for us to get to see some of the latest aeroplanes out at Floyd Bennett Airfield. We were photographed on top of the RCA building (Rockefeller Centre.), saw Arthur Murray's 'Leg Show' the Rockettes, had frogs' legs at Jack Dempsey's (ex World Champion boxer) Restaurant, visited Jimmy Rose's 'Diamond Horseshoe' night club and restaurant, and went to a dance put on by the 'English Speaking Union', where the female partners were gathered from the theatrical industry of Broadway!

Another interesting excursion was out to Liberty Island, and climbing up into the Statue of Liberty, where two people at a time were allowed to climb up the steps in the arm of the statue, and take in the view to be seen out through the openings in the torch. I believe that no one now is permitted up in the arm, on account of the weakening of the internal steel structure.

There were two sisters with whom Bob and I had become acquainted at the Airport, Helen and Pat Quillan. One drove an ambulance, and the other worked out there. They took us to Forest Hills, near where they lived, and we watched Donald Budge and Pancho Saguro battle out the final of the United States Tennis Championship. I think, from memory, it was Budge who won. On another occasion we spent the best part of a day with Helen and Pat out at their fifty-yard section of private beach at Long Island, complete with overnight accommodation. Sunbathing and playing in the surf, rum and Coke and cookies, it seemed all too wonderful to be true.

Another day, with of course female escorts, we spent out at Coney Island Amusement Park, and tried all the most hair-raising rides, winning prizes and boxes of chocolates at some of the ball or dart throwing and rifle-shooting entertainment stalls. What with being taken to all sorts of cabarets, dances, floor shows etc, we rarely got to bed before 2 or 3am.

One memorable show we were privileged to get to was the premiere of the classic film *Holiday Inn*, which was opened by Bing Crosby and Fred Astaire. It is the show in which Bing sings the everlastingly popular song, 'White Christmas'.

Four of us New Zealanders took a Yellow Cab to a bar in a sleazy area down Harlem way. In our laughter, chattering and antics, I accidentally knocked over the drink of a burly-looking bloke. I immediately offered to buy him another drink; but he immediately hurled his empty pint handle along the bar, and informed me he wouldn't accept a drink from 'a bloody foreign bastard.' So a fight started, in which we didn't seem to be particularly involved; but not looking for that kind of a fight, and being young and fit we managed to duck under most of the flying fists, headed for the door, and got to hell out of there and up the street to where a cab happened to be. Its doors swung open as we approached, and the four of us piled in. It was the same taxi we had gone down there with 20 minutes before! The driver remarked, 'I didn't think you would stay there long.'

One evening we performed a haka at the entrance to the Piccadilly Hotel about midnight, and in a matter of seconds, taxis stopped and a crowd gathered. By that time of course, our version of the Timaru Boys High School haka had finished. We were requested to wait a minute or two, while lights and cameras were set up, then we were obliged to do the haka again. A large crowd had gathered by this time, and 5th Avenue was completely blocked by traffic and people! It was truly amazing to us; but I suppose not many hakas would have been witnessed by people in New York.

One other event worth recalling was a lunch on September the 3rd 1942 at the Hotel Piccadilly, hosted by a kiwi resident in New York, Nola Luxford. She did this regularly for visiting RAAF and RNZAF airmen. There were about 70 attending the luncheon I went to.

After about ten days, our time to return to Canada was approaching, and our money was running out. So Bob Cotton and I elected to hitch-hike back up the Hudson River, and over to Montreal. We said our goodbyes, sent radio messages back home from the WHS Studios, gave Mr. Ogden a good luck silver Maori tiki that I had got made into a tie pin, hopped on the subway and up north as far as it would go, and started hitch hiking. Sixteen hitches and 24 hours later, we were back in Canada. Petrol was limited to 4 gallons per family a week, so none of the obliging private drivers were going far. We did get one or two longer lifts with milk tankers, and an enterprising prostitute, who was getting her clients to drive her from area to area; but we waited for a lift a long time at the turn-off to Chicago from the highway to Canada that we were on. So when a vehicle finally did come our way, we stood out on the thoroughfare with hands upraised, and brought it to a halt. The chauffeur-driven Cadillac was transporting a U.S. Senator to a high level conference in Montreal. He occupied the whole of the rear compartment of the Caddy but was only too pleased to allow us to travel in the front with the driver. The Senator himself had been a Colonel in the U.S. Army in the First World War.

At the border between Canada and the U.S. we had to go through Customs, while they drove on. However, while at the counter in the office, a young Canadian honeymoon couple heard our tale, and told us they were only going over to the States to purchase a carton or two of cheaper cigarettes, and would be back in about a half hour. Bob and I, in the meantime, had to walk the half-mile or so between the U.S. and Canadian Custom Houses. True to their word, when we had completed our declarations, the newly weds picked us up and delivered us right to the door of the De Carterets, cousins of my Mother's, and almost in the middle of Montreal!

Across the Atlantic

We spent a day or two in Montreal with the De Carterets and their two charming daughters. We were shown round the town, taken out for meals, thank goodness, as we were a bit strapped for cash 'till we could get to an

Air Force Base. We were also taken to watch the launching of a corvette which Mrs De Carteret had the honour of launching by smashing a bottle of champagne upon the bow.

After that we caught the train to Saint John, New Brunswick, and were taken by buses (there were about 30 of us now) to a barracks at Penfield Ridge, about 40 miles south of Saint John. We paraded next morning, and had roll call to see how many of us there were, then pottered about most of the day looking for somewhere to get some decent tucker. After a couple of days there, we all got bused back to Saint John, and then by train, about another 200 miles to Monckton. The barracks there were filthy, but we Kiwis and Aussies cleaned them up a bit and went to bed.

At Monckton I had four days in Hospital with a tummy bug, but managed to get up to see the excellent and moving film, *Mrs Miniver*, at the local cinema. I also met up with Alan Harrison from North Canterbury, whom I hadn't seen since Levin days, almost a year earlier. We had a few days at this dump of a camp where we thought we were to convert on to Coastal Command Hudsons, but it turned out that the Station couldn't cope with another intake of pilots.

So after numerous parades and roll calls over the next few days, we were taken to the harbour-side at Halifax by train, and boarded the Castle Line ship, *Athlone Castle*, along with about 5,000 other servicemen. It was crowded, with 366 of us in bunks in the Boat Deck Lounge. The bunks were six layers high with a 2 ft alley between the rows, and 18 ins between the layers. I was lucky, as I got a top bunk which had about 30 ins from the bunk to the ceiling, and with my legs over the side and head bent forward, I could sit and watch what was going on at floor level, whether it be poker or other card games, two up, seven up or darts. The dart board in our alley was on the wall about 2ft below my bunk. Ricocheting darts either off the dart board or the steel bulkhead behind it, were a constant danger to those in their bunks nearby, whenever a dart game was in progress.

We all had life jackets, and boat drill for us up in the lounge was 'Put on your life jacket, and lie on your bunk.' There certainly would have been no room out on the deck in an emergency for all of us lot until they had got the boats lowered. At least though, we had a sporting chance of getting outside. I didn't envy the blokes in cabins down in the bowels of the ship.

The *Athlone Castle* went out in the harbour a bit and anchored overnight, and we had Boat Drill practice, and air raid alarms etc. After a couple of days at anchor, another ten huge troopships with battleships, cruisers, and eight destroyers, set out in convoy at 9 am on the 29th of September 1942.

The first night at sea made us realise we were really in a war zone. In spite of the number of vessels in close proximity to one another, it was a complete blackout. Mind you, on the *Titjalengka* we showed no lights across the Pacific, but considering the number of ships around us, the blackout seemed more intense out here in the cold grey Atlantic. A companion standing next to me out on the deck had come out with a lighted cigarette in his mouth, (I didn't smoke then) and a Pommie deck hand grabbed him by the shoulder, and in a no uncertain tone of voice with a Merseyside accent, admonished the unsuspecting fellow by shouting, 'Put that f***ing smoke out. You make the ruddy ship look like a f***ing lighthouse!' The game was now being played under British rules!

We went back inside and played cards, yarned, played darts and watched other gambling games; but most of the time was spent standing in queues, either for the toilet, the shower, the Dining Room or the Canteen. These queues were continuous and snaked up and down and all over different deck levels. If you were bursting to go to the loo, you just had to control yourself, or acquire an empty bottle or other suitable container to carry with you.

During the early hours I got in the breakfast queue which moved along at a snail's pace all morning, finally getting me to a dining table where I asked for what was chalked up on the menu board. 'Porridge and sausages and eggs please.' 'You've had it mate' was the reply. 'There is spam and lettuce and spuds on now for lunch.' 'But I haven't had it', I replied, 'I've only just got here.' It was there at that time that the expression, 'You've had it mate,' first came into our air force jargon.

And so we spent most of our time standing in queues as we steamed across the Atlantic. Sometimes you might get breakfast, or it could well be the evening meal by the time you would reach the Dining Room! On one occasion I queued for half a day to get to the Canteen. A number of my friends noticed I was in the canteen queue, so I was supplied with a empty kit bag, a hand full of money, and a list of requested purchases, which I proceeded to obtain when I finally arrived at the half door counter. I then distributed my supplies of sweets, chocolate biscuits, cigarettes etc, at a small profit of course! We of course kept all our valuables in a secure money belt round our waists at all times.

Our convoy moved along at the speed of the slowest ship, so we didn't break any Atlantic crossing records. There were however some submarine alarms, which alerted the destroyers into dashing in and out amongst the main body of the convoy at great speed, and dropping depth charges every now and then.

As we were nearing the coast of Northern Ireland, it was broadcast over the Tannoy system that Lord Haw Haw had declared over Radio Hamburg that the German High Command was pleased to announce that a courageous German submarine had torpedoed and sunk the British troopship *Athlone Castle* –the boat we were on! They were just a little premature, as I think it was just soon after our voyage that another Castle Line boat was unfortunately sunk, though thankfully without five or six thousand people on board. During our convoy journey we were under almost continual air protection of the faithful old Catalina, or Sunderland flying boats. No doubt they kept the Jerry subs out of sight, and well down below torpedo firing depth.

During our last evening at sea, five of us Kiwis assisted the Entertainment Committee with an item in the Concert for the officers' final night party, by making ourselves up as Maoris with burnt cork and lipstick and then performing a haka or two.

Operational Training in England

After nine days at sea, the ship pulled alongside the landing building on a dismal afternoon at Liverpool. My everlasting impression of our arrival there was that everything appeared to be built of bricks! The buildings looked tired and old and well-weathered, but had stood the test of time, and there was a war on.

We filed down the gang planks, were sorted out into our various categories, waded through a mountain of kitbags, (we only carried a small amount of gear with us) to claim ours containing all our flying gear, boots, helmets, goggles, gloves, sheepskin flying suits, overcoats, best dress uniform, other personal gear and in my case, a smallish five valve mantle radio wrapped up securely in all my spare jerseys.

We pilots, about fifty in number then as I recall, were assembled, had a roll call, and then were herded over to a waiting train bound for Bournemouth down on the Channel Coast. During the journey we had a meal on the train, and arrived at our billets, a converted block of flats, at 2.30 am. We had a meal and went to bed.

Over the next few days webbing gear and gas masks were issued, and there were parades for medical and teeth inspections. I think just about everyone picked up some sort of ailment during the trip over on the boat, mostly skin complaints. So we were treated for athletes foot, mycosis groin (same thing but in the crutch) and crabs, also in the groin or armpits. Crabs were damn awful itchy little sods. To keep to attention while on parade, was a severe test of mind over matter! The service treatment seemed to rely predominantly on a violent red solution of Condy's Crystals. It helped a bit, but I had far greater success with Whitfields ointment, which I got from a Chemist. After 3 or 4 days treatment, the crabs simply crawled out from under the skin and dropped off, seemingly dead. Incidentally, there was notice inside the toilet door reading: 'You may as well sit right down on the seat, 'Cos the crabs in this joint can jump six feet'. Another inscription read: 'Judging by the display of wit, Shakespeare must have come here to shit'.

Between parades we went shopping, to the movies, and to a dance or two etc. The little five valve radio that had come over with me from Canada I took to an electrician at a radio shop to get converted to England's 230 volt power. I was quite amazed at the simplicity of the task. The electrician there simply measured off a ten foot six inch length of a particular type of flexible electric cable, put a male and female plug on the ends, and that was it: 110 volts converted to 230 at very little cost!

We were given ten days leave which took me to London to visit aunts and cousins who had vacated their residence, Saint Ouen's Manor in Jersey, and come over to England before the Germans occupied the Channel Islands. Incidentally Saint Ouen's Manor featured in the TV series *Enemy at the Door*, filmed in later years. During my time in London I was shown around fairly extensively by tube and bus, but poor old London was still suffering and reeling after the onslaught of the German bombing raids. And it wasn't all over then!

Leave over, caught a train back to Bournemouth and we packed up our gear. Bob and I set off for a walk in the general direction of a ruined castle that we had heard about. On the way we observed a policeman about a hundred yards along the street, so began making our way towards him to ask for directions. Suddenly with a deafening roar and a staccato chatter of machine gun and cannon shell fire, a Messerchmitt 110 from across the Channel had come in below the radar screens on an opportunist raid, zoomed up over the cliff, and blasted everything in sight, including the unfortunate policeman, who in just a few moments had two or three Air Raid Wardens gathered around his shattered remains. We never did get to see the castle ruins, but just went straight back to our billets, with the realities of war uppermost in our minds.

Later on we took our kitbags etc, along to the railway station. Our destination was Church Lawford, an AFU (Advanced Flying Unit) near Rugby in the Midlands, and we arrived there on the 27th of October '42. The temperature had dropped, and the six of us who shared a Nissen Hut were frozen! We piled all the clothes we could under our battledress, and continued station life again with lectures, Link Training and flying, this time in twin-engined Airspeed Oxfords. The hazy misty conditions of wartime England were a far cry from the clear skies of Canterbury or Saskatchewan! Flying was very intermittent due to the lousy weather, but lectures and Link training continued.

We also 'swung' a couple of compasses. This involved taxiing the aircraft away out onto a concrete area that was clearly marked with the 'Points of the Compass,' and well away from any magnetic interference. The aircraft was then manhandled until it was facing exactly north and it was then that the compass in the aircraft could be adjusted to give a true bearing.

Another day or so was taken up with a short Commando Course and giving assistance in the defence of the airfield, when we were engaged in a mock attack by paratroops.

Bob Cotton, author and George Helm, training for combat at Church Lawford, near Rugby, England, November 1942

It was a good scrap while it lasted; but eventually the referees declared that the airfield had been captured, and we were either dead or taken prisoner. I wouldn't have liked to have been in a real engagement against one of those highly trained fellows back in those days! Their Tommy guns were in action from the time their parachutes opened, and in their position above they had a wonderful view of any movement below! There was of course only blank ammunition used on this occasion.

We were required to go to Church services, and be pall-bearers at the funerals of the various unfortunate pilots, who hadn't managed to cope with some of the atrocious conditions we encountered with the changeable weather we were experiencing at that time. B.A.T. (Beam Approach Training) came on to our agenda at about this time. It was similar to what we learnt with the Link Trainer, only now it was for real. The system enabled a pilot to approach an airfield that had the system in operation and let down onto the airfield and touch down between the runway lights, in almost zero visibility. It worked fairly well, but if a pilot got a bit disoriented, and got a bit below the flight approach line, instead of on it or slightly above, the landing tended to be a bit hard! We also did quite a bit of night flying on the Oxfords at Church Lawford, but managed a bit of time off now and then. We took a bus trip out to Coventry then Birmingham, and back to Rugby. We also went to the odd dance, and had numerous singsongs in the local pubs, with Vern on the piano, and me leading off the words on the vocals. The publicans encouraged us with free drinks to get the singsongs going, as the joyful sounds encouraged patrons in out of the blackout on the street.

A good Christmas dinner party was put on by the Station. We waited on the other ranks, then the officers waited on us sergeants, then the other ranks waited on the officers. (From memory I think that was how it was. Mind you I'm going back 56 years.)

Flying training continued to about the end of January '43, during which time I had a stint up in the control tower as Duty Pilot. I was lucky no major incidents occurred during my period on flying control. There was of course a senior officer hovering round at the rear in an easy chair, ready to take over in the event of unusual incidents occurring. At one stage, too, I was off flying duties for a few days while I was recovering from an inoculation shot.

With just over 300 flying training hours entered in my log book, I had completed the training at Church Lawford AFU. I had a few days leave then, before being posted to 21 OTU (Operational Training Unit) at Moreton-in-Marsh.

21 OTU, Moreton-in-Marsh

The serious side of wartime flying was now before us, and the morning after our arrival, we were called from our barracks out on to parade and roll call. We twenty or so pilots were told to go to the Canteen, and select the other four members of our crew, so off we went to find our crews. There were about a hundred air crew milling around in the Canteen: navigators, bomb aimers, wireless operators, gunners, and of course by now, our bunch of pilots as well. It was then we discovered that a crew hadn't been selected for us individually; we had to find and choose them ourselves! This seemed to me to be the most organised disorganisation that had been encountered so far, in our flying careers!

I found my way over to the bar, and purchased a drink. With my back to the bar, I watched this jabbering, gesticulating and shouting mass of blue-uniformed personnel. How the hell, I thought, are you supposed to pick, and then, if successful, entrust your life to a crew acquired out of a crowd of seemingly irresponsible youths like that?

Halfway through my second drink, my question was answered. Three bright-looking bods, in the darker blue uniforms of the RAAF, enquired if I had a crew yet? When I answered in the negative, these three Aussies asked whether, as I appeared to be a likely sort of pilot, I would accept them in my crew. Having introduced ourselves, we set off in search of a bomb aimer. Our search ended with the acquisition of a farm lad from Lincolnshire with the single stripe on his sleeve of a P/O (Pilot Officer), who introduced himself as Jeff Tomlinson. That completed our crew, with P/O Alan (Plum) Warner, a school teacher from Sydney, as navigator, Sgt Alan Goodall, a barber from Bendigo, as wireless operator / air gunner, and Sgt Bernie (Penny) Farthing from Dubbo, not long out of high school, as rear gunner.

Two of my crew: Allan Goodall, wireless operator, and 'Penny' Farthing, rear gunner, Moreton-in-Marsh, December 1942.

Well, we were crewed up, so we had a few drinks to get to know one another, then it was off to bed. There really was no other, or better, way to get bombing crews selected, I think. It wouldn't be desirable or practical to have someone else choose whom you were to fly with.

On February 15th '43 our bunch started flying in Wellington Mk 1C bombers. The Wellington bomber was the brainchild of Barnes Wallis back in the mid-thirties, and was Britain's front line bomber until 1942, when the four-engined Halifaxes, Stirlings and Lancasters took over the major bombing roles in the European theatre. It was Barnes Wallis who designed and perfected the 'Bouncing Bomb' which was used successfully on the Dam buster raids.

The wingspan of the Wimpy was 92ft. It weighed about 15 tons and used about 84 gallons of fuel an hour, which gave you 1.9 air miles per gal.

The Mk IC was powered by two Bristol Pegasus engines of 1050 hp, and was a bit underpowered.

*'The Loch Ness' Wellington.
As reconstructed at the Brooklands Museum, England.*

The ones we had at OTU were mostly tired old aircraft retired from operational flying. The Mk X, which we flew out to North Africa, and on operations, was a vastly better aircraft. It was powered by two Bristol Hercules twin row fourteen cylinder sleeve-valved air cooled radial motors, of 1,675 hp each, and turning thirteen foot three-bladed constant speed propellers. Wimpies were robust aircraft of unique geodetic construction, easy to fly and quite reliable generally. They could take a terrific amount of abuse from enemy action and flak, and I've seen them limping back to base with holes blown through the wings and or fuselage that you could have walked through! I became quite fond of Wellingtons during my comparatively short length of time that I had with them.

One of the exercises that pilots were required to become familiar with was low level cross country flying, so one day when the weather was particularly inclement, my instructor suggested, seeing as no other aircraft were off the ground (even the birds were walking!) it would be a good time for me to have the opportunity to do some low level flying. We got a parachute each, though what for I don't know, except that Kings Regulations required all airmen to have one when off the ground. But I guess we weren't figuring on being high enough up in the air for a parachute to be any use to us anyway!

We climbed into the aircraft, I started up the motors and taxied to the end of the runway. Then with F/O Lewis in the co-pilot's seat with a topographical map of the local area on his knee, I opened the taps, and we took off. Visibility was approximately the length of the runway, about a mile, and cloudbase not much over a hundred feet. It was fun skimming over houses and trees, flicking a wing tip up over church steeples etc, and following the contour of the rolling hills and valleys. I had been flying on a compass course for about twenty-five minutes, when F/O Lewis informed me to be watching out for a major transmission power line, which we would soon be in the vicinity of. 'Shit', he immediately exclaimed as we went under the wires between two pylons, 'I think we'll go back now.' So I did a 180 degree turn, and headed back to the training base on a reciprocal course, making sure we were high enough up in the mist to clear the power lines on our return journey. We arrived over Base, did a half circuit and landed. My instructor was clearly shaken! After all he had already done a tour or two of duty over enemy territory, and to have been killed on an exercise like that was I guess not part of his plan in life.

After about 8 hours dual I went off solo in the Wellington, then after another 70 hours flying with my crew we were considered experienced enough to go off on operations. My crew and I were given the option as to the Theatre of War we would prefer to participate in, and at that time the Japanese threat to Australia and New Zealand was a far greater issue to the Aussies in my crew and to me than the German invasion of England! Anyway we had seen England. So we thought, let's go out to Burma or somewhere down that way. Even Jeff, our Lincolnshire-born bomb-aimer, was keen to get out of England for a while, and see some different countries.

Pilot's instrument panel of the Wellington

1. Bomb steering indicator,
2. Bomb/depth charge jettison control.
3. Auto-controls pressure gauge.
4. Instrument flying panel.
5. Starter and booster coil pushbuttons - port engine.
6. Propeller feathering switch—port engine.
7. Port engine speed indicator.
8. Undercarriage warning horn test pushbutton.
9. Fuel contents gauges pushbutton.
10. Windscreen wiper controls.
11. Undercarriage indicator.
12. Boost gauges (two).
13. Starboard engine speed indicator.
14. Cylinder temperature gauges (two).
15. Propeller feathering switch - starboard engine.
16. Oil tank low-level warning lights (two).
17. Starter and booster coil pushbuttons - starboard engine
18. Pneumatic pressure gauge.
19. Fire extinguisher pushbuttons (two).
20. Air temperature gauge.
21. D.F. indicator.
22. Fuel pressure warning lights (two).
23. Pilot's call light.
24. Flare launching warning light.
25. Suction gauge.
26. Oil pressure gauges (two).
27. Oil temperature gauge - starboard engine.
28. Boost gauge reversal control.
29. Flap control lever.
30. Compass.
31. Undercarriage selector lever,
32. Rudder pedal - starboard.
33. Windscreen de-icing pump
34. Oil temperature gauge - port engine.
35. Rudder bar adjustment wheel.
36. Flap indicator.
37. Cowling gill controls (two).
38. Intercomm. microphone pushbutton.
39. Torpedo release pushbuttons (two).
40. Brake lever.
41. Brake locking slide.
42. Bomb release pushbutton.
43. Bomb doors control.
44. Landing lamps switch.
45. Bomb master switch.

After completing our operational training towards the end of March, we obtained a couple of weeks leave to have our last look around England, and swill down a few more pints of their wartime beer. As we were required to have our gas masks with us, it was a simple procedure to remove all the contents of one's gas mask haversack, and replace them with your personal gear. It made a very handy carry-all bag. And of course, provided an Air Raid Warden didn't wish to see what your gas mask bag contained, you could save yourself a bit of extra baggage. Of course you always had it packed so that its appearance made it looks as though it contained a gas mask etc! I was never unfortunate enough to be caught without a gas mask; but the Lord only knows how I would have fared if Jerry had initiated a gas attack!

So with the Air Force issue food coupons for a couple of weeks, off we went visiting relatives, friends, old haunts and sight-seeing. Leave over, we returned to Moreton-in-Marsh, and waited around for three or four days until a brand new Wellington Mk X was flown in for us. It had barely an hour's flying time on the clock, and required to be completely tested out to our satisfaction.

And so we all went on a few trips in HF797 to check her out. We took her out across to the magnetic-free concrete pad to swing the two compasses, one in the cockpit, and the other in the navigator's compartment, then out over the Wash in the East of England, to test the six Browning machine guns, two in the front turret that Jeff operated, and four in the rear turret under the control of Penny, our rear gunner. Another navigational flight of eight and a half hours took us round the northern parts of the British Isles on a petrol consumption test. Sparks (Alan Goodall) also had a further opportunity to make sure that his radio equipment was sparking on all valves, that the intercom was operating clearly from all outlets, and among other things, that the hand pumps for the emergency fuel tanks operated freely. He also had a chance to use the Brownings in the front turret, as that would be his position on the run up to the target while Jeff was busy over his bomb sight. He was also quite adept at the use of the four Brownings in the rear turret, though he did happen to mention that his long legs did not fit comfortably in the confined space back there. Hence, no doubt the reason why rear gunners were short, tough little blokes, as was Penny.

Plum, of course busied himself with the navigation, and brushing up on all the myriads of navigational hints, examples, shortcuts and pitfalls that he had learnt during the previous months. It never ceased to amaze me how, after flying for 7 or 8 hours over unfamiliar country, often at night and on dog leg courses, I would hear his voice over the inter-com: 'Hey Skipper, such and such should be coming into view about now.' And sure enough, as we pushed on at our economical cruising speed of 150 mph, our expected location would appear within a few miles below us. Whether it be our intended landing strip, bombing target, particular landmark or whatever, Plum always got us there, with I guess a bit of help from me. Except on our last flight together many months later!

During the latter part of our flying training at 21 OTU a large number of our operational training flights involved bombing practice on marked targets in a designated waste-land area, and it was on these occasions that Jeff honed his already excellent bomb-aiming skills. The 'bombs' were of course dummies, either 1000 pounders, or a mixture of 500 and 250 pounders to make up a load of a couple of tons of bombs plus 950 to 1,000 gallons of fuel which we would be requiring if on a long bombing mission. These practice bombs didn't explode, but did throw out a sizeable area of whitish chalk-like powder, which made it easy, when turning away from the target, to see where the bombs had landed. On the run up to the target, which I would have identified from my pilot's seat, through instructions and photographs referred to us at briefing prior to takeoff, Jeff would be lying on the floor below the front gun turret, setting his bomb sight to our height above ground, air speed and wind drift, size of bombs and spacing between them. If required, and it always was on a genuine bombing raid, the camera would also be timed to coincide with the bomb drop. The camera would take six pictures, the fourth of which would show the area where the bombs would fall. That was of course if Jeff had got all his adjustments, dials and switches set right, and I kept the Wimpy straight and level, and obeyed Jeff's instructions of 'right, right, steady, left, steady, steady, - - - Bombs away.' I then continued straight and level for a further twenty seconds or so until the camera had taken its pictures.

To the Middle East

When all was in order, we loaded all our kit etc into HF797, said goodbye to Moreton-in-Marsh, and flew off down to 3 OADU (Overseas Aircraft Delivery Unit) at Hurn in Dorset. We remained here for about a week while weather conditions further south improved, and we got a clearance to land at Gibraltar.

At this time, Hurn was being used to train pilots in the flying and landing of troop-carrying Horsa gliders, which were being towed by Stirling bombers. To make the handling characteristics of the glider somewhat similar to a troop-carrying operation, rides were being offered to interested personnel for these take offs and landings. We joined the queue. Eventually it was our turn along with about another twenty or so other odd bods. Our large and cumbersome looking machine came quietly in over the boundary fence at about 20ft, stalled, and landed before us with a resounding crunch, completely breaking its back! Some very shaken and bruised passengers emerged through the normal, and not so normal apertures in the craft, and made their way from the wreck. Those gliders by the way, were constructed to be as light as possible, and were made predominately of plywood. We broke out of our line in the queue and decided to go to the local for a quiet drink. And now even after 57 years, I still have never been up in a glider!

Eventually weather conditions improved, and on the night of April the 27th 1943 we took off from Hurn in HF797, heading for Gibraltar. It was 11.30pm. Our flight path required Plum to put us on a dogleg course well out over the Atlantic beyond the Bay of Biscay to avoid Jerry night fighters from German occupied France picking off lone aircraft such as us. We never saw any, and obviously none of them saw us. The Wimpy was of course in night-flying mode. She was painted black, we displayed no navigation or identification lights, and the engine exhausts were shrouded to eliminate any sign of flame or red-hot pipes. Cockpit lights were off, and instrument lighting was little more than the glow of the luminous painted dials! We were invisible in the darkness of the night.

As the starlit darkness of the night slowly turned to the grey light of dawn, from our altitude of 9,500ft three islands appeared out of the grey expanse of sea about 50 miles east of our port wing. Upon my informing Plum of my sighting, he came out of his chart room, noted what certainly appeared to be some islands, and a decision was made to change course and head over towards them, as the only islands that they could possibly be were the Azores! We were hundreds of miles off-course and had only about two and a half hours fuel left! Panic! I can only imagine what Plum would have been thinking at that time. We were I guess a pretty green crew, and here we were on our first overseas operational flight, miles off course! But after a few minutes on our new course daylight increased, and what had appeared to be islands were the tops of some Portuguese mountains protruding through cloud, which in the dimmer light of dawn resembled the sea. A break in the cloud below us revealed the coast of Portugal, a semi-friendly nation. I put the Wimpy into a spiralling turn and descended through the hole in the cloud to a few hundred feet, at a short distance out from the coast. Plum's navigation had been spot on! We could map read now from here on down to Gibraltar.

As the sun rose over the peaceful Portuguese inhabitants along this rural coast, the war was out of our minds for the time being. There were animals grazing on the early morning dew-spangled grass, and tidy white cottages with their red-tiled roofs. Children were out on their ponies for an early morning canter, or perhaps off to school and a woman with a bucket on her arm waved to us on her way to milk the waiting cow as we passed nearby. It was a relaxed atmosphere in the 'plane now as we sipped on hot coffee from our thermos flasks, while rounding Portuguese Cape Saint Vincent and headed for the Straits of Gibraltar.

I dropped 797 down to just a few feet above the waves to go through the Straits, and Jeff, who had taken up his position in the front turret at that time, was heard to remark, 'We must be flying over a school of whales, as I can see them spouting in the sea below.' He was sadly mistaken. The 'spouts' were from anti aircraft shells being fired at us from the shore batteries on the northern tip of Morocco. Thank goodness they missed us, but by crikey, from a distance of 10 or 12 miles and firing at a target moving at 150mph they didn't miss us by much. We hadn't been warned of their presence before we left England, otherwise it would have been more prudent to have kept a bit closer to the Spanish side of the Straits. The Spanish were quite openly pro- Nazi, but nevertheless were not openly aggressive to the Allies. It was becoming increasingly evident that flying in a war zone could be a danger to your health!

As we rounded the Cape and started the run up to the Rock the main fuel tanks started running dry, so Alan swung into action on the Zwicky fuel pump of the emergency supply to keep us in the air 'till we reached the strip at Gib. We were going to have nothing to spare, and would have to make a landing on the reputedly short strip on the first attempt. There would not be sufficient fuel left to go round again! We had been warned before leaving England that there would be very little fuel to spare on this leg of our journey, so I knew the obligations I had to my crew, a brand new aircraft, and myself. I had to get it right the first time. After nearly nine hours at the controls, I was no doubt feeling a bit tired, but the excitement of making a landing at such an unusual place as The Rock had the adrenalin pumping through my veins.

The approach to the airstrip was over the harbour, which was crowded with ships, some even moored to the end of the runway which protruded out into the harbour a short distance, in an effort, no doubt to make a touchdown and slow up sufficiently to turn round before going off the other end into the sea. I recall it wasn't a reassuring sight to see the remains of a number of wrecked aircraft protruding out of the sea at the far end of the runway as I made my approach over a thicket of ships masts. I certainly would have liked to have been able to make my approach a good deal lower than mast height! However with full flap on and wheels down, air speed about 90mph (having used practically all our fuel we were pretty lightly loaded) and with brake pressure well above the recommended minimum of 120 pounds per square inch, I set her down short, cut the throttles and hit the brakes. Thank goodness they were new and worked well! We had a bit of runway to spare, but not much. Chattering over the intercom started up again after the silence of the last five minutes, as I taxied over to the vicinity of the Control Tower and a bunch of airmen waiting to greet us. We had successfully completed our first operational flight!

We were obliged to hand in all valuables from the plane, which included a couple of Omega watches, and our own personal RAF issue .38 Smith and Wesson revolvers. There were a few hundred Spaniards from La Linea who had permits to work in Gibraltar. They were checked by the Border Guards as they went to and from work through the barbed wire barricaded border alongside the runway, but things still mysteriously went missing.

In Egypt

We spent nearly a week in Gibraltar. I can't recall why; but it was a nice sunny place for a rest. Then we hopped from there to Biskra in Tunisia, to Castel Benito, on to El Adem, and finally via Cairo West to Fayid in Egypt. The plane was due for its 50hr inspection, and would not be ready for a couple of days. When we went back again to pick it up, we were informed that the plane had gone on out East.[1] A crew on the top of a list had been allocated it and our names were on the bottom. We would just have to wait until our turn came. So we hitched a ride back to Cairo again with some other airmen, also with all their kit in the back of an Army 3 tonner.

While the truck was stopped at a busy crossroad in a barren area, a hand suddenly reached up over the tailboard and grabbed the sheepskin flying jacket of a young South African Spitfire pilot. The teenage Wog made off down the road with his ill-gotten gain but he didn't get far. The South

---

1. In fact HF797 stayed in the Middle East, operating with 104 Squadron in Tunisia and Italy until Struck off Charge in December 1944, presumably worn out.

African pilot, quick as a flash, whipped out his .38 and with two quick shots at about 25yds dropped the bugger. Then yelling out to the driver to hang on a minute, he hopped out and went back for his jacket. He didn't spend any time with his victim, just snatched up his jacket out of the dust and blood and hopped back up in the truck as we drove off into Cairo. His only comment was, 'Well the bugger won't be doing that again.' He was much more concerned over the fact that his nice leather flying jacket had 'f***ing wog blood on it'. After all, I suppose, they were just about as thick out there as their blasted flies were, and were helping the war effort about as much.

Our tented camp was near the end of the northern tramline out of Cairo, at Heliopolis. There were hundreds of us there: trained aircrew, but with no aircraft.

'Browned off': The author at Almaza Camp, Egypt, 1943.

After about three weeks we acquired another Wellington, and were all prepared to have another go at getting out to the Far East; but that morning I developed an ear infection from the swimming pool water, and as we taxied out for take-off my eye-sight blurred, so I taxied back to dispersal.

I had a temperature of 104° and was admitted to the Army Base Hospital in Cairo. Apparently I looked ghastly. My crew, who kept coming in to see me, didn't expect me to live. And I must admit that I wasn't counting on surviving either, with a temp eventually of 105°. I lost 27 lbs in ten days! I was getting medical inspections every hour or two; but when the medics agreed I was about ripe, was given a shot of Pentathol, wheeled down to the theatre, and was back again in 20 minutes. The pain was all gone and I was ravenously hungry. They had no doubt sucked out the infection causing the swelling at the back of my eardrum. I had a few more days in hospital before getting some sick leave.

During my leave I had an unusual experience at a concert, stage and floor show put on by professional artists for the entertainment of the thousands of Allied troops in the area. The group came to do a show at the hospital, and I was wheeled along in my bed with many other wheel-chaired and walking wounded. One item that sticks in my memory was of a fellow going about among the audience while his partner was on the stage blindfolded. He would handle articles produced by members of the audience and she would describe what they were. I had started smoking then, and before being wheeled down to the show, had gathered 9 or 10 cigarettes in a Craven A packet. I had smoked one. The showman had by this time moved around to the area where my bed was. He picked up the cigarette packet and asked his blindfolded accomplice, 'What am I holding,' To which she replied, 'A Craven A cigarette packet.' He next asked, 'How many cigarettes are there in it?' She replied 'Nine'. When he asked, 'What sort are they?' I thought, this will fool her, but no it didn't. She replied 'There are four Craven A, three Woodbines and two Players.' which upon opening the packet, we saw was quite correct. He next put his finger under the strap of the watch I had on my wrist, and asked 'What am I holding now?' It was quite an elaborate stop watch; but she described it perfectly, even the French logo round the dial, which would have required a microscope to read. Then when she gave the serial number on the back, my hair started to stand on end. Now this watch had not been off my wrist for days, as it wasn't even then; but when she said my initials and name which were also engraved on the back, as well as my Air Force number, NZ415318, I very nearly fainted. It certainly was eerie! Supposedly she was reading my subconscious mind. I don't know, but it was damned queer. I of course knew my name and number etched on the back, but not the other logo on the watch There were no wonderful electrical gadgets around then, as there are now, and in any case there was no way anyone would have been able to tell what was on the back of my watch, or even known exactly what cigarettes were in that packet. I've asked dozens of people since, but no one has been able to explain that event. With others that were involved, I just considered it must have been a pre- arranged put up job; but in my case I know darn well it couldn't have been! The two performers were, I think, Greek.

Ten days sick leave was granted me at a nice little hotel on the beach at Tel-Aviv, in Palestine. Wireless operator Alan and rear gunner Penny came with me on the train too. We had a great relaxing time there, swimming and lying on the beach amongst the girls sunbathing. I quickly started getting my weight back up to normal again. We took a few bus trips round the area, out to the Dead Sea, Bethlehem, Jerusalem, the Garden of Gethsemane and other biblically historic places, such as The Wailing Wall, Rachel's Tomb, the Church of all Nations etc.

Church of All Nations, Garden of Gethsemane & Mount of Olives, 1943.

Leave over, we took an overnight train back down and across the Suez to Cairo. The train was crowded with troops, Jews, Arabs, goats, chooks, cats, canaries, kids of all ages etc. To get out of the mayhem during the course of the sleepless night, one or two of us got up in the overhead luggage rack. We had almost got to sleep up there when the jolting and swaying of the carriage, plus our weight, brought the whole lot down on the menagerie below. If we hadn't had the assistance of other Allied personnel, I guess we could have been involved in a sticky Arab incident! So we luckily escaped the wrath of the unfortunate passengers and animals etc on which we had landed, and with but a few bruises and no bones broken we continued on down to Cairo, and back to camp at Heliopolis.

There was, apart from the 9am daily roll call, the odd medical check, and on this particular occasion all 500 of us were lined up in two rows facing each other between the tent rows. We then stripped off with our clothes at our feet, to await the medics' giving us a thorough physical do over. We were inspected for syphilis, clap and other venereal diseases, crabs, lice, piles, mycosis feet or groin, and every other ailment that could lurk in any hidden place or orifice. It was an eye opener to be part of a parade of 500 plus naked young men. I had always understood that all men are born equal. It was obvious on viewing this line up that it is not the case. Some are far better endowed and equipped than others of us! Mind you we did have a few Egyptians who worked on the camp in our line up. They obviously believed in the theory that biggest is best!

An amusing incident occurred about the time of our encampment near Cairo in 1943. An easily recognized Flying Officer (due mainly to his bushy RAF style moustache) was observed by one of his senior officers on an upper floor in Shepheard's Hotel, completely naked, and following a flimsily-clad young woman to a bedroom. The senior officer was horrified, and knowing who the offending young pilot was, put him on charge for 'being improperly dressed in a public place', ordering him to appear at a Court Martial on a certain date and place.

The offender was duly escorted under guard to the appropriate place at the appointed time. He stood to attention before the high-ranking members of the Court. The charge was read out. 'Flying Officer So and So, you are charged with being, as an officer and a gentleman, improperly dressed in a public place, namely Shepheard's Hotel. What have you to say?'

The young officer replied, 'Sir, King's Regulations state that an airman is considered to be correctly dressed if he is suitably attired for the sport he is engaged in.'

After a moment's silence, the presiding officer declared 'case dismissed' and the Court adjourned. It certainly pays to know King's Regulations.

Towards the end of July '43 the survivors of the New Zealand Division had returned to Cairo with other Allied forces for some R & R, and things in town livened up considerably. After all these fellows had been fighting Rommel and his Afrika Korps for the last three years across the North African deserts, and had finally driven them out of Tunisia and back into Italy and Sicily. These now exuberant young fighting men almost took over the town. Take-overs of pubs and other liquor outlets were not unusual happenings. You would find a crowd of Army fellows gathered on the street outside, while one or two others held the owner or proprietor up against the wall with a gun, and others handed out all the available beverages to eager but unwilling to pay customers. When that place went dry they would move on to somewhere else. Of course the Military Police tried to maintain law and order, but at times fought losing battles. After all the troops had been engaged in fighting for a year or two so what was a bit of a scrap with the MP's to worry about? After one particularly large involvement between raucous revellers and the MP's, about 110 troops and 90 MP's required hospital treatment. It was a good scrap but luckily there were no deaths!

Back to the United Kingdom

These fellows had been in the thick of the fighting, while for the last three months my fully-trained crew and I had done nothing to help the war effort. Something had to be done! Plum and I checked out the Adjutant's Office at our Air Force Headquarters over a day or two. We figured he was usually out between 12.30 and 1.15pm. So next day, dressed in our best Air Force issue khaki tropical uniforms, and armed with an official looking document, we bowled up past the guards on the steps of the Headquarters building. Plum returned the salute the guards gave him, and we went inside. It was about 12.45, and no one seemed to be about. No doubt they were all over at the Mess Tent, fighting the flies for their lunch! We entered the door marked 'Adj', which was ajar, rummaged round in some cupboards and drawers to get some Air Ministry paper and envelopes, then hid our loot amongst the official-looking documents we already had, walked back out past the Guards, whose salute Plum returned, and back to our tents. We then proceeded to compose a letter to be presented to Wing Commander Lane, Air Officer Commanding, No 21 OTU, Moreton-in-Marsh. The letter stated that Sgt Pilot J B Hayman and crew were to be supplied with a Wellington Mk.X aircraft from the Vickers factory at Bristol, test the said aircraft, and fly it out to the Middle East to further the efforts of the fighting forces in that area. It was signed, Air Commodore (an indistinguishable signature) Officer Commanding Tactical Forces Eastern Area.

We informed our Camp commander of our posting, packed our necessary kit, and put the remainder in storage at Cairo base camp. Actually that kitbag, containing my surplus gear, arrived back home here in 1946, a year after the war ended. We said our goodbyes round the camp at Heliopolis and hitch-hiked over to Cairo West airfield with, of course, our precious letter. Hitching a ride round that area was never a problem back in those days with military vehicles in large numbers on the roads at most times. We got to the airfield in pretty good time; but what were our chances of hitching back to England?

There were a few military aircraft to be seen as we made our way to the Control Tower with our kitbags. Our fears of perhaps having to hang around for days, possibly weeks, for a ride back to England, were soon dispelled when the Duty Flight Control Officer revealed the good news that an American DC3 cargo plane would be taking off in about an hour on a flight back to Hendon Aerodrome, London. But he told us we had better get out there quickly and ask the pilot if he was willing to have us on board, as it was a cargo plane with no spare seats fitted. We went over to the vicinity of the aircraft, where a small group of U.S. airmen were. I went up to the one with the silver wings of a pilot on his jacket, and asked if there was any chance of getting a ride with them back to England? The Captain replied in the southern drawl of a Texan, 'Shure Bud. Hop in. You'se all 'll find it a bit uncomfortable. There's no seats in this goddam kite, just grab a cargo strap and tie yourselves to the floor at take offs and landings.'

Throwing our gear down for a seat on the shiny, well-worn aluminium floor, and tying ourselves down with the hefty cargo straps which were strategically located about the interior of the wide-bodied craft, we congratulated ourselves that at last we were on the move again! It was August the 6th '43.

The flight back to England took a little over two days, and we touched down at practically the same refuelling bases that had been used by us on our flight out, three months previously. What a waste it was of fully trained airmen, to be sitting down at Cairo all that time, while the war was raging both in Tunisia against Rommel and his Afrika Corps Panzers, and also out in the South West Pacific and South East Asia, against the aggressive and tenacious Japs. And of course we weren't the only ones. There seemed to be hundreds of airmen in the camp out at Heliopolis with nothing to fly. No wonder the war dragged on for such a long time. No doubt everyone concerned with the conflict was doing their best, and aircraft factories were working day and night, but while everything during the past fifteen months of my training had seemed to have been so precisely and meticulously organised, hold-ups like we had experienced in Cairo shouldn't fit into the scheme of things. Mind you, my getting an infection no doubt contributed quite a bit to our inactivity in the air war. However we had had the chance to climb the Pyramids and see the Sphinx, and visit many other historical and biblical places. I'm a great believer in the thought that there is an invisible hand that to a large extent steers us along life's path. Were we being steered now? When I look back over my life I think we were.

The flight across North Africa was naturally quite warm, but the night flight from Gibraltar out over the Atlantic and high over the Bay of Biscay was damned cold on a kitbag on the aluminium floor! On arrival at Hendon near London, we took the Underground to the New Zealand Forces Club at 18 Charing Cross Road. We were particularly conspicuous in our khaki shirts and shorts, and sun-tanned appearances, amongst other service personnel in war ravaged, smog shrouded London, with their pale hands and pasty features. On account of our obvious overseas activities we were showered with questions as to what we had been doing?

There had recently been news reports of Allied air raids on the Ploesti oil fields in Romania. So we settled on that line of bullshit. Yes we had been on a raid over Ploesti from Israel, and carried on to England to refuel. An impossible flight actually, but it went down well, and we were plied with free drinks to tell of our experiences out in the Middle East, until the lateness of the hour and lack of more tall stories dictated that we depart before we blew our cover!

On our arrival at Moreton-in-Marsh by train next day, we handed our letter to S/Ldr B.S. Leslie, Officer Commanding 311 Ferry Training Unit. He never queried our forged letter and signature, but directed us to draw bedding out of Stores, find ourselves an empty billet, and await instructions. It was no trouble getting somewhere to sleep, as empty beds were always becoming available as unfortunate air crew terminated their flying careers prematurely, or training-completed crews moved on to other areas.

We didn't have to wait long. Only about a week later a messenger came to inform me that a new Wimpy was on the tarmac ready for us to take up and test fly. Over the following few days we did the usual cross country fuel consumption tests, tried out the guns over The Wash, tested the wireless equipment, swung the compasses etc.

And Back to North Africa

On the 2nd of September we left Moreton-in-Marsh and flew down to No. 1 OADU at Portreath in Cornwall. Our Wimpy was fully fuelled up, and next day, on the 3rd of September, we went off on the night flight down the Atlantic past the Bay of Biscay to Ras-el-Ma, near Fez in Morocco. I recall on that occasion for some inexplicable reason we had run out of tobacco and cigarettes and apparently we were unable to obtain any locally. Shops must have been shut or something. However I still had some tissue papers for roll your owns, so there we were in the streets of Fez picking up cigarette butts out of the gutters and retrieving the useful bits of tobacco from them to enable me to roll up some fags for the others and me to smoke. What sticks in my mind is that they were the most awful cigarettes I've ever tasted. I think if anyone ever wanted to kick the habit, that would be not a too bad a way to go about it! Our craving for the habit must have been pretty strong in those youthful days. I had only started the habit a few months previously when encamped at Cairo, and New Zealand Forces Patriotic Society food and comforts parcels started arriving. These invariably contained, among other things, cigarettes and tobacco. I got a bit cheesed off at the way my crew pounced on these items, and so started smoking them myself, and shortly became so addicted to the insidious habit that my crew started referring to me as Smokey, as against my normal handle of Skipper. I smoked for about twenty years, but thank goodness I quit the habit then!

The author's crew photographed in front of a wrecked German aircraft. Left to right: Allan, Plum, Jeff and Penny.

After our overnight stay at Ras-el-Ma, and with full fuel tanks, we continued our journey on East. But after a couple of hours out over the Sahara Desert a panel light went red, indicating that we had lost the oil pressure in the starboard engine. Not wanting to ruin a practically new engine, I stopped the motor and feathered the propeller. We continued on then with one motor for another couple of hours to the emergency landing field at Biskra. We were to stay there for over a week while the oil pressure problem was sorted out.

At Biskra

Billets at this desert oasis were in a commandeered Arab Sheikh's mansion, and our bunks were in some of the (unfortunately now devoid of women) harem ladies' boudoirs. The doors of these rooms led out onto a balcony completely surrounding, but on the floor above, an ornately mosaic-tiled central bathing pool which wasn't empty. The nearby township of perhaps a few hundred locals was I guess at this time of military activity mainly under the control of eight or ten British Army personnel, whose duty it was to guard the acre or so of 44 gallon drums of 100 octane aviation fuel. The main purpose of this field was for returning bombers from raids over Italy etc, to land at if their own aerodromes nearer the coast were shrouded in fog. The head of this little Army detachment was the Warrant Officer DAPM (District Army Provost Marshal). We were well fed and looked after while the technicians who had been flown in sorted out our aircraft's problem.

Even though the fuel dump was pretty much under surveillance at all times, and especially at night when the two guards on night watch would start from the front and patrol round either side of the Dump, meeting at the back about every half hour, there was still the odd drum that mysteriously seemed to be missing. Suspicions were further aroused by the activities of vehicles in the village that seemed to be about a lot more than their wartime petrol allocation would have allowed. One day Penny, Alan and I were invited to go with the DAPM, a driver and a gunner, in the back of the 4x4 Chev Quad that was used to show a sense of authority to the local inhabitants. We drove slowly along the main thoroughfare and pulled up opposite a Citroen Ute parked outside the General Store. It was a suspect vehicle. The DAPM went over to the vehicle with a glass syringe attached to a rubber tube and extracted some fuel from the Citroen's tank. It was bright green 100 octane aviation fuel! At about that time the, I presume, owner of the vehicle came back out of the shop with his purchases, saw what was happening, hopped in the Citroen, stoked it up and took off at high speed in a cloud of dust. As soon as the DAPM could get back in the Quad we did a U turn and took off in hot pursuit of the fugitive but even with the Chev flat to the boards the Citroen was increasing its distance ahead of us. It was apparently going pretty well on the Avgas! However as we got out beyond the outskirts of the village, the track became more choked by drifted sand, and the 4x4 started catching up. When within 50 to 60 yards, orders were given to the Gunner on the back with us to 'Give it to the bastard.' The Lewis Gun opened up with its characteristic staccato chatter, and through the dust the tyres at the rear of the Citroen were seen to puncture and the driver slumped over the wheel and the vehicle came to an erratic stop near the side of the ill-defined track. We went slowly round the bullet-riddled vehicle, noting that the unfortunate miscreant's body was also well punctured, and that he was obviously dead. No one bothered to get out of our vehicle; but a compliment was passed to the Gunner on his excellent marksmanship! We simply drove back to our headquarters mansion and had a drink. We, inexperienced to that kind of rough justice, certainly needed one! The point had been made. Justice had been done, and law and order would prevail at least for a while.

 The drums were scattered about, and I guess it would be no problem for an experienced native thief to lie out of sight behind a drum of fuel, and while rolling it towards himself, smoothing out the resulting marks left by the drum with a palm frond. Even though the Guards patrolled the perimeter of the area every half hour at night, I guess a crafty thief would manage to roll the odd drum away undetected. In spite of the consequences, the temptation of acquiring some free fuel in an area of short supply could prove too much for some of the locals.

We learnt, during our stopover at Biskra, that there was an excellent fortune-teller who operated on some afternoons over in a shady area called the Park. We went along there one afternoon to make his acquaintance.

Fortune-teller in the Garden of Allah, Biskra.

We paid a few francs, and through an interpreter we had our futures looked into. I don't recall what was said of the other members of my crew's futures, but events that he predicted of mine proved to be surprisingly true! At the time of course, I didn't think too much about what he had told me, except perhaps that I would survive the war, which was I suppose a bit of a cheering thought when one considers that at that time an aircrew member had only a 50–50 chance. He operated by pushing your hands down firmly onto a tray of sand. Then when your hands were removed an accurate impression of all the lines of your hands were plainly visible in the fine sand on the tray. He then started erasing the impressions with a small stick. Then talking to the interpreter, he informed me that I would have a bad accident, but would survive the war. I would marry a dark-haired girl and have four or six children. That seemed a bit indecisive, but as it has turned out, now when I look back 57 years later it is surprisingly true. I had a bad accident, then later on my first dark-haired wife and I had four children. When I married again later, my second wife Linda and I have had two more children. It seems as though your whole life is in the palm of your hand! If you want to find out, go to Biskra. No doubt his son or grandson will be carrying on the business. If you are travelling by car though, don't try stealing petrol!

It seemed as if some no longer employed members of the Sheikh's harem had set themselves up in business on their own account down in the village. They no doubt made a reasonable living at their trade, as at that time quite a number of allied airmen passed through there, as well as numerous convoys of Army vehicles and personnel. Prior to our stopover there, up to a few months before, the customers would have been drawn from the German and Italian Forces. I wasn't tempted to sample the women's trade! However, on the last evening of our stay at Sheikh's Palace, which was what we were now calling our accommodation, our military hosts enlisted some local talent for our entertainment. This consisted of two pleasant-looking and shapely dancing girls, and two not so shapely or good looking local blokes to supply the music. To do this, these fellows squatted on the floor of one of the larger rooms of our Palace in which we were to be entertained. They held a Snake Charmer-type instrument which they rested on their crossed feet at one end and blew into at the other. There were a few holes down the side of this hollow instrument over which they moved their fingers, in an unsuccessful attempt, at least in my way of thinking, to play any semblance of a tune, or even any rhythm. To give them their due though, they did produce quite a fair amount of noise of a considerable wailing variety. However what the show lacked in musical entertainment, the dancing girls made up for with visual enjoyment. With the wine flowing freely, as the evening went on, the girls were persuaded to turn their dancing programme, though exceedingly entertaining, into a sort of Dance of the Seven Veils, in which eventually they dispensed with the veils, but carried on dancing in just their ear rings and shoes.

There were about 15 or 18 of us in the audience, and we were seated mostly towards one end of the spacious room in which the entertainment was being held. At pauses in the music, when the musicians needed a spell from blowing down their wailing pipes, the dancers would gracefully dance over and make themselves comfortable on someone's knee. It certainly boosted one's adrenalin to have a glowingly warm sensuous female land on your lap. One of them, who was half French, and had a 12 year old daughter back where she lived somewhere in Biskra, told me in quite good English that she had once been one of the dozen or so members of the Arab Sheikh's harem in that very building! When the war ended she hoped to go back into that secure life again. 'But what of your daughter' I asked? To which she replied that she would endeavour to the best of her ability to get her to become a useful and trustworthy member of a wealthy person's harem. 'It was a good secure life, but you had to learn to get on with the other girls.' I thought at the time that it would be great to be a Sheikh, or some similar person with a harem; but now, looking back on life, I have concluded that one wife is enough to handle!

150 Squadron, Kairouan

The oil pressure problem on our aircraft now having been sorted out, we were given instructions to fly north-east about a couple of hundred miles, to a airstrip near Kairouan, and report to the Commanding Officer. So after giving our Wimpy a test flight, we went off up to land at the hard-packed clay strip, a couple of miles west of Kairouan. We reported in, and were ordered to stay on the establishment, which was 150 Squadron, Royal Air Force.

Squadron badge.

In spite of our protests that we had been directed to fly out to Burma or beyond, we were outranked, and ordered to settle ourselves in with the rest of the squadron, and leave the Japs predominantly to the U.S. Forces.

Our hopes of getting out to India or beyond had now been dashed. The oil pressure light going red on our Wimpy down Biskra way was purely an electrical fault in the wire to the indicator light, caused by a loose nut. There was nothing wrong with the oil pressure in the motor at all! I've often thought about it since. That indicator light wire shorting and making that little light go red changed my whole life! What could have befallen me had we continued on out to the Far East, I wouldn't know; but no doubt it would have been different from what happened to me in the Italian Theatre of War. It must have been something to do with that Fortune Teller and the guiding hand of fate!

While Plum and Jeff, the two officers in our crew, moved off to the officers' tented camp, Penny, Alan and I drew a couple of blankets each and a 10 by 12 ft tent. We asked where we should go with our tent and gear, and with a wave of an arm, were told anywhere out there. So we went. There were 25 or so Wimpies lined up between Mussolini's North African Highway, (a 12ft tar-sealed strip) and the Squadron's airstrip, a hard- packed clay strip, a bit over a mile long. We pitched our tent on the other side of the road, not far from where some other tents were, and within about 100yds of the Sergeants Mess Marquee. With our belongings piled in one corner of the tent, the three of us chose another corner each to put our two blankets in.

We stayed where we had pitched our tent for the next couple of months. With lengths of aluminium framing retrieved from wrecked aircraft, old 500 lb bomb cartons, and a hundred yards or so of disused field telephone wire, which could be found lying around anywhere the armies had been engaged in battles, we were able to construct pretty comfortable beds with a wire base! It was certainly a whole lot better than lying on the hard ground. The long part of 500 lb bomb containers we also made use of as a wash and shaving stand. By removing the headgear straps and padding from a tin hat and sitting it in the hollow end of a container, it was ideal for the job. That was of course if we had any water! It seemed to be a pretty scarce commodity. We got issued with a mug-full per day, so washing clothes and personal hygiene didn't rate very highly on our list of priorities.

But though water was rationed, there was certainly no shortage of aviation fuel. Air Force Regulations required that all aircraft be refuelled immediately on returning from a mission. Our black-painted night operating bombers, after being topped up with petrol in the cool early morning hours, and then becoming exceedingly hot during the scorching temperatures of the day, would pour a constant stream of fuel from the overflow pipes of the wing tanks.

This proved to be an ideal place to remove the sweat stains from the cuffs and collars of your shirts, take the grime out of your socks, and get some of the original colour back into your underwear! This laundry system worked very well during our time there, near Kairouan. A certain amount of stiffness remained in one's garments; but they dried quickly, and retained that delicate aroma of aviation fuel! Surprisingly none of us, or any of the aircraft caught alight, which was a wonder as we all smoked pretty heavily in those days!

A Flight Sergeant navigator in a nearby tent had purchased a very classy dress shirt recently, made of some new sort of synthetic material (synthetics were still being experimented with in those days), so rather than wash his precious shirt in Av-Gas, decided to wash it in some sort of fire extinguisher foam spray. To his delight it turned out snowy white when hung on the line to dry. However when the proud owner returned after lunch to collect his shirt, it was nowhere to be seen, but upon inspecting the area more closely for signs of thieves' foot marks, he discovered to his dismay just seven or eight buttons below his improvised clothes line. His shirt had completely dissolved!

It always pays to read washing instructions given with any new article of clothing you buy! Fire extinguisher foam was apparently not one of the recommended solutions for cleaning that particular material.

Food

Probably because I was the only New Zealander on 150 Squadron at that time, I was commandeered on to the Sergeants Mess catering committee. There were a half dozen of us who would go off with a three-ton truck round the local villages on their Market Days. Fresh vegetables and eggs were very much in demand and sought after to augment the dehydrated vegetables, bully beef etc, which our diet mainly consisted of. On one occasion when we were negotiating a narrow dirt road through a pass in the foothills of the Atlas Mountains, we went close by some fat-tailed sheep. No doubt owned by someone in the area, they didn't appear particularly disturbed by our presence. It was mentioned in passing that a bit of fresh meat would be much appreciated in the Mess, but how could we go about getting any? I then volunteered the information that killing, skinning, and dressing a sheep for mutton had been a weekly chore for me back home on the farm. I only had a very small pocket knife with a 2in blade, but the cook's assistant who was with us produced a pretty decent sized knife with about a 6in blade. And so we shot a couple of these (unfortunately for them) inquisitive sheep and I cut their throats. By honing up the knife edge with a roadside stone, in a matter of minutes I had the skins off and the unwanted innards out, much to the amazement of those in our party who had never witnessed that sort of carry on before! We wrapped the carcasses back in the skins to keep them clean, and keep the flies off until we handed them over to our Mess Cook for his culinary expertise to work on. It was a very tasty and wholesome sort of stew that we were served up with next day: a much appreciated change. No doubt incidents like this didn't enhance relations between Tunisia and the West, which appear at times to be more than somewhat strained.

The Mess cooking facility was pretty basic. It consisted of two 12ft lengths of old railway iron placed side by side on the sand about 12ins apart. Before the cooking for the next meal began, a few gallons of ordinary petrol would be poured along on the sand between the rails. This volatile liquid of course immediately soaked into the sand; but not to worry! With an assortment of pots and pans, camp ovens and dixies, and other numerous containers of the type suitable to provide meals for a few hundred hungry bods, it only required a lighted match to be thrown down near one end of the rails, and the whole cooking operation was started up. Naturally some of the containers needed more heat than others, but as the flames died down to less than required at any place along the line, it only took a bit of a stir up with a poker to bring some fuel soaked sand to the top, and the chef was literally cooking with gas! I only knew our cook as Jack, and I can think of nothing but praise for the way he could turn out the satisfying meals for us that he did, with the limited variety of supplies at his disposal, and under such primitive conditions! Guys like Jack never got any medals, but they deserved to, working as they did in the stinking heat, though it did rain once or twice out there at Kairouan. One of my favourite puddings that Jack served up to us was simply a bread and jam (sometimes raspberry) sandwich, dipped in batter, fried to a golden brown and served to us on our tin dish with a very nice sweet-tasting and smooth custard. Yummy! Good old Jack will no doubt be dead by now. After all I'm writing of events that took place 57 years ago. But in spite of our good-natured banter at the time, I'm sure he knew how much we appreciated his noble efforts!

Acquiring (and Losing) a Jeep

With the invasion of Sicily, and the Allied landings in Italy on the way, there was a bunch of American Air Force personnel who it seemed had been left back at the base from which their Airborne Division had departed. They could get into Tunis to draw normal supplies from the American supply depot there, but apparently were unable to get any whisky! Two or three of them drove on down to our base to see if they could do a swap of 15 or 20 gallons of orange juice for a bottle of Scotch. My tent being the first they came to, and as I was on the Mess Catering Committee, I agreed that it could be arranged. Our Mess was issued with just one bottle of Scotch per week, so it only took 4 or 5 fellows on a night off Ops to decide to have a bit of a party and clean up the whole bottle! Fifteen or so gallons of grapefruit or orange juice gave everyone the chance of a decent thirst quenching, though not an alcoholic drink. There was still the odd bottle of beer we were issued with, or sweet North African wine if alcohol was required to drown one's sorrows.

This arrangement continued for a few weeks, but there came a time when our American benefactors were unable to supply any fruit juice. They had no shortage of money: 'Just name your price.' But money was not much use to us down there. Our pay easily supplied us with our casual wants and drinks at the Mess Bar. It was one of their buddy's 21st, and nothing but a bottle of Johnnie Walker would be good enough for the occasion. The four or five of them who had come along on this trip were travelling in a couple of U.S. Army jeeps. So I suggested that if they could spare one of them, they could have the whisky. They readily accepted the deal. After all, there were lots of wrecked, blown-up and burnt-out jeeps scattered about areas where the War had been across North Africa, so what was one more? And so they piled into their remaining Jeep and happily drove off to celebrate the occasion of their mate's 21st, with the assistance of the bottle of Johnnie Walker, while I proudly claimed ownership of a clearly designated U.S. Army Military Jeep. It was a simple transaction: no receipts or change of ownership papers to fill in and sign. Just a casual handshake was all it took to complete the deal! However, as I discovered eight or nine months later, the 21st birthday was a happy event, but the loss of the Jeep was not.

The crew and I spent most of the afternoon driving round the Squadron camp area, down to Kairouan a time or two, and generally showing off our new toy. We parked close by our tent, immobilised the motor, and secured the chassis by the bumper bar to the tent pole with a chain and padlock.

We weren't on Ops that night, but immediately after breakfast in the morning, our 150 Squadron C.O.(Wing Commander Morris) pulled up near our tent in his Corporal-driven Quad. After returning the customary salute that I had given him, and glancing at the Jeep he remarked, 'Nice little machine you've got there, Hayman.' 'Yes Sir' I replied. 'I understand you got it pretty cheap.' 'Yes Sir.' I could guess what was coming next. 'A U.S.

Army Jeep for a bottle of Johnnie Walker would be I think a pretty good deal!' 'Yes Sir.' 'As all items and commodities on this Squadron are under my authority, it is therefore only right that any items purchased through the sale of any Squadron property, should be placed at my disposal.' 'Yes Sir.'

What else was there for me to say? I was just a Flight Sergeant and he was a Wing Commander. End of conversation. So he took the Jeep away over to Maintenance, and a few hours later was seen doing his rounds with it completely repainted in Air Force colours and roundels. It was used on the Squadron for the remaining time we were in North Africa, and the C.O. took it with him on the boat when the Wing moved over to Italy just before Christmas '43.

Having had a taste of the convenience of a personal vehicle, we persuaded one of our transport fellows to take us along to a war equipment dump about 10 miles beyond Kairouan, to see if any vehicles there could be coaxed back into life. They were mostly pretty much knocked about, but there was a DKW motorcycle that had once, no doubt, been a Jerry dispatch rider's. Its tyres were not too bad, just needed a bit of a pump-up, and it was minus a battery. We had to fork out £5 for the Corporal guarding the dump to let us wheel it out through the usually locked gate in the surrounding barbed wire entangled fence. The money I guess just went straight into his hip pocket! We hoisted our bike up onto the truck and took it back to Squadron Maintenance. A battery was found that suited from the Station motorcycle section. The tyres were pumped up a bit, we acquired some petrol, and coaxed it back into life. By Jove that thing could scamper! 100mph (160 kph) was well within its capabilities. We took it in turns, or in pairs, to go on excursions along the road to other Wimpy squadrons or military camps, and other excursions round the area, including of course visits to Kairouan on minor shopping expeditions.

There was actually precious little of any use to us that could be procured in Kairouan. I think we could get camera film there, but there was no developing facility. That however didn't pose much of a problem, as film could be developed at the Squadron Photographic Section. However we were unable to have them printed, as the only photographic paper available there had A.M. (Air Ministry) engraved all over the back of it. It was a pity that we hadn't been able to get those negatives printed, as those views of life, and scenes of activities and disasters while out in Tunisia, were all lost later in an aircraft crash.

Air Tests

Squadron life didn't consist entirely of flying around and dropping bombs on enemy targets. In the three months from the 15th of September 1943 to the 21st of December, the Squadron only had us up on 14 bombing missions, the main reason being bad weather over the target area, which made it impossible to see the exact location of the target. What a difference it would have made if the G.P.S. (Global Positioning System) had been available to us in those days, and you knew within a metre or two exactly where you were. It certainly would have prevented us from having the crash we were involved in at the end of my flying career.

Wellington Bomber

However as all aircraft were to be flown every four days while on standby, we were continually offering ourselves to take Wimpies up for test flights. This honed the crews' flight training, and gave us all the opportunity to go through and practice the various procedures required for bailing out, ditching, fire-fighting procedures, and actions to be taken if crew members were injured, incapacitated or killed. I wanted to be sure all crew members knew exactly what to do in any emergency, could do it thoroughly and without any panic. This included the bomb aimer being able to keep the aircraft in a reasonable straight and level course until the remainder of the crew could bail out somewhere over some land. Thank goodness these emergencies never arose, but we all felt sure we would be able to cope if they did.

These air tests were amongst some of the most memorable occasions of my flying days. You were required to take the Wimpy up off the ground and test it for an hour. And that's just what we did. Low level flying always has its appeal, as it's only when near the ground that one realises the sensation of speed. So all of these tests would include a bit of low-level stuff. It was fun flying over the practically uninhabited areas around Kairouan, and beating up tented areas where other groups of military personnel were camped. On one occasion an American encampment appeared ahead. We were already down at about 20ft, so I dropped down even lower, out of sight behind the tents, and taking care to avoid their flag pole with its American flag waving lightly in the almost imperceptible breeze, we roared over the outer surrounding rows of tents and dropped down again to almost ground level over their quadrangle, before powering up over the tents on the other side. Obviously it was about their mealtime, as a hundred or so Yanks with dixies in hand were standing in a wavy line, edging toward their Mess tent. I could see as we approached they were starting to scatter, and as Jeff in the front turret remarked, 'We've broken up their places in the queue;' but as we departed from our beat up, it was Penny in the rear turret who witnessed the full demoralising effect that our beat up must have had on their otherwise peaceful day! The Mess queue of course, scattered, with fellows falling over one another, and going off in all directions, throwing themselves down on the bare ground, and some diving into foxholes that happened to be near where they were. The whole area erupted in clouds of dust and sand, which I'm sure didn't enhance the quality of the otherwise excellent meal that some of them no doubt, had already placed in their dixies. However, Penny said, the funniest sight was two or three fellows attempting to run from the flimsily constructed log-over-trench latrine, which turbulence from our now under full power ascending aircraft had blown the screens from, with their pants still down round their knees! It was a good beat up. Not that I had anything against the Americans; they were a wonderful bunch of fellows to be associated with. It was just that those happened to be in the wrong place at the wrong time, and my youthful exuberance had become manifest!

On these test flights one of the tasks that both Jeff and Penny looked forward to doing was testing the Browning machine guns. These we used to do over a largish shallow lake between Kairouan and Sousse. There was quite a large amount of bird life there, but as that was where we were told to test the guns that was where we tested them. One end of the lake seemed to be the favourite area for thousands of Flamingos to congregate. There were just acres of these beautiful graceful white birds to be seen there. However when they were disturbed and raised their wings in flight, they displayed their beautiful pink plumage. It was a wonderful sight, and we steered well clear of them. However on a lot of the other parts of the lake there were literally millions of ducks. These little blighters apparently played havoc with the local farmers crops in the area, so we considered them fair game! I've always been keen on getting the odd bird or two for a Sunday roast, and I still am; but I had never envisaged the slaughter a couple of machine guns would inflict on ducks in the air fifty to a few hundred yards ahead, and so thick, the sky was black with them. Each 303 bullet would probably knock down ten or a dozen birds before it was spent, and as they were being squirted out at the rate of a thousand or so a minute, it certainly was mass destruction. I only hope the local farmers appreciated what we had the pleasure of doing for them. The nearby military camps were quite pleased with our duck shooting efforts, as they would collect hundreds and hundreds of the birds as they drifted in near the shore, and it was possible to wade out after them, as the lake was only a few feet deep. Unfortunately the results of our shooting were just a bit too far away for our squadron to receive any benefit. We did hear on the grape vine that the birds made a very welcome change to others' monotonous diet. So to borrow a phrase we were 'Killing two birds with the one stone.' We not only tested the Wimpy's guns, but eliminated some of the grain eating pests from the neighbouring farmers' paddocks, as well as supplying a welcome change of diet for nearby military personnel.

Another thrill-seeking escapade that I indulged in on a few occasions was flying just above the sealed surface of the road (thanks to Mussolini's pre-war efforts) east from Kairouan, with the propellers' blast churning up clouds of dusty sand out of the ditches on either side. Crazy, I know, but I would have had to ascend a couple of feet if I had wanted to lower the undercarriage! These exploits naturally scared the living daylights out of anyone driving along the road. Traffic was reasonably few and far between, but there was always some unsuspecting individual in a military vehicle that we could zoom over from behind with a rip and a roar and smother him in dust. Vehicles coming towards us, thinking we were about to crash land on the road, usually abandoned their vehicle, and took refuge by throwing themselves into the roadside ditches! It was exhilarating sport to be apparently going along a road at more than four times the usual speed for those days. There was never anything said by authorities back at Squadron Headquarters about these exploits, and I guess we wouldn't have cared much if they had. After all things weren't particularly rosy at that time, and life expectancy didn't appear to extend very far into the future! We would of course have been easily recognised as a Wellington aircraft, but from below at our low level it would have been well nigh impossible to have noted the serial number. A memo may have been sent from other military authorities to 205 Group, but we heard nothing of it.

During one unusually hot afternoon, our test flight took us out near the seacoast south of Sousse. A crew member mentioned that a swim in the 'Med' would be a welcome way to wash off some of our accumulated grime. So I said 'Let's go down and check out the beach.' The tide appeared to be out a bit, so picking a mile or so straight stretch of wave-washed sand, I put the 15 ton Wimpy down within 20yds of the gloriously inviting water. The crew were stripped off, and frolicking in the gentle warm surf in a matter of seconds. I turned the aircraft round, and leaving the motors ticking over I climbed down and joined them in the water. It was without a doubt, the most delightful few minutes in the sea that I, and no doubt the others, had ever enjoyed! We could have spent hours there, but we were supposed to be on only about an hour's flight, and besides that I daren't leave the Wimpy's motors idling too long on a hot calm afternoon like that. So after a quick drip dry we dressed and prepared for take-off. We very nearly didn't make it! The eight to ten minutes parked on the sand, plus the gentle vibration of the idling motors had settled the tyres quite a few inches into the sand. She wouldn't move. However with full flaps on and full boost on the motor on the side that had the wheel less embedded, we managed to get rolling, and take off back to base. I should have noticed before climbing back on board that the wheels had settled a bit, and a minute or two with a good pair of hands could have scooped sufficient sand away to eliminate the problem.

It was all a bloody risky thing to have done. After all there was no way of knowing whether the beach was suitable for landing on at all! We could have got hopelessly bogged, and I shiver to think what the authorities would have made of a situation like that. If we had been returning from a raid or a long distance transport flight and were running out of fuel, we would no doubt get congratulated on saving the aircraft from crash landing; but to get stuck on a beach while going for a swim would be a different story. Luckily not many heard of our exploit, and we never considered going out there again for a swim. Sousse is now probably a tourist trap: perhaps another Surfers Paradise. There certainly must be some wonderful beaches around that area. I should know. After all, I've tried one! Miles more beaches looked equally as inviting from the air.

Thieving

There was a spate of thieving reported to have been happening in the tented area of our Squadron camp. So the order was issued that any stray persons seen about after dark, and acting suspiciously, were to be shot. After all, just a couple of nights previously, the four occupants of the tent just two away from ours had woken up in the morning to find all their gear had been taken during the night while they were asleep; even the clothes they had been wearing the day before had vanished off the ends of their bunks. We figured a bit of small arms shooting practice was called for. A small empty tin was put out on the road in front of our tent. Sometimes the tin was hit, but if not the lead made an interesting ricocheting sound until it expended its force out on the desert beyond the tarseal, from where its ricochet had started. We of course soon expended the few rounds we had been issued with for our .38 Smith and Weston six shot revolvers. However by distorting the rim of Sten Gun ammo', it could be used instead of regular .38 revolver Ammo'. There were thousands of rounds of Sten Gun Ammo' about, so our revolver practice continued, even to putting ricocheting shots off the road between donkeys' legs as they were ridden past. This didn't seem to upset the donkey much, but its rider certainly was inclined to endeavour to encourage a bit more speed out of his mount. And so we were prepared for any unwelcome intruders during the night hours, with revolvers ready in our beds.

A night or two later, I awoke to a rustling sound coming from the vacant corner at the back of our tent where most of our kit was kept. The rustling was interrupted occasionally by a metallic tinkling sound. Someone was stealing our possessions! I eased my revolver out from under the bundle of clothes I used as a pillow, and pulled the hammer back. My movement apparently disturbed the miscreant, as once again everything was quiet. However in just a few moments the tinkling and rustling sounds could once again be heard. If only I could see exactly where the thief was, and I wasn't going to shoot one of my crew members, I'd shoot the bastard! It was just about full moon at that time, but a bit of cloud about. I waited my chance, and with revolver aimed in the direction from which the sound was coming, and finger on the trigger and my heart pounding, I was in a high state of nervous anticipation! At last the moon-obscuring cloud moved away, and the moonlight clearly revealed the culprit. I carefully let the hammer of my gun back down to the safe position and watched what was creating the unusual noises. Would you believe, it was only a mouse! He was gnawing away at a greasy piece of butter paper as he pushed it round on a tin plate, and creating the tinkling sounds as it was manoeuvred past a knife and spoon that were also on the plate. I've often thought since that has been the only occasion in my life so far, when I have been mentally prepared to shoot someone like that in cold blood. Mind you, up here in our isolated High Country farmhouse, I would have no compunction, if an intruder were appearing to be offering any threat to our wellbeing, to terminate his existence. I believe in the old law, that an Englishman's home is his Castle! There had been notices erected warning the locals of our objection to their presence about the camp, and to my failing memory, I can't recall any other reported incidents of off camp thieving.

We were situated about two miles west of Kairouan. The cemetery was unfortunately a bit closer. The local culture dictated that burial grave mounds have a small ventilating hole left for the 'spirits' to exit. When the easterly wind blew, the aroma mingled with the aerodrome smell of hot oil, fuel and aircraft repair dope, certainly was a heady mixture! There being no navigational aids as such, in the area, it was jokingly suggested that incoming aircraft could home in on the Kairouan cemetery nasal beacon! As strict blackout was in force at that time, one's nasal directional aids certainly seemed a distinct possibility.

Night Operations: Take off and Climb

Night operations were carried out with absolute minimal lighting. Crews assembled at their allotted aircraft a half hour before take off, so your eyes became accustomed to the darkness. No lights or matches were to be lit. Cigarettes could be lit from one another's cigarette butts. I often have wondered since how we were permitted to smoke in the vicinity of fully fuelled and bombed-up aircraft; but everyone seemed to do it. As time for take-off neared, cigarettes were stamped out or extinguished under the hesitating stream of one's last nervous pee. The crew would then climb the ladder under the nose into their aircraft and pull the ladder up inside after the last one on board. Everyone then would settle into their respective compartments and confirm over the intercom that they were ready for take off.

A signal from a ground staff LAC by means of a shielded torch with a tiny one sixteenth inch aperture allowing a tiny light would convey to me that the battery boosters for the starter motors were plugged in and fire extinguishers were at the ready. A circular motion by the torch holder indicated that all was ready for me to press the starter button for the starboard motor, which would then fire up. When it was ticking over sweetly, the procedure would be repeated with the port motor. I never had a motor refuse to start, a great credit to the maintenance staff and the design of the Bristol Hercules fourteen cylinder sleeve-valve motors. After the engines had warmed up for a few minutes, they would be tested at operating revs, and the dual ignition systems would be tried individually for faulty plugs etc. The chocks would then be removed by ground staff, and we would await our turn for take off.

The dozen or so aircraft of 150 Squadron would now be ready, and when our turn came we would be signalled out the 30 to 40yds by the torch bearer to the runway where the shrouded runway lights would be then visible. Cockpit drill would be completed: H.T.M.P.F.C.G.S. Hydraulics, trim, mixture, pitch, flaps, fuel carburettor, cowling, gills, switches. A Canadian Instructor told me an easy way to remember this formula was, quote, 'Hot tempered men prefer f---ing college girls slowly.' It has certainly stuck in my memory. Unfortunately during my life I never did become acquainted with a willing college girl!

We would be held there with the beam of a red Aldis Lamp till the previous aircraft had cleared the far end of the runway, then the red would be changed to green and it was then your turn to give the heavily laden

Wimpy all she could take and thunder away into the darkness of the night. The shrouded runway lights disappeared once you were 20 feet in the air. When coming in to land you would need to be down to below 500 feet at an approach distance of three to four miles. The blackout restrictions were pretty much in force at that time.

So after lift-off we just bored off into the pitch dark, wheels up, flaps up, navigation lights off, and hoped to goodness you didn't fly into anyone else. From our airstrip there would be planes strung out about a mile and a half apart which was I guess, a reasonable safe distance according to the boffins. We would all be climbing at 500 feet a minute at 130 mph. (These were the most economical speed and rate of climb for a loaded Wimpy) until we had reached our chosen height.

I never chose a height of a rounded off figure like 7,000ft or 8,500ft; but something more like perhaps 8,775ft. Of course altimeters could never be relied upon to be accurate to within 50ft or so, as variations in atmospheric pressure alter their readings a little as you travel. However, I felt safer if, in my way of thinking, I wasn't following the crowd. As we neared our designated target for the night, there would be a large number of aircraft in the area.

Night Operations: Over the Target

205 Group, of which 150 Squadron was part, comprised six squadrons located in pairs in three separate locations near us in Tunisia. We shared our base with 142 Squadron. At two other bases were 37 and 70 Squadrons, and 40 and 104. All told, on many occasions, between 70 and 80 Wellingtons would converge over the same target! As you could imagine, this congestion of aircraft over the one target at the same time, posed a considerable danger to one's health! Up to the E.T.A. (Estimated time of arrival) over the target, usually around midnight or one or two a.m., we all had navigated our way during the previous 3 to 4 hours by dead reckoning over the sea, and perhaps recognisable landmarks if visible by starlight. The navigator would sometimes get a fix with his sextant from the stars

through the perspex astrodome if we were above cloud. We would have been given an expected wind speed and direction at briefing an hour or so before take- off, and radio contact mainly consisted of getting a recall if the weather had deteriorated significantly over the target area. The loop aerial direction location device was seldom used confidently, as the broadcasting radio stations from which a bearing could be ascertained were not considered reliable, with the Germans frequently broadcasting programmes similar to the BBC in London from other locations, but on the same wave length, simply to confuse us up in the air! Dead reckoning was therefore basically the norm.

We would usually locate a position twenty or so miles from the target, and stooge round there until 10 minutes or so before bomb drop. With eyesight completely accustomed to the dark, and very pale green instrument lighting, map reading was not too difficult. At briefing, a map would be on the wall behind the Briefing Officer, with the target pinpointed, and a tape pinned out from base, usually in a dogleg fashion, showing a recommended flight path. I found it no trouble to visualise this later on, and could accurately pinpoint the various landmarks as we approached and passed over them, usually between 7 and 11 thousand feet. Coastlines were pretty easy to recognize as were promontories and bays etc., which were easy to distinguish. Railways, roads and rivers could be picked out on clear starry nights, but were difficult under high cloud.

As the time for bomb drop neared, we headed for the target, and as we approached at a minute or two before the hour, one of the Wellingtons (sometimes us) would be tasked to drop a few 4 million candle-power flares on parachutes over the target. So much for sneaking up on the enemy! The bombers were of course now in full view of the anti-aircraft batteries and night fighters! That of course seemed bad enough; but to be milling around in the same area amongst 60 or 70 other aircraft, with bombs dropping all over the place, was to me by far the greatest danger. On one occasion we were over the target on our bombing run and I was taking directions from bomb aimer Jeff, of 'Right, right, steady, left, steady steady,' when I observed another bomber about 10 feet directly above us with bomb doors open, and rows of bombs ready to be dropped in a matter of seconds! We were too close to turn away. The only evasive action open was to close the throttles and drop away, and come round again for another bombing run. Jeff of course was exasperated at my actions as he was just about to drop our bombs, but when I explained that another plane just above us was also about to drop theirs, he accepted the situation. Penny, the rear gunner, noted other aircraft behind for me to avoid, but coming round for a second run was always risky, as by now the enemy were more in command of the situation. However, we managed to get round again in the next few minutes and did a very successful incendiary drop over the aerodrome that was our target on that occasion. I don't think that there was a building, or aircraft, on that 'drome that wasn't burning when the last of us left. Unfortunately there were also the remains of some of our aircraft also burning in the area. The thought always passed through one's mind that 'There, but for the grace of God go I.'

Night Operations: the Return Flight

The flights back in the early morning darkness were a bit boring; once the coast had been crossed and we were stooging down over the Mediterranean back to North Africa, there appeared to be little chance of enemy action. The adrenalin had lost its impetus and the odd cup of coffee was required to ease the boredom of the return journey. Night fighters were of course always a possibility; but with flame shielded exhausts, no navigation lights, and no visible cockpit illumination, a black painted Wimpy would be pretty hard to detect.

Returning from a mission well up the leg of Italy on a dark starry night, Penny's voice came over the intercom stating that a Fw190 was approaching from the rear, but about 50ft above our flight path, and enquiring if he should give him a burst. I instantly replied, 'If he hasn't seen us, leave the bugger alone.' I was sorry for Penny really; but a burst of tracer from the four rear guns would have immediately given our presence away to the enemy, and even if that particular Focke-Wulf was put out of action, there were probably others ready to pounce on unsuspecting lone Wellingtons such as we were. We could have perhaps downed one of their fighters, but a Wellington with a crew of five would have been a far greater prize for them. After all, we had done a good job on that night and knocked out a span of a vital bridge that carried supplies to Rommel's army, with the seventh 500 lb bomb of a stick of nine. I recall an expression of my Mother's: 'He who fights and runs away, lives to fight another day!' Discretion, at times, can be the better part of valour.

Actually a sequel to that particular raid was brought to my mind again about 15 years later when I pulled into the Kimbell pub on the way back from Fairlie with a load of super. I got into conversation with a few locals, including a former Private Ross, who mentioned that a Wellington bombing raid back in October '43 on the nearby bridge had knocked down part of the wall of a Italian-controlled prison of war camp. The Italian guards who were mostly in air-raid shelters at the time didn't notice that a few New Zealanders managed to escape. They found a boat in the dark and drifted down the river and eventually got back to the Allied lines. Some people are born lucky!

I could distinctly remember the last of that stick of nine 500lb bombs hitting the outer wall of that compound with a shower of dust and masonry. I didn't mention that fact at de-briefing that morning, as seeing that Italy had capitulated the month before, we weren't to bomb other than military targets. I hope the 'Ities' have forgiven my indiscretion by now. To compensate, I have bought one or two Fiat Tractors in more recent years, plus a SAME tractor on an earlier occasion. Italians are lovers not fighters. But now in the year 2000 they have proved that they are also pretty good at sailing yachts. New Zealand only just beat them for the America's Cup.

Another night, the target was a railway bridge at Civitavecchia, which a group of us managed to destroy. It was apparently undefended or the anti-aircraft gunners were asleep, or having a party or something; it just seemed too quiet to be real. As it was a beautiful moonlight night I decided we should go down a bit lower after bombing, and let the gunners have a go at any targets that might present themselves further down along the railway line. After all there was a war on, and it seemed we should have a go at waking some of the bastards up! It was exhilarating following the curves of the railway line at about 20ft above the tracks. As we rounded a low hill a marshalling yard containing numerous railway fuel tankers came in view. Jeff got a bit of a burst at them, but Penny in the rear turret didn't get a decent deflection shot, so I said, 'We'll go round again,' which we proceeded to do, and as we turned away across a level area, actually a Jerry airfield, still at about 20ft, all hell broke loose for a few seconds. The boys responded with all our six Browning machine guns could give; but man there was some lead flying. I reckon, if we'd had the wheels down we could have taxied across on the tracer, and the tracers were only a fifth of what was flying about as there was usually four others between each tracer. We had certainly woken them up. There were guys stumbling out of barrack block doorways, climbing out of windows, jumping into slit trenches and falling over one another. It certainly sticks in my mind as a very vivid few seconds or maybe nearly a minute. We didn't get back to the rail tankers. Possibly one or two Jerry fighters got a few bullet holes in them, but Penny noted that we had left no fires burning. So we headed for home with our tails between our legs, but at least we woke some of them up and spoilt their night's sleep. We of course were courting disaster, but were lucky that time. Oh to experience that youthful exuberance again!

Flooded Out

A gap in my Log Book of flying activities from the 24th of October to the 12th of November '43 marks the time when the airfield was put out of action. On the 24th there was a night of heavy rain. The area quickly turned to a bog, with pegs pulling out and tents collapsing and chaos reigning as everyone endeavouring to keep their kit up out of the wet and under cover from the rain. The temperature, however, was warm so it was not a great hassle to spend the rest of the night out in the rain, ankle deep in mud keeping our gear dry under the collapsed tent. Dawn broke and the rain stopped; but then water started trickling past us, and slowly started rising! The hierarchy in their wisdom, or lack of it, had located our airfield on the low-lying flood plain of a river, sourced fifty miles back up in the Atlas Mountains! There had apparently been a lot of rain back up there, and during the course of the morning, its evidence showed as the muddy water rose about us. At least it wasn't raining any longer and with the aid of boxes and empty bomb cartons we kept our gear up out of the water, which at its peak rose to just on two feet in depth. The water receded by evening and we got ourselves semi-reorganised, but the mud was diabolical and stuck like the proverbial 'Shit to a blanket.' When walking about, one's footwear would carry great slabs of the stuff, the size of snowshoes and two or three inches thick! Needless to say we didn't try walking far until things had started drying out a bit. It really didn't take long. The ground was really pretty porous, in fact so porous that it had allowed seven or eight of the Wimpies to settle right down on their bellies as if their undercarriages were retracted! All flying activities were at a complete standstill! All available personnel were required to assist in digging the planes free, and getting them back up on the surface again. The ground had soon become hard again, as we discovered with our digging efforts. Sloping ditches had to be excavated at not too steep an angle from the surface down to the level where the wheels were embedded. It took hours and hours. Eventually when all was ready, yokes were fastened to the lower ends of the undercarriage legs, and with long ropes attached from down there up to a couple of three ton trucks, the stage was set to get the first Wimpy out. The trucks revved up, the wheels churned and we all found suitable handholds from which to assist by lifting and pushing. The results of all this was about three inches of movement! More power was required. Two more trucks were sent for and with more ropes, attached to the pair already hooked on. Another combined effort was put in motion, but still to no avail. Still more power was required; but from where? The answer was right before us. Each Wimpy had a couple of Bristol Hercules motors, giving a combined horsepower of 2,850hp. We couldn't start the motors up, though, until another major amount of soil had been removed, to enable the 13ft propellers to rotate with no fear of their coming into contact with the ground. We had done enough for that day, so went back over to the Mess to enjoy whatever interesting items Jack had cooked up for us under his also disrupted conditions. As long as the matches could be kept dry, he could always be sure that the petrol would ignite for his cooking fire.

Next morning found us excavating a colossal amount of material from in front of the engine nacelles so the props were free to rotate, and also some more, so the flaps could be lowered to give more lift. When all this had been completed, the engines were started and warmed up, the towing trucks were at the ready on the tow ropes, and with numerous helpers pushing, the first Wimpy slowly was raised back up onto level ground again. Over the course of the next few days this procedure was repeated until all the other bogged aircraft were back up on to the surface of the airfield. When all had been checked over and test flown, the Squadron was ready to go back on night bombing operations again.

Oudna

We only flew one more sortie off that strip near Kairouan before 150 Squadron shifted out to Oudna Two, an airfield near Tunis, which we shared with Americans doing daylight bombing raids with B-17 Flying Fortresses and B-24 Liberators. There was a bit of friendly rivalry between the crews of our separate camps there, they of course complaining of our night flying operations disturbing their sleep, while we complained of their daytime activities disturbing ours! But we got along well with the Yanks, and I enjoyed our five weeks there.

One interesting phenomenon that we observed on a warm sunny afternoon was the vapour trails of a plane flying aimlessly round high above the airfield. I assumed it must have been doing some sort of high altitude testing; but upon enquiring I found that wasn't the case at all. What they were doing up there was freezing the ice-cream mixture to have with the dessert for that evening's meal! This operation happened on quite a number of afternoons while we were there. The 10 to 15 gallons of the creamy mix was put in a suitably sized canvas kitbag to be hung outside the Flying Fortress when it had attained sufficient altitude for the temperature to be well below freezing. Three or four hours up there and it would be ready for the GI's who would already be in the 'Chow' line waiting for their meal to be served. No doubt this was an expensive way to freeze ice-cream, since probably seven or eight hundred gallons of fuel would be consumed on each freezing operation! But I guess it was worth it. It was damned good ice-cream, as on occasions we were invited over to have some.

The Americans seemed to have a bigger allocation of water than we did, and we could sometimes make use of some of it for a shower. This consisted of a bucket with a few small nail holes punched in the bottom and hung up at about head height in a screened-off area. A smaller bucket was also there in which to get a bit of water from nearby, at outside air temperature. Actually it was just refreshingly cool. This ration of water was tipped up into the one with the holes in, and you quickly moved under the trickling refreshing water. If you didn't spend too much time getting the soap lathered up, there would still be sufficient water trickling down to wash the soap and grime off. We appreciated these occasions with the friendly and cheerful Americans very much, and it was good to feel reasonably clean again.

The Yanks, I think really thought we were great airmen and navigators, but considered us to be crazy to fly out at night over enemy territory, find and bomb a precise target, return to base and land again in the dark! I myself however considered their daylight bombing raids to be more hazardous than ours. They certainly seemed to get more shot up than we did, but the overall losses, proportionally, were probably much the same.

The Turin Raids

The Ities had capitulated in September '43, and so were no longer an enemy. Therefore we were instructed not to bomb built-up areas. Our targets were now mainly road and rail bridges, aerodromes, and railway marshalling yards. There was an exception to this ruling, though, when we were tasked to bomb the Villar Perosa ball-bearing factory at Turin in German-controlled northern Italy on the 24th of November. The factory buildings were right on the apex of the junction of the Dora Riparia and Po rivers. I know it was very easy to identify the exact location of the factory buildings when we finally reached the area. I don't know how many Wellingtons from 205 Group took part in this raid, or how many altogether failed to return. I know 150 Squadron lost quite a number that night![2]

At our briefing, to mislead the Germans as to our target for that night, we were advised to keep out to sea off the West coast of Italy and then turn inland as if going to Alessandria before making the run into the target at Turin. And so on the night of the raid we flew up under the cloud and crossed the coast south of Genoa, then climbed up into the cloud to clear the high ground ahead. At three and a half to four thousand feet we started losing speed and height. We were iced up! We got back to the coast and down to sea level, where the ice soon melted and got shaken off as it unevenly came off the propellers, and the motors must have been nearly shaken out of their nacelles. The chunks of ice being thrown off them and crashing against the protective plating on the Wimpy's fuselage, to protect the pilot and also any airman who was sitting in the co-pilot's seat, was a nerve wracking experience. So, with ice all off and still out over the sea we climbed up into the clouds again, but were very soon iced up, so it was back down and out to sea again. This time after getting rid of the ice, I climbed back up further out to sea, and broke through the cloud at about seven thousand feet, and then headed back on our original course in bright moonlight above the clouds. Plum Warner, our navigator, did a great job on his dead reckoning, after all this too-ing and fro-ing! He gave me the course to turn on to for our run into Turin, after his navigation should have put us over Alessandria. Shortly after we turned towards our target, he announced that we should now be on the outskirts of Turin. 'What's the visibility like?', he asked. 'Ten tenths cloud' I

---

2. In fact 150 Squadron was lucky, losing no aircraft, but 205 Group as a whole lost 17 out of 88, five of them from 142 Squadron, which shared Oudna with 150 Squadron.

replied; but just at that moment there was a slight break in the cloud cover, through which there showed the odd speck of light from a blacked-out town. I nosed the Wimpy down below the cloud, and sure enough we were over Turin. 'Congratulations navigator; good work!'

Somehow it seemed eerie. We were eight or ten minutes late over the target area, but there should have been a bit more sign of previous activity from the 70 or so Wellingtons of 205 Group that were supposedly tasked to bomb this ball-bearing factory in Turin. It was ominously quiet: no flak, no searchlights. We were a bit late; but were definitely at the right place. Even under the cloud, by the filtered light from the stars and moon, the target was clearly able to be distinguished sitting in the fork of the Dora Riparia and Po rivers. To make it easier and more distinct for the bomb aimer to accurately line up his sights, and also for our camera to get a good shot of our bomb drop, we dropped a four million candle-power parachute flare down the flare chute. I then turned back to do our bomb run. Jeff gave me a couple of 'Right rights,' then 'Steady steady, steady' and finally 'Bombs away.' You could feel the Wimpy getting lighter as the six 500lb and four 250lb bombs dropped away at one-second intervals. I continued on straight and level for the required number of seconds in accordance with the bomb sight settings for our air speed, altitude etc., so that the camera would get an accurate picture of where our bombs were about to land. Then it was back up into the clouds, and back to Oudna No. 2, Tunisia. It really seemed to be, apart from the trouble with icing up on the way to the target, just too straightforward a raid. What could we have done wrong? Was it the wrong city, and target? No, couldn't be. We had been shown an aerial photograph of Turin, with the factory to be destroyed clearly marked, so why were there no other Wellingtons from 205 Group to be seen in the area at the time we had been authorised that night to do our bombing? Also why no opposition? We discussed the various possibilities over the intercom at intervals during the 4 hour flight back to Oudna.

At briefing, we were laughed at when we told the Flight Commander that we had successfully located and bombed the designated target. Apparently a number of aircraft had returned early, with the crews reporting severe icing conditions, and inability to reach any suitable alternative targets due to extensive cloud cover over the whole of Northern Italy. The only proof we would have was the photos our camera should have got of our bombing run. We hurried back from the customary after-sortie bacon and eggs to the briefing hut, to await the shots of our raid to come over from the Photographic Section. We sweated it out waiting, and hoping Jeff had got our camera co-ordinated correctly with the bomb-sight in the short time he had to make adjustments for our between three and four thousand foot altitude bombing run. There was no need to worry! Jeff had done an excellent job, as had we all. The fourth photo showed where our bombs were about to land. It was right on target! So we had got to the right place at nearly the right time; but apparently, on that occasion no one else had![3] We were then very thoroughly questioned and interrogated as to why, in our opinion, such a large number of aircraft were lost that night, 24th-25th November '43. The only reason we could give was of pilots pressing on into the icing up cloud conditions, losing altitude, and crashing into the rising ground ahead. Maybe, somewhere in the archives there has been recorded what perhaps happened to those unfortunates that night.

Two or three nights later, 205 Group was tasked to bomb the ball-bearing factory at Turin again. Our Wellington was loaded up with a Cookie, a 4,000 pound bomb with a delayed action timing device. We took off in the late afternoon, and flew to Elmas in Sardinia, refuelled and continued on to the target. However we encountered thick cloud again, so the raid was aborted, and all aircraft were recalled to their bases. I guess we were expected to have jettisoned our bombs into the sea. I considered this to be a terrific waste, and detrimental to the war effort, so I returned to Oudna with the Cookie still slung underneath. I recall there was a great scatteration of personnel into the slit trenches when it was observed that we still had the four thousand pounder on board. I guess everyone was a bit uneasy

---

3. In fact Flying Officer Bint and his crew had also bombed the target, as had four crews from other squadrons.

until the armourers had got the thing safely defused. As I understood it, the delayed action device on these larger bombs was activated by a glass vial, which broke on impact, releasing some acid, which in an estimated time ate through a certain type of metal, allowing the detonator to be activated. There was of course, always the possibility that a heavy landing could have started this reaction, and certainly a crash landing with bombs on board was fatal, not only for the crew, but also for many people in the surrounding area. No doubt it wasn't a wise idea to have brought our Cookie back; but I hated the thought of wasting it!

The Crash

On the 20th of December we flew over to Cerignola, an airfield near Foggia that our Allied armies had captured from the Germans in central Italy. I left Penny and Jeff there, along with two or three of my ground crew. Alan Goodall, Plum Warner and I then went back to Oudna for the night, packed our gear and our tents etc., and gathered up our five remaining ground crew and all their gear and equipment, plus half a ton of Bully Beef and biscuits, which were the emergency rations for the Mess. Larger necessities for the Squadron were being transported by sea and road.

With tents and gear piled high in the fuselage, and kitbags filling the bomb-bay we took off into the misty drizzling murk, flew at tree-top height out over Cape Bon and in the direction of Foggia. We stayed below cloud at about 150ft above the sea. With no Met Office back at base for weather information we dropped a smoke float to get a wind speed and direction as we were nearing the Southern shores of Sicily which I could dimly see in the distance. While I flew on straight and level it was the rear gunner's job to keep his gun sights trained on the floating pot of smoke until it was no longer visible. The amount of time that this took was noted from his watch along with the angle of his guns and with our air speed also given, a chart on the side of the gun turret would then give our wind drift. Plum, who had crawled down the almost-loaded-to-the roof, fuselage to Alan Goodall our wireless operator, who was in the rear turret, to assist in this operation, got a wind speed and direction of 15 miles per hour from the south. If only they had said so over the intercom I would have corrected that finding as the white caps on the waves clearly indicated a northerly wind. Plum hadn't emerged from inside the aircraft, so no doubt he hadn't noticed his mistake. As we approached the coast of Sicily at Cape Rossello, Plum gave me a course to fly calculated on a wind from the south that would take us 25 miles north of the 10,000 foot high Mount Etna.

I put LN433 G-George into a climb and bored off up into the overcast. I had complete faith in the navigator. He had never put us more than one or two miles off track in all our long distance trips, which had been mostly at night. So why should I worry now in the daytime? Mind you it was thick cloud, and we were just on instruments. Plum came and sat in the seat alongside me and was soon asleep, while LAC Ginger Dugdale came and stood between us. And so it transpired that having flown over, and round, this area on dozens of occasions, always in the dark and often in atrocious weather as well, our luck finally ran out. I had been flying on instruments for about 25 minutes and was at about 7,000 feet, when as the light seemed a little brighter, I looked out to see if perhaps we were breaking through above the cloud, when to my horror an ugly cluster of jagged snow-covered rocks flashed passed about 10 feet below the port engine nacelle! I looked forward over the front gun turret in time to see part of the snowy rock and lava-strewn cone of Mount Etna rushing towards us from about 75 yards (the extent of visibility) at 130mph. In a split second I assessed the situation. The altimeter had read 7,000 feet a few moments before. Instinct and self-preservation took over. Both throttles rammed hard forward breaking past the copper wires that normally preserved the motors from over-revving through too much boost from the superchargers. Control column hard back against my chest with my right hand. Even though fully, if not overloaded, the Wimpy responded instantly and roared up the at least 45 degree rock-strewn snowy slope, missing some of the larger boulders by inches.

Which way to go? We were running out of air space fast! Visibility about

60yds. A little bit more clearance under the starboard wing so starboard it was. A little bit of aileron and a bit of rudder but as the turn started a larger 8 to 9ft rock went past below us and took both props off. The engines under full power and no load on quickly flew to pieces with con rods, pistons, and cylinder heads flying in all directions. With all power gone and at an angle of 45 degrees or so we went crabwise half sideways and half backwards down the slope a bit, and came to a crashing, bashing, tearing, screeching stop in a semi-sideways motion. There was utter silence, save for a few loose stones still following our path down the mountain; but they soon came to rest amongst the lightly falling snow. A few pieces of shattered aircraft tinkled as they swayed in the light breeze. There was also the trickling sound of running water! I could see it running over the stones below me, where the floor of the pilots compartment had once been. Also down there were the huddled shapes of my navigator who was either dead, or unconscious, and partly on top of him was LAC Dugdale, who was obviously dead, the top half of his head having been completely removed, exposing the remaining half of what had once been a very able and trustworthy brain.

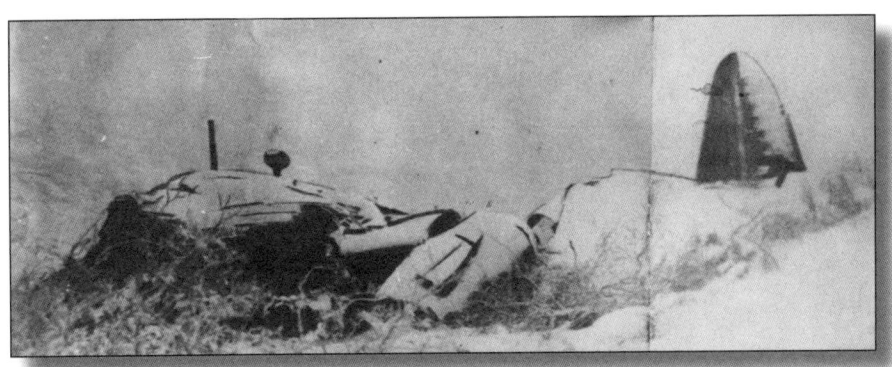

RAF photograph of the wreck of the author's Wellington, Mt. Etna, 21 December 1943.

That trickling stream of water? Unusual up here! Holy hell! It's 100 octane aviation fuel! There's another six or seven hundred gallons where that lot is coming from, and it is turning to white fumes as it splashes past the still almost red-hot remains of the starboard motor which is partly under my seat, and just to the rear of the two inert bodies. Fire! Got to get out of here! No problem really. The rudder pedals, control column, instrument panel, along with 12 feet of fuselage and the front gun turret have all disappeared. Undo the quick release on the flying harness, jump down the 4 feet or so off the seat and scramble away. However a funny sensation has come over me. No feeling anywhere. Move forward. Just feel as if I'm floating. My God! I think I must be dead. I look back to see if I'm still sitting in the seat; but no I have moved forward a bit. So must get out; but what's this funny floating, numb feeling? Don't know. Slide a bit further towards the edge of the seat. Head jerked back. Oh hell! Still plugged into the intercom', and oxygen outlets. Must get the helmet off. Got to undo the buckle under my chin. Not easy when you can't see or feel what you are doing, and the middle left hand finger is practically devoid of flesh and nail back to the first joint and is spraying a thin stream of blood about a yard in all directions with every heart beat! However I eventually got my helmet off and jumped down.

It was not a highly successful manoeuvre. My left leg had lost a considerable amount of muscle and tendons, due to a nasty gash below the knee and when I landed on my right leg, which had been broken six or seven inches above my ankle, the tibia and fibia protruded through the bottom of my battledress trouser leg and stuck into the gravel as my shoe encased foot swung up and hit me on the knee. My God! Not a pretty sight. Still there was no pain. In fact no feeling in me anywhere at all! I was shocked into anaesthesia I guess; but oh hell did the sight of that make me feel sick? One thing I could feel. I was soaking wet. No not rain or melted snow; but sweat. Those last few seconds. How many? Maybe fifteen or twenty from the first inkling of disaster till the crash. And I had wet practically all my clothes right through. The sweat of cold panic-stricken fear. But I was alive, although it still felt like, or maybe it was, just a ghastly dream! Whatever, I must get away. There could still be a fire. I know that instinctively I would have turned off the switches at the last moment; but that would be of no use on this occasion with the complete instrument panel etc., ripped away.

My hands and knees were semi-functional so I crawled and scratched my way over the rocks and rubble up across the area the crashing aircraft had cleared of ice and snow as it finally came to rest. After about 25yds I was exhausted, so I turned and sat with my back against a boulder and surveyed the devastating scene. Of course I'd seen plenty of crashed aircraft before but they were always someone else's affair. That sort of thing would never happen to Mrs Hayman's little boy Bruce! It must be a nightmare surely! Yet it seemed real enough. Oh my God what a thing to happen! And what an inhospitable place for it to happen: between eight and a half and nine thousand feet up on Mount Etna. It could only be there, as it was the only mountain that high within a hundred miles, and it was my bloody luck to have hit it. Perhaps I'm the only survivor, I thought. Heavens above, what a prospect. Just have to wait until this awful weather clears, and then a search aircraft may be able to discover the wreckage.

The drone of an approaching aircraft could be heard in the vicinity, getting closer, then an awful crashing bang, then utter silence! Etna had claimed another victim. I wonder who that was? I actually found out 58 years later, when an American visitor came and stayed here for a night in February 2001. He was Britt May from Boise, Idaho. He told me a flight of American B-24 Liberators were also transferring from Oudna II in Tunisia to Foggia in Italy that Sunday. He recalled the atrocious weather that he and his crew encountered on that trip. Their flight lost two Liberators that day. Without doubt the aircraft I had heard crash shortly after we had would have been one of them..

I was left with my thoughts again. Then after maybe 20 minutes or so, two snow-covered figures clambered up into view round the crumpled starboard wing, looking for other survivors. I called out to them to go and see how Plum was. He had started to recover consciousness, so they helped him up and made him more comfortable back in the aircraft. They then came back to me with a blanket, some bully beef, and a tin of biscuits from the half ton or so of emergency supplies that we were carrying for the Sergeants Mess. The two of them reckoned that they were perfectly OK and so it was agreed that they would push off down the mountain to get help for the five of us who still remained alive. So after getting us reasonably comfortable, they disappeared down through the mist and snow surrounding our location. It was about 2 pm. and they hopefully thought help would get to us before nightfall, which was little over three and a half hours away!

They were soon to be proven wrong. However, out of the eight of us that had been on board, they were the luckiest, having been flung out of the aircraft and landing side by side in 4ft of snow two hundred yards below the aircraft, without a scratch or bruise on either of them! For one ground crew member who had been dozing amongst a pile of tents and kit one minute with the noise and sensation of flying all about, and then the next, to be sitting in snow, enveloped in mist, and utter silence, with no sign of an aircraft to be seen, would have been unusual to say the least! He told me later, he thought for a start he must be dead, and was floating off, up in a cloud to heaven!

His companion in the snow, Alan Goodall, who had been in the rear gun turret, was equally confused. He had realised all was not well when we had flown over the first outcrop of snowy rocks, and I had taken violent evasive action, and so to get a better view of what lay ahead, had turned the turret at right angles to the fuselage, which enabled him to look along the port side. I remember him calling over the intercom, 'What the hell is going on skipper.' To which I had no time to reply! Then the next thing he knew there was no sound, no aircraft, just softly falling snow on top of the 4ft or so he was sitting in. When the two of them had recovered their senses, they judged by the slide marks in the snow which way they had come. And so, giving themselves a quick check for fitness, started clambering up the steep slope to where they estimated the crashed aircraft must be, and after struggling for 150 or so yards, the twisted remains came into view.

It was a long night for those of us alive up at the scene. However, one other ground crew victim, LAC Moore, died about 12 hours later, when his wheezy gurgled breathing no longer could be heard during the course of the next night. That left four of us.

I had trimmed the dangling tip off my middle finger with a little pocket knife that I always carried, wrapped the stump and protruding bone with my handkerchief to quell the bleeding, straightened out my broken leg, and propped it up in a reasonable position with snow. I pulled the blanket over myself, put my injured hand under my right armpit, and settled in to wait. There was upwards of a foot or so of snow that night which kept the biting wind off; but the warmth of my body melting the snow further soaked my already sweat-drenched clothing.

Early the following morning, Plum Warner, who had a fractured jaw, face lacerations, some teeth knocked out, and a sprained ankle, along with another one of the ground staff, who considered he was fit enough to walk in spite of some fractured ribs, and other abrasions and bruises, decided to, in their own words, 'Make a break for it,' and see if help was perhaps on the way. With visibility still only about 50yds, they soon disappeared down into the mist.

It was a long day, listening for the sound of anyone's approach. The dismal scene slowly faded as night approached again and it started getting colder. My remaining living companion, LAC Tommy Parr, who was still in the aircraft fuselage, had apparently suffered a semi-fractured spine, which gave him considerable pain when moved. We were within shouting distance of one another; but didn't spend much time conversing, and mostly just brooded over our own thoughts and wretched situation.

After another long night, morning revealed another foggy day and a long one at that. Still no sign of any rescuers. The night closed in around us again. Would I be able to last another freezing night? After all, the only protection I had was a wet blanket over my already soaked clothing.

Why hadn't a search party got back up to us by now? After all, the first two had left 36 hours ago to raise the alarm. Surely they would have got down to civilisation by now, and the Italians had at this stage come over to our side. But then, on the other hand, it would not be easy to get down an icy mountain, in poor visibility, from a height of 8,000ft! And indeed, it hadn't been easy, as we were to learn later. Both Alan Goodall and his ground crew companion, and Plum and his companion, had to spend a night out on the lower slopes, before they made contact with the Sicilians, and were guided down to meet up with the Allied Forces. They made contact with some Sicilians near the village of Bronte, I have since learned.

During the night as I slowly became colder, the desire to drowse off became more intense. I recalled the last entries in Captain Robert Scott's diary, when he slowly froze to death in Antarctica in 1911, and realised that if I went to sleep in the present circumstance, there was little if any chance of my waking up again. The cold was creeping up my legs, and almost a warm feeling was stealing into my body. I had to keep awake! I tried singing all the songs I knew and at that time I could recall hundreds. Then I recited poems, funny stories, monologues etc. When that form of forced wakefulness became exhausted, I began recalling the events and memories of my life! I remembered hearing once, that your whole life passes before your eyes just before you die, so I quickly got my mind back on to singing, and practical things, calling out to Tommy, my fitter and rigger.

Eventually the night passed, to reveal another murky day with visibility only extending from one side of the Wimpy's 90ft wingspan to the other. The day wore on. I opened a tin of biscuits and tried one; but it wasn't what I wanted. I tried some bully beef; but that was no good either. Besides it was frozen! So I sucked on lumps of snow. That seemed to quench the thirst, no doubt caused by loss of blood etc.

Rescue

After a dreary morning, suddenly two rifle shots rang out from quite close quarters, followed by a single shot from a bit further away. I started blowing my 'Ditching to dinghy' survival whistle to attract attention, and presently three snow-covered bedraggled figures loomed up from behind the aircraft. No doubt they had followed our downward trekking crew members' footsteps in the snow to get to the wrecked aircraft. Their clothes were pretty much in tatters. One poor fellow had ropes, laced together with string, wrapped round his feet for 'boots;' but they were fairly well equipped with rifles, binoculars, and revolvers, one of which I found myself staring into the muzzle of when I pushed back the snow-covered blanket under which I had been sheltering. They slowly approached, chattering amongst themselves in Sicilian. I couldn't understand a word of it; but got the impression that my presence wasn't assisting their plan. To add weight to this theory, the Luger-wielding member appeared to be punctuating his remarks by flicking the Luger's safety catch off and on. My God. After all this I am now going to be shot!

My instincts for self-preservation started the adrenalin flowing in my half- frozen body and alerted my mind to action. Prior to flying in this Middle Eastern area, I had been issued with a playing card-sized card, on which was written in about six different languages the information that to save my life, or any other person's who had one of these cards was worth, if I remember rightly £1,000 sterling. I figured this was an appropriate time to cash in on it. When I moved my hand to get my wallet out from inside my battledress tunic, the gun wielder became a bit more agitated and the Luger was held even closer to my face. However when it was discovered that I was only getting out a card to hand to them, a moustached individual who turned out to be their leader indicated the gun to be put away.

Order appeared to be restored. In fact from amongst their equipment a half bottle of Johnnie Walker was produced, which I managed to get the top off, and gleefully put it up to my mouth. The bottle was snatched from my hand by their leader, who indicated its contents were some sort of antiseptic and should be applied to my wounds. No doubt Plum and Alan and the others had indicated to the Sicilians they had made contact with that there were probably still some wounded survivors alive up at the crash site. I guess though that I must have looked a bit of a mess. My left eye was only partly open with a circular glass filled cut practically right round it. A gaping gash on my cheek, and my pulverised nose occupying most of the area where my right eye was and completely blocking its vision! I poured a little of the brownish liquid on the severed end of my finger, thanked them, and handed the bottle back. I guess I would have appreciated it more if the contents had been genuine 'Red Label' instead of Savlon or Dettol or whatever it was. I never was to find out as my knowledge of Italian, or lack of it, created a practically impossible barrier of understanding between us.

The leader of the trio (whom I later found out was none other than Salvatore Liberetti, at that time the leader of the Mafia!) indicated that they would get the two of us down off the mountain.

One of those who helped Tommy Parr and me down from the wrecked Wellington. Biagio Greco (aged 87) and his son Giuseppe.

The Greco brothers, Francisco (left) and Biagio, with their wives, extreme left and right.

The remaining two corpses could stay till later: which indeed they did for a few days, 'till the weather cleared sufficiently for an RAF party to reach the scene. No doubt they were well preserved up there in the freezing conditions.

And so I was rolled onto my blanket, pulling the two back corners round me with my arms crossed and thus hanging on in a sitting position, while Salvatore grabbed the other two corners and started sledging me down over the rocks and snow. It was I guess, somewhere round about midday. Progress was slow, and visibility practically white-out conditions. On some of the steeper parts of the descent, Salvatore carried me on his back which was in my way of thinking, extremely hazardous in the icy conditions, with precipitous faces disappearing into the mists below us.

My injured companion, Tommy Parr, was being helped down in the same manner by the other two rescuers. Though not being close enough for me to see them much of the time, they kept within shouting distance at the rear.

Eventually the snow gave way to patches of alpine plants and bracken, and we descended below cloud level. Before us stretched the vast expanse of the mountain base stretching out to the farmland and vineyards in the distance. I would estimate we were still at about 5,000 feet.

Presently we descended into a small depression, in which was growing a single pine tree, beneath which a lad of about 12 years was tending a small fire, with a couple of tethered donkeys nearby. We were dragged up to the fire, where we appreciated the warmth.

I managed to get a 'Silver Fern' tobacco tin out of my pocket in which I had about 60 cigarettes of various brands. I had been dying for a smoke for the last two days or so; but had no means of lighting one. With the burning end of a stick from the fire, I was soon drawing the longed-for smoke down into my lungs. The remaining cigarettes were grabbed and quickly disappeared. I could only wish them well with my last smokes, as they had well and truly earned them by getting us safely this far down the mountain.

After some animated discussion amongst themselves in Italian it appeared we were to continue the journey by donkey. And so, when we had been hoisted on board, and with my companion's donkey tied to the tail of mine and the boy leading we continued on down the steep and uneven slope. What a journey! No home comforts here! The donkeys were skinny, the terrain steep, and to stop sliding over the animal's withers onto its neck, I found I had to hang onto an ear with one hand, and the tail with the other. To make matters worse, my fractured leg kept catching on the bracken, and stunted scrub, and swung wildly round and about the animal's legs. Not a very reassuring sight! There didn't appear to be much pain; but the sensation of the broken bone ends grinding together, and the sight of my foot no longer appearing to be part of my leg was not very reassuring. The pain was mainly confined to my groin, where the sharp withers of the donkey threatened to ruin the 'family jewels'.

Nevertheless we were making progress, and by the time it started getting dark the terrain was becoming less steep. The lights of a vehicle appeared in the distance, swung across our path, then swung back and held us in their glare. An RAF Jeep quickly drove up and a corporal got out. He was part of a search team out looking for us, but was of course about 5,000 feet below where we had crashed. He told us however that the other four members of our crew had been picked up and taken to hospital, suffering from some exposure, besides the fractures and wounds received in the crash.

We were transferred to the jeep, my companion occupying the back seat, as it was more comfortable for him to be able to lie down on his back, and I was lifted into the front.

We thanked the lad with the donkeys, who no doubt went back to his camp to join his companions, who (so we were told later) were deserters from the Italian Army who were hiding in the mountains from the authorities. Their group was known, would you believe, as the Mafia!

By the time RAF personnel were able, when the weather cleared a few days later, to get to the plane to recover the two bodies still there and collect any of our personal belongings, our rescuers had completely looted everything of value, even to cutting the tyres off the rims. What a haul they would have had, with four tents, all the flying kit, clothing, personal belongings etc., of the eight of us on board, as well as half a ton of Bully Beef and biscuits. There was also all the repair and maintenance equipment for servicing the aircraft, including batteries, drills, grinders, riveters etc. And then there was the aircraft itself, containing six Browning machine guns, with half a ton of ammunition plus radios, instruments and many other saleable items, not least of which would have been the half dozen or so parachutes,. Silk was gold during the war for clothing, especially women's. It no doubt gave the Mafia a good boost to their illicit operations; but that was no concern of mine. I could only wish them well. After all they had saved my life and that of my companion. I certainly would not have lived through another night on that exposed mountainside.

Actually all the RAF salvage crew recovered of mine was my Flying Log Book and an album of personal photos. Unfortunately all my unprinted negatives of North African operations were lost, also my much-prized official RAF photos of our various bombing operations taken from our plane as we struck our various targets, were also lost. However we were still alive and that was the main thing.

We proceeded down the mountainside at a faster pace and only slightly more comfortable. As both my legs were practically useless, I found that, to remain on the seat, I had to hold on to the windscreen support with what strength I had in my left hand, and the Jerry Can handle, which was carried at the rear of the vehicle, with my right. It was a rough ride, with rocky patches, and shingle slides, some of which seemed almost vertical! In the beam of the headlights it could be seen by the marks where the corporal had had numerous attempts to get his vehicle to the crest of some of the more difficult inclines; but the American Jeeps were tough little machines, and it did its job well!

Eventually we dropped down over the side of a cutting and onto what had once been a reasonable country road, though now, after the passing of the tide of battle a few months before, was reminiscent of a section of the Moon! It was pock-marked with shell holes, disused gun emplacements, shattered trees, and battle litter. However there was a reasonable track, albeit mostly one way, and as at that time of night other traffic was non-existent, progress was not too bad.

We eventually came to what had once been a little country town, and the driver suggested I visit the local doctor, who still resided there. So we duly pulled up at a heap of rubble with a garden gate hanging drunkenly off a broken post with the remains of a picket fence attached. Not the picture one brings to mind for a country G.P.'s residence. The driver dragged the gate aside on its one remaining hinge, went down some steps and knocked on a door, which opened presently, the light revealing a pleasant-looking, middle-aged man. I was assisted down into the remains of his home, placed on a clean bench, and the Doctor proceeded to put a temporary splint on my leg. He also bathed my more visible wounds with the last of his antiseptic. I later requested that the Military Authorities replace his medical supplies for his kindness.

Hospitals and a Hospital Ship

We got back into the Jeep, and three hours later we arrived in the city of Catania, where we pulled up outside a large school building. We were transferred to stretchers where army orderlies carried us up the stairs. The bells were striking midnight on Christmas Eve 1943. Sicilian Nuns with candles followed us up the stairs to a schoolroom turned into a ward. They were singing Christmas Carols with the same tunes but Italian words. Very touching. Almost it seemed like going from the Gates of Hell up to Heaven!

There was great jubilation in the ward when we were carried in, as the others of our crew were already in bed there. They certainly were surprised and pleased to see us, as they thought we would have succumbed to the cold by now.

This British Army hospital would no doubt give me some decent treatment, I thought. My battledress was cut off me, and I was suitably robed, and placed in a warm bed with hot water bottles down near my legs and feet. What a glorious feeling it was to be dry and warm again. But as I started to thaw out, the pain in my lower limbs became excruciating, and morphine had to be administered so the rest of the patients in the ward could get some peace from my agonising moaning and writhings!

By morning I had settled down and was ready enough for a series of patch-up operations. Pentathol had become the popular anaesthetic for short operations and that day, even though it was Christmas, I was put out to it every hour or so. My left hand middle finger had the bone removed back to the first joint, and the end stitched up. Then glass was removed from my face, and gaping wounds were stitched up. Next tendons and lacerations in my left leg were pulled together and sewn up again. Then my nose was pushed back into place, and an instrument was poked around inside my nostrils to make a couple of holes for me to breathe through, and it was taped and plastered back into place.

These operations were explained to me by the other boys in the ward, as they all took place on my bed! The wound in my right leg, where the tibia and fibia had broken through, was sewn up and bandaged, and the lower limb was put in a cradle-shaped sort of splint arrangement, no attempt being made to align and set the bones into position. That lower limb swelled up considerably, and was to remain that way for about seven months!

I stayed at that hospital in Catania for five or six days before it was decided that I should be transferred back to England for better treatment. After saying goodbye to the crew, who shortly after returned to 150 Squadron at Cerignola, I was taken out in miserable freezing conditions on a stretcher, by a field ambulance to a airport where I was left on the tarmac covered by a blanket, which kept flapping and blowing off in the freezing wind. I thought I must surely catch pneumonia; but I didn't.

Eventually a DC.3 aircraft pulled up nearby and I was pushed in on the floor and strapped down amongst numerous other war casualties with varying degrees of disablement. We took off and after a short flight landed back in North Africa at a Field Hospital, the part of which I was in consisting of a large Marquee. I remained here for another four or five days with forty or fifty other bods where our basic wants only were attended to. Then it was on the move again.

So out on stretchers to the tarmac we went, and again by DC.3 we were taken to Algiers. I was field ambulanced to a large white building in a palm-lined compound that had been a very exclusive French girls' boarding school, then carried up some stairs by orderly-carried stretcher, into a very pleasant, sunny and warm, white painted room containing beds with sheets on them! What bliss! I hadn't slept in a bed with clean sheets on since leaving England, months and months before.

I was settled in and made comfortable with a dozen or so other disabled companions, and then wonder of wonders, music! I hadn't heard any music for months, except a few occasional scratchy items on the Wimpy's loop aerial-equipped, direction-finding radio. The first recording that was put over the speaker system was the mellow tones of Perry Como's latest hit, 'Prisoner of Love.' Now whenever I hear that number the strains of the music take me right back to a clean white bed in the sunny corner of that peaceful building.

I stayed there about a week I think, and then a big flap started. A hospital ship had arrived in port and every patient was to be transferred by boat back to England. We were all permanently disabled, or else on long-term treatment. We were taken to the ship's side down at the docks, on stretchers, by ambulances. There seemed to be thousands of us to go on board, and the waiting appeared to be endless. However our turn eventually came to be taken, by stretcher up the gangplanks and down into the bowels of the boat. I was in a room with about thirty other patients, in beds that hung on davits, which could be allowed to swing free when the ship was in rough seas and rolling badly. From our ward we couldn't see out, but eventually the hatches were banged shut, the whistle blown, ropes cast off, and we could hear and feel the big steam engines starting and the propellers churning the water below. It would have been about the 15th of January 1944.

We were away, and with a bit of luck back to England. It didn't bear thinking of our fate, if German U boats had decided to torpedo us. We made an easy target. For in contrast to everything else in wartime that was blacked out, we were ablaze with lights, especially the ones shining on the red crosses on the funnels, sides and deck. However the enemy honoured the Geneva Convention, and left us alone to get safely to Liverpool.

The trip was uneventful except for the usual Bay of Biscay storms when, because of the rolling of the ship, our bed fastenings were released and the beds could swing freely on their hangers. It was an unusual sensation to see all the beds in the ward lying over at about a 25 degree angle one way and then go slowly to about the same angle the other and so on until the storm was passed; but it kept the sea sickness down to a manageable level, and food and drink would stay on the bed trays without spilling, even though it seemed as if it was the beds that were at an angle and the ship was level. However it could be realised that this was not the case when the stewards came in carrying their trays full of food etc., and other requisites. They were marvellous and never appeared to slip or spill anything!

We amused ourselves by singing, telling funny stories, recounting our experiences, or general discussion. No matter what your own circumstances are, there is always someone who is worse off than you are. I can recall one unfortunate Tommy who had a hand grenade explode prematurely, which had badly disfigured his face, blinded both eyes and taken his hands off. He was the most cheerful lad in the ward, always starting up a singsong or keeping us in fits of laughter with his funny stories. He was so pleased that the war was over for him, and that he hadn't been killed and was going home to his wife and daughter whom he hadn't seen for two years. He was never going to see them! I wonder what his homecoming was like. It would be a remarkable woman to be able to cope with a situation like that; but I guess there were hundreds of similar cases.

The voyage lasted about ten days before the rolling of the boat steadied, the engines slowed, and the news was announced that we were shortly to berth at Liverpool. There was feverish activity as we were transferred from the boat to the waiting ambulances and ambulance trains. I eventually was put aboard a train along with hundreds of other war casualties who were also stretcher cases. The train pulled away from the murky and drab Liverpool docks and we sped off through the misty and wet winter countryside. It was dark well before reaching our destination where we were met by fleets of ambulances.

Horton

Along with many others I was taken to the Horton Emergency Hospital at Epsom in Surrey, just on the outskirts of London. Pre-war, it had been a mental institution, but had now been converted to an emergency hospital for civilian casualties of the London bombings. Why I was sent there I never found out, and at the time, who was I to query where my hospitalisation was to take place? In hindsight, however, I realise I should have had the best treatment that England could offer as already I had gone for over three weeks with the compound fracture of my leg with little more done to it than being bound up in a splint! I was to remain here for 6 months.

Conditions were pleasant and adequate, but the medical facilities were apparently not as of a high standard as was available in the top-class military establishments, to which the better Harley Street Specialists had been transferred, to enable them to get the wounded back into battle as quickly as possible. However, it was an enjoyable time while there, with lots of visitors, friends, WAAF's and relatives.

An amusing incident I was involved in while there took place on April the 1st. To exercise my left leg, which wasn't in plaster, I had a small sack of lead weights that I could hang over my ankle and exercise my knee joint etc by swinging it over the bedside. After breakfast I requested a bedpan, which incidentally at the time I did not require. After having this receptacle for a given period of time under the bedclothes, I placed the twelve or fifteen pound weights in it, covered with a few scraps of toilet paper, and put the whole thing on the end of my bed, covered with the usual small towel. My usual busy little nurse grabbed it in passing, but had to pause for a second to adjust her reactions to the unusual weight, and carried on out of the room.

Nothing was said. The trolley came around after doctor's visit, with morning tea and biscuits, which I duly tucked into, swigging them down with a large gulp of tea. It was then the joke was on me. Instead of sugar, the tea was liberally laced with salt! I think I laughed louder than all those who were in on the act. I did eventually get a decent cup of tea, and the lead weights, which missed going down the drain, were eventually thrown back to me. Another April Fools Day had passed successfully.

I was allowed up quite a lot of the time when my leg plaster would allow and could get around in a wheelchair, and later on, on crutches. The ward I was in contained about 30 beds placed down two sides of a large rectangular room. We were all orthopaedic cases and were a happy bunch. For us, at least temporarily , the war was over or so it seemed, though not quite, for one or two reasons.

Firstly, in the compound just outside our ward and about 10-12yds away from our blacked out windows, there was an anti-aircraft gun continuously manned by three or four tin-hatted and well-camouflaged gunners. Most of the time I guess they had very little to do; but when an air raid was on, which was quite often, they were all action. If an enemy aircraft came within range all hell would break loose, as this AA gun started pumping shells skyward at the rate of about one a second! Apart from the noise, which was ear-shattering, the muzzle blast and vibration threatened to bring our three story brick building down about our ears or in our case, beds. After about a minute of this barrage, which seemed to be the average time that an enemy aircraft was in range, we invariably found when the inside lights were turned on again by the nurses returning from the air raid shelters, that all our beds had congregated in a rough circle in the centre of the floor! I can tell you that an average New Zealand earthquake had nothing on that for vibration noise and terror.

Secondly, apart from the air raids, the other form of enemy action, which I suppose basically is a form of air raid, was the V1's or flying bombs. I can tell you from experience that it was not a very reassuring sound to hear one of those fiendish contraptions put-putting on its awesome way, or, when the motor stopped, to have to wait through that agonising time of silence lying in bed on your back, for it to come through the ceiling, or to hear the explosion blasting some other poor unfortunates out of existence along with half a city block of real estate.

Our establishment survived unscathed apart from a few broken windows during the term of my stay there. As the weeks ran on into months, and still my lower right leg remained infected and swollen, I seemed to be granted more and more time out of hospital on crutches, and time would be spent visiting my Aunt Lily Le Gros just near the tube station at Finchley, or down at the local Kings Arms or some such name, until one day it was completely demolished by a V1 flying bomb. Another 150yds and it would have been the hospital!

It was estimated that there were about three miles of corridors in this establishment, and many happy times were spent wheeling ourselves, or being pushed by other patients round visiting the numerous wards, and catching up on the latest lewd stories etc. Time could also be passed helping the nurses; rolling bandages, folding linen, taking round cups of tea or pushing round the meal trolleys, also taking out to patients and retrieving bed pans (Flying Forts) or bottles (P-38's). With not all of these activities was I able to be of much use, on either crutches, or in a wheelchair, but we all did what we could to help the wonderful nurses who were practically run off their feet due to necessary wartime understaffing.

The operating theatre on our floor was a largish room with 9 operating tables in it. There were movable folding screens between the areas, which did little to suppress noises or reassure the next patient as he waited on a trolley alongside for his whiff of anaesthetic or shot of pentathol. Moans and groans, wheezes and gurgles, electric bone saws, hammers and chisels chipping away at unnecessary bone growth, mixed in with the staccato barks and orders of the surgeons to the theatre nurses were all part of the scene of a trip to the theatre.

My leg wasn't responding to the limited treatment and drugs I was getting, and it was put to me that amputation of the lower right leg appeared to be the best alternative. I assured them that I wasn't overburdened with enthusiasm at the prospect of having my foot and lower right leg removed. They obviously didn't have the expertise or wherewithal to eliminate the infection in my lower limb and reset the tibia and fibia! Why not? There were some unusual, and to me unique operations performed on many other patients. Why, after six months had virtually nothing been accomplished to improve my situation? I was still on crutches or getting round in a wheel chair. I should mention, however, that my billiards and snooker technique had improved immensely in the past months, and I was playing a pretty mean game from my wheel chair! I guess my opponents weren't in the establishment long enough to get in the practice that I was able to.

However to get back to operations. There was a dispatch rider who had survived a glancing blow with a brick wall on his motorcycle in the blackout. He had lost a considerable portion of his upper right leg including a large amount of the femur. The orthopaedists had gathered up the best of the remaining shortened bone and got it set in position for the broken ends to re-unite. It would be about four and a half inches shorter than before; but muscle, being a bit like rubber, would soon compensate for the shortening. This, in a few weeks happened and he was able to start weight bearing on it again. The result of course was that he now had one leg four and a half inches shorter than the other! But not a problem. He was prepared for another op, wheeled down to the operating area and four and a half inches of femur bone was removed from his good leg. They made a first class job of this by making a half lapped mitre join with a screw in it to hold the bone ends in place. The removed bone ends were returned to the patient to be proudly displayed in liquid, in a glass jar. He was up and walking about in a very short while none the worse for his stay in hospital except that his trousers were about four inches too long. Nothing that a pair of scissors couldn't fix.

Pierre, a Frenchman of the Free French Army, did stints for the British military on occasions where he would be tasked to obtain information pertaining to the German defences along the German occupied Normandy coast. He would get taken by submarine in the middle of the night to within a short distance from the shore where he would transfer to a one man rubber dinghy and paddle noiselessly in to the beach, deflate the dinghy and bury it in the sand, taking his chances of course, as to the whereabouts of enemy mines! He would do a bit of a reconnoitre as to the placement of German pill boxes, gun emplacements, sentries etc., then hide till the following night. He would then approach a sentry at a nearby pillbox creep quietly up behind him and noiselessly kill him, usually by a sudden slash to the throat. However, Pierre's extermination trick that he was most pleased with himself about was when he was approaching the sentry from the rear he observed against the starlight, that this particular fellow was steadying himself with his rifle and resting his chin on the bayonet. It only required a violent pull backwards by the man's armholes and he impaled himself on his own weapon. From Pierre's point of view, very satisfactory!

Once the sentries were eliminated and any useful documents removed from them, the next operation was to go to the nearby concrete pill box, ascertaining what was going on inside, by peeping in through the machine gun slits in the walls. Usually two or three Jerrys would be playing cards or something. It only required the act of pulling the pin out of a hand grenade and tossing it in amongst them to have them disposed of. Then all maps, documents and useful information would be collected and tied in a waterproof container. It was then back down to the beach, dig up the dinghy, inflate it, and head back out to sea before he was caught. There would be a deadline to keep with the submarine and a password to be flashed to verify his identity, with his tiny torch. The time of pick up would generally be 2 am, and if contact with the submarine hadn't been established within half an hour, the sub' would return to base. It would return again the following night; but if no contact was made then it was assumed that things had gone wrong and that he had been captured or killed.

Pierre was always lucky on the few excursions that he was tasked to make; some others weren't! However in between these hair-raising excursions Pierre would be back with his regiment or route marches, drill parades, lectures, rifle practice etc. It was after a rifle practice excursion that he ended up in hospital. With his first shot down at the butts on target practice, he had apparently forgotten to remove the cleaning rod from his 303. The barrel exploded and removed practically all the flesh from his left thumb. A flesh graft was called for. An incision was made in his lower abdomen. The damaged remains of his thumb were inserted and sewn up, with his lower arm and hand securely tied in place. He got around like that for a couple of weeks by which time his thumb was securely grafted into his stomach wall. Pierre was then operated on again, and his thumb removed with a suitable amount of flesh on it and the skin from that part of his abdomen suitably shaped, stitched up and bandaged for ten days. When the bandage was finally removed, he being a fairly dark hairy bloke, his new thumb was sprouting quite a prolific amount of hair on the ball, and surrounding area. His girlfriend who came to visit him at his bed next to me, was most intrigued. No doubt with use the hair would wear off over time!

Another unfortunate fellow who had lost a goodly portion of his nose, including the bony part at the bridge, had to get some bone transferred back to that area of his face. His left forearm was opened up and stitched to a similar opening in the vicinity of his lower left rib, where it remained for a week or two and had completely healed itself in place. His next operation involved removing his arm from its temporary location and with it, a suitable piece of his lower rib. This, including his arm, was then attached to a prepared area between his eyes where it was to be grafted in place. He then went round with his forearm attached vertically in the centre of his face. In a week or two the piece of rib bone had attached itself firmly in place and he was then on the way to getting a new nose built up with further grafts.

To give myself a bit of a break from hospital before my impending amputation, I was given ten days leave. Bill Hermanson, an amputee who was due to leave hospital shortly, and I decided to have a night out in London before going our separate ways We dined at the Ritz, later getting told politely to leave, as our rendition of the Ink Spots singing 'Whispering Brass' was not being appreciated by some of the more stiff-upper- lip London patrons. I don't know why! Our immediate and accompanying friends seemed suitably impressed with our vocal efforts. However, rather than create an incident, we left, and went to another watering hole a bit further along the Strand. The evening passed quickly and as the beverage took its effect we almost lost track of time. We would have to run to catch the last tube train out to Epsom. We had gone but fifty yards when Bill fell to the pavement. His aluminium artificial leg had come off. There was no time to strap it back on or we would miss the train! I picked up his leg hung it over my shoulder, and gave him my crutches. We made it to the train just in time, causing much amusement to other late night revellers who were also hurrying to catch the tube'. We just managed to get in before the doors slid shut. My crutches, which Bill had held horizontally under his arm while he gripped an overhead strap with the other, were apparently protruding a foot or so beyond the rubber buffers on the carriage doors. When we stopped at the next station they were both about a foot shorter!

From our destination back to Horton Hospital we were an even more comical sight with me bobbling along on a leg in plaster and Bill's 'leg' over my shoulder, while he hopped along on one leg and crutches that were now about child's size. We didn't exactly get greeted with open arms by the Night Sister back at our Ward; but in our merry state the tongue lashing fell on deaf ears.

My plaster was patched up a bit and I was issued with another pair of crutches and Bill and I went our separate ways. He no doubt was supplied with a more secure arrangement to attach his aluminium leg to the stump of his femur, with some sort of waist harness.

Rauceby

With my small amount of gear in a backpack, I went by train to Sleaford in Lincolnshire. I was met at the station by Mr Harry Tomlinson, father of Jeff, my bomb aimer. I threw my crutches into the back of the old Ford Thames truck and climbed in. Mr Tomlinson started up the motor, and then got out again as he had forgotten to turn over on to the other side, a tractor radiator. When I asked why he had done that, the story emerged. When going from the farm at Osbournby into town he would have the radiator with the side up showing a large rusty patch where it leaked. On the return back to the farm the side was showing that had a patch of shiny solder where it had been repaired. This arrangement was so that, due to petrol rationing he could explain, it stopped by an over zealous police or traffic officer, his journey was necessary because if going towards town he was getting the radiator repaired, or on the return journey, it had just been repaired. The radiator in point of fact was beyond repair! The truck was running on distinctively coloured fuel for use in tractors, farm machinery and other industrial purposes. I guess that taking me from Sleaford to the farm could have been classed as part of the war effort. I certainly couldn't have walked that far on crutches. Not when sober anyway!

'Grove Farm' at Osbournby was typical of many English farms, with a yard surrounded by buildings and a two storied house nearby, all built of brick. Mrs Tomlinson was a cheerful homely lady, and she and her husband were a lovely couple to be associated with. It was a marvellous thing for me to be back on a farm again with people I could relate to. Besides Jeff my bomb aimer, who was now flying with another 150 Squadron crew at Foggia in Italy, the Tomlinsons had two others in their family, Young Harry, who would have been about 17 or 18 at that time, and Peggy, a girl of about 19 or 20. I was now definitely looking forward to my week or so's leave there.

During the course of the evening meal, the story of my hospital treatment was explained, and the Tomlinsons assured me that I should get into the No. 1 RAF Hospital at Rauceby Hill, just at the bottom of the Tomlinson's farm. So Mr Tomlinson said, 'I'll give Nobby Clark a ring.' Which he did. Having got through to the Hospital he enquired, 'Can I speak to Air Commodore Clark, please'. When the Air Commodore came on the phone, Harry said 'Is that you Nobby? I've got a young pilot here who has been getting anything but the best of treatment down in London. So do you think you would have time to have a look at him?' After a bit of a pause for the reply, Harry said 'OK, we'll see you in the morning, Nobby.' I remarked to Mr Tomlinson that he seemed to be on fairly friendly terms with the Air Commodore, to which he replied, 'Oh Nobby and I play golf together at the weekends, if we're not busy!'

So next morning at 10am, I was taken in the Fordson to see Air Commodore Clark (an ex Harley Street orthopaedic surgeon.) I was admitted straight away. This top RAF Hospital was at that time equipped with absolutely the best medical equipment that was available.

When the usual tests had been performed on me and documents signed, a Sister came to my bedside with a vial about the size of a lipstick, containing a brownish liquid. She informed me that little container of fluid was worth two thousand pounds, and I was to get half of it! It was the new wonder drug of Mr Fleming's, penicillin. This drug was drip-fed into my bloodstream at a controlled rate during the course of the next day or so. The drug had a remarkable effect. The inflammation on my lower leg started subsiding, and was down to an acceptable level in a matter of days. I had a minor op. where they drilled a hole in my lower leg bone with a hand drill, and inserted a steel pin just above the ankle joint. A stirrup arrangement was connected to this pin, in such a way that a 28lb weight could be attached by means of a stout cord bung over a pulley at the end of my bed. I remained attached to this arrangement for the next 21 days to enable my fractured tibia and fibia bones to be pulled back down to where the ends could be reunited again. The X rays indicated that the shattered ends had telescoped past one another by about 3 inches in the last seven months, by the elastic effect of the surrounding muscles, which had to be stretched out again.

The mobile X ray machine was wheeled up to my bed at weekly intervals, to check on progress, and after three weeks I was detached from my weights and stirrup, and taken to theatre to have the pin removed from my ankle, and a bone graft performed. My case was apparently somewhat unique as a large number of medics had been invited to witness orthopaedic surgeon Air Commodore (Nobby) Clark perform the graft. My last recollection before going out with the initial shot of Pentathol was the rows of faces peering down over the railings of the balcony that surrounded the theatre table, which was on a lower floor.

The operation involved taking a seven inch section of bone out of the tibia of my good left leg, and attaching it across the fracture in the right leg with the aid of 4 stainless steel screws. Copies of coloured photos taken at various stages of the operation were eventually included in my medical file.

The bone graft was a success, and I was out of bed in about ten days and partially weight bearing on the injured leg. However, recovery was slow and it would be ten more months before I was recovered enough to leave the rehabilitation centre that I was at to go back to NZ. The war in Europe was over by then.

Pre-war, Rauceby Hall had, like Horton, been a Mental Institution; but on account of its location, well out in the Lincolnshire countryside and close to numerous RAF bomber and fighter aerodromes, it was ideally situated to be the chief hospital to get airmen back onto their squadrons again. The turnaround of patients was constant, and hundreds passed through the wards during my five or so months there.

The weather was beautiful that summer and autumn of '44, and many a glorious afternoon I spent, being pushed round in a wheelchair along country lanes, and down the farm tracks, amongst the fields of ripening grain, by Peggy Tomlinson. The war seemed very distant in spite of the almost constant sound of heavy bombers and other aircraft.

One night we were awakened by the thunder of a heavy plane roaring overhead at chimney height followed a few seconds later by a tremendous crash! The burning remains of the crashed aircraft lit up the remains of a farmhouse and the surrounding countryside for a while, as we watched the fire engines and ambulances converging on the scene.

We didn't expect the ambulances to pick up any survivors, and indeed they didn't. The story emerged after a day or so. The aircraft, a B-17 Flying Fortress of the USAAF was pilotless. It had been badly shot up, and with no hydraulics, undercarriage or flaps the crew had headed the plane out to sea and baled out! It had however slowly curved round and nearly demolished one of the main hospitals that was endeavouring to get airmen back on the squadrons! It had almost completely destroyed a farmhouse, the occupants of which luckily escaped with their lives. The upstairs room in which they were sleeping was left with just sufficient floor in one corner to support the double bed which they were in. The fire crew brought them down, demoralised but physically unharmed.

An interesting sequel to an event that I was involved with in North Africa occurred one afternoon when a bunch of us airmen from the hospital were down at the local pub about a mile away. Some of us were on crutches or sticks; but I was helped along in my wheelchair by an airman who had lost an arm. We were sitting at a table having a quiet beer and a talk, when I had the feeling someone was staring at me. I looked round the room crowded with airmen, WAAFS, WAC's, land army girls etc. and caught the eye of an American a few tables away. As he rose to his feet, he said to his US buddies while pointing at me, 'There's the bastard over there.' They had evidently been discussing the bottle of whisky and Jeep transaction back in North Africa. They then came over to our table where I was sitting in my wheelchair, and this one fellow who I could vaguely remember, then accused me of taking his jeep off him in North Africa about 19 months before. I reminded him that I hadn't taken his jeep, but that I had bought it off him for a bottle of Johnnie Walker. He still was not too happy about the whole affair, as shortly after the transaction, his Company Commander who had gone on to Sicily with their Airborne contingent, had returned and when this poor fellow couldn't explain satisfactorily what had become of his jeep, he was put on a charge, was confined to camp and had to march around with a pack on his back for 10 days. They had since been transferred to England for the airborne landings in France. After resolving the past situation we swapped a number of drinks with the Yanks, and later on I was glad to have someone to help push me back to Rauceby Hall Hospital in the evening. It really was a one in a million chance that the American and I would have ever met up with one another again. But that's life!

Nick Alkemade

An interesting patient I had the privilege to be in hospital with at a near by bed, was an RAF rear gunner, Flt Sgt Nick Alkamede, who had survived a miraculous fall from an aircraft. He had been the rear gunner in an aircraft on a raid over Berlin. The plane was badly damaged by enemy gunfire and was burning profusely. The skipper gave the order to bale out. Nick Alkemade opened the doors of his gun turret to reach out to get his parachute, only to discover that the flames had already burnt his parachute. They were still at 18,000 feet, so he considered his options. He could either be burnt to death in the next few moments or he could turn his turret round to the side and jump to his death. He chose the latter option!

It was reasonably peaceful during the fall apart from the sound of aircraft overhead, and the crump of bombs bursting below. Then came oblivion. He awoke to find a reasonably friendly German nearby, but was amazed that he was still alive. To cushion his 18,000 ft fall, he had descended onto the side of a hill that was growing a plantation of 3 to 4 ft high pine trees, on top of which had fallen about a foot of snow. He had a few bones broken and was badly bruised. After all, he would have hit the ground at about 120 miles per hour!

He was taken to a hospital and patched up and became a prisoner of war. The story of his survival from a fall of 18,000 feet got around Berlin, and eventually was heard by Adolf Hitler. He was so amazed at this miraculous case of survival that he had a certificate printed confirming the fact of his fall and personally signed by himself, Adolf Hitler!

The Canadian rear gunner eventually became very ill with pneumonia and was repatriated back to England during a POW exchange exercise. These exchanges were organised occasionally with POW's who were considered unlikely to be of any further military use to their respective homelands. It was while on his brief stay at Rauceby Hospital that I met him and saw this precious certificate signed by Hitler, before he went back to Canada. If that document is still around, I'm sure it would be worth a fortune today. There was an article in the Readers Digest about that whole affair 25 or 30 years ago, so no doubt the full story could be obtained.

Hoylake

Towards the end of 1944 I was discharged from Rauceby to go to a convalescent centre at Hoylake, in the Wirral, across the Mersey from Liverpool. On the way across by train another patient and I, on account of our disabilities, were taken in hand by the Guard, and travelled with him in the Guards van. This avoided the mad congestion of personnel travelling by train in wartime England. We were well looked after by the Guard, who served up tea and biscuits every couple of hours. We also, with the aid of his boiling kettle, were able to steam open our personal medical files and inspect the considered learned opinions of our chance of survival. In mine, apart from the normal facts, and description and photos of my bone graft, there was a copy of a scathing letter to the Superintendent of the Horton Emergency Hospital from Air Commodore Clark, telling him in no uncertain terms that there were never to be any of 'his boys' admitted to that hospital, and that they were to go straight to Rauceby.

I had Christmas and the next five months at Hoylake. There were 25 or 30 of us at this establishment most of the time, which was a large manor house on the main street but overlooking the Royal Hoylake Golf Course. My legs and especially my right foot had been immobilised for so long that the joints had all adhered and considerable massage and exercise were involved in getting me back on my feet without sticks or crutches.

Some of the rehabilitation exercises were performed out on the golf course on fine days. We cut plough furrow type strips of turf and rolled them back, levelled the ground underneath and replaced the turf, taking the surplus soil away in wheelbarrows. There happened to be two fellows there who had lost an arm each, one the left arm, and the other the right. They were put in charge of a wheelbarrow. To witness two people trying to wheel the one wheelbarrow was a sight that is still firmly etched in my mind. It usually took a number of attempts, and a few reloadings to get a barrow-full to the stockpile.

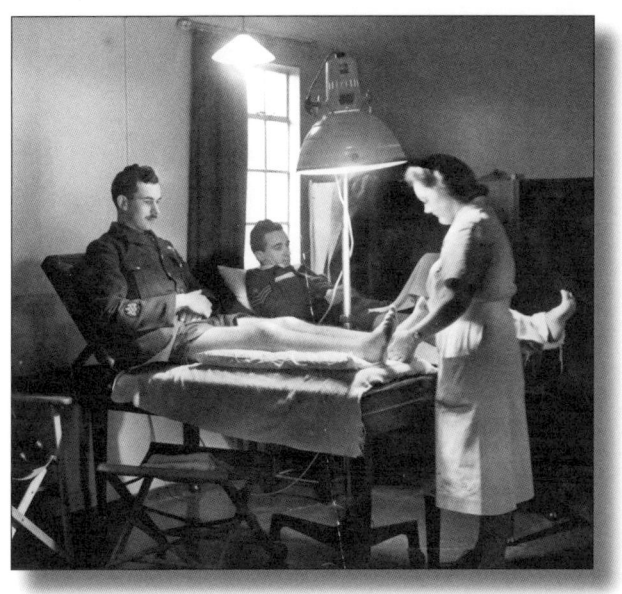

Warrant Officer Hayman in hospital at Hoylake, near Liverpool, 1945.

When the few offending humps had been levelled, the powers that be decided that a few more bunkers would enhance, and upgrade the character of the course, and so we set to work to put bunkers near some of the greens. I have never been back; but no doubt it would all be unrecognisable to me now after 54 years.

The War in Europe ended while I was at Hoylake, and we celebrated with the crowds in the streets of Liverpool. I went back to Moreton-in-Marsh for a week or two. I also got married to Toni, a girl from West Kirby, near Hoylake, and had a short honeymoon before I was posted back to New Zealand.

Part Four

Life Since the War, 1945– 2003

Return Home

I returned to New Zealand on the troopship *Andes* in June–July '45 with a happy bunch of returning servicemen, including a large number of the Maori Battalion. It was a joyful musical five-week journey back through the Panama Canal and arriving at Wellington the day after the disastrous wind and snowfall of July 1945.

I caught the ferry to Lyttelton, and then the train to Timaru. The train had a bit of a battle down across the plains through feet of snow and downed telephone and power lines. There was a big welcome from Mum and Dad at Timaru, and then it was back to 'Tasman Downs' by Lake Pukaki.

'Welcome Home': *the author and his parents, Timaru Railway Station, 1945.*

Life back on the farm proved to be the best physiotherapy one could get. Nevertheless I never got more than five degrees of movement in my right ankle, and also had some toe joints removed that had been misshapen from the frostbite I had suffered on Mount Etna.

For a year or so after returning to NZ I had the opportunity to go in the ballot for farms that came up for sale. I put my name in many times, but was unsuccessful at being drawn a winner. But Dad and Mum retired in 1952 and I took over the farm, assuming that the Government Rehab. Loans Board would arrange financial assistance for me to do so. This was flatly refused, much to my dismay. They considered that a 1,900 acre property in the Mackenzie Country was an uneconomic unit. The average size for a grazing run in this area is twenty- five to twenty-seven thousand acres, with one of our neighbours in control of sixty thousand. Since then, with the raising of Lake Pukaki for electric power development, our place has lost 800 acres, leaving us just 1,100 acres.

The Rehab. Course

When I returned from hospital in England in July 1945, I was given the opportunity to brush up on farming improvements etc. that might have developed during the war years. About fifty returned men were encamped at Burnham for twelve weeks to take part in a Rehab (i.e. Rehabilitation) agricultural short course at Lincoln College, where we were trucked to and fro daily. I had the little Austin up there with me and occasionally three or four of us would go into Christchurch of an evening to a show or pictures.

The course was no doubt beneficial to us and got our minds focused back onto rural activities again. There was however, one occasion when Professor Clay was extolling the virtues of poultry-raising. I had never developed a very close relationship with the scatty feathered creatures, and so after half an hour or so, of to us, a very boring lecture, a couple of us started playing cards between us on the form we were sitting on. This activity apparently hadn't gone unnoticed by the worthy Professor and so suddenly he shouted, 'Hayman! How much wheat does a hen require in one year?' Taken completely by surprise, and not having the slightest idea, I simply and facetiously replied, 'About a couple of pecks.' I was sure I was in for a tongue lashing for not paying attention, but as it turned out that was about the right answer, as two pecks is half a bushel, in the Imperial system. So I did pick up something about the food intake of hens. Incidentally, volume-wise, a bushel is the same as four gallons. No doubt that is for most of us another useless piece of information!

Post-war Transport

In 1937 I had purchased a derelict 1918 Harley Davidson motorcycle and rotted sidecar for £5-10-0. I coaxed it back into life, stripped it down, painted and rebuilt the sidecar.

Jack Hayman on his son's Harley Davidson, 1944.

It did me good service, but in late 1945 I sold it to buy a 12-foot clinker-built boat that could be fitted with a three and a half horsepower Briggs and Stratton motor. Stan Guard and his associates were building these boats at Fairlie under the wing of Jones Motors. Dad and I had gone to Timaru with the four ton International C30 truck for a load of fuel in drums, coal etc, and had taken the Harley down on the back for a prospective buyer to look at. A Mr. Rodgers duly arrived at the appointed time and I gave him a brief run down on the workings of the machine so he could go for a test drive round the block in the vicinity of the Railway Station. He went off and I waited for half an hour or so but he never returned. The Police couldn't trace him either! He had given his address as R A Rodgers, Pareora West, South Canterbury. There was such a person in that area once but he hadn't been seen for a long time. I never saw the bike, or him, or the £20 that he owed me. He and the Harley simply vanished without trace!

I have kicked myself over that affair ever since. The 20 quid though, nearly half the amount the boat was to cost, was not a lot really. If the Harley had been left in the shed, it would be worth at least twenty thousand dollars today. By the way the machine was painted a light grey colour with green mudguards and trim. Perhaps in his unfamiliarity with a bike and sidecar, he went off the end of the wharf into the harbour. Who knows? I guess though he just did a runner! However, I did get the boat and had a lot of fun fitting it out with motor drive shaft, clutch, rudder etc. During the time I had it, hundreds of Canada Geese were culled during the moulting season, and many trout were caught on idyllic evenings down at the lake.

The little Austin Seven became my transport for a year or so; but when my wife, Toni, arrived with hundreds of other war brides on the *SS Dominion Monarch*, which berthed at Wellington on the 23rd January 1946, and we began a family, the Austin was traded in for a slightly bigger 1938 Morris 10 saloon. The faithful Hudson was of course still available for our use when required for transporting heavy or bulky equipment etc, until Dad and Mum's retirement to Timaru in 1952, when they traded it in for a new Austin A40.

I should mention here that a feature of the Hudson was the ability of the back of the front seat to fold down flat, and with the rear seat squab turned round, an exceedingly comfortable bed could be made up with appropriate bedding requisites. Dad and I did a tour of some of the South Island in this manner just prior to my going away to the War. Mum and Dad had also done a bit of camping out in this manner. Toni and I also had a week or so away camping this way before it became apparent that Alan, our first child, was due to arrive in the latter part of 1946.

The Hudson in Retirement

The Hudson had its semi-retirement in Timaru, where for many years it was to be seen at the harbour end of Strathallan Street, to which location it was required to tow the popular and busy piecart every evening after (in those days) the closing of the Pubs at 6.0pm! The name piecart didn't really convey the full extent of the type of sustenance available at these mobile-eating places. Just about every medium-sized town in New Zealand probably sported one, where sausages, tomatoes, bacon and eggs, fish and chips etc could be served up, or taken away in a matter of minutes. Tea, coffee, and soft drinks were of course also available and no doubt of course, pies. During the 1950's and 60's the opening of more Fish and Chip shops and Fast Food outlets and then MacDonalds and Kentucky Fries saw the demise of the good old piecart and I don't suppose there are any in existence now. The health authorities wouldn't permit that sort of eating establishment on the streets these days.

In the 1920's my Dad's Uncle Ern. had fallen on hard times in the farming business round the Ashburton area. The local Police Constable could see the need for evening and late night eating and non-alcoholic refreshments in the town not only for locals but also for the odd passing motorist. It was he who suggested to Uncle Ern. the feasibility of getting a pie cart organized and on the street. Ern, like most Haymans, was pretty good with his hands and with the help of the Constable, a good-sized pie cart was soon set up just off the main street of Ashburton. With Ern and his wife preparing foodstuffs in the afternoon and getting set up in the evenings, the Pie Cart soon became a thriving business, especially during the war years with the passing military personnel. When Ern sold the business he had made more than enough to retire comfortably on!

Taking over 'Tasman Downs'

When I took on full responsibility of running the farm in 1951 and then without the Hudson, I traded the Morris for a 14-year-old 1937 Ford V8 sedan, which proved to be an admirable farm vehicle for Toni and me and our growing family. We then had Alan, Bernard and Nicola. Wendy came later, in 1954. At that time with the recently repainted Ford V8 car, a 17-year-old International 4-ton truck, and the 10-year-old IHC Farmall M tractor, I was ready to give farming a go.

As a Returned Serviceman I was eligible for a rehabilitation loan to assist with financing myself into the property on Dad's retirement. However, on my visiting the Rehab. Loans Board to apply for a low interest loan, I was flatly refused when asked for the location of the farm. When told it was on the shores of Lake Pukaki, they simply replied that no money was available for any properties in the Mackenzie, as no land up there was economic.

I had recently returned from a war where I had voluntarily put my life on the line flying Wellington bombers in North Africa and the Italian Campaign in 1943, and now, in 1952, I was handed the reins of 'Tasman Downs', plus its substantial mortgage and a grant of sufficient funds to enable Mum and Dad to continue with a decent lifestyle during their retirement in Church Street Timaru.

I realized it wasn't going to be an easy task to keep my head above water, and the difficulties I faced were accentuated by the fact that the property had been reduced by 500 acres with the first raising of Lake Pukaki for power development. The property was now 1400 acres: not much when one considers the average size of Mackenzie Country run properties is twenty five to thirty thousand acres, with some more than twice that size!

Would I be able to make a go of it? My war-damaged legs didn't encourage me to do much walking, but the reduced area enabled shepherding etc to be tended to in double quick time on horseback. The Cassies had left 'Guide Hill' Station next door, and John Hogg, in his early twenties, was assisted on to 'Guide Hill' by John Scott of 'Godley Peaks' Station. John was not married and during his 12–14 years next door usually had a married couple to assist him on the property.

Haymaking and Harvesting

In those years I did a lot of work for the neighbours at haymaking and harvesting times. For instance the Farmall M and I were called upon to do all the reaping and binding of the extensive oat crops grown then on 'Braemar', 'Guide Hill' and of course 'Tasman Downs'. I also did all the hay baling and the heading of the crops in the area. It also fell to my lot to do all the stacking of the sheaves of oats for the three properties and then of course organizing and running the chaff-cutting operations. These haymaking, harvesting and chaff-cutting operations required a number of men to be employed. With Dad's retirement I was then just a one man band, but with one or two from 'Guide Hill' and two or three from 'Braemar', a full gang could be organized to get these time-consuming, tedious and physically exhausting jobs completed during the drier spells of weather.

The crops of oats which the reaper and binder left tied into thousands of about 7 or 8 pound sheaves had to be all picked up by hand and stood heads up with about a dozen in each tent-shaped stook. These stooks were then left for the grain and straw to mature and dry out completely for ten days to a fortnight so the sheaves could be forked on to drays, wagons or in our case mostly on to whatever motor truck we had at the time. They were then taken to a suitable part of the paddock to be built into weather and wind-withstanding stacks. The stacks would be left maturing for a number of weeks or even months until a suitable time came, in the case of the oats, to be cut with a power driven chaffcutter and bagged and sewn into 75 to 80 pound bags of chaff, which was the basic food for horses.

With the crops and stocks of wheat, barley and of course oats etc, which required the grain to be saved for seed and commercial purposes the sheaves were forked into a threshing mill driven by a steam traction engine, though by the 1930's tractor power started coming into use. Steam powered engines are now collector's items, but can still be seen in operation at country field days, Agricultural and Pastoral Shows etc.

The introduction of the horse and later, tractor-drawn header harvesters and then the self-propelled header that came on stream during the latter half of the twentieth century saw the demise of the six or eight and ten or twelve men gangs in the harvest fields. Harvesting the crops of grain for example, when the standing crop was nearly ripe, required the horse- drawn reaper and binder to be driven to the paddock by the operator driving a couple of, usually, Clydesdale horses. These machines, either Massey-Harris or McCormack Deering, would take a 6 foot cut of the crop and tie it into sheaves, which could be carried on a bundle carrier across the paddocks by the operators' control of a foot pedal. This of course in an average to good crop required the bundle carrier pedal to be activated every 15 to 20 seconds. That as well as operating the other half dozen levers to adjust the flow of the cut crop and get the twine tied as near the middle of each sheaf as possible, and drive the horses was a skilful, tiring but interesting job.

In the mid 1930's Dad acquired a tractor-powered McCormack reaper and binder with a ten-foot cut. This proved to be too wide a cut for our hummocky moraine-deposited land so we cut a couple of feet off it, changed the iron rimmed and spoked main wheel for a pneumatic tyred one for operator comfort and we were in business! We operated this machine behind the International T20 crawler tractor for a season or two before we got a rubber-tyred little International Fairway 12 tractor. I was nearly 16 and had left the Timaru Boys High School boarding establishment to come home and help Dad, and no doubt, no longer having to pay my school boarding fees inspired Dad to get the Fairway 12 tractor, which was my pride and joy. What a wonderful breakthrough it was in 1935 to put tractors on rubber tyres. No more clattering banging and rattling over rocks and hard shingle roads. More comfort for the operator and a softer ride? I don't think operator comfort was much of a priority for tractor manufacturers back in the early 1900's. The T20 crawler did come with a padded seat and Dad had built a canvas-covered cab complete with a Model T Ford windscreen. But though this kept the rain off and most of the wind out, it did little to stop the swirling clouds of dust choking the operator.

I started driving the crawler tractor during the school holidays and at weekends when I was about 13, usually on straightforward jobs like disking, harrowing, rolling etc. It also was hot on the crawler with the seat just above the transmission final drives and one's legs and feet down on either side of the gearbox. So on fine days the curtains would be wound up and the windscreen opened to let a bit of the two to three mile per hour breeze of the tractors forward motion drift through under the hood, which I must say kept the sun off. But the dust!

Threshing wheat at 'Tasman Downs' 1927. The threshing mill was driven by the T20 caterpillar tractor.

I think crawler and caterpillar type tractors were designed specifically to create masses of dust for operator discomfort when cultivating soil for cropping. I recall Dad's brothers and cousins and brother's-in-law complaining about the dusty tractor jobs they were engaged in round Waimate and the Canterbury Plains and Dad replying, 'Good Lord! You call that dusty. A blooming sheep walking across a worked paddock up here would create a bigger cloud of dust than your tractors do down there!' The nor'west wind-blown glacial rock flour off the Tasman River during the last few thousand years had deposited a foot or so of very fine soil over the glacial moraine deposits on the eastern side of the Tasman Valley and beyond to other pockets of the Mackenzie Basin. This was the type of soil that had been cultivated in the area since the 1870's.

The 1500 to 1800 acres of 'Tasman Downs' were, up to 1914, used as a winter feed block for the sheep from 'Tekapo' Station, with which it was run in conjunction. Turnips and Swedes were the predominant winter feed crops and after they had been eaten the ground was prepared for crops of oats to be fed, as chaff, to the hacks and working horses. These crops of course were cut and tied into sheaves with the reaper and binder which was pulled by a couple of good sturdy Clydesdale draught horses under the control of the operator (teamster) who controlled the many levers, rods, pedals etc., that enabled the crop to be tied in neat sheaves according to the standing crop's height, and the bundles of sheaves left in neat rows from round to round, for the other harvest men to set up in stooks to dry before being built into twelve to fifteen ton stacks.

These harvesting operations of course required the use of a number of helpers. Up here, where 'Braemar', 'Guide Hill' and we worked together, we could usually muster seven or eight able bod's for much of the physical stooking, stacking, forking sheaves or hay, sewing bags etc.

In my childhood days in the 1920's, hay making started with someone with a couple of horses pulling a four and a half foot sickle bar mower to cut the hay. Usually two of these mowing rigs would be on the job as progress in 60 or 80 acre paddocks was not particularly fast, with hard cutting patches and the odd loose stone etc, holding up progress, and of course the twenty odd triangular sections on the cutting bar had to be sharpened every hour or so by hand with a file. Damaged sections had to be removed and new ones riveted on.

After the hay was starting to dry it would be raked with a horse-drawn rake, and as it dried more horse powered hay sweeps were operated to push hay over to the stationary hay press, belt driven by a portable steam engine or other type of engine drawn into position with horses. The hay press itself required six people to operate it, two of them hefty fellows with pitch forks to fork the hay left by the hay sweep operators up on to a platform attached to the hay press where another man with a fork fed the hay into the press. These forkfuls had to be timed to coincide with the action of the vertical 'monkey' which pushed the hay into the bale chamber where the horizontal plunger pressed it into a suitably adjusted bale pressure.

These forkfuls would be put into the machine between its strokes every four to five seconds. This always appeared to me to be highly dangerous. My Dad usually occupied this position and never suffered any injury. I think that would have been an understatement. One false move and the machine grabbing an arm or leg and you would be gobbled up in a few seconds! A few forks met their demise so a few spares were always carried. Broken ones usually only required a new handle to be attached to the tines.

At about every three foot length of pressed hay passing through the bale chamber, a monitoring wheel would ring a bell which indicated that a wooden block required to be tipped in before the next bale of hay was started. These wooden blocks the size of the 18 inch by 14 inch bale chamber were slotted on either side where wires could be threaded through by less muscular individuals with nimble fingers, but not necessarily a high I.Q., The persons on either side would get the wire end that had been threaded through and thread it back through the slots in the block at the other end of the bale as it came along in its erratic plunger-driven movements, depending on the size of the forkfuls of hay being put in by the hay feeder. The two separate wires were then quickly joined with a few quick twists and the next pair of wires were readied to be threaded through for the next bale. These 14 gauge wires were previously cut to a length about nine and a half feet and a loop twisted on one end then straightened and put in bundles of one hundred.

The other man in the hay baling operation was the fellow who stacked the bales of hay in an oblong shaped stack seven or eight bales high. His job also entailed collecting the wooden blocks as they emerged and putting them back into the hand operated tipping mechanism ready for the next separation of further bales. As each bale was made in about forty to forty-five seconds all hands were kept fairly busy.

I came on the active scene when I was eight or nine and was strong enough in the hands to tie wire satisfactorily. At that age I had been milking cows for a year or two so my hand strength was no doubt adequate for the job. Though tying wires on bales at a stationary hay press was not a physically demanding job, I considered it the most unpleasant. The hay press was always positioned by the wind direction to favour the ones forking the hay. This meant that the wire tiers were always in the dust and loose windblown hay. On breezy nor'westerly days it didn't take long for the ones tying the wires to become completely covered in loose hay. This did keep the wind off one, but of course didn't enhance visibility! However, if the wind velocity got above about 20 mph, the hay baling operation would have to be abandoned, as the raked hay would soon be blown away.

When I was twelve, I took on the job of stacking the 75 to 80 lb bales, which was of course a lot physically harder work but at least you could keep your face facing towards the breeze. Handling the wire-tied bales soon had one's hands in blisters if gloves weren't worn; but with an arm under the bale at one end and a large bale hook in the other hand, stacking or carting bales was not too bad a job.

The author's father, left, haybaling at 'Tasman Downs', 1940's.

The wire-tied bales were the norm until, in October 1945, the International Harvester Company and also the New Holland Company of America came out with self-pickup and twine-tying balers which could be pulled behind a tractor and the hay baled and tied immediately it was fit enough in the windrows left by the operator with the hay rake. This was of course a big saving in manpower; but the bales now scattered around the paddocks still, of course, had to be picked up and transported to barns or stacked and covered in the paddock before rain got a chance to spoil them.

From 1945 Dad and I did all the baling for 'Braemar', 'Guide Hill' and 'Tasman Downs', as well as the mowing.

The author's father on the new Farmall M tractor, 'Tasman Downs', 1941.

The Farmall M tractor, which Dad had purchased in 1941 in place of the ageing T20 Crawler, was a big step up with its rubber tyres and faster gearing. I joined the Air Force that year, but Dad contracted to do the mowing, plowing, reaping, heading, chaff-cutting etc with that tractor. The war in the Pacific broke out at that time and the price of Browntop grass seed increased considerably, as it was an ideal grass to get a good tough turf surface quickly on the hundreds of airfields that were required to be constructed on the islands in the Pacific and elsewhere in the world as the conflict spread. A smallish IHC 52 header was purchased, and the first year that Dad operated it that little header paid for itself. One small benefit of War! That header was power take-off, driven by the tractor. Just another job for the Farmall to do. For the next 25 years that tractor did a large proportion of the work in the district. Thousands and thousands of hours are behind it now, but in its semi retirement it still gets used every few months to grade our mile or two of roads with a grader blade I constructed to work hydraulically beneath it.

There has not been a battery to go flat on the Farmall now for 30 years, but it has always been easy to start with just a couple of pulls on the starting handle. The impulse devise on the magneto ensures a hot spark every half turn of the starting handle. It has had three sets of sleeves and pistons, two sets of brake linings, three sets of tyres and one fan belt. Its original price was about ten bales of wool. The last tractor we got a couple of years ago cost the equivalent of about a hundred bales of wool!

Operator comfort was not a priority 60 years ago. There was a hard seat to sit on, and though a folded jute grain sack did give a bit more comfort, I wonder how many of those I've worn out with my bottom! A few dozen I guess. When I returned from the War I decided a bit more comfort was required so I built a flimsy cab of wood and canvas and an old Ford T windscreen, which kept off the sun, rain and wind but not the dust. Goggles protected your eyes, and a good pick every once in a while enabled you to keep your nasal passages clear enough to breath through. I wonder how the human body copes with the conditions it sometimes is called on to endure. Unprotected farm equipment is bad enough; but walking or perhaps sitting on implements behind teams of horses in dusty field conditions would no doubt have been just as bad.

What bliss now the tractor and harvester operators enjoy with air-conditioned cabs, radios, heaters etc. I don't consider life was that good back in the 'good old days!' Nevertheless with many hands helping from neighbouring properties at harvesting, stacking haymaking, chaff-cutting etc, there was wonderful communal friendship to be had.

In the early 1950's, when Dad and Mum went to live at Church Street in Timaru, the Cassies, then with their family grown up, left 'Guide Hill' and

John Hogg was assisted on to 'Guide Hill' by John Scott of 'Godley Peaks' Station, 35 miles away on the north west end of Lake Tekapo. The set-up was that if John Hogg could make himself available at any time when mustering of the merino sheep on 'Godley Peak' Station was to be done, John Scott would let him have the annual draft surplus merino wethers. It was quite a generous arrangement on John Scott's part.

As 'Guide Hill' was running mainly dry sheep, John offered to supervise the lambing etc, for me on 'Tasman Downs' if I could assist with his agricultural work, harvesting etc. It was an admirable arrangement and we got on well together, as I did with his married couples and single men he employed from time to time.

Two Disasters

1961 saw the break-up of my marriage to Toni, my English war bride of 16 years. As apparently is the way of things, I had no idea that our family life was about to be torn apart. It was on June the 14th. I had taken the truck to Fairlie for a load of coal and tractor fuel. Upon entering the house about 5pm. things seemed strangely quiet. There was no welcome home or children coming to meet me. The governess, Christine Newton, whom we were employing at the time to supervise the teaching of correspondence to Nicola, aged ten, and Wendy, aged seven, informed me that Toni had left with the two girls, and that there was a note pinned to the pillow on my side of the bed. It read: 'Goodbye Bruce, I'm leaving you. I've got the girls. You can have the boys.' (At the time, Alan, aged 14, and Bernard, aged 12, were boarders at Timaru Boys High School). Well, that sure knocked the wind out of my sails! To say I was shattered when I found out that Toni had taken our two little girls and gone off with Andy Poharama, a Maori, who had been round the district for a year or two in the shearing gangs, would be the understatement of the year. But the house cows still had to be milked and the dogs, hens, pigs etc fed, and Christine collected and taken to 'Guide Hill', where Joe and Sidney Fraser were the married couple for John at the time.

It was a day or so after Toni's departure that Ian (Inky) Wardell phoned from the Pukaki Hotel, wanting to know when I was going to come and get my Chevy car. So that was where the pickup place had been! John took me down via Tekapo, because there was no road down the east side of Lake Pukaki then, and I retrieved my car. After a packet or so of cigarettes and a few beers that night I decided to have a go at seeing where they had gone. John kindly agreed to care for the animals on the place and look after everything while I was away, as I had done for him at times when he was away from 'Guide Hill.'

I had been away a few days and had found the family at a house in Christchurch, and seen the children at school, but they had declined naturally to leave their mother and come back with me. I then phoned John, back at 'Guide Hill', to see how things were going at home, as on the radio news there had been reports of gale-force winds in the back country. The news could not have been worse.

At that time the district was being reticulated with electric power from the National Grid and John and I had felled a few trees to make way for the power line. The surplus twigs and branches had been burnt and the area tidied up. But the wind must have caused some sparks to fly. For when John had gone down to milk my cows etc that morning, utter devastation had greeted him. The hay barn with the winter supply of 2,000 bales of hay was just a heap of twisted iron and smoldering ashes. As if that wasn't bad enough, the chaff house and stable, (which included the old school room) were also burnt. The stable etc I had converted to house the header, baler, topdresser and chaff-cutter. What a shock! Especially on top of the recent events. Should I just give up and get to hell out of it? After all it was but 40 odd years previously, during my Grandfather's ownership when the manager was due to leave, that Dad and Mum were told to leave 'Opira' and go up to 'Tasman Downs' and as Walter said, 'Look after the Godforsaken place,' till we can get rid of the bloody thing!'

It was tempting to just pack up and go. But no, I wouldn't. Hadn't I put my life on the line to go and fight to keep this land in British ownership?

Then on return had I not been refused a Rehab Loan to help pay off the mortgage, on account of the property's location in the Mackenzie Country, classing the land uneconomic! No, I wouldn't go! In spite of my war injuries classing me as 75% disabled, I was determined to prove to the bloody bureaucrats that this bit of God's Earth had been worth fighting for. After all, the house, workshop, tool shed and car garage were still intact and I still had the car, Farmall tractor and four-ton C30 International truck. I might mention here that nothing that had been burnt had been insured! It takes a fire to change one's ideas on insurance. In later years I've been paying hefty premiums on complete farm insurance etc, but have much more peace of mind.

My divorce was shortly settled in Court at Dunedin. Nicola and Wendy were to stay with their Mother, leaving Alan and Bernard with me. They continued as boarders at Timaru Boys High till they were seventeen or eighteen and I arranged employment for them until they married and were off on their own. There was also maintenance to be paid for Nicola and Wendy until they were sixteen years old.

A goose drive had been organized for about ten days after the fire, at which about 30 shooters turned up under the direction of a long time associate and returned serviceman, Bill Stone. Bill had also arranged for some assistance from them to help clear up the mess left after the fire. They also raised £500 for me to get an Allis-Chalmers Allcrop 60 header from Angus Copeland, who had no further use for it. This very generous gift gave me a great start to getting the farm ticking over again.

Rebuilding and Upgrading

It was a time of intense activity for me that year. Getting hooked up to the National Grid with electric power was a most wonderful event, but also created a lot of extra work for me to do. I pulled out the coal store and dismantled the brick fire surround on the chimney, put in an electric hot water cylinder, and replaced the kauri sink bench top with stainless steel. I also built another bathroom and toilet in an old bedroom and generally reshaped a lot of the house.

I brought up a load or two of concrete blocks and built a grain and seeds etc storeroom 22 feet square, attached to which was a four-bay implement shed. I must admit that I did employ a block layer for a few days to assist in putting up the block for walls for the building, but the foundations and the rest of the building construction I did myself. Lloyd Carlton was also here for a day or two to put the wiring in the house, woolshed and workshop.

Before the power was turned on, our private telephone line had to be upgraded from a single-wire, earth return system to a double copper-wired set up. This was privately owned and maintained by the four property owners up here: namely, Donald Burnett at 'Mount Cook' Station; Vic and Lucy Robertson and son John, managers for the Australian and New Zealand Land Company on 'Braemar' Station; John Hogg on 'Guide Hill' Station, and me on 'Tasman Downs'. John and I cut all the three-inch by three-inch cross arms into two-foot lengths and bored the five holes of various sizes required in each one. There were about 1150 of them. John and I then took all the 3 x 3 hardwood timber to the Tekapo A Power Station, where Mr. George Scott, Engineer in Charge, very kindly offered us the use of the Station's electric drills and power saw. A few afternoons out there and we soon had all the cross arms sorted and ready. Then with John's married man, Joe Fraser, we joined up with one or two of the others and checked the existing phone poles. These Australian Jarrah poles tapered from 5 x 4 inches to 4 x 3 inches had already been in use for just on fifty years, but were in remarkably good condition. With a few doubtful ones we dug in a stub post and bolted it to the pole.

Donald Burnett undertook the job of tying the new wire on to the insulators while we wound up the now no longer needed number eight galvanized wire and ran out the new steel-cored and copper-coated twin telephone wires. We ran them off the back of my old International truck with the use of a wire spinning Jenny to avoid pulling the copper covered wire over the ground and damaging it on protruding stones. As the work progressed the last job in the evening was to connect up a wire again so the phones could be used again until work resumed again. After a few weeks the new double wired line was completed and the faithful old Evi battery-powered phones became redundant and were replaced with the more modern dial phones and the party line of the district was a thing of the past. We made a good job of that line and I remarked that it should last for another fifty years. To which Donald Burnett replied, 'I would like to see it last for a hundred years.' Indeed it probably could've, but it wasn't to be. Modern electronics made our private telephone line obsolete in little more than 25 years and we up here in the Tasman Valley are now served with a dish, high up on a pole in the yard, which picks up the signal from a translator on the top of Mount Mary about ten miles away. We are up with the field with digital phones, fax machines, computers, cell phones etc, and what next in the future? The mind boggles when one considers the tremendous advances made in the electronic field since the discovery of the untapped power of the silicon chip!

Remarriage

After my wife left me in 1961 my widowed mother came up from Timaru to keep house for me, and ensure that I had at least one square meal a day! But when Alan and Bernard came home from school for the holidays the housekeeping burden became too much for my mother, then in her sixties, and assistance was required. Accordingly, my mother asked around, and contacted Linda Cargo, who was looking after children at 'Haldon' Station. Linda agreed to come for a short period to help my mother, before moving on to be companion help to Mrs Robertson at 'Braemar' Station. Linda and I became engaged and in 1963 were married at the Presbyterian Church, Highfield, Timaru.

Wedding Day, 1964. Bruce and Linda Hayman

In due course we had two children, Jane (born 1967) and Ian (1971). Both were taught by correspondence until Jane went to Selwyn House School in Christchurch and Ian to Waihi School, in Winchester, taking his pet rabbit with him in a hutch! Jane went on to Rangi Ruru College, and Ian to Christ's College, Jane following this with a BA at the University of Otago. Ian, however, returned to 'Tasman Downs' on leaving school, to help out when I had a series of problems with my damaged leg. He was really thrown in the deep end while I was in hospital having skin grafts.

Relocation

In the mid seventies Lake Pukaki was raised for the last time, and this meant that the homestead had to be re-built on higher ground. The money being offered to build a new house was $18 a square foot for 3/4 the size of the home we were living in. This was way below the current building charges up in that area at that time.

The Old Homestead and workshop, early 1970's.

So some of the less urgent farm work was put on the back burner, and I went into the timber business. I cut down about 45 trees, 25 of which were ones I had planted as my first job, when as a 15 year-old I left school to help Dad on the farm. By the 70's they had grown into massive Oregons.

Cutting timber for the news homestead at 'Tasman downs', 1970's.

Having already drawn the plans for our new home I cut the logs into the required lengths for the job. For the beams spanning some of the larger rooms they required to be over 20 ft long. With the aid of the tractor I got them loaded on the old Bedford truck and took them to the little sawmill at Fairlie, 45 miles away, and had them cut to the dimensions required to complete the building of the house to the requirements of the plans I had drawn. Each load of timber I brought back was strip-stacked and covered for 18 months to let it season.

The building took two years to complete. At that stage I employed a couple of carpenters to drive most of the nails; but I was involved with cutting timber to lengths, mixing the concrete, collecting rocks for the cladding, doing all the carting etc, as well as supervising and advising the Ministry of Works on the shifting of the farm buildings that had to be relocated. Thank goodness that at the time, I was a young fellow of only 55!

Getting ready to erect the framing of the new homestead, 'Tasman Downs', mid 1970's.

I might add that I did all the plumbing as well, and also a vast amount of steel reinforcing in the structure to withstand the snow loading and 100 mile an hour plus winds that are a feature of this area; but it was fun. We experienced one wind of 113 mph on the gauge here by the house just a few days prior to putting the roof on.

The new homestead completed: the author's daughter and Jane and son Ian, 1977.

At another site about a mile away on the farm where we thought we might have relocated, the gauge there had registered 122 mph! There were of course no trees in the area at that time. Fortunately there is some shelter now from the trees around that I've planted.

The Farmstay

In 1982 Linda and I made the decision to operate 'Tasman Downs' as a farm stay, and this has proved a wonderfully rewarding one.

Over the years we have hosted individuals, couples and families from all over the world, from Moscow to Tokyo and Santiago to Berlin. Meeting such a variety of people from such diverse backgrounds has enriched our lives and, it seems, from their comments in our visitor's books, enriched theirs also. Again and again visitors speak of the 'million dollar view', of the quiet, and of the visit as a New Zealand highlight. Many have returned, one couple thirteen times!

Linda and Bruce Hayman and the new homestead, 1978.

Recent Years

Over the years I've avoided employing help except of course the gangs that came for a week to do the shearing. My damaged leg if walked on extensively used to swell up and was prone to having the skin broken if knocked at all. These abrasions often turned to ulcers, which could take months to heal and often required skin grafts. On the last occasion this happened, in 1995, I had become fed up with it and told the skin specialist, who was considering another graft, not to waste his time on it anymore, and to get an orthopaedic surgeon to cut the damn thing off. The offending portion was removed about six inches below the knee and with it went the stainless steel screws and the pain. I don't think that I limp as much now as I did before because I've now two legs the same length! I'm not much hampered with an artificial leg. I have still got the knee joint with about six inches of lower limb below. I avoid walking too much, but at least it doesn't hurt, and I really don't limp and can still drive OK.

I never flew again after the crash on Mt. Etna. Civil aviation would naturally want only 100% fit pilots, and rightly so too! I sometimes thought of getting a small plane, but family life and paying off the mortgage restricted the availability of surplus cash. I did, however, get into jet boating in the early '60s.

Author jetboating down the Chimney rapid, Pukaki River in a Jet 41, late 1960's. Photo by Guy Mannering.

The jet boat was invented on a neighbouring property, 'Irishman's Creek' Station", by Bill Hamilton, who, pre-war, I used to play ice hockey with, and also a bit of polo. It was the same Bill Hamilton who first took me at over 100 mph as a twelve year old in his Bentley during December 1932. Bill was later knighted for his invention of the jet boat. He and Lady Peggy have since died.

For 35 years my second wife, Linda, and I have had immeasurable fun and have made many acquaintances of and become firm friends with many other jet boaters during excursions up and down the many rivers in New Zealand's South Island. It is a challenging sport and certainly keeps alive one's youthful exuberance. I still have a jet boat, but our 27 year-old son Ian mostly drives it now, unless I am wanted to drive it for a bit of flat water boating while the young do a bit of water skiing.

We sold all our sheep in March 1996 and now run 500 odd cattle on a fattening basis.

The last load of wool from the old 'Tasman Downs' woolshed, 1970's. Jane and Ian in front of the Commer truck.

We do a bit of cropping and also make a lot of hay for winter-feeding. Then there are the guests on a farm home-stay basis.. Life is still interesting. My biggest problem is failing eyesight and without the pleasure of reading and the more dubious pleasure of watching TV, filling in time gets a bit boring in the evenings and long nights. I only seem to need about five hours sleep now I'm in my eighties.

I do much less about the farm now, but despite problems with my eyes, can still assist with ploughing, and using our quad bike, which took over from our old CT90 Honda Trail bike, which still goes well, and three wheelers, can still play a useful part in assisting Ian, Nicky and their wee Archie to keep the finances of the farm ticking over and giving us all a reasonable lifestyle. I think the quad bike must be the most cost-efficient machine on the farm.

A Postscript

I finished writing the story of my life in 2003. Life has gone on quietly since then, but it might be a nice way to conclude my memoirs by summarizing how things stand for me and my family in 2007, as the book is readied for publication. Linda and I still operate our farm stay, though we are happy now to have fewer guests than formerly. I can still assist Ian on the farm, too, though as my eyesight has deteriorated there is less I can do.

The 'Tasman Downs' Homestead, 1990's.

Of my first family, Nicola, sadly, died young, but Wendy and her family are in Christchurch, while Alan and Bernard both live in South Canterbury, and come up to 'Tasman Downs' from time to time, hunting and fishing. Of my second family, Ian now runs 'Tasman Downs' Station, and he, his wife Nicky and son Archie, live in a house about 100 yards from our homestead, while Jane, her husband Sam, who have two children, Thomas and Mary, are in partnership with his brother on a farm near Ashburton.

Life was never meant to be easy and challenges are put before us to be tackled, solved, avoided or accepted and made the best of. New Zealand is a wonderful country to live in, but now, in the first decade of the twenty-first century, with terrorism, suicide bombings, genocide etc in many places, one wonders what lies before us in this troubled world. It is difficult to comprehend the mentality of a religious sect that leads its followers to believe that the way to heaven is to destroy as many other people as possible who have different beliefs by blowing yourself to smithereens amongst them! However no doubt the world will carry on as it always has, and hopefully right will prevail, to the betterment of the majority.

Appendix One

JOURNAL of

JEAN DE CARTERET

His Voyage from Jersey to settle in New Zealand,

30th May 1859 - 23rd December 1859

Translated from French original by

OLIVER MOURANT

1859, May 30th – *We left St.Peter this morning at 5 o'clock. Francis Pepin my nephew had the kindness to convey our baggage by means of his horse and cart on board the "Wonder". We and our children were carried to the ship in the spring cart belonging to my nephew Josué Le Gros, and in a cab which our dear friend Henriette had hired to take us.*

We parted from our friends on the Victoria Pier at 7 o'clock and our separation was truly a bitter one for us and them.

After the "Wonder" had left the harbour, and even a little while previously, rain had begun to fall and continued nearly the whole way to Guernsey.

Emma was seasick nearly all the time and Samuel as well. The other members of our party were not sick, the sea being quite calm.

On our arrival at Guernsey the "Wonder" had to remain in the Roads because the tide was out. It then began to rain in torrents while we were landing in small boats.

As we could not all be taken with our baggage in the same boat, we disembarked in two. Emma, I and the baggage were in one boat; my wife, the other children and two ladies who accompanied us, namely Mrs. Miriam and Miss Parks were in the other. By accident the last boat to leave the ship did not follow the course that we had anticipated and as a result my wife and children: thought for a time that Emma and I had perished. They searched for us everywhere, but as a matter of fact, I, with Emma in my arms, was busy superintending the landing of our baggage and its transfer to the "Metropolis". Meanwhile the heavy rainfall was continuing and I had no umbrella, only a good stout overall; Emma was well wrapped up in a shawl, so neither of us was absolutely soaked to the skin.

After our baggage had been safely put aboard "Metropolis" I took refuge in the first open doorway I could find on the quay in order to shelter and to regain my breath. Whilst we were there Samuel, who was searching for us, passed. I hailed to him and we followed him to a café on the quay where the remainder of our party had taken up its quarters for so long as we should remain in Guernsey.

As soon as my wife had entered this house she set to work to strip the children of their garments. She put Matilda on a sofa from which the child fell on the floor without hurting herself, but the fright made her fall into convulsion which lasted six or eight minutes. She recovered later but remained in a very weak state.

In this house we dined on beef tea, and after resting until 3 o'clock we boarded the "Metropolis" on which I had secured the first cabin, which we were to occupy for the two following days.

The journey from Guernsey to London was also calm and agreeable, although during the night of Tuesday to Wednesday my wife and I felt rather seasick, which may have been caused by excessive fatigue in looking after our two youngest children. Anne, Lydia and Stephen were not at all ill; in fact they were very lively, but Samuel lay stretched out in the cabin almost unable to move.

I slept very little the first night although the beds were excellent. I got up at 3 o'clock and could just discern the Sussex coastline. I watched the passing shipping as I did for the remainder of the journey.

This method of passing the time was very interesting for the passengers, many of whom like ourselves were going to embark at London for New

Zealand, some for Auckland, others for Canterbury.

<u>Wednesday June 1st</u> – We began to go up the Thames at about 4 p.m. but we did not arrive at our destination until 11 p.m. It was then very dark and we passed through a variable forest of ships one of which was the "Leviathan". We slept on board our ship.

On Thursday morning early our baggage was examined by the Customs Officers, who had no fault to find. That portion of our baggage which we wanted to be put aboard the "Natoaka" we left on board the "Metropolis". We then made our way in two cabs to Mrs. Allbery's, No.1 St. Mark's Street, Great Prescott Street, where we were most hospitably received as friends whose arrival was expected.

She gave us a good breakfast and we remained at her house for a whole week at a cost of five guineas. She supplied us with beds and meals; she also took charge of the children, and frequently conducted us to places which would have been difficult for us to find.

During the week we bought several articles which we needed for the voyage, namely :

		£	s.	d.
8	metal cups and saucers		8	-
3	enamel dishes		4	-
1	dustpan			6
1	very fine coffee pot		6	-
1	teapot		2	-
6	soup spoons		3	-
2	dessert spoons			6
6	teaspoons			9
1	enamel saucepan		2	6
2	bread bins		2.	3
1	frying pan		1	6
1	stag carving knife		3	6
2	butcher's knives		2	-
1	slop pail		4	6

1	box iron		3	6
1	ship filter		9	-
1	spring balance		18	-
1	tool chest	3	-	-
6	saw files		3	-
1	sawset			9
1	turn screw		1	2
1	mortice chisel		1	8
1	" "		2	-
1	bench screw		2	-
1	cross cut saw		17	-
1	padlock		1	3
12	enamelled soup plates		11	-
12	enamelled dinner plates		10	-
1	meat dish		1	2
1	meat dish		1	4
1	meat dish		1	9
1	meat dish		2	-
1	meat dish		2	6
1	wash basin		2	6
1	basin		6	-
1	chamber		5	-
1	water bottle		3	3
1	spouted quart pot		4	3
1	pepper box		1	6
1	mustard pot		1	2
1	salt box			10
1	ring for basin		3	6

Less discount 8/7

<u>June 8th</u>

2	folding iron bedsteads	1	9	0
2	folding iron bedsteads	2	2	0

232

1	child's mahogany chair	16	6
6	portable chairs	16	6
1	looking glass	2	3
1	strong packing case	14	-
1	child's cot	5	-

The cot as too big for our cabin so we had to return it to the maker; it would have cost us more if we had not bought it, but we agreed for 5/-

<u>June 9th</u>

1	Hook pit	2	-
6	lbs. of soap (savon marin)	4	-

After having filled the water bottle, and having carried it with a certain amount of difficulty some distance to the ship I noticed that the bottle leaked. I therefore returned it to the Vendor and exchanged it, doing the business in an hour as the ship was on the point of sailing.

And so then was all our family on board at 9 am. At about 3 p.m. we had our first meal on board. Roast beef with bread which we had difficulty to obtain, all being confusion aboard.

After tea, we put the children to bed as well as we could. Anne, Lydia and Stephen in one beside my wife, with Emma and Matilda, Samuel with me. We had little sleep during the night and Matilda was very fractious.

Early next morning before the others turned out I dressed and began to write a letter.

<u>June 10th, Friday</u> - We had breakfast at about 8.30 and then we set about tidying up the cabin to the best of our ability as we were expecting the Government Officials during the afternoon. Meanwhile the ship was towed to London Docks and remained outside till the morning when two steam ships towed her to Gravesend.

Here the Government Inspectors arrived and the names of the passengers having been called we answered to our names. The Doctor noticed some little pimples on Lydia's face and inquired what they were. I replied that they were the effect of the voyage from Jersey. He thereupon told me to step aside and that he would further consider our case.

When all the names had been called I was requested to present myself in the first saloon where I found the Doctor, the Emigration Officer and the Captain. I was requested to parade my family before them which I did. The Doctor then declared that the children were suffering from chicken pox and that it was impossible for us to continue our voyage; consequently we must get ashore again. Our protestations were in vain, such is the English Law and none can change it.

I now said to them that if I must go ashore I want all my baggage before leaving the ship. A large amount of our baggage was in the hold among the effects of other passengers, and very difficult to find but the Captain, the Doctor and the first mate, after the Officers had left the ship, promised to try to keep us on board, or to find our baggage. Truly our plight was a very sad one.

Thereupon I resolved to get possession of all my belongings before leaving the ship and to return to Jersey, believing that course to be the will of God. That night the first mate John Harrison gave us a lamp in order that we might make our preparation to leave on the following day. We made a good use of the time and prepared everything as best we could, after which we turned in, we and most of our children being fully clothed.

Saturday morning early the deck was thoroughly washed down by means of hoses and long-handled brushes - coffee tea and biscuits were served up, the last mentioned so hard that they were very difficult to eat.

We continued until noon to make our preparations. The Officers returned and gave orders for us to appear before them. They then told us that it had been decided that we must come ashore as the ship would not be allowed to cast off until we had left it.

As we were not willing to comply until we had given effect to our plan, the first mate went to work to get out our baggage. After having made a vain attempt he returned and informed the Emigration Officers that he had not succeeded.

Mr. Savill then suggested that we should continue our journey by their next ship and that compensation should be given to us for our expenses while on shore. He offered us ten pounds to enable us to carry on, and a cabin on the next ship as good as the cabin which we had to vacate. As Mr. Savill did not wish to conclude the business without consulting the other members of the firm, he suggested that I should call at their London Office in order to arrange matters definitely.

We agreed to that proposal and the Captain having provided two boats we put the baggage which had remained in our cabin in one boat and we got into the other after having bid adieu to our companions who seemed quite sad to see us leaving them.

The boat in which we were came ashore first, so we left the two boys behind to mind the baggage, giving them strict order to remain in charge of the effects until we had found lodgings in the town.

We followed the boatmen through the town in order to find lodgings. The first house we were shown was locked, so I had to go to the agent while I left my wife and four girls in the road. The agent refused to let the house for the short time for which we needed it. So I had to set off again with the two boatmen to try and find what we needed, but no success rewarded our efforts and after one and a half or two hours search we were still on the road, nobody wishing to accommodate us, some afraid that our children would spread chicken pox among their children, and others not wishing to let premises for so short a time, quarter day being very near.

Finally, we were so exhausted that we decided to enter the first cafe we should see for we had had nothing to eat and it was nearly six o'clock. We came at last to Mr. Ingram's cafe; the servant told us to come in and bring our baggage.

I immediately returned to the landing stage and hired porters to carry our effects which proved a difficult task for them because the bundles had to be carried on their shoulders to the top of the steps and all the length of a covered passage as far as the road. The Customs Officer demanded one penny per bundle; I agreed to pay him 1/6 for the whole lot, and the porters having agreed to carry all my bundles to the Café for 8/- we arrived safely, distributing the parcels in the various rooms which we were to occupy, and I dismissed the five porters with a tip of 6d.

And so our labours having terminated we sat down to have tea and a little rest. After tea we made our beds and put the little girls to bed.

As we were very tired we were glad to follow them as soon as possible after having agreed with the proprietor of the Café for 5/6 per day, we undertaking to cook our own meals.

We changed into clean linen and turned in but as soon as we reached the bedroom we noticed that it was infested with bugs. We therefore did our best to destroy them before we went to sleep. During the night although we waged war on the insects my wife and child were immediately bitten and our rest was much disturbed.

Sunday. – I got up about 6 o'clock feeling not too well and without appetite. I went to the Wesleyan Chapel at 11 o'clock and in the evening at 6.30.

Monday. - I set out for the office. At the station I bought a return ticket for London for 2/-, I then crossed the river by Steamer to Tilbury where I changed over to the railway train which was crowded with passengers and arrived at Fenchurch Street Station in an hour. The railway runs through very flat country among meadows, wheat fields and pastures wherein are herds of oxen and sheep with here and there a village or farmhouse.

Upon my arrival in London I went to the office of Shaw and Savill at about 9.30 and after waiting a long time I saw at last Mr. Shaw who told me that he had not yet consulted with his partner and he requested me to call again at 12.30. Meanwhile I went to see the ship but I did not find the two cabins as well placed as those on the "Matoaka".

I took the opportunity of calling on Mrs. Allbery to tell her of our misfortune and to rest for half an hour. I then went again to the office which after a delay of two hours I had to leave for Gravesend with nothing done. I promised to write to the office in order that the partners might know my address and forward me their decision.

I then set out to find the station which I did after having asked three or four persons. With considerable difficulty I reached the station and took my place with about twenty other persons in a 2nd class carriage. After about an hour and after following the same route as in the morning, I reached the Cafe where I found my wife and children who had almost given me up for lost. That was my first rail journey.

After an early tea we began to remove our baggage to another house which my wife had found during my absence where we would be by ourselves. It was hard work and I found a young man to help me for 6d. but he demanded 1/- because there was more work to do than he had anticipated. The mistress of the Cafe was very angry at our leaving her establishment and demanded payment of one day extra and 2/- for our trunks. For sake of peace we paid her all she asked, and we took up our quarters in the new house for which we paid 5/6 per week.

<u>Tuesday</u> – I remained at home writing to Shaw Savill & Co and to my nephew and I commenced the journal which I had not yet had the time to begin.

<u>August 20th.</u> – We embarked at Gravesend on the ship "Nourmahal" after having been detained in this town from the day we were put ashore because of our children who had not been considered fit to remain on the "Matoaka". We had remained in Gravesend ten weeks in very unhappy circumstances and with few, conveniences but we enjoyed good health and made several friends who regretted our departure. Paid 3/6 to the carter, 2/6 to the porters, 1/6 to the Customs and 10/- to the boatmen to put us aboard. the "Nourmahal".

I should here state that I sent four applications to Shaw Savill & Co for our detention from 15th July to 9th August. They paid the first three very punctually amounting to £10.10.0 but the last one remains unpaid, no reply having been received to the letter which accompanied the application, whereas upon the former applications having been made, this, firm had sent me a postal order for the amount.

We began to put our baggage in its proper place as soon as we arrived on board and then we had a dinner of boiled beef and roast beef with a good dish of potatoes.

Before dinner the Emigration Officers had come aboard to examine the *state of health of the passengers. We had no difficulty to pass the test and we thanked God that we had not been condemned a second time to remain behind.*

After dinner we continued to arrange our cabin to make ourselves as comfortable as possible: the cook gave us tea which he himself had made in our teapot. Tea finished and night having come on, we put our children to bed in the cabin of which the following is a plan:-

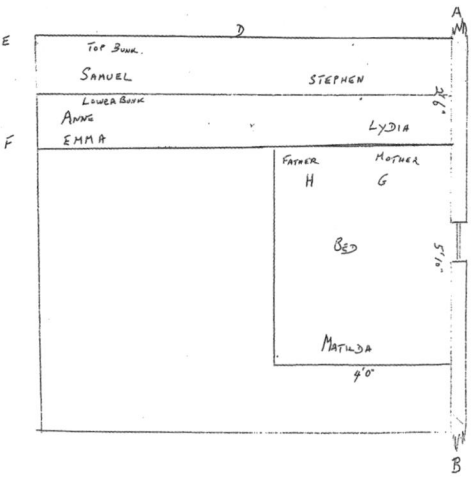

A to B side of ship
C – A window which can be opened to admit light and air
D – Two bunks one above the other. In the upper bunk the boys sleep end to end. In the lower bunk Anne and Emma sleep with their heads towards E.
F – Lydia sleeps with her head towards the line A, her feet being against her sisters' feet; and these bunks are 30 inches in width.
G, H – is a bed for me, my wife and Matilda; four feet wide and about 5 feet 10 inches long.

We lay down in these beds after having prayed to the Lord to take us under his loving care during the night. The children slept soundly until morning, but my wife and I were so disturbed by the noises made by our neighbours' children and by the crew that we did not sleep for more than two hours although Matilda remained quiet.

I had forgotten to say that while we were arranging our cabin, a steam-tug took the "Nourmahal" in tow until night fall, stopping near the mouth of the Thames but resuming early on the Sunday morning.

As soon as we were out of the river the "Nourmahal" set all her sails and continued the course until off Deal, where we dropped one of our pilots; we resumed our journey with a fair wind until Monday when the wind began to drop.

<u>August 23rd.</u> – The Isle of Wight in sight. Wind N.E. but nearly calm, so we have made little progress today.

<u>August 24th</u> – Fresh easterly wind, ship making fairly good headway. My wife is feeling seasick and so are the children. I have written a letter to my nephew, and have forwarded it by the Pilot who left us off Start Point.

<u>August 26th</u> – We are nearly all seasick and unable to eat. Lat. 48° 48' N, Long 6 W. - This evening we caught a small shark.

<u>August 27th</u> – My wife and I are somewhat better. The bad smell in the cabin is almost unbearable; we made use of camphor during the night and this did us good. Lat 470 22' N Long 8. The ship has travelled 196 miles.

<u>September 13th</u> – A ship in sight. I have written a letter to my nephew as I hope to be able to forward it by that ship. The letter is as follows:

"We all are still quite well, God by his mercy having preserved us until now. We are in Lat.16°N. 26°W. that is to say in the Tropics in the Atlantic Ocean. The weather continues fine. We had rain only on about the tenth day after leaving England, and then only a shower. The sea has been calm, we have had no bad weather, and the wind has been fair which has enabled us to make good progress. We left Gravesend 24 days ago. Since I wrote when we were in the Channel, we have been seasick for a few days, but not seriously; thank God I was able to attend to the needs of our sick ones, although I did not feel too well myself. We have been much distressed by the bad smell of the bilge water which is in the bottom of the ship- they pump daily, sometimes both morning and evening to try to overcome the difficulty but still the smell remains almost unbearable. Last night when it was time to turn in four passengers were obliged to change their quarters; the smell in their cabin was even stronger than in ours. The heat in our cabin is almost suffocating; this morning when we got up the temperature was 82 degrees in our cabin. We have to lie down with practically no coverings; even then our night shirts are soaking with perspiration when we wake up. Little Matilda suffers much from the heat; when she is below she usually sleeps all through the night; last night she had only her flannel on.

We have had not much rest because of her; we have to give her drink nearly every half hour. She had such a looseness that she gave us considerable trouble and anxiety; the little darling is not getting the food which she needs, nothing has been supplied to us for her although the Emigration Officers having the right to do so had ordered us to apply for milk. When we did apply we were informed that there was no milk on board."

September 29th - I got up at 2 am. as it was my turn for watch in our saloon, my turn comes every eight or nine days. Last night at 9 o'clock we crossed the Equator and Neptune was due to come aboard, but as we had turned in early I did not have the opportunity of making his acquaintance. The weather lately has not been so warm as before. The evenings are cold on deck so one has to wrap up more.

In our cabins we still feel the heat when we turn in, and we simply have one sheet for a covering. Thank God we are all well and no longer feel sea-sick, but we have little appetite for the ship's provisions. Few passengers have any liking for the preserved meat; we share our portion among the sailors. We do not take the salt beef because the first time we had some, the smell and the taste were enough to satisfy us. The ham and porfe are the only animal foods that we have had the courage to eat.

Our breakfast usually consists of biscuits and ham; our dinner, of pea-soup on alternate days, and preserved potatoes or rice and pudding made Of flour. Our tea consists of bread and butter or biscuit.

Yesterday a sailor was nearly killed, a pulley falling on one of his eyebrows while he was helping to replace a topmast; he seems better to-day.

The smell is not so bad now in our cabin, but matters are no better in the fore-cabins. The sailors were pumping as usual at 7 pm, as they do daily.

The ship has taken a long time to reach this point by reason of the long spell of head wind. For many days the ship has travelled only twenty miles South, although it has gone a hundred miles towards the West, but now we hope to make more headway. I have little time to read or write, my time being spent in minding Matilda and in domestic duties. My dear wife is worn out with washing, baking and preparing our meals. During the night our sleep is broken by Matilda whose looseness is such as to necessitate a change of linen nearly every hour; then Emma wakes up and asks for a drink etc. If the Lord had not given me strength I do not know what would have become of us, but praise his Name my strength has been sufficient to the day.

Hitherto, we have had no rough weather, this evening there is a fairly stiff breeze.

October 8th – I got up at 2 a.m. to take my turn for the watch, we may be out of the tropics today. Yesterday, we passed Trinidad at a distance of about 70 miles. We have had a few squalls since I last made an entry in my journal and now we are having a stiff breeze which makes the ship roll considerably. Anne has been very weak and depressed for five or six days; Matilda still gives a good deal of trouble during the night.

October 9th – The sea was very rough yesterday which has made it difficult for us to move about. The bad smell is not so noticeable, temperature is lower and we have had to put a blanket on us last night instead of a sheet as previously

October 10th – Very calm weather.

October 11th – Strong breeze and rain towards 3 a.m. Lat. 30° S.

October 12th – Stiff breeze, everybody better. Put another blanket on the bed and yet the weather seems cold; thermometer at 63 degrees. Head wind daily. This morning I put on my stockings; I had not worn any since we left the Channel. The children put on petticoats and drawers also a cloak when they went out of the cabin.

October 13th – Lat 34° 31' South; Long 24°21' West; our course being East by South.

October 15th – Lat 35°31' South, Long 16° West. One of the apprentices fell this evening from the rigging and was picked up unconscious. The doctor did all he could without reviving him; during the night he vomited blood and remained insensible, groaning at times.

<u>October 17th</u> – Sighted Tristan d'Acunha this morning.

<u>October 18th</u> – Got up at 2 a.m. to take my turn of watching in the saloon. Moon shining brightly in a clear sky. Last evening at 5.30 the ship reached the Island and took soundings but did not find bottom at 95 fathoms, so continued tacking with a few sails set in order not to drift on the rocks. At about 7 o'clock last evening one of the island boats came alongside loaded with geese, chickens and eggs, which the steward bought for the first class cabin - much to the disgust of the other passengers. The second class passengers tried to give orders to the islanders to bring provisions for them but the Captain refused to give permission saying that the ship would be filled up and that there would be room only for the supplies which he had ordered; he promised however to give the passengers some fresh meat. My idea was to have bought a sheep to share with some of the other families in the second class and to buy eight dozen eggs. The sheep for £1 and the eggs a dozen which would not have been dear if they were as big as those which had been brought which were bigger than those of a goose.

The boat is due again this morning and we will see what it has on board; my wife and children would like some new potatoes but there are none on the island, nor onions, nor any vegetable, as in the Southern latitude the Spring is just beginning.

There are six families making a total of forty persons in the island, the number of inhabitants used to be larger but several have emigrated to the Cape and to the United States. At about 11 am. the boat arrived alongside the "Nourmahal" bringing ten very small sheep, two pigs, geese, chickens, eggs, butter, fish, crayfish and milk. We managed to get only one and a half pounds of butter and one and a half quarts of milk in exchange for an old dress and old stockings. The eggs were secured very quickly by the passengers who climbed down to the boat, so we got none. Mr. Blackburn however gave us two hen's eggs later.

At about 1 p.m. our ship left the Island and continued on its course Eastbound for New Zealand, passing with a fair wind between the last island (of the archipelago) and two other islands to the South East.

In our cabins we still feel the heat when we turn in and we simply have one sheet for a covering. Thank God we are all well and no longer feel seasick; but we have little appetite for the ship's provisions. Few passengers have any liking for the preserved meat; we share our portion amongst the sailors. We do not take the salt beef because the first time we had some, the smell and the taste were enough to satisfy us. The ham and the pork are the only animal foods that we have had the courage to eat.

Our breakfast usually consists of biscuits and ham; our dinner of pea-soup on alternate days and preserved potatoes or rice and pudding made of flour. Our tea consists of bread and butter or biscuits.

Yesterday a sailor was nearly killed; a pulley falling on one of his eyebrows while he was helping to replace a topmast; he seems better today.

The smell is not so bad now in our cabin, but matters are not better in the fore-cabins. The sailors were pumping as usual at 7 a.m. as they do daily.

The ship has taken a long time to reach this point by reason of the long spell of headwind. For many days the ship has travelled only twenty miles South although it has gone one hundred miles towards the West, but now we hope to make more headway. I have little time to read or write.

<u>October 19th</u> – With a stiff breeze the ship is making rapid progress. The captain has given us about five pounds of mutton and six pounds of beef as our share of the meat distributed among the passengers. We have prepared the mutton part to be boiled in order to make broth which the children wanted very badly, and we baked the remainder. It was delicious and our children enjoyed it more especially as they had not tasted fresh meat for a long time, namely eight weeks. We bought two large eggs from a passenger for 6d and W. Hudson our neighbour gave one to Anne, their "mess" having obtained the greatest share yesterday when the boat arrived. Yesterday the Steward gave us one of his large eggs and half a bottle of milk. With the egg we made a good rice pudding which tasted very well and we drank the milk with our coffee.

Every evening except Sunday my wife has suffered a good deal of pain when going to bed, but all the family seems to be perfectly well this afternoon. Recently we have bought some port wine and ale for those who were weak, and even the small quantity which my wife drank last evening seems to have given her ease. We have also given some during a long period to Matilda and the good which it has done her is remarkable. The wine costs 3/- a bottle and the ale 1/-.

<u>October 20th</u> – *Weather calm, Lat. 38°4' South. Long. 9°25' West. Borrowed a saucepan to make broth with our fresh beef. We never ought to have forgotten to bring with us a large two gallon saucepan, it would have been very useful. We ought also to have brought a cabot of onions and a few bushels of potatoes as these are not issued to second class passengers; we only receive preserved potatoes and then not half as many as we require.*

<u>October 21st</u> – *The greater part of the water bottles leak which is not to be wondered at seeing that they are made of tin and become very rusty very quickly because we put them down on the deck which is wet with seawater when we go to draw our daily ration.*

At that time the sailors are washing down the decks with seawater pumped through leather hosepipes. At the end of the hose is a copper discharge pipe, by means of which one can direct the flow of water exactly on the object to be washed down. The water leaves the discharge pipe with great force and is directed here and there by one of the sailors who directs the jet of water on the deck, your clothing, your shoes etc. while two or three other sailors have brooms with which they swab down the decks. They do this washing-down regularly every morning and by this means the tin bottles as well as the shoes of passengers are ruined. I recommend any emigrator to have one or two earthenware bottles covered with wickerwork and shoes of indian rubber. About a fortnight ago my bottle began to leak and I had an idea to block up the hole with a sharp piece of wood and that has almost stopped the leak.

<u>October 22nd</u> – *Last night we were rocked to sleep as the ship rolled along, and we are all well thank God.*

<u>October 23rd</u> – *Weather very rough. We slept very little last night as we*

are on the weather side of the ship and have heard the waves break heavily against the side of the ship. We have stayed in our cabin all day, the weather being too rough and cold to go out, and there was the added danger of getting a wetting from the waves which broke over the decks. We spent the whole day reading and singing.

<u>October 24th</u> – Weather has moderated. We have now reached Long. 40 23 T East, having ran nearly due East since the 18th. We drew our rations this afternoon as we do every Monday.

<u>October 26th</u> – Last night was very disagreeable as the ship rolled so much; it seemed as if everything was being flung down; that kept us awake all night but by God's mercy we are all right this morning. Last evening Brooks the third mate came down into the saloon and forbade our boys to grind the Scotch Barley as we had been doing in order to make flour for bread seeing that we never had enough bread to allay the hunger of our six children. Four of them only receive half rations although they can eat the full bread ration of an adult. The ship's biscuit is so hard and coarse that they not wish to taste it, they would rather die of hunger, but Samuel, Lydia and I and little Matilda usually make our breakfast of biscuits after having put them to soak all night in cold water, and then warming them up in the oven in the morning with slices of ham or pork baked on them. When we left England little Matilda was reckoned a baby who did not receive a ration, but now she has a big appetite, and eats as much bread as our other children. Enough salted food, preserved meat and rice, etc. is issued to us, but such commodities are of no use for our children; the Captain refuses to exchange biscuit for flour although we had been led to believe by our contact that such exchange could be made.

This evening is the roughest we have had to face so far. Whilst the passengers were having tea, the ship seemed to make such a terrific leap that most of the dishes were thrown down with a tremendous crash. The water was at once cleared away so that it could not get into the cabins but an hour later a new wave broke into the saloon which again gave our friends plenty of work to do. Fortunately for us, we were on the sheltered side so we did not suffer. Lat. 41 31' South; Long 13 31 East.

<u>October 27th</u> – I turned out at 2 a.m. to take my turn at watching; after having turned in early but I had not been able to sleep because a passenger was creating a great disturbance and using very coarse language towards another passenger. The noisy man had obtained a bottle of liquor last evening and seems to have got drunk.

<u>October 28th</u> – A very fine morning, the ship is rolling like a drunken man. Brilliant sunshine, gentle breeze, during the afternoon the wind rose again and veered round from SM. to NW. so now our cabin is on the lee side and as the ship leans over on our side we are in danger of getting our cabin wet if a wave should reach the saloon. Long 21°31' East.

<u>October 29th</u> – Strong breeze, ship making thirteen and a quarter knots. Samuel stayed in bed all day as he was sea-sick and had suffered from stomach ache all night. Emma too is unwell and the doctor has given them both tincture of rhubarb. When on deck for a few minutes at dinner time I got a wetting as we shipped a sea.

<u>October 30th</u> Sunday – Very rough today. The se got into our cabin several times and we did not go out.

<u>October 31st</u> – Last night we had a very strong wind which made the ship rise and fall considerably and prevented our sleeping. Damage was done to the cabin seats by the passengers clinging to them for support.

<u>November 1st</u> – Long. 41° 321 East. Very little wind the ship rolls heavily as there is no means of checking the effect of the long waves. My wife has been trying to make bread by mixing soaked biscuit with flour. Emma has jaundice, the Doctor came yesterday to give her medicine. Matilda is doing well and eats almost anything.

<u>November 2nd</u> – Strong breeze. This morning, returning from the galley (which is a place on deck where provisions are cooked and water is boiled) with a saucepan full of boiled water I noticed a wave coming which threatened to give me a wetting so I hurried a little and as a result I fell full length and got the wave over my clothes. I hurt my thigh a little and also had a scratch on the leg. The water got into the cabin and I did my best to swab it up with a cloth but I soon got tired and passed on the work to Daniel and to our neighbours

to finish. Samuel also returning from the galley with a pot of peas lost all the contents of the pot when the string by which he was carrying it broke, so we had only half a dinner. During the evening, as we were making coffee for our meal the pot of hot water fell over so we had no coffee at the end of this day of misfortunes.

November 3rd – This morning as we were making coffee for breakfast the coffee pot tipped over; at the same time the carpet bag fell against the slop-pail and tipped that over - a chapter of accidents which made our cabin worse than ever. In the ceiling of our cabin there are three different places through which the water penetrates. Long. 46°21' East. The ship rolls very dreadfully: several dishes were smashed last night and we slept very little.

November 4th – Sea very rough. The deck is always awash and our cabins are wet by the water which enters by the sides and through the deck because the ship's timbers are not properly caulked.

A SHIP IS ONE OF THE MOST MISERABLE PLACES. Thank God we are pretty well. Lat. 45°South. Long 53° East.

November 5th – 1 turned out at 2 a.m. to take my turn to watch in our cabin. The night was very rough. The waves keep breaking on the deck and the water leaks into our cabin through the deck. I slept heavily until midnight. At about 9 a.m. the water got into our bedroom and the water was ankle deep among our boxes. I at once set to work to mop up the water while my wife and the children remained on the beds so as not to get wet. My work took a long time to finish because the water in our neighbour's cabin continued coming to ours from hers. As she remained in bed with her children I could not go into her cabin and remove the water from there. I was much fatigued when I had finished moving our boxes and cleaning up the watery mess as well as I could.

November 6th Sunday – Sea slightly calmer. We had no courage to prepare our meals so we remained in our cabin all day and for the first time dined off porridge.

November 7th – Finer weather. An occasional wave breaks on deck. We have been hanging a sheet for a few days now against a beam of our ceiling in order to keep our beds dry.

Lat. 45° 17' South; Long. 730 15' East. Weather very cold. Hail showers from time to time; a heavy shower this afternoon.

November 8th Tuesday – Strong breeze and rain this morning. Fine afternoon. Long 77° 15' East.

November 9th – Sea very rough. Waves often break on the deck and get into the second cabin where there is a porthole open. A wedding today between two of our second class passengers, Miss Meredith and Mr. Richard, by Reverend Blackburn who is on his way to Auckland with his wife, six children and two nurses. It seems that the couple were not acquainted with one another before they met on board.

November 10th – Last night the ship rolled more than ever so we had difficulty to remain in bed. Showers of hail fell quite frequently.

November 11th – More cold showers of hail. Long 97° East.

November 12th – Morning fine, evening stiff breeze.

November 13th Sunday – Long; 103° 41' East . The second cabin very wet this morning; my wife, feeling unwell, stayed in bed. The ship continued rolling heavily last night.

November 14th Monday – I turned out at 2 a.m. to take my turn of watching. My poor wife stayed in bed nearly all day because she felt so ill. During the evening I saw the Doctor who prescribed a little sage of which she took a small helping but she had not sufficient courage to eat it all. The water reached our cabin again this morning and our condition was most pitiful. The Doctor called again today and said that he had recommended the Steward to let my wife have some broth or fresh meat if he had any. But we took care not to ask the Steward; we wish to be treated like the other passengers; they do not go to fetch things, good food provisions are brought to them without their having to ask for them when they are sick. And that is why we did not go to the Steward.

November 15th – Fine morning, but the ship rolled heavily during the night. Long. 113° 33' East.

November 16th – Plenty noise caused by rats during the night. Their continued running along side of our cabin kept us awake during a great part *of the night. Long. 118° East. The hatch was opened this morning as fair weather was expected but towards noon two waves again broke into the second cabin. For that reason the hatch had to be replaced although the weather is fine.*

November 17th *– Fine day. Long 123° East. Lydia received a small quantity of grapes, almonds and walnuts from Mr. Macrichie who has been very kind to us during the voyage. He has given grapes to Lydia twice a week without fail which has given the children much pleasure. Long.139° East.*

November 22nd Tuesday *– Fine morning but little wind, same weather since Sunday. Much disturbed by rats during the night.*

November 23rd *– Long. 145° East.*

November 24th *– Long. 148° East, Lat. 45° South. A large bird was caught about noon. It measuring more than seven feet from wing tip to wing tip and is called a "Mabymarok". The ship has sailed one hundred and forty miles since yesterday. At sunset we noticed a shoal of porpoises around the ship, the sea seemed alive with them but they had soon outpaced the ship. Long. 150°East. Weather very calm.*

November 25th *– During the night at about 2 a.m. four planks in the bottom of the boys' bunk fell upon the girls who were asleep underneath, but by an interposition of Divine Providence no harm was done. Weather rainy, wind rather fresh but in the good quarter since this morning. We are all well thank God except my dear wife and Anne who have no appetite.*

Since our arrival on board, we have made slight acquaintances with our travelling companions. The majority are people without religion who live according to their unregulated inclinations. A large number of them spend their time playing at cards or chess. Other people singing songs or smoking. Messrs. Hudson, Jakins, Tester, Williams and Baxter are the only passengers who have the fear of God before their eyes. And because these men wish it, live a life different to the others, they are hated.

November 26th Saturday *– Weather very rough but the ship is bowling rapidly along with a fair wind. Long. 155° East.*

November 27th *– Fine weather. Mr. Blackburn preached this morning in*

249

the first class saloon and Mr. Smale in the evening. The former is an Anglican Minister, the latter a Wesleyan Minister. For the last two years Mr.Smale has maintained himself without being chargeable to the Wesleyan Society. Mr. Blackburn's wife has been very kind to us from the beginning of the voyage when Matilda was so weak. She gave us medicines which she had for her own children and these medicines had a good effect on our children; in fact she did all she could for us a circumstance which we can never forget. Her husband has rather exalted opinions concerning his church; so much so that neither he nor any member of his family has ever been seen at a service conducted by the Wesleyan Minister, although the latter has taught him the New Zealand language during the voyage. The Wesleyan Minister knows it better than English as he has lived in New Zealand for more than twenty years.

November 29th Tuesday – Yesterday and today we encountered a strong headwind the ship had to give way two points from her true course towards Cook's Straights. Two big albatrosses were caught this morning, they are beautiful birds being the largest that fly. They measured more than ten feet from wing tip to wing tip. The sea from the Cape has been covered with birds. Many passengers make war on them almost daily with their guns. Long. 164° East.

November 30th – Headwind still continues. This morning the wind backed to N.W. My poor wife is very ill and remained in bed all morning.

December 1st – Strong fair wind so we are making good headway in the right direction. Rain nearly all morning. Water enters our cabin more than ever through the sides of the ship. For that reason I kept my clothes on all night and my boots as well, the better to help my wife to mind the children, if I had not kept my boots on I would have had to have my feet in water half a dozen times while attending to the wants of the children as usually happens every night. In addition to all that it is my turn for watch from 2 a.m. I used part of that time in running off the water from our cabin into the second class saloon.

December 2nd – Fair wind. Lat. 35° 33' South; Long. 168° 42'.

December 3rd – This morning we arrived in sight of the Islands called Three Kings off the N.W. of New Zealand; we passed between the Islands and the coast during the day. During the evening we were in sight of the Bay of Islands. We are now busy in our cabins making up our packages in view of coming ashore.

<u>December 4th</u> – Early this morning we were off Great Barrier Island with a head wind. We tacked and came inside, but the wind dropping we made very little progress in the Thames Gulf. We passed many little islands of the New Zealand coast, forty miles from Auckland.

<u>December 5th Monday</u> – Early this morning we were in sight of the islands which form a sort of breakwater for the haven or gulf known as Waitemata.

We observed that we were signalled at the Signal Post and we passed between Rongitoto Island and the mainland. Continuing our journey with the land in view a sign which filled our hearts with joy and hope, we cast anchor in the roads a few hours later and I prepared to go ashore to find lodgings.

Soon a boat arrived alongside our ship and I jumped in with some of the other passengers to land at the jetty. The very first person on whom I set my eyes was my friend and neighbour Fred Burchell who seized my hand and helped me get ashore.

We then directed our steps towards the town and as we walked we met the missionary to whom Mr. Burchell introduced me as a member of the society. After having promised to go and see him we continued in the direction of the house of Mr. John Denize to whom I had written, knowing he lived in Auckland, asking him to try and get a house ready for us to occupy when we should arrive. When we arrived at the house Mrs. Denize informed us that her husband had gone to meet us and that we had missed one another; when we returned towards the harbour we met Samuel with Mr. Denize.

There and then we set to work to find a house suitable to lodge us and to accommodate our baggage, because the house which he had prepared for us had been taken by some of the passengers who had been with us on the "Matoaka". We were informed that that ship had arrived safely but that five passengers had died during the journey and that the wife of our neighbour Mr. Pritchard was one of the victims. The old lady who had accompanied us from

Jersey to London had stood the fatigue of the journey as well as anybody.

After having walked for more than an hour and seen almost all the town we at last found a cottage which we rented for one month. During the evening I returned on board where we lay down for the last time. At about 9 o'clock on Tuesday morning Mr. Denize came again on board to help us to disembark.

We collected our baggage on deck where the Customs Officers examined it and marked each package whether it was to pass duty free or otherwise. Two items were marked to be taken to the Customs House namely a box of carpenters tools and a gun which I had bought in Gravesend.

As soon as we had lowered our baggage into a big boat with the baggage of two or three other families we got in as well and were rowed to the Customs House and landed our stuff without any extra charges in accordance with the terms of our contract.

We loaded up a cart with our belongings and accompanied it on foot to our new house situate in the upper part of the town (as if it were Rouge Bouillon in St. Helier) from which place there is a fine view.

We spent quite a long time arranging the cottage placing our mattresses on the floor on which we slept soundly on firm ground after having rocked for one hundred and seven days on the bosom of the deep. Paid 4/- to the carter and 5/6 for the gun.

<u>December 7th Wednesday</u> – At about 10 o'clock we went to claim our boxes which had arrived on the "Matoaka". I had to pay freight, storage and cartage amounting to nearly £12. I went also to the bank where I did my business without any difficulty. I had to be introduced by someone living in Auckland and who knew me, and as I had anticipated that difficulty, I was accompanied by Mr. Denize who the Manager knew. After that formality I opened a current account until I knew what to do with my money.

We had two loads of boxes to bring home. When the first had arrived I set to work to open it while Denize and one of the boys went to fetch the other. We were thankful to find everything in good condition, nothing had suffered any damage during the voyage. Until nearly midnight we were busy employed unfastening the boxes and distributing the contents through he house. We were than very glad to lie down once more on a Jersey good feather bed, after all the discomfort which we had endured since we left the Island. My wife and Anne were poorly during the night; perhaps that was caused by change of diet and fatigue.

<u>December 8th</u> – My wife and Anne much better. Finished putting the house in order.

<u>December 9th Friday</u> – We borrowed some tubs for washing; our Jersey friends are very kind and do not seem to know what to do to help us. One of the passengers on the 'Nourmahal' is at our cottage washing our linen soiled during the journey.

We have at our cottage, just the same as at all the other houses I have seen, a well of good water for both drinking and washing. Nearly all the houses are timber built; a few are built of brick or of volcanic stone from the volcanoes which formerly existed in New Zealand. The weather has been fine all the week the temperature is rather high but bearable something like fine weather in Jersey during July or August. Bread is 2 1/2d. per pound. Meat 7d, candles l0d.

<u>December 10th Saturday</u> – Last evening Mr and Mrs. Otto came to see us with the mother of Mrs. Otto who was a Nicolle from La Davisonnerie near La Hougue Bie. She left Jersey fifty years ago and is 72 years of age. Mr. Otto assures us that the good land produces 14 tons of potatoes and that one can easily make 15% on one's money. This morning Mr and Mrs. Burchell and their niece paid us a visit; they are delighted with New Zealand. During the evening Mr. G. Gruchy came to see us and had tea with us; he invited me to call on him.

<u>December 12th Monday</u> – Yesterday I went with the two boys to the Wesleyan Chapel. Mr.Buddle officiated. On the way back to the house I made his acquaintance and was introduced to the "Superintendent of the Province", the Officer at the head of affairs in the Province after the Governor. He is a Wesleyan and invited me to call on him today. During the afternoon we went to Jean Denize's where we had tea. He is the owner of two good wooden houses and he is well satisfied to live in New Zealand.

<u>December 13th Tuesday</u> – We all went together to the Land Office in order to have our Land Orders endorsed. We met there a large number of our fellow-passengers who were examining maps of the country. Among others we met a Mr. Le Boutillier from Grouville who had been to inspect land at Wangarei where he had selected a holding. He assures me that land is very productive in that district and that the adjoining holding would suit me, but someone had already taken over 40 acres.

During the afternoon, we went to see Mr. Burchell who lives three and a half miles out of town. He has a comfortable little cottage in a retired spot which has a fine outlook on the sea, a good garden well stocked with fruit trees of all kinds, and with the usual vegetables which we have in Jersey.

In addition to his house he has six acres of land on which he keeps two cows but he does not cultivate the land as the garden takes up all his spare time; otherwise his time is taken up giving drawing lessons to other families.

<u>December 20th</u> – I returned from Wangarei about sixty miles from Auckland. The little schooner "Hate" took two days to reach the place, two days to return and I stayed there one day, my idea being to see two or three lots near Le Boutillier. I was the bearer of an introduction from the Land Commissioner to an agent in Wangarei who was to take me to wherever I desired to go. The "Hate" arrived at Tamaterau (which forms part of Wangarei) at about noon on Friday the 16th and landed about twenty emigrants; men women and children with their belongings. The countryside appeared very beautiful - high mountains covered with trees reaching right up to the summit. The lots which I was to visit were situated beyond those mountains, so that one had to cross them in order to arrive at the destination. I saw immediately that the position was unsuitable for myself and my family.

I thereupon boarded a small boat with two other passengers and the mate to go into the interior, six miles up the river which is about as wide as the Thames flowing in some places between high mountains but for the greater part amid marshes covered with forests of trees evergreen. At high tide the water is two or three feet deep in the forest; between the trees there are clearings through which the boats may pass but care has to be used not to collide with tree trunks. It was a lovely sight.

When we had left the boat I followed one of the passengers Mr. Rust (an old colonist of Wangarei) and another passenger a Wesleyan missionary whose acquaintance I had made during the journey, and we went along a fine road sixty feet in width bordered with a hedge of roses in flower. There was a fine enclosure here wherein a dozen sheep were grazing. There are cottages occupied by shoemakers, a baker and a blacksmith and others along the road. In one place there is a fine orchard planted out with apple trees, peach trees and other fruit trees which seem to thrive remarkably well. Mr. Rust's house is situated about half a mile away, he keeps a general store where he sells ironmongery; glassware, earthenware, groceries, cottons, woollens and all kinds of merchandise. As we arrived at dinnertime we were invited to partake of the meal which consisted of pork, new potatoes and cabbage served in good old Jersey style, and we did justice to it.

After dinner I directed my step to the office of Mr. Charon, land agent for Wangarei. When I got there I found the house open but no-one there or near, so while waiting I walked around the house ant waited for him in the barn. I waited there to no purpose until the evening when I returned to Mr. Rust's house where I met two strangers one of whom I was informed lived with Mr. Charon. I thereupon asked his permission to sleep in the barn for the night, telling him I would be much more comfortable there than I was on board our ship. He acquiesced and promised to take me the next day to see the lands if Mr. Charon should not yet have returned; I thanked him and we went off together after supper and I lay down on a bed in the barn.

There were two other beds in the barn which I suppose other visitors like myself could use. I had breakfast in this room and then I walked out into the yard where I saw a man singing like a Frenchman. I saw at once that he was the man I was looking for so I greeted him in French as "Monsieur Charon" and informed him of the purpose of my visit. He received me very well and said among other things that the lots which I was interested were not worth looking at; he said he was well acquainted with these: high steep mountains, rivers running through, no level ground, mountain sides covered with almost impenetrable forests, and that he was certain that before I had reached half way to the lots I would wish to trace my steps.

He then offered to show me the Credit Lands which could be purchased outright by paying a rent of 6d per arpent for five years with a final payment of 10/- at the end of five years.

I accompanied him to the lands in question and satisfied myself that they were good lands; part is fairly level sloping gradually up the mountain side towards the summit which is covered with forest. In the midst of the lands is a stream which could be used to irrigate the land if necessity should arise. The only disadvantage is that no practicable cart road has yet been made to reach the land; at present there are two or three descents into deep valleys, streams have to be forded which at this season and during this dry year is an easy matter, but when it is wet it must prove to be a difficult task.

So for that reason I informed Mr. Charon that I thought that those lands would not suit my purpose. We then returned to his house to eat a piece of bread which I had brought with me and directing my steps towards the boat which was to bring me back to Auckland, I got aboard at about 3 o'clock and we started back soon after. Another boat had the start of us but after about a mile it struck a mud bank and it remained there while we passed it. The wind being contrary we were two days making our homeward trip.

December 23rd – Yesterday I returned from Mrs. Gruchy's. I had left home on the 21st at about 8 o'clock and arrived at her home at about 11 o'clock. During the afternoon we went for a walk in the neighbourhood along paths through a large plain covered with bushes and fern where one finds large tree trunks ten or twelve feet in diameter lying on the ground. No-one knows how long those wonders of the forest have been lying there, possibly centuries.

The plains where those trees are lying belong to divers private persons who do not cultivate the land although it would be capable of producing enough to feed a town. It seems a great pity that so many thousands of arpents of good land should remain uncultivated.

Mr. Gruchy owns in this district (Papakura) two farms where cattle are reared. This year the earth is dry because very little rain has fallen, it is therefore impossible to estimate how much the land can produce in an average year. None the less I noticed on the road a field of wheat of some 50 arpents, as fine as you would see in Jersey. Last year the same field produced eleven tons of potatoes per arpent.

Further on the road I saw hay, very fine in spite the drought, and I rejoiced to see herds of cattle and sheep grazing.

The land here is covered with volcanic stone and rocks cast up by eruptions of the adjacent mountains in remoter ages, trees and bushes have since grown up amongst those stones. In the land where the stones have been cleared away and the ground has been cultivated the soil proves very fertile and the land is sold at an exorbitant price.

Appendix Two

Excerpts from the 150 Squadron Operational Record Book

Base: **Kairouan West**

21.9.43 The following captains have been selected for tonight's operation, the target of which is Bastia: F/O Kalberer, Sgt. Wilkes, Sgt. Hales, W/C Southwell, F/Sgt Sullivan, Sgt. Viveash, Sgt. Smithson, F/L Boxwell. All successfully located the target, illuminating flares being well placed over the target area. On arrival several fires were seen burning in the area W of the main Harbour and a large explosion following earlier bombing was reported by several crews, either on the quayside or from a ship moored alongside, this being followed by a fire and a series of smaller explosions. Sticks were laid across the N end of the main harbour and in the dock area, but smoke over the target area prevented bursts generally being seen or results observed. A good fire was pin-pointed in the vicinity of the fuel tanks at N end of the Jetty. Some crew reported up to three ships in the harbour, one of which was burning. Bombing was carried out from 5000/7000 ft. Opposition L/FF hosepiping at 7000 ft from the hills S of the town and medium inaccurate H/FF from batteries N, NW and S of the town. Visibility moderate to good. One Wellington was detailed to drop nickels over the 9th Army battle area. The a/c took off at 0057 and landed safely at base at 0836. 500,000 Special German Nickels were dropped from 7000 ft in the area ordered. No opposition was encountered.

[Sgt Hayman flew as second pilot with F/Sgt Sullivan in Wellington X, serial number LN482. The aircraft was designated as illuminator, and hence carried 36 flares. The flight was 7 hours 40 minutes in duration].

22.9.43   No operations

23.9.43   The marshalling yards at Pisa were tonight's target and the following captains were detailed:- Sgt. Valentine, Sgt. Stone, F/S Tunstall, F/O Bint, Sgt Bluhm, Sgt Holmes, S/Ldr Brown, F/S Adams, F/Lt Jones, Sgt Felstead, F/Sgt Daly. One a/c, piloted by S/Ldr Brown, returned early owing to engine trouble. The remaining ten aircraft landed at base between 0155/0305. They found the target admirably illuminated and dropped their load from 4000/6000 ft. These fell along the marshalling yards and the Station where several fires were started and explosions caused. The whole target area was left covered with a pall of smoke. Opposition was only slight and was probably defending the L/G. Fires were visible on the way home for 70 miles - either from the target or on the adjacent L/G. The target was cloudless and visibility was good throughout apart from haze patches along the Sardinian coast.

[Sgt Hayman flew as second pilot with F/O Bint in LN381. The bomb load was 6 x 500 lb and 2 x 250 lb bombs, and the duration of the flight 8 hours 10 minutes.]

24.9.43   Ten a/c attacked barges and the harbour installations at Leghorn. One a/c (F/O Williams) missing and one (F/Sgt Hodgson) crashed just outside the airfield perimeter. The crew of the latter were uninjured.

25.9.43   For tonight's target, which is the crossroads and coastal road at Formia, the following ten pilots have been detailed: - Sgt. Hayes, F/O Bint, Sgt. Stone, Sgt Hayman, F/S Tunstall, Sgt Kennedy, F/L Jones, Sgt Hales, Sgt Adams, Sgt Clarke. All

crews claim to have identified and bombed the target and its immediate vicinity. Reports indicated a successful attack and sticks were seen to straddle the crossroads and main coast road to S and W of this point. The cluster of buildings on either side of the crossroads and also immediately to the E were seen to be hit and as a result several explosions were observed by green and blue flashes and sparks resembling electric power cables short circuited. The majority bombed in two to three sticks: some of the bursts were not observed. 2 x 1,000 lb were dropped close by cross roads. One a/c dropped one stick on Railway Yards NE of target due to smoke obscuring detail of the latter. E of target a semi-circle of fires was observed by all crews, believed bush fires and approx 5-10 miles inland. No opposition was encountered. There was practically no low cloud over target and visibility was moderate to good. All aircraft landed safely.
[On this first operation as captain, Sgt Hayman piloted Wellington X LN318, carrying 9 x 500 lb bombs. The flight was 6 hours 30 minutes.]

26.9.43	Stand down
27.9.43	Stand down
28.9.43	Stand down
29.9.43	Stand down
30.9.43	Twelve of our aircraft have been detailed for tonight's target [again Formia] captained by the following pilots:- F/L Jones, F/O Kalberer, Sgt Daly, Sgt Holmes, Sgt Felstead, Sgt Viveash, F/Lt Boxwell, F/S [sic] Hayman, Sgt Bluhm, F/O Bint, F/S Barber and Sgt Hayes. One a/c returned early (Sgt Hayes) due to engine trouble whilst a second landed at Borizzo, due to the same cause, before reaching the target. All the remaining a/c located target by the aid of flares and the illumination was stated to be excellent. Reports indicate

that the bombing was rather scattered. Some good sticks were observed on the target and the road to E. The buildings in the vicinity of the target were also hit. Several sticks were seen to drop in the water just off shore from the target. Two crews report seeing one or two craters in the centre of the road in the target. Weather. Severe thunderstorms were encountered on outward flights from Cap Bon to about 39o W with very bumpy conditions. On return storms had moved away to SE of track. All a/c returned safely from the target, which was the main coastal road at Formia. [Flying HZ305, Sgt Hayman and crew carried 2 x 1000 lb bombs, and 5 x 500 lbs. Flying time was 6 hours 35 minutes. The Form 541 recorded Sgt Hayman's crew as hitting buildings.]

1.10.43 Nine a/c attacked two pontoon bridges over the River Voltunro at Grassanice.

2.10.43 No operations

3.10.43 Eight a/c attacked the southern marshalling yards at Civitavecchia.

4.10.43 No operations

5.10.43 Grossetto L/G [Landing Ground] was tonight's target and nine of our aircraft have been ordered to attack under the following captains. F/O Bint, G/C Southwell, Sgt Stone, Sgt Hayes, Sgt Hayman, Sgt Felstead, F/O Rogers, F/ S Daly and Sgt Hodgson. All aircraft identified and bombed the target aided by the illuminating flares, which were excellent. Hits were secured on a/c on the SW, N and NW corners of the runway. Several explosions were observed among a/c and in all some 11 to 15 a/c were left burning. Both S/E [single-engined] and T/E [twin-engined] a/c were observed by all. Three of the a/c burning on the NE end were seen by crews with verey cartridges going off. A hangar at the W end was blazing well and the roof falling in. A large a/c believed Me323 was observed at E end and in front of hangar. One stick was dropped across workshops and buildings. In this area a large fire was seen and several explosions occurred at intervals. No opposition was encountered. Weather was cloudless over the target except for traces of cloud at 4000 feet. Visibility was good throughout. All aircraft returned and landed safely at base.

[Sgt Hayman's crew flew LN318, carrying 14 x 250 lb bombs, and 18 x 40 lb. The flight was of 7 hours 10 minutes duration, and the Form 541 recorded his crew as scoring hits 'On workshops, bursts seen'.]

6.10.43	No operations
7.10.43	No operations
8.10.43	Eleven a/c attacked a choke point in Isernia.
9.10.43	No operations
10.10.43	Nine a/c attacked the coastal road at Terracina.
11.10.43	No operations
12.10.43	Nine of our aircraft have been detailed to attack two northern railway bridges at Civitavecchia piloted by the following captains:- F/O Bint, F/O Kalberer, Sgt Stone, F/S Tunstall, Sgt Heyes, Sgt Hayman, Sgt Hales, G/Capt Southwell, F/S Felstead. One aircraft failed to take off whilst another had a starboard engine catch fire near Cap Bon. The latter a/c jettisoned bombs and flares safe and landed on unused A/D on Enfidaville Road. All crew are safe. The remaining seven landed at base between 0652/0725. One aircraft bombed on D.2 - bursts were not observed. The other six identified and bombed target and bursts were observed in the target area, straddling bridges where near misses were seen. Two cookies were seen bursting - one S of Aiming Point and the other N of aiming point. A large

fire was observed slightly N of Aiming Point. There was no opposition. One aircraft visited Furbara A/D and machine gunned billets from 100 feet. The same a/c visited Cerveteri A/D and saw 9-10 S/E aircraft and two burnt out a/c but could not attack as guns seized. At Civitavecchia a large fire was burning at the Cement Works whilst another was seen near shore, believed to be the barracks. One 1/2000 ton cargo vessel was seen in harbour. Weather was excellent over the target.

[Sgt Hayman's crew flew LN482, carrying 7 x 500 lb bombs, and 4 x 250 lb, all with delayed action fuses. The flight was 6 hours 45 minutes. Form 541 noted: 'Straddled RR bridge'. It was his aircraft which machine-gunned billets at Furbara aerodrome, and was frustrated by jammed machine guns at Cerveteri aerodrome.]

13.10.43 Six a/c attacked the railway near Lake Orbetello.

14.10.43 Tonight one of our aircraft has been detailed to drop nickels on Rome, the captain being F/O Rogers, whilst thirteen others had been ordered to attack the road bridge across railway south of Statione di Talamone. One aircraft failed to take off due to engine trouble, the remaining twelve however all located and identified the target, carrying out a very successful low-level attack. Bombing was well concentrated in the target area. Sticks were seen to straddle the line W & S of the bridge. Other sticks fell in near vicinity of the bridge and in area of line and road up to 200 yards SW of the bridge. The station buildings were hit and fires started. 2x4000 lb in in [sic] near vicinity of canal bridge, a further 4000 lb fell S of the target area. one crew reported that canal bridge is down. No opposition was met over the target area. Approx 4/L/FF guns, firing tracer, inaccurate and 4-5 S/Ls at Catebello Seaplane Base, machine gunned by 1 a/c

- 300 rounds - results of which were unobserved. A few MT [Motor transport] on road approx Montalto de Castro were also machine gunned from 2/300 feet by two aircraft, expending 2,350 rounds. Buildings at Porto Clementino A/D and railway station buildings also machine gunned, 4000 rounds being used. Three oil tankers were observed in siding at station. No activity at Grossetto L/G is reported. Visibility was excellent and the target was clear. All aircraft returned safely.

[Sgt Hayman and crew flew ME596, carrying 7 x 500 lb bombs and 4 x 250 lbs. Form 541 noted: 'Straddled bridge and line: craters seen'. It was their aircraft which machine-gunned the Catabello Seaplane Base.]

15.10.43 Ten a/c attacked a/c at Marcigliano aerodrome.

16.10.43 Aircraft on the Rome/Casale L.G. is tonight's target, for which ten of our aircraft have been detailed under the following captains:- F/O Rogers, F/S Tunstall, Sgt Clarke, F/O Kennedy, Sgt Allum, Sgt Stone, Sgt Bluhm, F/O Skehill, Sgt Hayman which took off. One a/c is missing captained by F/Sgt Clarke, the remainder of the crew being Sgt Mears (navigator) Sgt Britton (Air bombardier) Sgt Stewart (W/op.A.G.) and F/Sgt Lawson (Rear gunner). Three other aircraft abandoned task owing to weather conditions, one jettisoning its bombs on land near coast W of Rome. The other two a/c brought bombs back. Four aircraft located and bombed the target and some burst were seen, mainly in N.E. area of L/G. A green coloured fire was observed. One aircraft came down to 200 feet and straddled trees with 2000 rounds of machine gun fire, but no results were observed. One aircraft bombed a L/G definitely either Rome/Casala or Marcigliano, dropping bombs from 2500-3000 feet. Bursts were seen on trees. One other a/c bombed on D.R. after locating river and dropped from 3000 feet but no results were seen here. There was no opposition over the target though L/F and H/F was observed in Rome area, and about six light and four heavy guns in Viterbo area. One a/c saw a ball of fire strike the ground - position 4200N/220S at 200 hrs - believed to be an aircraft. Heavy rain and lightning was encountered on route and cloud and rain covered the target at first but by 20.00 hrs it almost cleared. Visibility was poor. The weather was similar for the nickelling raid on Milan where the target was not identified but 177.000 nickels were dropped on ETO from 8000 feet. Nine of the aircraft landed safely at base.

[Sgt Hayman and crew flew in LN385, carrying 12 x 250 lb bombs and 98 incendiaries. Form 541 noted: 'Bombs fell in perimeter'. The flight was of 7 hours 50 minutes in duration.]

17.10.43　Wg. Cdr W.M. Morris DFC assumed command of the squadron vice S/Ldr E.W. Brown, who had been acting C.O. since the departure of W. Cdr. Southwell on 10.9.43. No operations.

18.10.43　No operations

19.10.43　No operations

20.10.43　Two a/c attacked a/c on Furbara L/G and a third carried out a nickelling raid on the battle area of Mondragone, Valrano and Bolano.

21.10.43　No operations

22.10.43　F/Sgt Barker, F/S Stone, Sgt Hayman, Sgt Hayes, F/O Thompson, F/O Skehill, F/Lt Boxwell, Sgt Bluhm, F/O Kalberer, F/S Hodgson, Sgt Mattingley, Sgt Holmes, Sgt Adams and F/Lt Jones are the pilots detailed to attack the railway bridge at Portocivitanova whilst F/S Anderson was detailed to nickel Rome but returned early owing to an unserviceable turret. The aircraft operating at

Portocivitanova all were able to clearly identify the target aided by good illumination and many bombs were seen to fall very close to the bridge and a few direct hits were claimed. Several bombs fell on the railway lines, in particular those dropped by two aircraft which were detailed to make a low level attack on the main railway and the line to Macerata. Hits were also claimed on Portocivitanova road bridge and on the railway bridge S of Porto S. Elpido di Mare. Two S/E aircraft were observed n the target area, but no attack was made. A small fire was observed in a farm building S of the primary target. Defences were nil. A series of lights were observed to apparently follow the track of the a/c as they crossed Italy. Over Italy the only cloud was in the valleys, and visibility was 15-20 miles. All aircraft returned and landed safely at base.

[Sgt Hayman and crew flew in HE596, carrying 6 x 500 lb bombs and 2 x 250 lb. The total flying time was 9 hours 20 minutes. The crew reported sighting an enemy aircraft. Form 541 records: 'Hit bridge'].

23.10.43　Eleven Wellingtons from this Squadron have been detailed to attack a/c on Guidonia A/D. Owing to sickness in on a/c one was unable to take off. The ten remaining aircraft were captained by:- S/Ldr Brown, F/Sg Kennedy, F/O Skehill, F/O Bint, Sgt Barber, F/S Viveash, F/O Thompson, F/S Daly, Sgt Hodgson, Sgt Allum and Sgt Hayman. One aircraft is missing from operations, the crew being S/Ldr E.W. Brown (Pilot) F/O I.M. Godby (Nav), P/O E.A. Hackshaw (W/Op), Sgt E Harlington (Bomb Aimer) Sgt E.H. Edmonds (F/G) and F/Sgt J.C.R. Robertson (R/G). The remaining nine aircraft were able to identify and bomb the target by the aid of illumination which was considered quite good. Bombing was carried out from between 5000 and 7000 feet - many sticks fell in front of the hangars and in the NE dispersal among some 30 single and twin-engined aircraft which were widely dispersed in these areas. Thirteen of these were seen burning at one time. Although smoke and dust prevented really accurate observation of results the attack was believed to be successful. Nearly all crews confirmed a report that a terrific explosion occurred in the special assembly shop. The only flak came from 2/3 heavy guns 3-4 miles NW of target. Practically all crews saw two aircraft in difficulties over the target and one blew up in the air and the other was seen to catch fire and fall in flames. An aircraft - believed Mc202 - was observed at this time but no air to air firing was seen. One unidentified S/E a/c with light in nose was seen in target area but no attack developed. Weather was fine and clear at the target but ground mist patches in neighbourhood. Nine a/c landed safely at base. [Sgt Hayman and crew flew in MF489, carrying 12 x 250 lb bombs, and 48 x 40 lb. Flight time was 7 hours 5 minutes, and the crew reported an enemy aircraft sighted. Form 541 recorded: 'across centre of LG'].

24.10.43	Nine a/c attacked Pistoia marshalling yards. One a/c (Sgt Bluhm) is missing.
25.10.43	No operations: landing ground flooded.
26.10.43	No operations: landing ground flooded.
27.10.43	No operations: landing ground flooded.
28.10.43	No operations: landing ground flooded.
29.10.43	No operations: landing ground flooded.
30.10.43	No operations: landing ground flooded.
31.10.43	No operations: landing ground flooded.
1.11.43	No operations.
2.11.43	Fifteen a/c attacked a/c dispersed on Rome/Romano L.G.
3.11.43	No operations

4.11.43	Fourteen a/c attacked Corte marshalling yards.
5.11.43	No operations
6.11.43	No operations
7.11.43	No operations
8.11.43	No operations
9.11.43	No operations
10.11.43	Six a/c attacked the Recco railway viaduct.
11.11.43	Eleven a/c attacked the Prato marshalling yards.
12.11.43	Ten of our aircraft have been detailed to attack tonight's target, namely the Pontassieve marshalling yards and railway bridge. The captains are F/Sgt Kennedy, Sgt Holmes, F/O Thompson, Sgt Moffitt, Sgt Susmann, F/Sgt Viveash, W/O Tunstall, F/Sgt Allum, F/Sgt Adams, F/Sgt Anderson. Most of the aircraft identified the target clearly but cloud interfered with observation in several cases. The target was, however, well covered and many fires and incendiaries were seen in and around the marshalling yards. One stick started a fire and flung up debris and blue sparks whilst another caused vivid flashes and blue sparks close to the junction. Several crews believed their bombs fell near the bridge but no definite hits were claimed on it. Three sticks fell on the E bank of the Sieve, near the bridge, the road junction and buildings. The barracks were reported to be on fire. There were several reports of bombing and good fires by the Arivo about 5-8 miles S of the target. No opposition was encountered. One Wellington was detailed to drop 167,000 Italian leaflets over Bologna and this was carried out from 6-8000 feet. About 12 blue S/Ls were coning over Bologna and touched the aircraft on two occasions, whilst there was fairly intense heavy and light flak. About six balloons were reported at about 7000 feet. Two unidentified aircraft were also seen over the area, one following our a/c for some minutes, but there was no

encounter. All aircraft returned safely.

[Though the Form 540 entry (above) does not include his name, the Form 541 lists Sgt Hayman and crew: 'Dropped bombs on target'. Their aircraft was LN347, carrying 4 x 500 lb bombs, 2 x 250 lb, and 16 x 30 lbs. Flight time was 8 hours 50 minutes.]

13.11.43	Six a/c attacked the road and rail bridge over the River Vavat, near Nice.
14.11.43	No operations
15.11.43	No operations. Squadron moved to Oudna II.
16.11.43	No operations
17.11.43	No operations
18.11.43	No operations
19.11.43	No operations
20.11.43	No operations
21.11.43	No operations
22.11.43	Eleven a/c attacked the Ciampino Railway junction and aerodrome.
23.11.43	No operations
24.11.43	The ball bearing plant at Turin is tonight's target and the following eleven pilots have been selected as captains:- F/Sgt Hodgson, F/Sgt Kennedy, F/O Hammond, Sgt Moffitt, F/O Bint, F/Sgt Allum, W/O Tunstall, Sgt. Holmes, F/Sgt Viveash, F/Sgt Barber and F/Sgt Hayman. One aircraft carrying 1x4000 lb went to an advanced base - Elmas A/D in Sardinia - but did not take off presumably owing to bad weather. The remainder took off between 16.25 and 16.37 but eight aircraft returned early, one owing to electrical trouble and seven owing to bad weather encountered N of Corsica. Two aircraft, captains F/O Bint and F/Sgt Hayman, bombed Turin after identifying the R. Po and the bridge which lies immediately N of the target. One aircraft bombed

through cloud in the vicinity of the target, the other attacked a factory on the right bank of the Po upstream of the bridge and opposite the given target. No results were observed. Defences:- Ten H/FF guns around Turin, 3-4 miles from the centre of the town and no searchlights seen. Miraflore A/D had a flarepath lit up but put it out soon after attacking aircraft arrived over the target. The two aircraft which bombed landed safely at base.

[Form 541 gives no details of this raid at all for any crew, but F/Sgt Hayman's logbook records that he and his crew were flying LN323, carrying 6 x 500 lb bombs and 2 x 250 lb, as well as 2000 nickels (i.e. leaflets). Flight time was 9 hours 20 minutes.]

25.11.43	No operations
26.11.43	Seven a/c attacked the Grosseto Rail and road bridge. One a/c nickelled the battle area.
27.11.43	No operations
28.11.43	Ten a/c attacked aircraft and installations at Rome/Ciampino A/D. One (F/Sgt Barber) missing.
29.11.43	No operations
30.11.43	The Operational Record Book records no operations, but in fact this was the night of a second, aborted raid on Turin. F/Sgt Hayman and crew, flying HE581, were detailed to carry 1 x 4000 lb bomb, and in order to do so had to fly to Decimumannu, in Sardinia, to refuel. Because of bad weather, however, the operation was aborted and aircraft recalled. Flight time for HE581 was 5 hours 30 minutes.
1.12.43	Ten a/c attacked Pontassieve Marshalling Yards.
2.12.43	Eight a/c attacked Arezzo Marshalling Yards.

No further operations were carried out prior to Christmas. The squadron was busy preparing to move to mainland Italy.

20.12.43	First flight from Oudna to Foggia [not mentioned in Forms

	540 or 541] The aircraft was LN433 and the flight to Cerignola, near Foggia, took 3 hours 25 minutes. Return flight?
21.12.43	Second flight from Oudna to Foggia, and crash on Mt. Etna [not mentioned in Forms 540 or 541]. Again the aircraft was LN433 and the flight time to the crash was 2 hours. No operations from 3.12.43 until after Christmas.